BETWEEN REGRETS AND PROMISES

BROOKE FOX

Dear reader,

Between Regrets and Promises was originally published as a duet: *Truly Mine* and *Truly Yours* by Kennedy Fox in 2019. It's been re-edited, re-titled, and merged into one longer standalone. If you'd like to listen to the audiobooks, you can search them up by the original titles on all retailers.

Although this series should be read in order for the best reading experience, *Between Regrets and Promises* does overlap from the previous book's timeline to show you what happens prior to the first book and then up to the scene where it ended and into the present day.

This is recommended for mature audiences due to sensitive subject matters, open door sex scenes, and adult language. This book has heavier themes than book 1 and a suspense subplot, so please be cautious before continuing.

This book contains domestic violence (on page, not between the MCs), emotional and verbal abuse (not between the MCs), unintentional homicide, crime scene details, mentions of suicide (via dreams and during crime scene shifts), physical violence, gun violence, abduction with on page harm, assault, threats and mental health rep: PTSD, anxiety, emotional trauma and grief.

This is an angsty, slow burn romance between two people with a history that evolves into more and ends in a happily-ever-after.

If you'd like more detailed information or specific chapters of events, feel free to DM me on Instagram @brookewritesromance or email me at brookewritesromance@gmail.com.

Happy reading!!
-Brooke

I wanna be more than friends
    I wanna tell everyone you're taken
    And take your hand until the end
    I wanna be more than friends
    At the risk of sounding foolish
    I don't wanna fool around no more
    So if we're gonna do this, then let's do this
    You can fix my broken heart, if it's all yours

More Than Friends
Jason Mraz, Meghan Trainor

PLAYLIST

Listen to the full playlist on Spotify

Hurt Somebody | Noah Kahan, Julia Michaels
More Than Friends | Jason Mraz, Meghan Trainor
Back to Friends | sombr
Ordinary | Alex Warren
Like I'm Gonna Lose You | Jasmine Thompson
Don't Leave Me Alone | David Guetta, Anne-Marie
Never Be the Same | Camila Cabello
Story of My Life | One Direction
Some Girl | Andy Grammer
Stargazing | Isabella Celander
Nothing to Regret | Robinson
Love Lies | Khalid, Normani
Somebody's Heartbreak | Hunter Hayes
Love Myself | Olivia O'Brien
Party For One | Carly Rae Jepsen
Someone You Loved | Lewis Capaldi
One Shot | Hunter Hayes
Party For One | Carly Rae Jepsen
You Are The Reason | Calum Scott
Never Really Over | Katy Perry
Talking Body | Tove Lo
Call You Mine | The Chainsmokers, Bebe Rexha
Heaven | Avicii
More Than Friends | Mokita
Sorry | Halsey
Legends | Kelsea Ballerini
Lie | Shallou, Riah
This Feeling | The Chainsmokers, Kelsea Ballerini
One Shot | Hunter Hayes

PROLOGUE

MASON

PRESENT DAY

"You almost ready?" My roommate, Liam, stands in the doorway of my bedroom chugging a beer. Both dressed in suits, we're ready to go to the wedding reception our friend Hunter invited us to. His brother, Hayden, is finally getting married to his high school sweetheart, Savannah, and that's definitely something to celebrate. Plus, free booze.

I straighten my tie and look at him through the mirror. "Yeah, give me two minutes."

He nods and walks off with his nearly empty bottle. I hear the glass clank into the trash can in the kitchen. I sit on the bed and slide on my dress shoes before running my fingers through my hair. I scrub a hand over my face as I yawn, needing to wake up, though I'm exhausted from a long ass week. Between working for my dad at the District Attorney's office and training in the testing lab, I have minimal free time, but it'll be well worth it when I'm officially a forensic investigator in the fall.

After tucking my wallet into my back pocket, I meet Liam in the living room where he's lounging on the couch. Once he notices

1

me and I nod that I'm good to go, he stands to follow me and locks the front door.

"Think Sophie will talk to us tonight?" Liam asks, frowning. When we met her three years ago, she and Liam became instant friends. Hunter's engaged to one of her sisters, and they've both been in our inner circle for years. I wish I could say our friendship has been great, but the only way to describe it would be rocky and unpredictable, which is mostly my fault for how I treated her.

We're both a bit tense about seeing everyone tonight. Our group of friends hasn't hung out in a while, mostly because Sophie's been avoiding everyone. She didn't appreciate the way Liam and I tried to warn her about Weston, her douchebag boyfriend, over a month ago and has pretty much written us off. The guy is a maniac who I'd punch out again if the situation presented itself. Love has blinded her from seeing his manipulative ways. I care a lot about her, but she doesn't see that. She hates me right now.

Soon, we're across town and pulling into the parking lot at the reception hall. It's early evening, and the party's supposed to last all night. Though I'd rather be in my bed, recovering from this long ass week, I've been looking forward to seeing everyone and celebrating.

"Think she'll bring that fuckwad?" I ask since she and Liam are always texting each other. If she wasn't with Weston, I'd assume they were secretly dating, but he has a thing for Maddie, Sophie and Lennon's youngest sister, though he'd never admit it. Most days, he acts as if she doesn't exist, which drives her insane.

"Well, he didn't come to Hunter and Lennon's proposal so who knows. He'll probably be 'working' again. After you punched him out last month, I don't know what to expect. Sophie hasn't been responding to my texts lately," he admits, which worries me even more.

We head toward the entrance where the music's already blaring. As soon as we walk in, I see Hunter across the room. Almost instantly, Liam gets distracted by a tall blonde and leads her to the bar. The dude is a chick magnet, always has been.

Shaking my head, I walk over to where everyone is sitting. I grin when I meet up with Hunter and Lennon, who's holding Alison, their six-month old baby. Maddie forces a warm greeting, but I can tell she's annoyed. If I had to take a guess, it's because she's spotted Liam at the bar flirting with Blondie. I hold back a chuckle, knowing it all stems from jealousy, and settle for a smirk, which causes her to groan. Subtle is not her strong suit. She's made it known she wants Liam, yet he continues to ignore her advances.

Deciding I need a drink, I order a beer from the bar and look around. "So where's the third musketeer?" I ask Lennon and Maddie when I don't see Sophie.

Lennon glances down at her phone and shrugs, her smile slightly faltering since her sister's supposed to be here too. Her phone vibrates moments later. Lennon announces Sophie's finally on her way and that she's going to wait for her in the hallway. Lennon hands the baby off to Maddie, and Hunter follows Lennon out of the room.

Sipping my beer, I narrow my eyes on Maddie, knowing I'll get the truth from her.

"Has Sophie talked to you lately?" I ask directly. If I've learned one thing over the years, it's that these Corrigan sisters are terrible liars.

"Not much, honestly. She's been avoiding us. But you already know that." Maddie puts her attention back on the baby, and I can tell she wants to change the subject. They're all being strange and walking on eggshells, which gives me a bad feeling.

I grind my teeth, holding back what I really want to say about Weston. All I've ever wanted is for Sophie to be happy and in a relationship she deserves. Something I can't give her regardless of our past. When we met, I was still too damaged and needed more time to heal. Sophie's a forever girl, but I could only give her one night. Now she's taken, and while I miss her being around, I'm concerned about her well-being more than anything.

The moment Sophie started dating him, things changed. She moved in with him only three months into their relationship, and that's when shit got worse. I didn't trust him, and rightfully so, but instead of listening, she accused me of being jealous. Though I wish I could've been what she needed, that wasn't my reason for snooping into this guy's background.

Before I can ask Maddie more questions, Liam walks over and joins us, the blonde long gone, which Maddie notices. Though Liam tries to act like a hard-ass most of the time, I notice how his face softens when he sees Maddie holding Allie.

A moment later, my eyes land on Weston as he forcefully drags Sophie into the ballroom. My nostrils flare as the scene unfolds in front of me. The way he jerks her around infuriates the fuck out of me. After confronting him a month ago, and the way he responded, I know how bad this guy is for her, dangerous even.

Hunter and Lennon walk back to our table as I keep my eyes on Weston and watch him pull Sophie to the bar. The greedy asshole orders two drinks for himself as Sophie keeps her head down. She doesn't order anything, and that alone is strange because we've partied with the girls dozens of times, and she usually has at least one. Sophie briefly makes eye contact with me long enough for me to see straight through her façade. My chest aches at her expression, all happiness gone from her soul.

I notice her eye is swollen and red though she's tried to cover it with makeup. My jaw clenches at the thought of him hitting her. Hunter glances at me, and I stiffen, causing Liam to zero in on Sophie and Weston, who are having a not-so-quiet argument. Her voice is hushed while his is loud, and I can tell she's embarrassed by the attention he's bringing to them. She frowns, and it's obvious she's trying to ignore him, but he's not having it.

Eventually, Sophie comes over to our table, leaving her dickhead boyfriend at the bar. As soon as she's away from him, Lennon takes the opportunity to grab Sophie and takes Allie and Maddie with her to the ladies' bathroom, knowing damn well Weston wouldn't be ballsy as fuck to follow them there.

"Lennon's going to get her to open up. Don't worry," Hunter tells me, but I barely hear him. I'm focused on Weston, who's snarling before he chugs a beer. He may not be saying a damn word, but his body language is screaming to test him, and I want to get in his face the way he got in Sophie's.

Liam crosses his arms over his chest and warns me. "Don't, Mason. Not the time or place."

"Did you see Sophie's face?" I hiss, looking back and forth between the two of them. "He fucking *hit* her." My jaw clenches, remembering the threat he promised when Liam and I got in his face last time.

Hunter frowns with a short nod.

"I've seen way too many domestic cases, and she has the signs written all over her. The way he jerked her toward the bar and how she cowered around him makes it more than obvious," I say, my voice shaking with anger. Manipulation combined with a controlling personality can lead to abuse—or *worse*.

Her boyfriend orders another beer before stumbling to the table.

"What're you looking at, you pussy ass bitch?" he asks, his voice laced with arrogance. "Wanna try me again?"

My brows shoot up. The fucking audacity. He's goddamn lucky we're in a public place right now, or I'd lay him flat on his back.

Liam steps in the way, hovering over Weston like a statue to put space between us. Considering he's built like the Hulk and was a bouncer through college, he's the last person anyone wants to fight.

The music in the room fades away, and all I can hear is my heart pumping blood through my body. Hunter tries to calm the situation, but it's already escalated. The last thing I want to do is ruin Hayden and Savannah's reception, so I step back.

Weston releases a maniacal laugh and raises his voice, garnering the attention of some of the guests. He's intoxicated and out of control. "Where's my whore at? I'm ready to get the fuck out of this lame-ass party."

Hunter stiffens, and I can tell he's ready to kick him out. Weston glances around again, his eyes are bloodshot. The fact that he's already shit-faced makes me fear what Sophie has already dealt with today. Sophie's reclusion and not acting like herself makes so much sense. She's afraid of him, of what he'll do, and the bruises on her face and swollen eye are proof of that. My nostrils flare, and I clench my teeth, anger mixing with my adrenaline. Balling my hands into fists, I try to calm down, but I want to kick this motherfucker's face inside out.

"Did you hit her?" I ask flat out. I'm not going to play games with him.

"What the fuck is it to you?" He steps around Liam and gives me an evil grin. Stepping closer, he lowers his voice. "And I'll do it again if she gets in my way." Then he slams his palms against my chest, causing me to stumble back slightly before he walks out of the room, laughing. Though I shouldn't allow my emotions to take over, I stalk after him. Hunter and Liam follow me into the hallway.

"Hey!" I shout from behind Weston as he exits the main doors that lead outside. Once I'm outside, I continue, "Don't you ever lay another fucking hand on her," I warn him with Hunter and Liam standing behind me.

"Or what?" He spins around and faces us. "What're you assholes gonna do about it? Push me around again, you pussy? Pfft. You should mind your own damn business or else…" Weston sizes me up and straightens his shoulders as if he's ready for a brawl. Unfortunately for him, I know how to fight, having had a boxing trainer for years. I may be slender, but my hands and body are weapons.

"You like punching so much, why don't you hit someone your own size?"

"That all you got?" He stumbles as he takes a step closer.

"Don't make me have to tell you again. This is your official warning: you touch her again, and you'll be dealing with me."

"With all of us," Liam adds, stepping to my side with his arms crossed over his broad chest. He wasn't a bar bouncer all through college for nothing.

Weston scoffs, rolling his eyes as if our threats mean nothing to him. He moves closer again, and the smell of alcohol oozes from him. "Keep it up, and she'll be dead before you have the chance to save her," he says with zero emotion in his voice. His words immediately cause me to see red, and I lose control of my actions. My anger guides me forward, closing the gap between us, daring him to throw the first punch.

Do it, motherfucker. Hit me. I puff out my chest, hoping his drunken ass does it.

Weston narrows his eyes and raises his arms. He swings at me, grazing my cheek enough to feel, but it barely makes a dent as I step back slightly.

"Bad idea, fuckface." I lift my hands before he can even register it. My fist connects with his jaw, causing an ear-piercing crack. It should've knocked him out flat on his ass, but somehow, he only stumbles. When he regains his footing, it's as if he snaps like a crazed psychopath. His pupils are full of rage, and he transforms from human to monster in seconds. I allow him to swing at me again, but he misses when I move. He tries again, but I throw another punch. This time, my fist smashes into his nose, and Weston releases a strangled cry as he curls down and covers his face. As soon as I do, Hunter and Liam pull me away, but I don't budge. I need to make sure he stays down this time. Just when I think the asshole is done, and I step back to walk away, Weston fidgets and reaches behind his back.

"Hey!" he shouts, grabbing our attention, and that's when I find a Glock pointed directly at me.

Where the fuck did that come from? I freeze, my heart pounding so hard I'm sure he can hear it.

"Now what, pussy boy?" He turns to the side and spits out blood. "You brought your fists to a fuckin' gun fight." Blood drips from his nose and lips that are split open and swollen, and his eye is nearly sealed shut. I slowly hold up my hands, hoping he's not crazy enough to shoot me but knowing he just might be. You don't pull a gun on someone unless you plan to use it, and I'm not stupid enough to call his bluff.

That insane cackle returns, piercing through me. I glance over and see Hunter and Liam standing behind me, both with their arms up too, and realize the situation I got them into. *Fuck.*

I think about Sophie's beautiful face and how amazing she is, and how long she's been with this terror of a man. I wonder how many nights she's gone to bed scared of him, or worse, scared for her life. Just the thought of him hurting her has me seething all over again. She's the reason I confronted him in the first place, because she deserves better than this piece of shit who lays his hands on her.

"Not so brave now, are ya?" He steadies his hand, continuing to aim at me. I look down the barrel, hoping these aren't my last moments alive.

"Just put the gun down, Weston," Hunter says calmly. "You don't have to do this."

"Shut the fuck up," Weston snaps. "If any of you says another goddamn word…I'm pulling the fuckin' trigger. Three bullets is all I'll need for each one of you."

My blood pumps faster when he narrows his eyes at me. I've seen enough shit to know what happens next. In my mind, I can imagine it all so vividly, the evidence they'll collect, and the pictures they'll take when they find my splattered brains on the concrete. Everything seems to happen in slow motion, but whatever I do next has to be calculated with no sudden movements.

The gun clicks as he chambers a round, and the sound echoes in my ear.

This isn't how I want to die.

This can't be the way my life ends. The way all of our lives ends. Fear, guilt, shock—my emotions hit me in full force as I think about the Corrigan sisters and how this will destroy them. He'd kill us and then kill Sophie too if he gets the chance.

Fuck. I should've just let him walk away and let Lennon handle Sophie since they left the room anyway.

In my peripheral vision, I see Liam move slightly behind me, and Weston quickly points the gun at him. He aims right above Liam's head and fires off a warning shot.

"I'll fuckin' kill you all if you try anything," he threatens. "All. Three. Of. You."

"Weston, we can all walk away from this," Liam says slowly. "Don't do anything you'll regret." Fear smothers Liam's voice, but his actions are steady as he tries to gain control of the situation. I want to turn around and tell them both how sorry I am, how much I fucked up, and how much I love them as brothers. If these are my last moments, I'd at least want to make them count. However, I don't want to add more fuel to the fire by talking and pissing off Weston.

"Now. What was that you were saying earlier?" Weston glares at me. "I'm gonna be dealing with you if I lay my hands on Sophie again?" His head falls back with psychotic laughter. "You don't scare me, but by the look on your face, I scare the fuck out of you."

"You've proven your point," Hunter interjects. "Let's just all calm down and leave."

"Not fuckin' happening," Weston hisses.

I contemplate my options, which aren't many at the moment. I could risk everything and charge him, fighting for the gun and taking him out, or it could all go horribly wrong and he could pull that fucking trigger. I'd take a bullet for Sophie if it meant keeping her safe, but if I'm going down, then so is this motherfucking bastard.

"Weston…" I start.

"You're gonna listen to *me*," he cuts me off. Weston continues running his mouth, feeding from the control and attention almost as if he's performing for an audience. If only he was a paid actor with a fake gun sent here to play a sick prank, but he's not. Instead, he's a maniac with the need to feel power. That much is obvious. Weston continues to wave it round, talking shit and calling me every name under the sun. A car pulls into the parking lot, causing him to lose focus, and in that split second, I make a move and charge him with all my strength.

We fall to the ground with me on top of him, but he keeps his arm above his head, causing me to struggle to reach it as he tries pushing me off. I knee him in the gut, and his arm bends just enough for me to reach his hand. He notices what I'm doing and pulls back, then points the barrel at me.

Hunter's on the phone, begging for the cops to come as I push against him. Liam shouts at both of us to stop, and I'm literally living my worst nightmare. I'm glad they don't intervene, though, because Weston could easily turn it on them. I manage to grasp the gun in his hand so it's no longer pointing at me, but his strength doesn't seem to be waning as he continues to fight for control.

Moments later, police sirens can be heard wailing in the distance, but there's no end to this game. There will be no winner. They'll either arrive and aim their weapons at us or Weston's gun will go off.

We continue to wrestle on the ground, and somehow, I manage to twist the gun to face him, but he's relentless as our hands tangle for it.

Then it happens too fast.

I hear the shot.

I feel warmth.

I see blood and skin.

Then all that can be heard is my erratic breathing. Am I shot? Did he shoot me?

Hunter and Liam pull me off him, and it's then I see Weston's lifeless body on the ground. I've never seen them so shook up in my life. Adrenaline pumps through me, but my mind can't seem to handle the rush or the shock as I push them off me, rubbing my blood-covered hands down my chest and stomach.

"I'm fine. I'm fine," I reassure them.

The three of us gaze down and see the bullet wound to his head.

Oh my God.

"Fuck!" Liam yells, running his fingers through his hair as he paces. A few people from the reception walk toward us, horror written on their faces as they screech. Hunter begins to panic as half a dozen squad cars race into the parking lot.

"Calm down," I tell everyone, knowing shit's about to get

hectic as fuck. The cops are going to take our statements, and a team will analyze the crime scene. The people who surround us look at me like I'm a monster, like I'm a murderer. With red on my hands and clothes, I look guilty as fuck.

It was self-defense. I can claim it all day, and I have witnesses. But it doesn't mean a man didn't die because of me, regardless of the fucking circumstances. I didn't like the guy, but I didn't want things to happen this way. The emotions swirl inside my head, unable to sort them properly as the shock of this whole thing soars through me.

Several police officers whip open their car doors with their guns drawn, shouting at us to show them our hands and not to move. We lift our arms, surrendering so they know we're not a threat. They can see Weston on the pavement, the gun next to me, and how I'm covered in his blood and confirm I'm the guy they want. The cops keep their guns pointed as one officer rushes over, shouting at me to get on my knees and put my hands behind my head.

I do as I'm told, and he forcefully cuffs my wrists behind my back.

As the officer helps me stand, I look at Hunter and Liam who look distraught and scared as hell.

"Wanna tell me what happened here?" the officer asks.

I ignore him, knowing my rights. I'm not saying a damn thing without counsel, even if it was self-defense. I know how fucked up the justice system can be, and I'm not about to incriminate myself.

"Call Serena!" I yell at Liam as the officer starts pushing me away from the scene. "Tell her to come to the station, but not to tell my father!"

He nods, knowing why I'd trust her. Before I can say anything else to them, the officer jerks me toward his car.

So many thoughts run through my head. Anger mixes with regret, but I remind myself why I confronted him in the first place. I did it for Sophie, for her safety, and I'd do it again if it meant keeping him away from her.

Glancing over my shoulder, one officer covers the body while others put up yellow caution tape around the crime scene. I catch sight of Lennon, Sophie, and Maddie talking to Hunter and Liam. The girls look confused and shocked. I wish I could hear what the cops were saying to them. Sophie's hysterical, so I'm sure they just told her the news about Weston. I look away, unable to watch her cry for that piece of shit who hit and threatened to kill her. I have no doubt it would've led to that.

Right now, I want to be invisible. The world around me begins to fade, and I try to tune out the screams and cries of the guests as word of what happened spreads. As I'm forcefully shoved into the back of the squad car, realization of what took place begins to set in as an officer jumps into the front seat, then drives us away.

I killed Sophie's boyfriend.

I fucked up, and I'm going to pay for it.

CHAPTER ONE

MASON

THREE YEARS EARLIER

As sweat drips down my forehead and into my eyes, I punch the bag with as much force as I can, knocking it harshly from left to right. The burn in my knuckles is a welcome pain, especially after the shit day I've had.

I didn't bust my ass for four years and graduate from college two months ago just to fetch coffee, dig important docs out of the trash, or be someone's personal secretary. I knew I'd be starting at the bottom and have to prove myself, but it's a little difficult to do that when I'm the bitch boy.

Once I finish my reps, I grab a towel and wipe off my face. Working out is the only thing that keeps me sane these days. Between the demons from my past and the guilt I continue to live with, I need this outlet. Since I joined the real world of adulting, and college football is no longer an option, boxing has saved me.

"Not bad, Holt," Max says, patting my shoulder. "A little aggressive today." A couple of months ago, I started working out with a boxing trainer, but he's already taught me so much. "Session's over."

I could go for another thirty minutes, but I shouldn't overdo it again. The last time I insisted I was fine to continue, I nearly passed out from losing my own breath. My heart pounded so fast and hard, it couldn't keep up, nearly causing an anxiety attack.

Though it wouldn't be the first one I've had. And I doubt it'll be the last.

"So how's the internship treating ya?" he asks as I remove my gloves.

Keeping my gaze focused on my hands, I grunt out my response. "I do what I'm told, day or night."

"That brutal, huh?" Chuckling, he hands me a bottle of water, then grabs one for himself. Considering he's been watching me for the past hour, I laugh.

"I want to do more," I explain. "Get my hands dirty, use the shit I learned in school, and work on cases, but that's not how it works."

"You'll be back at school in the fall, right?"

Putting the cap back on the bottle, I nod. "Yeah, grad school plus taking on internships and gaining work experience will be intense as hell." Just the thought of the insane schedule I'll have makes my chest tighten even more, but it's what I want to do more than anything.

"Wow, man. That's quite impressive." He grins.

"Don't say that yet. I'll probably flunk out before I finish the first semester." I snort, seriously wondering how I'll manage it all. Thankfully, these are paid internships, though it's not much. Unfortunately, that's where my father steps in and plays the proud dad who's footing the bill for my tuition. Outsiders say I should be thankful for his help, but I'm just a pawn in his career to make him look good. It gives him bragging rights that I went to a good university, had good grades, and landed an internship. However, he's disappointed I didn't follow in his footsteps and become an attorney too. He treats me as if his legacy will live through me even though I don't want that.

"Doubt it," he says. "See you next week?"

"You got it." We bump fists, and I take off for the showers.

Once I'm cleaned and dressed, I check my phone and see a

group text from the guys. I've known them all since freshman year when we rushed a fraternity together. Brandon, Hunter, and Liam are my ride or dies, and I'm grateful to have them help balance the personal shitstorm that consistently fucks with my life.

BRANDON

Drinks tonight? Meet at 8.

HUNTER

I'm working late tonight, but I'll try.

LIAM

I'll see if I can fit it into my very busy schedule.

MASON

Don't be a dick, Evans. We all know you're sitting on the couch with your hand down your pants. In fact, I'm on my way home, so I better not walk in on you fondling yourself again.

BRANDON

Again?

LIAM

That was one time…

MASON

One time too many!

BRANDON

I'm bringing Lennon, so could you both keep your hands out of your pants?

LIAM

And for your information, I'm not home. Currently preoccupied by a lady friend.

MASON

Then why are you on your phone if you're sooo busy?

LIAM

Fuck off. I have one free hand.

BRANDON

Dude. Lennon read that.

LIAM

Grow some balls, Locke. Going to be doing a
couples massages next?

BRANDON

Don't be jealous, Evans. Open your heart to love,
and you could get a couples massage too.

I snort at the thought of Liam being with any girl longer than a
weekend.

LIAM

Hard pass.

MASON

Just leaving the gym. Meet you guys there.

LIAM

Come pick me up before this chick ties me up
and does some weird, freaky shit to me.

MASON

HARD PASS.

BRANDON

Thought you liked that?

LIAM

Fuckers. Hate you both.

I chuckle, shaking my head as I stuff my phone in my pocket.
Liam's been my roommate since we moved out the summer after
freshman year. We didn't want to live on campus anymore and
found a three-bedroom house close enough to walk if we wanted.
The following summer, we added a third roommate, but she's
busier than both of us, and we hardly ever see her anymore.

Once I'm home, I shower, eat, get dressed, then hang out for a
bit before I get too bored and leave for the bar early. It's Friday
night, and after the week I've had, I need a drink or two.

I walk into the Coliseum and see the guys haven't arrived yet. Not that I should be too surprised. Liam's always late, and Brandon probably got lost in his bed with Lennon. They've only been dating for a few months, but I can tell he's head over heels in love with her already. It's sickeningly cute, but I'd never admit that aloud.

Lennon's a year younger than us, and now that she's on summer break, she and Brandon are attached at the hip. When he suggested a time to meet up, I should've known that actually meant an hour later.

Instead of calling them out for their tardiness, I order a beer. We've been coming here since before we could legally drink, so the bartender knows us all by name.

"Riding solo tonight, Holt?" Dan asks as he grabs me a beer.

"Nah, just waiting on everyone." He hands over a bottle, and I ask him to start a tab.

Ten minutes pass, and I check my phone to see Hunter got caught up at work and will be late. We graduated two months ago, and the asshole already has a full-time job in construction management. Not that he didn't work his ass off for it. I'm just bitter that I still have to finish graduate school, complete internships, and gain more work experience before I can apply for my dream job as a forensic investigator. Three more years and I'll hopefully be doing what I truly want with my life.

I send him a snarky text and tell him to hurry. However, knowing Hunter, he's probably just making excuses so he can skip. He's been doing that a lot lately, mostly since Brandon started dating Lennon, and I'm convinced it's not a coincidence. In fact, I think he's avoiding her on purpose, which means one of two things: he thinks she's annoying to be around and can't stand their PDA, or he secretly wants to fuck her.

My money's on the latter.

Though he'd never admit it since his loyalty to Brandon is solid. He's a smart guy for staying away as much as possible, which will be a lot easier once she's back at school in the fall.

Just as I'm finishing my first beer, a brunette bombshell comes to the bar, and it takes me only seconds to decide I need to buy her a drink.

Dan asks what she wants. She sucks in her plump bottom lip, hesitating.

"Jack and Coke, please," she finally orders, setting down her clutch. I take the opportunity to run my gaze down her body and notice how beautiful she is. She has a section of her hair in a braid that wraps around the top of her head like a headband, which looks sexy as hell.

"Put hers on my tab, Dan, and bring me another, please."

"And who might *you* be?" She raises a flirty brow.

I study her features as if I'll be tested on them later. Her sun-kissed skin looks so damn smooth that I'm tempted to reach out and touch her just to see if I'm right.

"Mason," I respond, smirking at the way she's looking me up and down. Leaning toward her, I whisper, "And what's your name?"

"Well, I guess since you bought me a drink, you've earned the right to know," she taunts as Dan places the glass on a napkin in front of her and scoots another beer toward me. "Thank you, by the way."

"You're welcome…" I linger, waiting as she takes her first sip.

"Sophie," she finally responds with a sweet smile.

"That's a beautiful name," I tell her. "Sophie."

"Thank you." She grabs her clutch and glass, then steps back.

"Wait." I reach out and gently grab her arm. "Aren't you gonna stay?"

Sophie's gaze lands on my hand before shifting to my eyes. "It takes more than one drink to seduce me." Her voice is filled with temptation and fire. "But since I'm waiting for my sister, I guess it won't hurt to sit here."

"Wow, thanks for making me feel like an obligation," I tease as she takes the seat next to me. "I wasn't trying to seduce you, by the way."

"That so? Because I think that's exactly why you bought me a drink," she accuses, the corner of her lips tilting up. "But if it makes you feel any better, it's not much of a hardship, considering the view."

I cock my head, taking the small victory. "Good. Cheers then." Clinking my bottle with her glass, we both take a drink. "So how many would it take?" I wink, and when she blushes and laughs, I know she's as interested as I am.

We talk for a few minutes before I ask Dan to get us another round. He gives me a knowing look and arches his brow when he sets them down in front of us.

"So you're meeting your sister here? Is she late, or are you early?"

"Early. I didn't feel like going all the way home and then driving back the same way, so I came straight from rehearsal," she explains, playing with her straw.

Fuck me. It's hard to concentrate when all I can imagine is that mouth around my cock.

I swallow, blinking and bringing my eyes back to hers. Sophie smirks, obviously aware of the way my body reacts to her. "What kind of rehearsal?" I ask, then take a long swig.

"I play the violin for the Sacramento Philharmonic & Opera." She lowers her eyes briefly but when her deep brown eyes meet mine again, there's a faint blush covering her cheeks.

"That's quite an accomplishment," I tell her honestly. "Very impressive."

"Don't be yet. I only got hired a couple of months ago after graduation, and they could still kick me out on my ass if I suck."

"I doubt they would've hired you if you weren't good," I say seriously. "Getting paid to do what you're passionate about is pretty badass, though. I'm sure you're amazing."

Sophie bobs her head back and forth as if contemplating that, which makes me laugh.

"Yeah, you know you are."

"And what's your passion, Mason?" she asks over the rim of her glass, her drink nearly gone. Taking a sip of my beer, I keep my attention on her, too afraid that if I blink, she'll disappear right before my eyes.

"If you must know…" I pause, finishing the last drops of my beer. "Helping people."

Sophie arches her brows. "Is that so?" Her mocking tone makes it clear she doesn't believe it. "And let me guess? You volunteer in your spare time and donate to charity on top of it?"

Her condescending attitude has me barking out a laugh. Sarcasm sounds sexy as hell coming from her.

"Oh, sweet Sophie," I muse, leaning closer and grabbing a strand of her dark hair. "Don't confuse me with a saint. I'm a sinner."

"A sinner in sheep's clothing?" She arches one brow, her teeth biting down on that lower lip I want to taste.

I brush a finger over her cheek, then pluck her lip with my thumb. "Depends if we're wearing any."

Sophie's breath hitches, and I feel the heat from her body against mine. By the way her chest rapidly rises and falls, I know she feels the electricity buzzing between us too. It's hot, threatening to catch fire if I don't kiss her soon.

I tilt her chin, bringing our faces closer, seeking permission to give us what we both want. When she leans in, I don't hesitate to move my lips to hers. At first, I move slowly, but when she moans, my greed takes over, and I want her more than I need oxygen.

My hand wraps around the nape of her neck, feeling the softness of her skin as I slant my mouth over hers and deepen the kiss. Sophie flattens her palms over my chest, then fists my shirt as she brings us closer.

Then I remember we're in public.

I break away, pausing inches from her face and then glance around. People fill the barstools, loud music plays, and chatter surrounds us. While kissing Sophie, it was easy to ignore it all because it felt like we were the only two people in the room.

"Do you wanna get out of here? Somewhere not so public?" I ask just above a whisper.

She licks her lips. "My sister is expecting me to be here."

Oh shit. I search for the guys but still don't see Brandon or Liam. If Sophie asked me to, I'd ditch them—Lord knows they've done it to me plenty of times—but I can tell she doesn't want to do that to her sister.

"Alright." I nod and stand. "Come with me then?" Holding out my hand, I wait as she studies it for a few seconds before the corner of her lips tilt and she takes it.

"Okay." Sophie grabs her clutch, and I lead her around the bar toward the staff bathrooms. I know this place like the back of my hand, and though I've never taken a woman there before, I'm happy to have Sophie as my first.

The moment we step inside, I lock the door behind me and pull her into my chest. Tangling my hands in her hair, I cover her mouth with mine.

"I have a confession," she murmurs.

"Confession is for sinners, sweet Sophie," I tease, wrapping a hand around her waist, then sliding it down to her ass. "Are you a sinner?"

The corner of her lips tilts up seductively. "Aren't we all?"

Grinning, I nod.

"I've never done this before," she states shyly. I perk up a brow, then she continues. "I mean, with a stranger. Or in a bar bathroom." My shoulders relax at the nervousness in her voice. "D-do you have a condom?"

I nearly choke on the thick air surrounding us. Her bold question takes me off guard, but my cock hardens at her words. She wants this as badly as I do.

"Yeah, I do." I stare at her, unable to take my eyes off her beautiful face.

"Then you better kiss me, *Sinner*." Sophie grabs my waist,

closing the gap between us, and I cup her face, fusing our lips together in a heated battle of need.

Moving down her neck, I suck on her collarbone, then flatten my tongue and slide it up to her ear. "You taste delicious. So damn sweet, Sophie."

She moans as I take her earlobe between my teeth and bite. "I want to taste you every-fucking-where." I growl as she rubs her palm against my erection.

"Mmm yes." Sophie's head falls back as I suck on the spot between her neck and shoulder. My hands find the hem of her shirt, feeling her smooth skin beneath my fingers and craving more. I undo her shorts and feel her lace panties, and as soon as I slide my hand inside, she gasps.

"Are you wet for me?" My finger rubs down her slit and her arousal coats it. "Fuck, you are."

Sophie nods as I effortlessly sink inside her. She fists my shirt as a moan releases from her throat, her eyes rolling to the back of her head as I twist my finger and dive deeper.

"You like that?" I ask, my voice hoarse.

"*Yes.* Oh God, yes." Her eyes flutter as she bites down on her lower lip. I have no doubt she'd be moaning much louder if we didn't have to be cautious of a possible audience outside.

Pulling back slightly, I slide two fingers inside, then thrust harder and faster, wanting to feel her tighten around them. Sophie pants, and I use my free hand to cup the nape of her neck, kissing through her rapid panting.

I bring my thumb to her clit and rub circles around her throbbing bud. Moments later, her body shakes and squeezes me. I capture her long-drawn-out moan with my mouth, kissing the fuck out of her as she comes hard and fast.

"Jesus Christ." I remove my hand from her panties and wrap my lips around my fingers. "So goddamn sweet. Just as I knew you'd be. *Sweet Sophie.*"

Her eyes are hooded as she catches her breath. Without another word, she undoes my jeans and pulls them down just enough to grab my cock out of my boxer briefs. The moment she touches me, I lose my ability to breathe. Sophie wraps her hand around my shaft, giving it long and fast strokes, making me groan.

"Fuck, that feels so good. I want inside you."

Sophie responds with a strangled moan. "Yes, please."

I lift her shirt, cupping her breast and wrapping a hand around her backside, pulling her body closer to mine. Like Sophie, I've never done this in a grungy bathroom in an almost public place, but I'm not letting her go. Wishing I could devour her and take my time to cherish her the way she deserves, I vow to do just that if I'm lucky enough to see her again after this.

Before it's too late, I reach for my wallet and grab a condom. She takes it from my fingers with a smile. "Let me."

Fuck yes.

Lowering my shorts and jeans a bit more, she slides it over me, my cock hard and so goddamn ready for her.

"Oh, sweet Sophie," I muse, capturing her mouth. "I have a feeling you're going to ruin me in more ways than one."

"All sinners have their kryptonite," she taunts, then pulls off her shirt.

"If I didn't know any better, I'd say you were the devil in red lace." I admire her bra and the way it shows off her perfect breasts.

"Guess you'll just have to find out." Sophie steps back, keeping her eyes locked on mine as she peels her shorts off and admire everything about her. She's so fucking stunning. I can't take not touching her for another second.

Closing the gap between us, I walk us to the counter, then lift her on top of it. I loop my finger into her panties and move them to the side as I align my cock with her entrance. With my free hand, I stroke myself a couple of times before pushing inside her pussy.

Sophie wraps her legs around my waist, pulling me closer. The moment she tightens around me, I nearly lose it. No words are spoken as we claim each other's mouths, our bodies joining together in the hottest way possible.

I palm her breast before pulling down the cup and taking her hard nipple between my lips. She arches her back, whimpering as I squeeze her hip and drive into her harder and faster.

"Mason." She whispers my name, and it sounds like fucking heaven coming from her lips.

"You feel so fucking good," I tell her, bringing our foreheads together. Our breaths mingle as I drive us closer to the edge. "Christ, I wish I could stay here all goddamn night."

"Losing your stamina already, Sinner?"

"I'm about to fuck that smirk right off your face." Reaching under her, I cup her ass cheeks in my hands and buck my hips against her—rotating between harder, faster, and deeper.

She latches onto my biceps, her legs tightening around my waist as I claim her mouth and taste her moans. "Oh my God."

We move together, finding a rhythm that has me seeing stars as I touch every smooth inch I can. *Sweet Sophie.* So fucking gorgeous. I don't know how the hell this even happened, but I've never wanted anything more in my life. One minute, I'm drinking alone, and the next, I'm being swept off my feet with her flirty comebacks and seductive eyes.

"Jesus. You feel so damn good," I tell her before pressing my lips to hers for a searing kiss. She arches her back, and then she's falling, her body meeting mine at every thrust, every demand, every greedy movement. She exposes the length of her neck as her head falls back, and when her body shakes, I know she's there.

"*Yes*," I encourage.

As her pussy tightens, her arousal coats my cock, and within seconds, I'm following suit. I come hard and long, grunting as she pulls our mouths together.

Breathless, we push apart and stare at each other. Her lips are parted, swollen. Silently, our foreheads press together. The dinging of my cell breaks our gaze, and the realization that we need to get out of here before we're caught hits me in full force.

"My friends are probably here now. Fucking good timing." I roll my eyes, cracking a smile.

"Yeah, my sister is no doubt wondering where I am."

We pull apart, both of us dressing in awkward silence. Sophie checks herself in the mirror, finger combing her dark strands and dabbing a tissue over her face. Sex hair is hot as hell on her, but I keep that thought to myself. As much as I want *that* to happen again, I'm not going to assume it will.

"Do you want to go out first?" I ask. "I'll follow in a few minutes to keep the bartender from getting suspicious."

"Uh, sure. Good idea. Doing the walk of shame in a public place is already going to be humiliating. I don't need to be called out on it too." She brushes her hands down her shirt before grabbing her clutch. She meets my gaze. "Sorry, that came out—"

"No, it's fine. I get it," I reassure her, then unlock the door, peek down the hallway, and open it wider. "All clear."

Sophie purses her lips and drops her eyes, acting shy around me for the first time tonight. "Thanks."

She walks to the bar area and I wait to see if she glances back, but she never does. To know she's never done this before fills me with satisfaction. It's affirmation she felt the same connection as I did. We couldn't wait a minute longer to be alone, but now I'm wondering if it was all a front, and things between us have changed. I have mixed feelings about her abrupt change and hope she's not going to tell me it was a huge mistake or something. Though that might be for the best considering I'm not looking for a relationship.

After two minutes, I leave the bathroom. Wondering if she'll still be at the bar or if she took the opportunity to bail, I stop dead in my tracks when I find Brandon, Liam, Lennon, and Sophie standing together at a high top table.

What the fuck?

"Dude, about time!" Liam shouts, and they all turn and stare at me.

"I was starting to think you bailed," Brandon adds.

Swallowing, I stalk toward them. "You assholes were taking forever. I was here ages ago," I tell them, hoping my words are steady.

"Oh damn. Had I known you were so early, I would've told

you to keep my sister company. She was early too," Lennon says, snapping my attention to her. Then to Sophie sitting next to her.

Sister.

Oh my God.

Sophie is Lennon's sister, and I just fucked her in the bar bathroom. Shit, I still have the taste of her on my tongue.

Feeling like a fucking douchebag, I don't know what else to do besides reach my hand toward her and introduce myself. "Hey, I'm Mason."

She sucks in her cheeks, eyes narrowing in on my hand that I'm sure she wants to fucking bite off, but then she flashes a slow, weary smile. "Nice to meet you, *Mason.* I'm Sophie."

"Since she's new in town and I've been spending so much time here, I figured it was time for y'all to meet," Lennon explains giddily.

I pinch the back of my neck, wishing I could rub out the knot that's starting to form. This is so fucking bad.

"Sophie's a professional violinist," Liam states proudly, but I already knew that. "Isn't that badass?"

"Oh wow. That's amazing!" I clear my throat before it goes dry. "I'm gonna grab a beer. Be right back." I excuse myself before any of them can say another word.

I ask Dan to get me a beer and a shot of whiskey. Just as I'm feeling the burn down my throat, Liam comes to my side.

"You fucked her, didn't you?" he goads.

"Shut up, asshole."

"Thatta boy." Liam slaps a hand on my shoulder. "Don't worry, I won't tell. Especially not Brandon."

"There's nothing to tell." I take a sip of beer, hoping he can't see through my lies.

"Oh yeah? So you didn't just fuck his girlfriend's sister?" His shit-eating grin tells me he knows damn well I did.

"I didn't know she was Lennon's sister," I hiss between my teeth. "Stop talking about it before I junk punch you."

Liam scoffs, knowing he's much larger than me. "Hey, I said

your secret's safe with me. But that doesn't mean she won't tell Lennon."

Shit, he's right.

Brandon *will* kill me if he finds out. He loves Lennon so damn much that he'll swing at anyone who threatens their relationship. Having sex with Sophie in a bar bathroom would definitely merit his ass-kicking. Once she tells Lennon, I'll be painted as an asshole, and my past doesn't help my case either. Brandon will inevitably find out, and our days of hanging out will be over. Lennon would hate me for using her sister and never want me around. If Brandon's forced to pick between Lennon or the guys, he'd choose her. I haven't gotten to see him as much since they've been together.

"So was she a fling of the past or more recent? Like…*tonight*?" He flashes a knowing smirk, one he's perfected over the years. He's such a dick.

"Are we gossiping about our sex lives now?" I deflect. "It's none of your damn business."

Liam raises his hand to get Dan's attention and orders a couple of beers. "Well, if I guessed within thirty seconds, the rest of them will too."

Groaning, I roll my eyes as I take another sip. Once he grabs his beers, Liam pauses before walking away. "Time to put on your poker face, Holt."

CHAPTER TWO

LLENNON INVITED me to a party tonight, and since she's leaving for her senior year of college next week, I want to spend as much time with her as I can. But the party's at Mason and Liam's house, which is the last place I want to be after what happened last month.

Mason. *Ugh*. I'm a fool.

After our awkward greeting in front of everyone, we ended up getting a few minutes alone at the bar. Stupidly, I gave him my number, and he admitted he's not 'good at relationships.' I cracked a stupid joke about how I wasn't asking him to marry me or anything, which only made things weirder.

"Sophie, I'm sorry. I don't want to hurt you. Your sister is dating my best friend, and Brandon will murder me if he finds out. He knows I don't do relationships anymore and will be pissed if he thinks it'd interfere with his relationship with Lennon. So I don't think we should tell them and just be friends." He flashes a half-ass grin, an attempt to soften the blow, but it doesn't.

The word 'anymore' isn't lost on me when he describes how he doesn't do relationships, though it only leaves me with more questions than answers.

"Friends?" I force out a smile as if he hadn't sliced a knife through

my heart. "Of course, I get it. No worries." I take my drink, but before I can walk away, Mason grabs my elbow, and our eyes meet.

"It really was nice meeting you, Sweet Sophie."

Swallowing the lump in my throat, I replay the hottest sex of my life and lament how it would only ever be a one-time thing. I told him I'd keep our secret, but it feels wrong not to tell Lennon. However, I've never seen her happier than with Brandon, and I don't want to jeopardize that by turning him against his best friend. If Mason doesn't do relationships, then it's better I know now before I had the chance to fall in too deep.

Yep. That's what I'm telling myself. Doesn't mean I wasn't hoping he'd still call or text at some point.

He never did.

I have no reason to be disappointed, considering he warned me, but I still am. Our encounter was short-lived, but I thought we shared a connection.

I never dated in high school or, rather, was never *allowed* to. Perks of being a pastor's daughter with strict rules. After high school, I fled to Utah and started college at California State University in Fresno.

Although I met tons of single guys on campus and even lost my virginity to my boyfriend of a year, I didn't feel the same way about him as he did for me, so I ended it.

I went on a few dates with decent men, and formed some solid friendships, but nothing compared to *that night* a month ago.

Flirting and sharing details with someone I'd just met was out of my element. I'm usually the shy girl who stays home to practice my violin and binge-watch Netflix with a pint of ice cream. Lennon's the only reason I left the comfort of my cave.

Since getting hired to play in the symphony three months ago, I've dedicated myself to my job and haven't worried about having a social life.

My disappointed heart is Lennon's fault. I've been so busy protecting my sisters that I let my guard down that night. She calls me the 'mother hen' of her and Madelyn, our younger sister—and maybe I am— but I proudly accept the title like a badge of honor.

Maddie's still in high school, but I check in with her throughout the week. She lives in Park City with our parents. After I left, our mom became even more overbearing, and it only got worse when Lennon moved out a year later. Maddie's going crazy without us and tells me as much each time we chat.

I get lost in my thoughts again, and for some reason, they go right back to Mason. Though I have a squeaky-clean reputation and am typically shy around men, Mason made me feel like someone else that night. He didn't know anything about me, my past, or the stigma that comes with it. I felt brave and bold, and the way he kept eye-fucking me gave me the confidence to follow him into that bar bathroom. What came next still haunts me in my dreams.

Dirty, filthy, sexy dreams.

"Heading out?" my roommate asks. I only moved in with Maria after graduation, and we're still developing a friendship, which is why I don't invite her to go with me. She's a few years older and works as much as I do, if not more.

"Yeah, my sister is nearly forcing me out," I tell her, grabbing my keys. "See you later?"

"We'll be here," she singsongs, petting her cat, Nemo.

Once I'm in the car, I crank the music, hoping that'll get me in the partying mood. However, my stomach is in knots at the thought of seeing Mason again. I don't know how to be "friends" with a man I banged on a whim, but to hell with it. I'll just make a beeline for the booze as soon as I get there.

"Sophie!" Lennon squeals the second she sees me walk in.

She's beautiful with her long, golden locks in waves down her back. Most people don't believe we're sisters, considering we look nothing alike. She's a blond-haired, blue-eyed beauty who's bubbly and outgoing. I have dark hair, brown eyes, and am mostly introverted. She makes me feel comfortable when we're out, though, because her laughter and excitement are infectious.

"Hey!" I reply when she squeezes me in a tight hug.

She pulls back, studying my face. "Everything okay?"

My eyes widen when I realize I'm frowning. "Yeah, totally! Just in desperate need of a drink."

Just as she leads me to the kitchen, I spot Mason standing next to Brandon, Liam, and another guy. I drink Mason in, admiring the way his shirt hugs his chest and hating that I want to run my nails down his abs. He meets my gaze and smirks. Fucking bastard. *Take that smirk and shove it up your ass*, I want to tell him, but instead, I flash a toothy grin and wave like a fangirl.

Ugh. *Stupid, stupid, stupid.*

"Who's that other guy?" I ask Lennon while she digs in the fridge for beer. "The one who looks like he could crush you in a second…"

Lennon flicks her eyes over, then groans. "Hunter."

"*The* Hunter?" I quip.

"The one and only. Asshole extraordinaire." She rolls her eyes, then hands me a can of Bud Light. "You were supposed to meet him at the bar last month with Mason and Liam, but he bailed at the last second."

She doesn't sound sad about that either.

"We're drinking the cheap shit tonight?" I tease, opening the can.

"Mason and Liam's drug of choice apparently. I bet you they have the good stuff somewhere, though." She starts opening cabinets until she finds a bottle of Jack. "*Voila!*"

I chuckle as she holds it up like a trophy.

"Now to find some shot glasses," she says.

"Next cabinet." A deep voice rumbles behind me and the hair on the back of my neck rises.

Mason.

"Ooh, thanks!" Lennon grabs two, then pours the liquid.

Daring to look, I glance over. He's leaning against the doorframe with his arms crossed and a smirk painted across his lips.

"What's up, Sophie?"

"Not much," I say, keeping my jaw locked.

Well, this is awkward as fuck.

"Shots?" Lennon interrupts.

"Let's do it!" Mason's head falls back as he shouts at the ceiling.

Kill me. Kill me now.

"Lennon, hook me up!" Liam comes charging through, knocking Mason right into me.

"Shit, sorry. Sophie, right?" Liam grabs my arm and holds me upright until I'm facing him.

"Yeah," I say once my feet are planted.

"Liam! Watch where you're going!" Lennon scolds. "Knocked my sister over so fast you nearly impregnated her."

A roar of laughter echoes, mine included. Lennon doesn't drink a lot, but when she does, she's an absolute hoot.

"Jesus, I said sorry!" He grabs one of the shot glasses filled with whiskey, then hands it to me. "Truce?"

Before grabbing it, I glance at Mason, who's shooting daggers at Liam, giving me all the fuel I need to be extra nice to Liam. He obviously doesn't like that Liam is being friendly with me, but too fucking bad. Mason doesn't get to have an opinion on that.

"Truce." I tilt my head back, then swallow it down.

"Yeah!" Liam shouts with both hands raised above his head, getting the rest of the partygoers going too. A round of hollers shakes the walls, and I smile at the obnoxiousness of my new *friend.*

"Another?" Lennon asks with a grin.

"Yep. Keep 'em coming," I order, handing her my empty glass.

"Soph…" Mason comes closer, then whispers in my ear, "You don't have to do this."

"Do what?" I pierce him with a sharp glare as he steps back. "You worried about me?"

He brushes a hand through his dark hair that's short on the sides and longer on top. Hair that I've pulled. "I just don't want you thinking you have to drink because of me or anything."

"Why would you think that, Mason?" I narrow my eyes at his insinuation. "I drank before I knew you. We're *friends.* I know that. So why don't you take your ego and sit back down?"

Liam overhears us and brings a fist up to his lips and smiles around it to stifle a laugh. "Daaaaamn. I like this chick!" He gives me a high five, then wraps his arm around my shoulders. "Mason can sometimes be a mood killer. Don't mind him. Come drink with me. I'm *way* more fun."

"Dude, what the fuck?" Mason glares at him, crossing his arms over his chest.

"Relax, man." Liam slaps his shoulder. "Let me get you a drink so your uptight ass can loosen up."

"I'm fine," Mason insists.

"You pussies done gossiping and ready to party?" Hunter comes barreling in. He holds up his beer can as he yells, spilling it on himself in the process.

Liam throws his head back and woots loudly, pounding a fist on his chest.

"Should've warned ya, they get a bit out of control," Lennon warns, scanning the room for Brandon. "I'm gonna go find my boyfriend. You alright in here?"

"She's fine, Lenny." Liam smirks. "I'll take *good* care of her."

Lennon furrows her brows at the unwanted nickname. "Don't call me that." Then she pushes Hunter out of her way and walks out of the kitchen.

Mason grabs a new beer from the fridge, cracks it open, and stands awkwardly as he drinks it. I'd feel bad for him, but seriously, what did he expect? Tell me we can be *just friends* and then act like he gives a shit what I do?

I don't think so.

"I bet I can kick your ass at pool," Liam blurts. "Wanna play?"

"You have a pool table?" I ask, pouring myself another shot. If I'm gonna get through this night, I can't be sober.

"Hell yeah. It's in the back room. Let's go, new friend." He flashes a wink, smirks at Mason, and then I put the pieces together.

He knows about us.

He knows we hooked up, and he's either trying to rattle his friend, or he's giving him shit for not pursuing anything with me further. Either way, I don't mind being his pawn in this game. I'm well aware of the bro-code and know that Liam isn't hitting on me, which only fuels me to play along.

"I'm in!" I tell him as we link arms, and he leads me to their game room.

"You know, this really isn't helping the whole frat boy image," I tease as we each grab a cue stick.

"You can take the college out of the frat boy, but you can't take the frat boy out of college. Pi Kappa Alpha! Pikas, baby!" And then the roars of his repeated words echo from the living room.

"I take it your frat brothers are here too?"

"Hell yeah. We only graduated a few months ago, and a lot of them stuck around. Hunter, Brandon, and Mason too."

Of course.

"Kilan is here, too. He lives across the street, and we've been partying with him since we moved into the neighborhood a couple of years ago. He's an investor or some shit, so he's always traveling, but when he's home, he likes to relive his youth through us since he spent his college days stuck in a book. He's in his thirties now, so we like to give him shit about trying to keep up with us." Liam cackles.

"Guess I never got into that stuff very much." I shrug, watching as he racks the balls. "I went to a few parties but never joined a sorority."

"We all played football, so it was kind of expected. But I don't regret it. Made a shit ton of friends for life and got into a ton of trouble, too. But you only experience college once, so..."

"So you went balls to the wall?" I chuckle as Hunter and Mason enter the room.

"Twenty bucks says she takes your ass to the cleaners," Lennon goads, dragging Brandon behind her.

"No way." Brandon laughs. "Sorry, Sophie. I'm gonna have to bet on Liam this time."

Lennon gapes at him. "Betting against my sister?"

"Babe, he's basically a pro." He waves his hand out for emphasis. "Been playing for years."

"I'm pretty sure he majored in pool," Hunter adds.

"He's also drunk as hell," Lennon counters, but we both know that's not why she's betting on me.

"I'll go in on that bet," Mason interrupts. "Fifty bucks on Sophie."

"Asshole," Liam mutters.

Yep, he definitely knows our dirty little secret.

"Seriously?" I finally say. "I thought this was for fun."

"It is. Show me whatcha got, Soph," Liam taunts with a devilish grin. "Hell, with that outfit, I'd bet on you too."

Mason growls behind me, making me smile. Liam's eyes meet mine, and he winks.

"Alright, let's do this." I stretch my arms out and link my hands together, pretending to crack them as if I'm about to do real damage.

"Ladies first," Liam says, removing the triangle and hanging it up.

Though I'm confident, I'm also wishing I hadn't taken those last two shots right about now.

"Kill 'em, Soph," Lennon cheers, and the guys all chuckle.

With my back hunched over and my legs parted, I line up my shot and narrow my eyes on the balls as I stroke the stick over my thumb a few times. Then I slam the cue ball and watch the striped and colored balls fly across the table. When a striped ball goes into one of the pockets, Lennon cheers.

"We calling it?" I ask Liam as I walk around, trying to find my next shot.

"Sure, let's play by the rules." He smirks, standing on the other side. The fact that we're secretly on the same side sends a thrill through my body. Even if it's just to make Mason mad or jealous or whatever, I'm game. He had the nerve to fuck me in a bathroom and then say we could only be friends—which is fine, whatever— but he doesn't get to act as though he's concerned about me now. I stupidly gave him my number, and in the past month, he never texted or acted like he gave a shit until the moment another guy gives me attention.

"Ten ball in the corner pocket," I say, then get into position, biting my lower lip when I realize my ass is right in front of Mason's view. With precision, I slam it in.

"Fuuuuuck," Liam groans. "Nice one."

"Told ya." Lennon beams.

"Want to increase the stakes?" I ask.

"Whatcha have in mind?" He arches a curious brow.

Biting down on my lower lip, I give myself a second to gain the courage I'll need to go through with this. Maybe those shots were a good idea after all.

"Strip pool? Make a shot, the other person loses an item. Miss a shot, and you gotta take something off. Understand?" Once the words are out, there's no going back, but I'm damn glad none of the other partygoers have come in here. They're too busy drinking in the kitchen and dancing in the living room.

Lennon bursts out laughing, knowing damn well I'm about to strip him down to his underwear.

"Well, well, well…you just made things interesting." He sets his stick against the wall, then leans down to remove both shoes for the last two balls I made.

"Should've worn layers tonight." He chuckles.

I call two more balls before I miss, then it's Liam's turn. He's stripped off both socks, and I've removed my right shoe for the one I missed.

He gets three in before he knocks one in with mine and forfeits his next turn.

"Strip," I tell him.

I've removed my left shoe and then both earrings during his rounds. Of course he gave me shit, saying I wasn't playing fair, but that's what he gets for not asking for specifics beforehand. I'll take off every piece of jewelry before I take off my clothes.

We all watch as he peels off his shirt, and God Bless the Ab Gods, because the man is ripped like Hercules. It shouldn't come as a shock, though, considering the tight shirt he was wearing didn't leave much to the imagination. Liam Evans is built like a linebacker I wouldn't want to piss off. He has tattoos on both arms and his chest, and if my little sister were here, I'd be wiping her drool off the floor. She has a thing for bad boys even though she's not been allowed to date either. I have a feeling the second she moves here next year, she's gonna be thinking of ways to get rid of her V-card.

I have two balls left, and he has three, so I take my time deciding on my next one.

"Getting worried?" Liam taunts. "Do you need me to show you how to work that stick?"

I blush at his sexual innuendo, knowing he's only doing it to piss off Mason, and by his audible grunt, it's working.

"You know…" I say in a seductive tone, flirting back. "I could use some help. The whiskey has gone right to my head." I straighten my spine with the stick in my right hand. "Do you think you could help me line up this shot? It's a tricky one." I'm playing dumb, and Lennon knows it too. She giggles behind me, whispering to Brandon. I notice Hunter leaning against the wall on the other side, glaring at the happy couple, and I wonder if there's more to the roommate story than Lennon's told me.

"I'd be happy to." Liam hands his stick to Hunter, then comes to stand behind me with a knowing smirk. I bend over the table with Liam's large frame covering mine, his arms around me as he helps guide the pole between my thumb and forefinger.

"Nice and slow…don't rush or you'll risk giving it too much pressure and it'll bounce off instead of falling right in," he directs, and I pretend to be helpless in his hold.

"Like this?" I stroke it back and forth, keeping my eyes on the ball.

"Perfect," Liam says seductively in my ear, then slowly backs away and stands to the side.

"Fifteen in the corner." After a few seconds, I take the shot, and it effortlessly sinks into the pocket. Then I'm left with one more striped ball.

"Your options are limited," I mock as he starts unbuttoning his jeans.

"Don't act like this wasn't your plan all along," he muses,

pulling them off his legs until he's standing in only his boxer shorts.

"Final ball," I say, grabbing the cue chalk and rubbing it on the end of the stick. "Fourteen side pocket." I look at Liam who winks at me. He doesn't care that I'm going to beat him, but when his gaze follows Mason, I instinctively turn and see the intense, pissed-off expression painted on his face. If they're as close of friends as they say, he should know Liam is purposely taunting him. But maybe he thinks I'm the one out of the loop instead and really believes Liam is flirting with me?

That makes this upcoming victory even better.

"Yes!" Lennon cheers the second the ball goes in. "Y'all owe me!"

"She still has to make the eight ball, babe," Brandon tells her, chuckling.

"True," I say. "But I'm certain Liam's out of clothes to take off."

We all look at him, waiting to see if he backs out.

"I've got nothing to hide." Without another beat, he pulls his boxer briefs down to his ankles, then stands up proudly.

"Oh my God…" I quickly cover my eyes and turn around, blushing that he actually did it.

"Dude!" Hunter shouts at him. "No one wants to see that."

I giggle. "I wouldn't say *no one…*"

"Okay, game over. Clothes back on." Mason's booming voice echoes over everyone.

I peek between my fingers and see he's standing inches from me. "Thank fuck you didn't miss or give him the chance to win." He lowers his voice so no one else hears, but it wouldn't matter, considering how loud everyone's being. Between Hunter and Brandon telling Liam to put his clothes back on and Lennon telling them to pay up, it's loud as hell in here.

"Why?" I drop my arms, looking up at him. "You're the only one allowed to hit it and quit it?" I raise my brows, challenging him.

"What? No. Soph…"

"Just stop." I turn toward my shoes and slide them on.

Grabbing my earrings off the table, I'm grateful when I see Liam getting dressed, though he was definitely nice to look at.

Marching into the kitchen with Mason on my heels, I grab the bottle of Jack off the counter and pour myself another shot.

"You don't need to drink that just because of me."

"Why? You don't think I've earned it?" I tilt my head back and swallow it down before he can respond. "Also, get off your high horse. I'm not drinking because of *you*. Actually, scratch that. I am…because you frustrate the hell out of me."

Mason glances around me, and when I hear my sister and the other guys chatting, I know they're on their way in here too. Mason grabs my elbow and drags me out, not letting go until we're in a quiet hallway.

"What're you doing?" I whisper-hiss. "I'm not a rag doll you can just manhandle."

"Soph, I know. Jesus. I'm just trying to talk to you without all of them hearing." He brushes his hand through his hair as if he's flustered.

"Okay, what do you want to talk about?"

"I understand you're pissed but trust me that not getting involved with me is for the best. If I was a selfish man, I'd say to hell with it and pull you into my bed right now."

My heart beats erratically at his words. Part of me wishes he'd do just that, but I'd only end up more hurt.

"I don't know how to be friends with you, Mason," I tell him truthfully. "Lying to my sister…"

"Which is why you should pretend nothing happened."

I flinch as if he'd just slapped me.

"Shit, that came out harsh." He fidgets with his hands. "I'm not in a place to have a relationship right now, and the last thing I want to do is cause you any pain. I would've never taken you into that bathroom if I knew you were Lennon's sister. Now everything is fucked up."

His honesty gives me whiplash.

"Seeing you get cozy with Liam pisses me off, and although I have no right to be—"

"Exactly." I cut him off. "You don't have any right or say. If I want to get cozy with the entire Pi Alpha whatever fraternity, you don't get to say shit."

"Liam isn't interested," he blurts. "He's just trying to fuck with me."

I roll my eyes, resisting the urge to smack him for his idiocy. "I'm not stupid, Mason. I figured that out within ten seconds."

"Wait. What? So all of that…" He waves his hand in the air. "Was what?"

"A show. A *game*. Whatever you wanna call it. Liam started it, and I played along. I'm well aware he's not into me that way, so get off your soap box. And here's a little tip. The next time you sleep with a girl you have no intention of calling, don't tell her it's because you don't do relationships. Put her out of her damn misery and just admit you're not that into her, or that you were too drunk, or hell, that she's not your type. But don't do this 'let's be friends' crap. Got it? No girl wants to hear that because we all know it's bullshit."

I hate that while I'm chewing his ass out, I remember what it felt like to be kissed by him and want to kiss him again.

Ugh. I'm pathetic.

"Trust me when I tell you it's better this way," Mason says sincerely, his voice low and pained.

I snort, not wanting to take the bait. "Sure. If that's what helps you sleep at night."

"I sleep like shit."

I square my shoulders. "Good."

He bites down on his lip, stifling a laugh. We both remain quiet, neither of us having any fight left.

"How'd you learn to play pool like that?" he asks, breaking the silence.

"Really?" I arch a brow, annoyed he thinks we're gonna be on talking terms now.

He shrugs, giving me a pitiful look.

Inhaling a defeated breath, I slump my shoulders as I release the tension. "I've always been good with my hands. Calculated and precise. It's why I started playing the violin. Once I got to college, it was the only thing I could participate in because I'm not an athlete, or a singer, or math wiz. So I'd meet with friends at the pubs, and we'd play pool. Surprisingly, I got good at it." I shrug. "Once Lennon was allowed in the bars, she'd play with me, and I'd demolish her—not that it was a true hardship—she sucks."

Mason's face splits into a wide smile, and I hate that I love it so much. "You certainly gave Liam a run for his money."

"Eh, I'm not convinced he didn't let me win. He's also pretty drunk."

"Don't be so modest. But maybe you should ask him for a rematch when you're both sober."

"Yeah, maybe."

Are we having an actual conversation?

We're silent for a beat, but if I don't go back to Lennon, she's going to come looking for me. I keep focused on my feet and contemplate how to wrap this up. Friends or not, this is still awkward when I continuously replay our moment together in my mind.

"Well, for whatever it's worth…" Mason's words bring my gaze back to his. "I hope we can be real friends someday. It'd be a shame if you hated me forever when we obviously have *great* conversation."

Snorting at his emphasis, I nod. "Looked like you were about to murder Liam in there. You sure you can do *just friends*?"

He groans. "Liam was pushing my buttons on purpose. And I didn't even tell him. He just figured it out. He's an asshole like that."

"Weirdest friendship I've ever heard."

He grunts. "Try being his roommate."

"Pass." I chuckle, admiring the way his jeans hug his thighs.

Fuck my life.

I need to stop checking him out.

Stop looking at Mason as anything more because he's made it clear there won't be *more*. If only my heart would get the memo, though, and stop reminiscing about every part of my body he burned with his touch.

Exhaling a deep breath, I let him know the terms of this *just friends* arrangement. "This doesn't mean I'm not still pissed at you. I won't tell Lennon, but I wouldn't be surprised if she figures it out too," I tell him matter-of-factly before adding, "And we're not exchanging friendship bracelets anytime soon." I put my foot down to let him know I'm not giving him the upper hand.

"No? Friendship anklets, maybe?" He raises his brows with a boyish grin. Damn him.

"You're a moron, Mason Holt."

"So I've heard." He smirks.

My shoulders rise and fall, accepting that this is it. "You did warn me, so I should've taken your word for it. You're definitely no saint."

He tilts his head, the remorse obvious in his expression. "I wish I could be—for you. But I'm a good friend. Just ask my dickhead roommate." He nods toward the kitchen where Liam's being loud and rowdy.

I snort, shaking my head at him. "We'll see about that."

CHAPTER THREE

MASON

TWO YEARS EARLIER

With my first year of grad school complete, I'm ready to party my ass off this summer. Only two more semesters until I'm done, which can't come soon enough. My internship ended on Wednesday, and now I have to figure out what the hell I'm gonna do next.

It's only been two days, but I've been taking time to relax and refresh before moving on to the next thing. I've been going nonstop since graduating college, so taking time off to recoup is needed, but it'll be short-lived. Gaining more experience is my number one priority, but I don't have any prospective jobs lined up—not even a temporary one. I recently submitted applications for six- and twelve-month internships, but I haven't heard anything back.

I check the time and realize I need to leave now if I'm going to be on time for lunch. My father doesn't tolerate tardiness from anyone, especially not his own son. While I hate the country club and everything it stands for, he insisted I meet him there to eat. Probably so he could brag and rub elbows with all the politicians and elected officials. It's disgusting how fake they are to each other, considering they'd climb the backs of their colleagues to get to the top. Nothing like a fifty dollar plate of shitty shrimp and booze to make a person feel elite.

While I drive across town, I think about my dad. I haven't seen him in a few months, using school and work as an excuse. Now that those two things have ended, he knew I couldn't say no although I wanted to.

Each time we get together, he reminds me of how much of a disappointment I am for not following in his footsteps and going to law school. I considered it, but after seeing how much the job took over his life, I knew it wasn't for me.

Being the district attorney always took priority over our family, no matter the occasion, and when work called, he'd bail. I promised myself I'd never put my career over my wife and kids, *if* I ever have those things. Deep down, a part of me feels like I don't deserve to be happy. I had happiness once and wishing for it again would be selfish.

The country club is set off in the distance on a beautiful golf course. If I were just an outsider looking in and didn't know anything about the members who frequented it, I'd probably think it was paradise. It's far from it. Before I get out of the truck, I sit in the parking lot and give myself a pep talk. No matter what my father says today, I'm not going to lose my cool. I repeat it a few times.

I walk inside and am greeted by a few people who know my dad. "Mr. Holt, welcome back."

It's been over a year since I've been here, so I'm impressed they remember me. Then again, it's impossible *not* to know who my father is, and I'm the spitting image of him.

I catch sight of my dad sitting at a table across the room. The years have been good to him even though I can't say he deserves it much.

"Mason," he calls out with a forced smile as soon as he sees me.

Heads turn toward me, and I'm that embarrassed kid again. He loves attention, but I can't say I do.

"Hey, Dad," I say, sitting across from him at the table.

He snaps his fingers, and the waiter comes over to take my drink order. I look down at his glass of bourbon and get one too, because I'm probably going to need it. Awkwardness floats between us when he answers his cell phone and begins talking to his wife. It takes everything I have not to roll my eyes, and I'm thankful when my whiskey arrives.

"I don't have time to talk about this right now, Hallie. I'm having lunch with Mason." He shakes his head, growing more frustrated with her. "We'll discuss it when I get home," he says between gritted teeth, then ends the call.

Seems he treats her like a child too, but it could be because she's only four years older than me.

"Women." He chuckle as if I'm one of his golf buddies.

"Hmm." I take another sip, wishing the alcohol would kick in sooner because I don't want to discuss *her*. The thought of Hallie has always left a bad taste in my mouth, especially considering how they got together.

Being the new attractive fresh out of college secretary for the DA really worked in her gold-digging favor. After an affair and a pregnancy announcement, he left my mother high and dry with nothing but resentment and a paid-off house. A year after the divorce, she threatened to fight him in court for half of his shit, and since he didn't want the negative attention, he caved and paid her off. Like he does everyone.

I haven't fully forgiven him for what he did. My mother is the strongest and smartest woman on the planet and was there for me when I had no one and when I felt the most alone. She's my biggest supporter, and when everything happened with my previous girlfriend, Emma, she kept me sane. My father was too busy pointing fingers and covering possible scandals because he's only ever concerned about number one—*himself*.

"How's Michaela?" I ask, changing the subject. Even if I hate

Hallie, I can't treat my five-year-old sister poorly. She deserves better than either one of her parents.

"She's good. Starting kindergarten in the fall. Can't believe it," he tells me, looking over the menu. I halfway wonder if he'll force her to go to law school since I didn't. It wouldn't surprise me since they named her after my father. It's disgusting, and I can only imagine how much pressure she'll have on her to be the best at everything. I've lived that life without the result my father wanted. She's his second chance.

The waiter returns and takes our order. My dad asks for another drink but makes it a double. It's almost as if he has to be wasted to be around me. Good to know I make him just as miserable. When his freshly poured glass of bourbon is placed in front of him, he cuts straight to the chase.

"So what're your current plans now that the semester has ended?"

I suck in a deep breath. "Not sure yet. I'm waiting to see if I get another internship since I found the last one so beneficial. I learned a lot and was grateful for the opportunity to work so closely with people in the field."

He nods. Doesn't say congratulations or that he's proud of me, not that I expect it anymore.

"I can get you an internship at the morgue to be a coroner's assistant. A position became available yesterday and it'll look good on your resume. I'll call when we leave here."

I open my mouth to speak up but then close it because I don't have any other options at the moment. Though it's not my first choice of places, death is an important part of a forensics investigator. It'll be a good experience, so I can't complain about the opportunity.

"It's settled then," he says when I don't offer any argument. I could explain how I don't need him continuously butting into my life, but at the moment, I do need his help, though I'd never admit it out loud. Each time I walk into a new job, one he's pulled strings to get me hired at, everyone instantly assumes I'm some privileged punk who doesn't work hard. One would think being the DA's son would make life easier, but the reality is, it doesn't. I have to work ten times harder than someone who comes from a normal family to prove myself.

Our food finally arrives, an indication that this meeting is halfway over, and Dad talks about his new secretary. I wonder if he's sleeping with her too, but I don't say shit, while he runs his mouth and talks about her tight ass. And in a snap, he starts in on me. I'm shocked it took him this long.

"I honestly don't know why you chose to go this route with your career. You would've made a great lawyer, Mason. You've got that no bullshit attitude, just like me. You could've climbed the ranks, worked on criminal trials, and made a name for yourself."

"Sounds boring as hell." I shrug, chewing a mouthful.

"It's not too late for you. Many people go to law school after they work in their field for a few years."

"It's not gonna happen. After I get my master's and a few more internships under my belt, I'll have enough experience to start fieldwork. I'd rather help understand the ins and outs and whys of homicides than putting the bad guy behind bars with paperwork. The evidence is what's important."

He scoffs. "It's just as important for justice to be served."

"I didn't say it wasn't. Investigating crime scenes directly relates to the cases, just not in the way you want. You can't keep pulling this shit. It's exhausting for you to bring this up each time we're together. Just accept what I'm doing and be happy that I'm happy."

He glances around the room to make sure no one is paying attention to our conversation because it's always about appearances to him. I made sure to keep my voice low, not wanting to set him off, but I can tell with every passing minute that he's growing more annoyed with me.

"It's a waste of your intelligence."

"And that's your opinion," I rebut. "And we all know what those are like."

I push the rest of my food away and place the napkin over my plate because I'm done talking about this. All I've ever wanted is his support or, at the very least, his acceptance, but I doubt I'll ever get either. After everything that happened with Emma, he's held my career path over me, and I think he's forgotten why I wanted to become a forensics investigator in the first place. It doesn't matter to him, though. His only concern is that I'm not walking in his shadow, making the Holt name proud.

The check is delivered just in time. Dad hands over his credit card, then signs the receipt, and we both stand. He speaks loud enough for everyone near us to hear. "We'll have to get together again soon, son."

He pulls me into a tight hug but shows no emotion. It's just an action for him without any meaning behind it. I force a smile and get the hell out of there as quickly as I can. He doesn't follow me.

Once I'm in my truck, I pull out of the parking lot and head toward the gym to work off some of my frustrations. Keeping an extra bag of clean clothes with me comes in handy at times like this. The lunch itself didn't go terribly bad, but too much unspoken tension has lingered between us for years. To my father, I'm a failure, or at least that's how he makes me feel. What sucks is, after all this time, a part of me still wants to make him proud.

It doesn't take me long to park, go inside the gym, and change. I grab some gloves and put them on, then enter one of the training areas. With everything I have, I work out all of my pent-up annoyance. I'm gasping for air as I push myself to the limit. It doesn't take long for exhaustion to hit, and I'm thankful I found this escape after graduation. While getting my undergrad degree, I kept busy training and playing football. It helped me cope, and I needed that when I left. Boxing keeps me sane.

My arms feel like Jell-O, and I suck in deep breaths, trying to cool down as I grab my bag and go back to the truck. I pull out my cell phone and text all my friends to see if they want to go out tonight. Considering I'm gonna be forced to work with dead people for the next six months to a year, I need to be with the living while I can. Before I reverse, text messages come like crazy. Brandon has plans with Lennon, but Liam and Hunter are down. The three of us together only means one thing—trouble. It's exactly what I need. Tonight, we're gonna relive our frat days. Fuck, I can't wait.

I go home and put my dirty clothes in the wash, then hop in the shower. After I'm dressed, I head to the bar and pre-game. Although that's probably a bad idea, I don't give a damn. By the time Hunter and Liam arrive, I'm three shots and a beer in.

"Dude, are you already fucking drunk?" Hunter asks.

"Not yet!" I shout over the music.

Liam places his hand on my shoulder. "Ready to get this party started?"

"Fuck yeah!" I tell him as he orders double shots of tequila for the three of us. We're the loud, annoying guys at the bar, but I give no fucks. We take our shots, and Hunter orders another round. I'm tempted to text our other roommate to come hang out with us, but she's been so busy with work that I'm sure she's already in bed.

"How'd it go today with your dad?" Liam asks before we shoot down the alcohol. I've already gotten to the point in the night where it all tastes like water, so I just grin like an idiot.

"The same as always. He reminded me of how much of a dick he is and how much of a disappointment I am."

"Fuck him!" Hunter says. "He's just like my dad. Both assholes."

"Totally." I nod and laugh. Since Hunter's dad is in politics, he grew up in the same type of household as me. Their relationship is just as rocky, but he's written his father off. I wish I could do the same, but since I hope to one day be working as a forensic investigator, and that department reports directly to the DA, he'll always be in my life in one way or another.

The music blares, and I find myself needing to sit because I'm too wobbly on my feet to stand. Hunter and Liam are both snagged by ladies and led to the dance floor. Instead of trying to follow along, I pull out my phone and scan through my contacts and come across Sophie's name. *Sweet Sophie.* Just seeing her name programmed in my phone makes my heart pound. Our friendship hasn't changed much over the last year, and I still think about her kisses and the way she tasted, though I shouldn't. I don't want to give her the wrong idea by getting too close, but anytime I'm with the guys and she's there, it's hard to take my eyes off her. I know my rejection stung, but I wish she'd believe me when I tell her it's what's best *for her*. That doesn't mean I don't wish I were capable of giving her more.

Since I'm a glutton for punishment, I find myself typing up a message because I want her here, right now. Though I've restrained myself from texting her after our amazing night together, the tequila is encouraging me to do it.

MASON

Whatcha doing tonight? Come meet me at the bar.

The text bubble pops up, and it makes me smile. I'm sure she's going to tell me to fuck off or throw it in my face that we're just friends.

SOPHIE

No thanks. Not looking for a repeat of the first night we met.

MASON

But you have to admit it was pretty unforgettable.

She sends me an eye roll emoji, and I find myself reliving those moments with her in the bathroom bar. Fuck, it was one of the hottest moments of my life.

SOPHIE

Error 404. Contact not found.

MASON

That's for websites, so nice try.

SOPHIE

Whatever. Go away.

MASON

Oh, come on. I'll buy you a drink.

SOPHIE

Isn't that what got us into this mess in the first place? Also, I'd prefer not to watch you flirt with every chick in the bar, you know, because you're not "relationship material."

I laugh because the only person I'm talking to right now is her. She's the only woman I've talked to all week.

MASON

I'll buy you two drinks then since, you know, you said it took more than one drink to seduce you 

SOPHIE

I must've blacked out during our first conversation.

MASON

Trust me, you were very alert...checking out every inch of me.

SOPHIE

How much have you had to drink?

Thinking about it, I honestly can't remember. A fucking lot.

MASON

Too many? Maybe I need you to be my designated driver

Knowing how motherly she is, I chuckle. If anything will get her here, it's that. She's too caring to ignore me, but we'll see.

My bladder is full, so I stand and tuck my phone in my pocket. I stumble on my way to the bathroom, bumping into shit. On the way back, I cut across the dance floor, which ends up being a huge mistake. I get knocked around like a ping pong ball and find myself laughing over the hilarity of it. There are so many people here, I might never make it back to order another drink.

I run into Hunter who's dancing close with some redhead.

"Lost?" He snickers.

Shaking my head, I flip him off and squeeze between bodies until I force myself to the other side of the bar. When I make it back, I plop down on my stool, and after I order another beer, a woman slides in the seat right next to me. The smell of her sweet perfume has me turning my head, and when I find Sophie, my eyes go wide.

"You came," I say, grinning.

She narrows her eyes at me. "Only because you pulled the DD card."

"I know you so well," I say, the alcohol swimming through my bloodstream, giving me way too much courage.

"You wish you did," she retorts. "Ready to go home? By the way your eyes are crossing, I think you've had enough to drink."

I nod, just wanting to be alone with her without having to strain to hear her over the music. Standing, I nearly fall over, and luckily, she catches me. Our faces are so damn close that I can smell the peppermint on her breath.

"Sorry," I softly say.

She wraps her arm around my waist. "Yep, you're so done. Where's Liam?"

I shrug, playing dumb because I'm sure she'd ream his ass, but we're all three sheets to the wind at this point. She shakes her head but doesn't let me go. On the way out, we pass Hunter and Liam dancing with two girls, and they give me shit as Sophie explains she's taking me home. As expected, she gives them a stern talking-to about drinking too much, which only makes them laugh their asses off.

"Don't puke in her car." Liam cackles, and I flip him off. Sophie holds me tight as I wobble beside her.

"Okay, okay. Time to go," she says, pulling me away from them. When we walk outside, the warm summer breeze blows through her dark hair, and I can smell her sweet shampoo.

"You smell so good."

She snorts. "You're so drunk."

When we get to her car, she unlocks the door and helps me inside, buckling me up like a little kid. She reaches over me, and I'm tempted to taste her lips again. It's been so long, but it's something I've never forgotten. Our eyes meet, and her breath hitches. I swallow hard, and she pulls away, shutting the door and walking around to the driver's side.

"You're too good to me. I don't deserve this. I don't deserve you," I mutter.

After she cranks the car, Sophie glances at me. "You might one day…if you grow up."

I smile, closing my eyes. "Hmm. Maybe one day, Sweet Sophie."

On the way home, I drift off as the booze takes over. It seems Sophie drives like a bat out of hell because it only takes all of a minute to arrive at my house. She pulls into the driveway and parks. I look at her, the streetlight casting an orange glow in the car.

"Damn," I whisper. "You're so beautiful."

"You're so wasted."

I shake my head. "Even so, you really are. I've got a few regrets in life, Soph. But one of my biggest is not being good enough for you."

Sophie leans her head back against the seat, and her eyes meet mine. There's disappointment behind them, and while I wish she would say something, it's not the time—not with me in my current state and my lips being way too loose.

"Good night, Mason. You should probably go to bed."

I suck in a deep breath before reaching for the door handle. "Good night. And thank you."

She gives me a quizzical look.

"Thanks for coming to my rescue. Hunter and Liam were preoccupied and intoxicated."

She giggles. "You're welcome. But next time, try Uber."

"Nah, there's no driver out there as pretty as you." I blink hard and smile, then stumble my way through the front door.

Once I'm inside, I kick off my shoes, then slowly make my way upstairs to my bedroom. Plopping on my bed, I close my eyes, and all I can see is the sad look on Sophie's face. I wish I could give her what she needs, but I can't because she deserves better than me.

Sophie deserves it all.

CHAPTER FOUR

IT'S BEEN a month since I drove Mason home from the bar. Though we have known each other for at least a year and have history, hearing him say he regrets not being good enough for me that night has replayed in my mind every day, and I can't seem to shake it. That night, he played me like a fiddle. He knew if he pulled the drunk card, I'd pick him up, and of course I did. Everyone knows to call me if they need a designated driver, even Mason. The next day, Liam gave me shit for it, and I was half-tempted to tell him what Mason said but kept it to myself. Though Liam can see through me and the way I feel about Mason, I've not admitted it because it's easier to keep those thoughts tucked deep inside.

My phone vibrates on my nightstand, and I grab it. I need to get out of bed and practice. Though I was hired to play in the symphony a year ago, I'm one of the youngest members, so I'm always having to prove my worth to those who have been playing as long as I've been alive. Unlocking my phone, I find a text from Lennon.

LENNON

Just a sisterly reminder. Don't forget it's Mom
and Dad's anniversary today.

Even though I had a reminder programmed in my phone. It's a
big one for them, year number thirty of being married.

SOPHIE

Calling them is on my list of things to do ☺

LENNON

Awesome! I'm gonna call them later after I finish
setting up my classroom and organizing the
instruments. We should get together soon too.

SOPHIE

Totally! Ugh, I have to practice for the next few
hours.

LENNON

Good luck!

We say our goodbyes, and I promise to go out with her soon.
Lennon recently moved to Sacramento to be with her boyfriend
and because she got hired as a music teacher for Hillsong
Elementary. My sisters are amazing, and I love how we'll all be
within driving distance from each other soon. Our youngest sister,
Maddie, is moving here in a week, and I literally can't wait. She
auditioned for a dance scholarship at Southern California
University before she graduated from high school, and right
before Christmas, she got the acceptance letter for a full ride. This
year, the Corrigan sisters will finally be together again, and I'm so
damn happy about it. Maddie is a free spirit, so I have a feeling I'll
be reining her in a lot, especially around Liam. He is one hundred
percent her type with that bad boy look and outgoing attitude.
I've always been the overprotective big sister—it's a part of who I
am and who I'll always be—but she's going to keep me on my
toes. I already know it.

After I dress, I walk into the kitchen and make a pot of coffee.

I'm going to need it to jolt me awake because I have a full day of practice ahead of me. My violin sits in its case by the door, and I set it on the kitchen table, then open it. The coffee finishes brewing, and I pour a cup, then grab the stand and my sheet music while I wait for the steaming liquid to cool. I usually practice while Maria, my roommate, is at her day job so I don't bother her while I play the same songs over and over until I memorize them. I try to be as considerate as I possibly can when she's home because I can't afford to live alone in this city on my salary. It's the main reason I've taken on side jobs like teaching kids how to play piano or violin and performing at weddings and special events with my string quartet.

I do a few stretches, knowing I'm gonna be sitting for hours, then take a sip of my coffee. Pulling my violin from its case, I place it on my shoulder and do a few warm-up scales. I play through each piece of music we're performing for next month's concert. At this point, I could play it all from memory, but I'm meticulous and make sure I hit each note perfectly. I'm my worst critic. Once I've finished each piece, I start from the beginning and go through my set two more times before my stomach growls, and I take a break to eat.

After I scarf down a sandwich, I grab my phone and FaceTime my parents. They answer after the first two rings and are all smiles.

"Sophie!" Mom grins.

"Hey," Dad says, standing behind her.

"Happy Anniversary, you two! Any big plans tonight?" I ask.

They look at each other and laugh, and I love how much they still enjoy each other's company. I hope to have a love like them one day.

"We're having dinner with some friends tonight and then after that…who knows." Dad chuckles, waggling his brows at my mother.

"Eww, TMI!" I shake my head and give them a face, which only encourages them to kiss like teenagers.

"Is that Sophie?" Maddie yells from behind, busting between them and taking the phone from their hands.

"Mads! Are you almost packed? You've got a week," Dad scolds.

She lets out a laugh. "You know it. I was packed before graduation day."

"Hey, give me the phone back," Mom demands.

"I'm counting down the hours," Maddie calls out, handing the phone to her with a snicker.

"Appreciate you calling, honey. Keep you in our prayers, and we'll talk soon. We love you," Mom tells me.

"Love you too. Bye, Maddie!" I say loud, and she yells it back right before the call ends.

Maddie's upcoming move has my parents struggling. It'll be the first time they'll be empty nesters, so it will be an adjustment for them both. Though my dad is the pastor for a mega church, Mom has devoted her life to us kids. She loves taking care of us, so it's going to be a huge change.

Growing up, we knew how much they loved us, but it didn't take away from the fact we were forced to live by their strict rules. Besides having early night curfews, we weren't allowed to date, wear clothes that showed any sort of cleavage, and attending church was mandatory several times a week. Maddie is ready for freedom, and Mom knows she's a handful. I've promised more than once to take care of and protect my little sister while she's here and look out for her and Lennon, but it doesn't seem like enough.

"Come visit us soon." Dad shoots me a wink.

"Maybe. You know how hard it is to break away with rehearsals," I remind them.

They nod, and we chat a little longer before saying our goodbyes. I tell them to have fun, but not too much fun. After the call ends, I go back to practicing but can't stop thinking about Maddie being here next week. It makes me so damn excited. Moving to California was one of the best decisions I ever made. I learned how to make choices in a world without my parents always nagging or guiding me and enjoyed growing up on my own terms. She's going to have fun, but hopefully not too much, though. The girl seems to love trouble.

"There's my favorite sister," I tease when Maddie plops down in the booth next to me. I can't believe she's finally here. She wraps her arms around me and laughs, then glances at Lennon. They're both my favorite, and I love them equally, but it's always fun to joke about favs. It's been a running thing since we were kids.

Maddie looks around with an eager expression. "I think the Coliseum is gonna be my new favorite place. Although they won't serve a minor…I guess it'll have to do."

"Yes, it will," I say. "You'll get to drink plenty after you turn twenty-one. Just enjoy being underage for a few more years." Even though I promised my parents I'd watch her, Maddie is gonna do what she wants to do. Always has, always will.

Lennon giggles. "Remember how things were when I first moved here?"

I grin thinking about it. "You acted like you found freedom for the first time ever."

"Pfft. It *was* freedom." She glances at Maddie. "Until I dated that asshole who nearly ruined me."

"See, Mads. This is why you need to take it slow and not rush into anything," I remind her.

"Yeah, yeah. Date with intention. Right, *Mom*?" She snorts just as Lennon's cell vibrates. Her face lights up as she unlocks it, which means it's Brandon. They're madly in love, and though it's almost sickening to witness, I'm happy for her. Lennon deserves a nice guy. Hell, we all could use one.

"Brandon's gonna stop by. That okay?" Lennon asks with googly eyes.

"Yep, the guys coming too?" I ask, curious if Mason will be joining us.

Lennon types away. "Just Mason and Hunter."

Maddie's gaze ping-pongs between us. "They're the hot ones, right?"

"They're all hot." I snort, hoping neither of them sees through my lies.

Shaking her head, Lennon goes back to her phone. "You are off-limits to them. *Especially* Hunter."

Maddie rolls her eyes, and Lennon instantly becomes frustrated. "I'm serious, Maddie. He's a player and will screw anything that has legs. I'll be damned if—"

"Okay, okay," I interrupt. "I think she's got the point."

Maddie shrugs. "Maybe if one of you gets me a drink, I'll understand better?"

"Don't piss her off," I say.

Lennon playfully flips her off, but she's not kidding about Hunter. She's ready to murder him.

I pull my phone from my purse and decide to text Liam because he likes the Coliseum. Over the last year, we've become great friends, and I enjoy his company so much. He's like the big brother I never had, and he's fun as hell. He gets me without wanting to get into my pants.

SOPHIE

Why aren't you coming to have drinks with us?

LIAM

Tied up on a job. You know how it goes.

SOPHIE

Like a real job? Or some chick?

LIAM

A real job. Unfortunately. Out of town again. I should be back in a few days, though. We should get together.

SOPHIE

We should. You still need to meet my little sis.

LIAM

If she's anything like you…hard pass. 🙂

SOPHIE

Don't worry. She's worse than me. Wayyyyy worse.

Maddie leans over and sneaks a peek at my phone screen, but I try to hide it from her. "Ooh. Who's Liam?"

Lennon arches a brow. "Just one of the guys. Seeing where he's at."

"And that's it?" Lennon asks, almost suspicious of our friendship.

"Yes, we're *just* friends. And I'm not just saying that. What we have is strictly platonic." I make eye contact with Lennon, and she backs off.

"Is he hot?" Maddie asks.

"Oh my God, Mads. You act like you're in heat." I let out a chuckle, but it trails off when Mason, Brandon, and Hunter walk through the door. The three of them look like superheroes coming to save the day in their tight T-shirts that leave no room for imagination.

Lennon waves when she makes eye contact with Brandon. He seems to glide across the room toward her and doesn't stop until their lips smack together. Brandon slides into the booth next to her, and Mason and Hunter go to the bar. Neither says hello.

"What crawled up their asses and died?" Maddie grunts, and I snort.

"This is my little sister, Maddie," Lennon introduces her to Brandon.

"Nice to finally meet you in person." He glances at me and Maddie, then back at Lennon. "They were right, babe. You really might be adopted."

Lennon slaps him on the arm, and I snort.

"You told him about that?" I ask.

We used to tease her when we were kids because she was the only blond in a family of brunettes. One time, she cried about it, and Mom took me to the side and told me to stop saying it. Our grandma had blond hair, and Lennon looks just like her, so there's zero doubt about her being my sister, but she always felt left out.

"He knows everything about me," she says, leaning into him for a kiss.

"You two are gross," I tease just as Mason and Hunter walk up with their drinks.

Hunter eyes Maddie, and she gives him a smoldering grin. Lennon looks like she's about to combust as she narrows her eyes at him.

"And who's this?" Hunter asks, and I snicker, knowing how he loves to get under Lennon's skin.

"My little sister, Maddie. She's off-limits, so don't even think about it." She stresses every word. "This is Hunter and Mason," she continues, waving her hand out toward them.

"Hi, boys," Maddie says, and Lennon gives her *the* look.

Mason glances at me, and for a split second, it feels like time freezes. His eyes meet mine, and I open my mouth to say something, but he looks away before I can speak. Awkwardness streams between us, and I'm happy when Brandon changes the subject, pulling the attention away before anyone notices the tension.

"Hey, Sophie. What's up?" Hunter nearly finishes his beer in one pull.

"Hey, how are you?" I ask, being polite.

He shrugs and gives me a smirk. "Just dealing with your sister who's a pain in my ass."

Lennon scoffs. "Excuse you? You're a pain in *my* ass." Brandon chuckles and wraps his arm around Lennon.

"Hey, Mason." I guess I'm going to be the one who tries to hold a civil conversation.

"Hey," he says dryly, then focuses on chugging his beer until the bottle is empty. He doesn't say another word to me, not even shitty small talk. I'm half-tempted to call him out and ask him what the hell his problem is, but I bite my tongue instead. Just friends, right? I repeat it over and over in my head.

Hunter looks just as uncomfortable as Mason, and Maddie notices. She leans over and whispers in my ear. "They always this awkward?"

"I need a drink," I finally say, letting out a huff. I stand, and Maddie follows me as I head to the bar.

She flashes a big cheesy grin. "Gonna buy me a drink now?"

"Hell no," I say with a glare.

"You are literally no fun. Lennon would've gotten me a drink." She's trying to guilt me, but I know better. Lennon wouldn't dare do that, and no amount of Maddie trying to play us against each other will work. "Then go ask her," I say, then order a double shot of tequila.

"You know you're not supposed to call my bluff!" She smirks as my shot is placed on the counter. I pay and shoot it down quickly, allowing it to burn.

"I'll just live vicariously through you." Maddie grins, sitting on the barstool, and I take the one next to her so I can clear my head.

"So…" She draws out. "You and Mason got something going on?"

I narrow my eyes. "Why would you think that?"

She shrugs. "Just the way you talk to each other."

"We barely exchanged three words." I roll my eyes and order another drink, and she gets water.

"Mmhmm. Whatever you say, big sis. But your face gives you away every single time."

I take the second shot and try to ignore her, but I can't believe she figured it out within the first two minutes of seeing him. It makes me wonder if Lennon knows and is just ignoring it. Or maybe she's too preoccupied with Brandon to notice. I look at Maddie who's giving googly eyes to the bartender. The girl is relentless.

"Guess we should get back to all the fun. I think I'm good now," I speak up, breaking her away.

"Drunk Sophie is my favorite!" Maddie claps, and I laugh. "I'm sure she's Mason's favorite too."

"I'm gonna ship you back to Utah if you don't stop," I warn.

She giggles and nearly skips back to the table. "Nope! You're stuck with me for at least four more years."

"Lucky me," I tease with a smile, hoping she doesn't make it awkward when we get back to the group, but I'm sure she will.

I should've ordered ten more drinks because dealing with Mason when he's in one of his moods is hell.

CHAPTER FIVE

MASON

ONE YEAR EARLIER

My heart pounds as I listen to Emma's voicemail. Her voice is cool and calm as if she's accepted her fate. Nothing like the several she previously left me when she'd stop taking her medication, then lose it after a few days.

But tonight feels different, *is* different. After a dozen missed text and voice messages from her and her sister, I race to her sorority house on a random bike I found outside the frat house. The music blares loudly for over a block, my body shaking as the blood whooshes in my ears. Although I have the worst feeling in my gut, I hope everything is okay.

The moment I walk into her room, the air rushes from my lungs.

I shake her. Pleading with her to wake up and cursing when she doesn't.

Her eyes. They look at me, begging me to save her.

Begging me to fix her.

I pump her chest, breathe into her mouth, and pray for a miracle.

Why, Emma? Why?

Everything fades to black, and my eyes pop open at the blaring sound of my phone alarm. Reaching over, I turn it off and wipe the sweat off my forehead and neck.

A dream. Another fucking dream.

Rather, a *nightmare.*

They've been more frequent over the past couple of months. In April, Brandon died in a tragic motorcycle accident, and it rocked us all. Hunter and Lennon are leaning on each other to grieve, but it's brought up memories from my past that I've tried to keep locked away. Memories I can't handle remembering.

Memories from four years ago that changed my life forever.

The image of her lying helplessly on the bed has continued to haunt me for years.

Brandon was one of my best friends and losing him has put me back into that dark place I've tried so hard to avoid. I can't afford to emotionally spiral out of control again, knowing my dad will be right there to put me in my place, so I do the only thing I can to relieve the stress and pain.

I kick my trainer's ass in boxing.

Waking up early means I can work out before going into the office, so I grab my duffle bag and drive to the gym with my nightmare and Brandon still lingering in my thoughts.

It doesn't feel real. I'm still waiting for him to walk in the door and dare me to do a keg stand. He was so in love with Lennon, and unfortunately, I know how she feels and what she's going through. Hunter, too.

All three of them were roommates, but Hunter and him were damn close. He's being strong for Lennon's sake. I've seen how he acted around her before, but ever since the accident, he's done a complete one-eighty and will do anything for her. I suspect he's had feelings for her, but knowing Hunter, he'd never act on them. He's not that kind of guy, but he'll sacrifice everything, even himself, to take care of her for Brandon's sake. That's how he is. And to make matters harder, Lennon found out she was pregnant shortly after he died.

Everything is a damn mess right now.

I graduated with my master's degree and wrapped up my internship at the city morgue last month, and had I been working the night Brandon died, his body would've been brought in before I had word of the accident. Knowing that pierces my gut because even after getting used to being around dead bodies, seeing his would've fucked me up worse.

This fucking head of mine. I wish I could turn it off and clear out the trauma that's made me the man I am today. The one who's a constant failure in my dad's eyes, the one who can't do relationships, and the one who numbs the pain by hitting someone.

I'm all worked up as soon as I get to the mat, which Tyler recognizes. He thinks it makes me better, but he doesn't realize how much pain I harbor, pain that allows me to punch the bag the way I do. After I do my reps, he wraps up his own hands and taunts me, knowing it won't take much to set me off. He taps my right cheek, then my left, pushes my shoulders a bit, and tells me to hit him.

He knows I won't *hurt* him, but we fight to win. Once I'm in that ring, I give it my all just as he does. His job is to make me better by strengthening my moves and critiquing my techniques. Tyler's at least five years older than I am and has been boxing for over a decade. I'd consider him a friend if I didn't need to keep our relationship at a professional level. Getting too close to people only gives them permission to let you down, and I've had enough of that to last a fucking lifetime.

"That's all you've got, Holt?" he mocks when he misses me, and I sucker punch him in the ribs. He barely winces although it was a decent hit. "My baby sister hits harder than you."

Grinding my teeth, I narrow my eyes into slits with my hands up. "Oh yeah? She legal?" I swing and miss when he steps out of my reach.

"Fuck off." Tyler goes for my jaw, but I duck and punch his other rib.

"I bet I could corrupt her. Give her a damn good time. Whaddya say? Give me her number." I smirk, knowing my words are distracting him, so when I punch him right in the gut, he nearly falls back into the ropes.

"Motherfucker, that was a low blow." He grimaces, pushing himself back up. "She's too good for you."

I shrug, letting his dig slide right off. And because I'm a glutton for punishment today, I keep punching and swinging. "Bet she gives good head."

Tyler pushes me back, nearly making me trip over my own feet until I'm bouncing off the ropes and he's in my face. I hold up my arms, covering my face as he lands punch after punch to my stomach.

After a half dozen jabs, I twist my body away from him and wrap my arm around his neck as my other hand decks him in the side. I manage to get him to his knees right before he takes my legs from under me. Soon, we're both on the floor, holding each other tight and trying to throw blows.

"If your sister cuddles half as good as you do, I just might take her ass too."

"Holt, I warned you…" he growls before kneeing me between the legs.

I groan loudly as he releases his hold on me, then stands as I lie helplessly below him. After blinking away the tears, I manage to get to my hands and knees, breathing heavily. Things haven't gotten this heated in months.

Just when Tyler thinks it's over and I'm going to surrender, I cut my arm under his knees and take him out until he's flat on his back. Then I place a knee on his gut, and as he grunts, I swing at his face, landing a good punch to his cheek.

The adrenaline from it all has me wheezing, and I fall next to him, my chest heaving for air.

"You're a real fucking asshole, you know that?" Tyler mutters between gasps.

"Does this mean you approve of me taking your sister out?" I turn my head to flash a toothy shit-eating grin. He jabs his elbow into my chest, then stands up.

"For the record, my sister would chew you up, then spit you

out before you even had the chance to ask her out. She's tougher than I am." He holds out his hand and helps me up.

"Alright. Point taken." I laugh, though we both know it was just the fuel that lit our workout. "I need to hit the showers and head to work. Now that I've kicked your ass, I won't feel the need to punch anyone out today."

"Don't push your luck, Holt."

I slide between the ropes, then jump out of the ring. "You know I always do."

Once I got the degree I needed to pursue a career in forensics, I had hoped my bitch boy days of making coffee runs and filing papers would also end. Each internship has taught me so much, even if parts of it sucked, and I'm grateful for the experiences. Putting them on my resume helped get a foot in the door for the job I wanted. Unfortunately, only a few forensic investigator jobs exist in the area, so while I wait for a position to open, I had to find other work to pay the bills.

I got a job at the Bureau of Investigations as an assistant in the homicide unit. It's right up my alley and involves more of what I went to school for, but that doesn't mean I don't get treated like a grunt. Being the DA's son comes with higher expectations, and while I don't mind the added pressures, I could live without the constant comments about how "Daddy got me here."

Working around men in suits all day is like being in the middle of a testosterone war. Everyone has a fucking point to prove.

Today ended up being one of those days I despise and was happier than a pig in mud to finally leave.

My supervisor lives to get under my goddamn skin and puts me in a piss-poor mood especially after it drives me to fuck up something. It was an easy task, but my mind was elsewhere after the way I woke up this morning.

I just want to go home, kick back, and have a beer to end this shit-tastic day. The last thing I need is company at the house, but that's exactly what I see when I pull into the driveway.

Fucking great.

Sophie *and* Maddie.

Normally, I don't mind their presence even when things get awkward, but it's been more than usual lately ever since Brandon died. They seem to think we need the distraction. Lennon has pushed everyone away except Hunter, so the girls come visit us. Losing Brandon was another wake-up call, one I didn't know I needed, but after what happened with Emma and helping with the homicide cases, I know all too well how short and unfair life can be.

Still, after the shit day I had, I just wanted to relax at home in quiet. Sophie and Maddie come with talking, *lots* of talking. Avoiding Sophie makes it easier to accept that we can never be together, but it gets harder when she's in my damn house invading my personal space.

"Hey, man," Liam greets as soon as he hears me.

"Hey." I keep my eyes focused in front of me as I walk toward the kitchen.

"Rough day, big guy?" Maddie asks.

I grunt. "Could say that."

Grabbing a beer from the fridge, I slam the door shut, then twist the cap off the bottle. I chug it, needing to erase the day away. Laughter echoes from the living room, and I grow more agitated that Sophie and Liam are so friendly.

I shouldn't give a shit, but after all this time, I still do. Though I don't show it, I care a lot for Sophie but having her around and in my house always fucks with my head.

She deserves better than I could ever offer her, better than someone who's fighting their own demons and is an emotional mess. The more I remind myself of that, the better.

Distance.

It's what I need so the temptation stops choking me.

The moment I walk into the living room and dart my eyes toward them, I instantly regret it. Sophie's lying on the couch with her feet in Liam's lap, and Maddie's flipping through the channels. I have no right to feel jealous or bitter, but that doesn't make seeing Liam's hands on her any easier.

"Wanna talk about it?" Sophie asks. Her big brown eyes look

up with so much kindness, and I just wish she'd stop looking at me like that. I don't deserve it.

"Nope," I say, sitting on the recliner that faces the TV, allowing me to avoid looking at them. "Would rather just forget it."

"You can't just drink every time you have a shit day, Mason." Maddie means well, but she's too young to understand a damn thing about the real world. She's only nineteen and just finished her first year of college.

"Would you rather I'd sit here and get high all night?" I bemuse.

"Oh, do you have any pot?" Her voice goes up an octave, which makes Sophie groan.

"Shut up, Mads. You know damn well you can't smoke pot during training, not to mention Mom and Dad would kill you if they ever found out," Sophie scolds her just as I knew she would. She's on the straight and narrow and would never do anything that crosses the line.

Except that night we met.

I still can't wrap my mind around why she did it. Knowing her now, I realize it's truly out of her character, which makes me feel like a bigger douche for telling her we should only be friends. I don't think she's dated another guy since the night we met, and while it's selfish of me to be glad she hasn't, she won't stay single forever.

Maddie, on the other hand, loves pushing boundaries, and knowing parts of their family history, I understand why. Not only did they come from a strict and religious home, but Maddie is the youngest and loves rebelling by doing everything her parents told her not to. I think she tries to get away with so much shit because she's been told how to act and what to say most of her life.

Maddie's a dancer, which also means she has a level of professionalism to uphold, but when she's off campus, she gives no fucks.

After Maddie finally settles on a show, Liam and Sophie chuckle at something. After some squealing and hearing Sophie sucker punch Liam, I glance over my shoulder and see he's tickling her feet.

Fuck me.

Why am I jealous? Liam claims he thinks of Sophie as his sister, but what if he doesn't? Or worse, what if she likes him too?

It wouldn't be that far-fetched, considering how much they have in common. They're both obsessed with Jackie Chan movies, which I found out months ago when they decided to spend an entire Saturday binging all his movies. They're both into classical music too, which I quickly learned when I first moved in with Liam. But when Sophie found out, she nearly flipped. The moment Liam mentioned one of her favorite composer's names along with an entire list of songs, Sophie lit up like a Christmas tree and couldn't stop talking about it. I sat there like a dumbass, not knowing a damn thing.

They constantly love challenging each other in games of pool, but fortunately for me, there's no more stripping. Now they just place bets for who's buying drinks the next time we go out.

Hell, maybe he *should* date Sophie. He probably thinks she's off-limits because he knows we hooked up, but that was two years ago. If nothing will come from it, why should he sit on the sidelines?

Fuck it. I need another beer so I can get out of my own damn head. So I can get *her* out of my head.

"So what do you think, Mason?"

"Huh?" I look over my shoulder at them on the couch and see the three of them staring at me. Fuck, I spaced out. "About what?"

"Did you not hear a word I just said?" Maddie curls her lips with her brow arched.

"No, sorry. Thinking."

Her face softens. "Sophie's symphony is playing at the park on the Fourth of July before the fireworks. Do you wanna join me and Hulk?"

I glance at Liam, who doesn't seem eager about being alone with Maddie, so I take pity on the poor bastard and nod. "Sure, I should be able to make it."

"Yay!" Maddie claps. "Then when she's done playing, we can all watch the fireworks together."

Yeah. *Yay.*

I groan, pushing myself up and walking to the kitchen for another beer.

"Can you grab me a diet soda, pretty please?" Maddie calls.

"Me too," Sophie chimes in.

"Me too." Liam chuckles, then adds, "Except I want a beer."

"What am I? Your drink bitch?" I shout, then grab two beers and two sodas.

"Well, we are your company, so you should be a good little host and fetch us drinks," Maddie says with a sweetness that has me snorting.

"Company? That would imply you were *invited*," I say as I walk back into the living room.

"You're in a mood tonight," Sophie says, lowering her eyes and not meeting mine. Fuck, now I feel like an asshole. I hand the girls their drinks and Liam his beer.

"Sorry," I say, taking my seat. "It's hard dealing with people who want to act like assholes because I'm a Holt."

"I'm so glad I'm allowed to punch people for my job," Liam says with a groan. "No wonder you hired a boxing trainer. Feels good to kick someone's ass at least." He chuckles as if he's just told the world's funniest joke. Though he's not wrong in the least.

"Just because you're a bounty hunter…" Sophie starts before Liam cuts her off.

"Uh, excuse me, it's fugitive recovery agent," he mocks. "I don't call you an instrument player."

Sophie snorts. "Not the same thing."

Then Maddie snickers, popping her can. "Potato *potato.*"

"Just because you're a fugitive-whatever doesn't mean you can just openly punch out people. Aren't there rules for that kind of thing?" Sophie asks. "Or, rather, laws?"

"I work for several bond companies who want their money, and when they don't get it, they want the fugitive back in jail.

They don't care how I get them or ask questions. And if no one's asking, no one's telling." Liam smirks, then sips his beer.

Sophie chuckles, and I hate how her face lights up anytime Liam talks. "You should let me shadow you on the job sometime!"

"Hell no," I say at the same time Liam says, "Hell yeah!"

We glare at each other.

"And why not?" Sophie directs her question at me.

"Because it's not safe." I give her the obvious response.

"I'm a big girl, Mason," she tells me assertively. "I don't need a babysitter."

I can't tell her the real reason—why I don't want her alone with Liam more than she already is, why I'm overly protective of her, and why I still struggle with my emotions and feelings for her. I can't tell her shit. The demons I battle on a daily basis are too much for me to handle, and I can't put that on anyone else, especially not her.

"Fine. Do whatever you want." I chug my beer, then stand, toss it in the trash, and head for my room.

CHAPTER SIX

SOPHIE

THE PAST FEW months have been hard for everyone, especially Lennon. Losing Brandon almost three months ago, then finding out she was pregnant not long after were hard realities to accept. She hadn't had time to grieve her loss or process anything that happened before she found out she would be a mother. Though I consider the baby a miracle already, I've been worried about Lennon and her health. I've been trying my hardest not to mother her too much and give her space, but it's been hard as hell.

Thankfully, Hunter has been there for her. He's been her saving grace, making sure she's getting sleep, eating, and taking care of herself, and I will forever be grateful for him. The man has completely turned his attitude and behavior around and has taken it upon himself to protect her. He's the only one who Lennon doesn't push away or ignore. At first, it hurt that she wouldn't talk to me about everything, but I understood why. The pain was too much for her, and I couldn't relate. All I could do was wait until she was ready, though I'm not certain she ever will be.

It's come to a point where our parents need to know. Lennon will eventually start showing, and lying to them will be impossible. Sure, they live in Utah, but we're all close, and they FaceTime us regularly.

Considering how religious and strict our parents are, they won't accept her being pregnant out of wedlock, so she hasn't told them yet. Lennon's concerned they'll write her off, and I have been too because the possibility of that is more than real. On a whim, Hunter suggested to be her fake husband and pretend the baby is his, and they flew to Utah this weekend to pull off one of the greatest stunts any of us have ever done. I haven't heard from her yet, but I'm anxiously waiting.

I stir, unable to sleep, and though it's early as hell, I get out of bed and make some coffee. Anytime I have a concert, I hardly get any rest the night before, so it's normal. Today is the symphony's Fourth of July program, and I want to run through my set a few times before heading to the park, so I may as well get started. When I round the corner to the kitchen, there's a sink full of dishes and a dirty pan on the stovetop. The trash is overflowing, and there's an empty gallon of milk sitting next to it on the floor.

"Are we fucking children around here?" I grind out, then get frustrated when I set my hand in smeared mustard on the counter.

I glare at the bright yellow paste on my palm and almost lose my shit. It's way too early for this, and I'm two seconds from waking the entire apartment. With everything I have, I try not to scream at the top of my lungs as I grab some paper towels and clean up the mess, but I refuse to do it all and leave the dirty dishes in the sink.

Soon, Maria and Carter will be getting up to go to work, and considering the mood I'm already in, it'd be best if I didn't see them.

Maria and I have lived together for a few years, and we had a good thing going until she became more serious with her boyfriend. When she asked if he could move in, I should've said no, but I couldn't afford this apartment on my own. If I would've been against it, she would've moved out and left me with the lease. I could've tried to find a new roommate but was worried that I wouldn't in a timely manner to help with the rent. With rehearsal and everything else going on in my life, I caved and have regretted it every day since. Carter's a slob, and I need to get the hell out of here as soon as possible.

After my coffee finishes brewing, I make a cup and go into my room and shut the door. I'm so damn angry as I sit on the edge of my bed, waiting for the liquid to stop steaming. Thankfully, my phone vibrates and pulls me away from my annoyance.

LENNON

Forgot to tell you we made it here safe and sound. Mom and Dad love Hunter (shocker, right?) and today is when the REAL fun begins.

Her message makes me smile, and I'm so relieved she's texting me. Today is the big Fourth of July celebration in Utah, and the day will be full of events. The church helps with a lot of activities, so Lennon and Hunter will be around my parents all day. I'm glad they love Hunter, but he can be very charismatic when he wants to be.

SOPHIE

About damn time, woman! I wasn't sure if they kicked your asses out or not. I mean, based on the situation, it was kind of a toss-up.

We make small talk, and I nearly snort when she asks me if all guys get morning wood. I know why she's asking too. She and Hunter are sleeping in her old bed that's so small it's laughable. Of course, I give her shit about it when she asks me if it's normal.

SOPHIE

Probably when there's a body pressed against it. Especially YOUR body.

I bet she's regretting texting me now, but we continue to chat about all things Hunter. Lennon cares about him deeply just by the way she looks at him when he's around. Though she hasn't admitted it, and I haven't pushed her on it *too much*, eventually, it will come to a crossroads because it's more than obvious how Hunter feels. They're in a weird non-relationship relationship. I just don't want my sister to get hurt. She's gone through enough this year.

We continue to go back and forth, and she promises to keep me updated. The fact that my parents love Hunter has me smiling, and it's a relief they don't see through the lie. They act natural and believable around each other because there's more there than either of them wants to admit. The underlying tone of her text messages makes me happy. She needed this break.

As I pick up my cup of coffee and take a sip, Maria and Carter scurry around the apartment. Part of me wants to walk out there and tell them both how I feel about this arrangement while ripping Carter a new one, but it'd be a waste of time. He's immune. No matter how much I complain or how nicely I ask, he's still a slob and refuses to change his ways. Maria accepts it because she's sleeping with him. I don't know how much longer I can stand it, but I'm trying to hold out.

Once the front door closes, I grab my violin and go into the dining room to practice today's lineup a few times. The music whisks me away from the filthy apartment and my annoyance. After three hours of playing, a sense of calm moves over me and then I get in the shower.

While I wash my hair, I think about my life and how I'm single as hell. Mason slides through my thoughts, but I push him away. As much as I want there to be something between us, I'm giving up hope. I've waited around for so long, and I'm sure he's wondering why I haven't gotten the hint yet. Knowing he'll be at my concert today makes me nervous, but it also gives me a glimmer of hope when I shouldn't have one.

I step out of the shower and dry off, then dress in the black uniform we're required to wear for concerts. Before I grab my keys, I text Maddie to see what she's up to. Considering she lives in the dorms and sold her car to move to California, I already know what the answer will be, but I text her anyway.

SOPHIE

Meeting me at the park?

MADDIE

Hell no. Come pick me up!

SOPHIE

You're so demanding. I'll be there in fifteen minutes. The show won't start for an hour, though. You gonna be okay while I warm up?

MADDIE

There are food trucks. I'll be fine.

I snort-laugh and pack my shit, then head out the door. As I drive to the dorms to pick up Maddie, my phone buzzes. At the first red light, I unlocked my phone and read the message.

LIAM

Mason and I are on the way. You there yet?

The last time we hung out, they both agreed to come to the concert and hang out after. It means a lot to me that he'll be there cheering me on. Liam's the brother I never had.

SOPHIE

Grabbing Maddie, then I'll be there.

LIAM

Alright! Maybe there'll be some hot, single chicks there? You think?

SOPHIE

Maddie will make sure to scare them off for you.

LIAM

NO.

I love teasing him because I see the way he looks at her, but he denies it. Though, it's not any different from me and Mason, and he loves to ride my ass about it. Maybe I'm in denial too. Before I can send him a text message back, the light turns green, and I go. My heart flutters when I think about Mason and how he'll finally get to see me play. Lately, when I've been hanging out with Liam, he's kept his distance, pretending I don't exist. The way he treats me is starting to wear me down.

Soon, I'm pulling up to the dorms, and Maddie is already outside waiting for me. Her shorts, if you can call them that, are nearly invisible, and she's wearing a crop top that shows off her perfectly toned body. Once she's in the car, I playfully scold her.

"Go up there and change, young lady. You can't go out in public wearing that."

"But how will I get any dick if I can't show off what my mama gave me?"

I narrow my eyes at her, scowling.

"Oh, come on. You know it's hot as hell out here. I'm already sweating." She fans herself with a laugh.

I grunt. "For a virgin, you're dirtier than anyone I know."

She shrugs, then puts on her seat belt, and I drive toward the park.

"Dance school. I learn about all sorts of terrible, horrible, and thrilling things backstage." When she waggles her eyebrows at me, I burst out into laughter.

"I don't want to know."

"Sure you do! Did you know there's a sex position called the Butter Churner?"

I glance at her. "Don't. Don't you dare."

"You're no fun." She snickers. "Bet you google it later."

"Bet you I don't!" I challenge, then change the subject and tell her about Lennon's texts this morning. She's all googly eyes when I tell her everything is going as planned. I give her the shortened version because Lennon will tell us more when she returns, and she better not leave out any juicy details.

"So Mom and Dad believe it?" she asks.

"One hundred percent."

Maddie sighs. "They just need to do it already."

I snort, shaking my head. Though I can't disagree.

"What? She's already pregnant. What's the worst that could happen?"

I park the car and glance at her. "You're grounded."

"For being right?"

"For being *bad*," I say, and she rolls her eyes before opening the door.

I grab my violin, then we walk across the park toward the stage. Families, couples, and tons of kids make up the crowd already here, which makes me super excited. Food trucks line the perimeter, and Maddie is already scoping them out.

"You hungry?" she asks.

"Nah. I ate already." My phone vibrates in my pocket and pulls me away. I remember I didn't text Liam back, but then notice I have another one from him.

LIAM

Here!

SOPHIE

We're by the stage. About to warm up.

LIAM

Heading that way.

Smiling, I look around, but the park is so crowded, it's hard to pinpoint their location. As soon as I tell Maddie they're here, she lights up with excitement.

"Now I'm glad I wore these shorts. Show Liam what he's missing out on." She's determined to crack his shell. I think it's hilarious how relentless she is.

"I doubt you're the first girl to show off her long legs. Liam's a robot when it comes to you," I tease.

"Well, good thing I'll be hanging out with them while you play. Perhaps I'll break through his walls. And if that doesn't work, I'll find a guy who's interested." She tightens her ponytail and smirks.

"They're gonna play big brother and not let any man close enough to get handsy," I say. They're just as protective of her as Lennon and I are, even when they act like she annoys them.

"Liam can get as handsy as he wants." She pops her hip.

"The only way Liam's hands are gonna be on you is if he has to carry your ass out of this park to keep the guys away from you. So don't push him," I only half-tease. I wouldn't put much past Maddie if it meant getting Liam's attention or having him finally admit he finds her attractive.

"I'm sure someone here would love to help me make him jealous." Maddie searches around, and I notice that look on her face. She's serious, and she might just do that. Maddie's beautiful, and I often worry about her. She's flirty, sometimes too much, but Liam and Mason won't let her do whatever she wants. Though, when Liam is around, Maddie doesn't have eyes for anyone else. She just likes to make jokes about it to get a reaction out of him.

From the corner of my eye, I see Mr. Tanner, my conductor, walk on stage while others arrange the music stands. "Crap. I gotta go. I love you. *Be good.*"

She grins. "Break a leg!"

"God, I hope not. I need my legs," I remind her for the thirteenth time. The saying is a thespian tradition, not one for musicians, especially considering I have my clumsy moments. I give her a quick smile before I turn and force my way through the crowd of people. When I make it on the stage, I look out into the audience and see Maddie chatting with Liam and Mason. I breathe a little easier, knowing they found each other, though she might have a tracking device on Liam at this point.

I arrange my sheet music and then grab my violin from its case and warm up by running through the scales. My heart beats furiously in my chest, and I'm somewhat nervous about Mason being here. Knowing he's out there watching me is a big deal to me even if it isn't for him.

Mr. Tanner moves to the front and gets our attention by tapping the baton on the stand in front of him. One by one, the instruments stop playing until we're sitting quietly, watching him.

"We're all here? Ready?" he asks. I glance around and don't

find an empty seat on the stage. If there's one thing about this group, we're punctual as hell.

We all nod, and he sucks in a deep breath and grabs the microphone. It's customary for him to do a small introduction and give a speech. I look out into the park and am blown away by how many people are waiting for us to play. The number of people in the audience this year are almost double of last year's attendance.

As I search over the crowd, I spot Maddie sitting between the guys close to the front on a blanket. Mason's laughing and so is Maddie, so I'm sure she said something inappropriate, as usual. Liam is as stiff as a board and it has me cracking the hell up. As I'm lost watching them, I look back at Mason and find him staring at me. I glance back at Mr. Tanner and try to pay attention to what he's saying.

"It's our seventeenth year to perform for the city of Sacramento. We're honored you're here. Sit back and enjoy the show." After a slight bow, he turns back toward us, and we all straighten our spines and get into position. He counts down, and we flawlessly start playing "The Star-Spangled Banner." The music whisks me away as I play, getting lost in it. I don't take a single day of having this as my job for granted. Performing, though it makes me nervous, also lights a fire inside me.

As I bow each note, a grin touches my lips, and I'm sucked into the melody. Though we've made it through most of our setlist, I'm shocked when the cellos begin the final song. After the cymbals crash, I look out at the nameless faces smiling, and it makes me so damn happy because I can see how the songs affected them. Once it's over and the audience applauds, I grab my sheet music and put my violin in its case, then tell several of my colleagues goodbye. My phone vibrates in my pocket and pulls me away as I walk down the stairs.

MADDIE

We're coming to meet you.

SOPHIE

K!

Before I can get lost in the hordes of people, Maddie comes bouncing up.

"You are a rock star!" she nearly yells, which causes me to blush.

I shake my head. "Nah."

"I'm impressed as fuck right now," Liam tells me, giving me a side hug. "I literally had no idea you were a part of something that good. I mean, Maddie jokes about you being a mistro all the time, but I don't think it's a joke anymore. That shit is real talk."

"I know, right?" Maddie says proudly.

I glance at Mason, and he's too busy staring past me, not paying attention to anything that's being said. Liam elbows him. "Right?"

"Oh, yeah. Great job," he says dryly, and even though I want to junk punch him, I refrain.

"Are you hungry?" Maddie asks, interrupting the awkward tension streaming between Mason and me. I'm not sure why or how it got to this point, but it's annoying as hell.

"Actually, I could use something to drink," I admit, feeling parched.

"They've got a daiquiri truck over there." Maddie points. "You could get me and you both one!"

"Not happening," I tell her, looping my arm through hers.

"One drink isn't gonna get me drunk," she states. Then she adds, "Well, it could, I guess. I'd probably be a lightweight." She giggles, then leans in and whispers, "You did awesome today."

"Thanks," I say.

Liam walks on the other side of me with Mason beside him. Liam's too busy texting someone to pay any attention to us.

"Mason was impressed. I know he was," she adds, only loud enough for me to hear.

I shrug, pretending not to care. I honestly don't need his approval—I'm good at what I do.

"But I could use a daiquiri," she says. "Want to get me one, Liam?"

He looks up from his phone. "Huh?"

I shake my head as we walk over toward the food trucks, and I buy a bottle of water and a burrito. The four of us find an open picnic table and sit.

"What did she say?" Mason asks Liam, and I try not to pay attention, but it piques my interest.

"We'll talk about it later," he says quietly, and I know it's something he doesn't want any of us to hear but leave it to Maddie to ask anyway.

"Who?"

Mason glances at her. "Our roommate. She's moving out."

"Roommate?" Maddie and I ask in unison.

They both chuckle. "Yeah. Well, only for a little while longer. She's moving out soon."

Maddie's eyes are the size of saucers, and I try to hold back my shock. I've been over to their house dozens of times, and I've never run into anyone other than them, and definitely not a woman. I like to consider myself an observant person too, but there's no sign of a woman living with them. I have so many questions, but I let Maddie take the lead. I love having her around because the lack of filter makes it easier to get details out of them.

"How long has she lived with you?" she asks. "How come we've never met her?"

Liam focuses on his burrito as Mason speaks up. "She's busy. Works a lot," he offers simply.

I glance at him, and his eyes linger on me for a moment. There are so many unspoken words streaming between us, and I need to know what his damn problem is lately. Maddie takes the focus away.

"This is weird. Does anyone else think this is weird?" she asks, but no one answers.

"I need a beer." Mason stands, then walks away to fetch one.

"Sorry about him," Liam says when he's out of earshot. "He's in a mood."

"Oh, that's what it is? Should've probably left Mr. Party Foul at home." I grunt with an eyebrow popped. Liam chuckles and stuffs his face.

After Mason returns and we've finished eating, I put my violin in the car, and we decide to find a spot while we wait for the fireworks to begin.

Liam places the blanket he brought on the ground, and Maddie and I plop down. Mason sits on the other side of me, shockingly. Liam's on the end, focused back on his phone.

Maddie leans back on the blanket. "Remember when we'd watch the fireworks show at home?"

I smile, thinking about Lennon. "Yeah. Sneaking up to our secret spot to get the best view."

"Yep. You know how many boys I've kissed up there?" She giggles, the corner of her lips tilting up devilishly. We weren't allowed to date, but that didn't mean Maddie didn't sneak around.

"I can only imagine," I truthfully say.

Mason's arm brushes against mine, and my body buzzes. I glance at him and wonder if he felt what I did. Thankfully, the fireworks begin and pull my attention to the sky, though I still think about that night we met. If he weren't friends with Brandon, and if Lennon weren't my sister, maybe things between us would've been different. He's never given me a real explanation as to why he's not relationship material, and after this amount of time, I don't expect one. It doesn't mean I can just forget about what happened between us, though I'm sure he wishes I would. To me, it was magical, unforgettable, and even if he doesn't admit it, the electricity still streams between us.

And I'm not sure the way I feel about him will ever go away, though I kind of wish it would so I could get on with my loveless life.

CHAPTER SEVEN

MASON

EIGHT MONTHS EARLIER

NO ONE WILL EVER TRULY KNOW what causes someone to take their own life, and as I stare at the scene of the accident and take notes, I'm sick to my fucking stomach.

Looking around the apartment, I notice everything is perfectly in place. A notebook lies on the bed along with her cell phone, a stack of schoolbooks, and an empty pill bottle. It was her third attempt, but this time, she succeeded. On her dresser are pictures of her with friends and family, and I wonder if she contacted any of them and told them what she was going to do.

My emotions begin to bubble to the surface, heat rushes to my face, and I have to excuse myself from the room. It's okay not to be okay, and right now, I'm definitely not. Too many memories flash before my eyes, and I'm weak in the knees as I think back to my college days.

"Mason," Detective Ducet calls out. I want to eventually go into investigations, and I have to be able to handle death and horrific scenes, but this one hits a little too close to home.

I scrub a hand over my face, then walk over toward him. "Make sure you observe how they collect the evidence. Smith is taking photos and marking the scene. I'll see you back at the office, but I think this is a cut-and-dried case. After getting statements from her parents and learning this wasn't her first attempt, I don't think any foul play was involved."

I nod.

"You look like shit. You eat something bad?" he asks.

"Yeah. I think so," I lie, not wanting to open the closet where I hide all my skeletons. "I'll be just a second."

I take a deep breath, pull my shit together, then go back to continue to help process the scene. Once I've done my due diligence, and watch the forensic investigators do their thing, I head to the office. My mind wanders, and I find myself falling into a dark place, one I try not to visit often. After the day is over, I grab my stuff and head home with a mind full of shit I don't want to think about. All I want to do is relax, wash off the day, and push it all away.

I think most people who have jobs of this nature have to compartmentalize it all. Otherwise, it's a lot of heaviness to deal with on a daily basis. But I also believe we're helping people when we solve cases and find the bad guys, or at least, that's what I tell myself.

The moment I'm home, I see Sophie and Maddie are here again hanging out with Liam. They've been around more and more, and though I purposely push Sophie away, wanting to keep her at arm's length, I can't deny that I enjoy her presence. Hearing her laughter, seeing her smile, listening to her talk about her job and how much she loves playing—all that brings me so much happiness. Sometimes when I don't think she's looking, I'll grin, but inevitably, she catches me, so I put my guard back up again.

The four of us have hung out before and watched movies. We've even been able to laugh and hold a real conversation too. At times, I notice myself failing at keeping her at bay, my resolve vanishing, and I have to remind myself not to give Sophie the wrong idea. The last thing I want is to lead her on and have her think I can give her more, when I can't. At those moments, I put my shield back up and push her away again.

Today was rough, bringing back memories I've tried to forget, and when I see them here again, frustration builds inside me. The demons I try so hard to control came back in full force today from just that one scene.

Liam greets me as soon as my eyes meet his, and Maddie mutters something under her breath about how I look like shit. Liam smirks in agreement, but he knows what my job entails and that it's bound to hit a nerve. Instead of responding to either of their comments, I grunt and head upstairs to take a shower. It's not their fault, but I need time after work to decompress and get the day out of my head.

I knew what I was getting into when I decided to major in this field and even more so when I realized where I could potentially work in the future. I knew I'd be dealing with horrendous situations like abuse and homicide, including kids, teenagers, and the elderly. In my mind, I knew what to expect. But today—today triggered me for the first time in a long time, probably years.

I stand in the shower and allow the hot water to roll over my tense muscles to try to settle my nerves, but it doesn't seem like enough. The weight of the day still sits heavy on my chest. Once I'm done and dressed, I head downstairs to the kitchen and pull a beer from the fridge. When I plop down on the chair, the three of them turn and stare at me, but I focus on the TV.

"Well, hello to you, too," Maddie chides in her snarky tone, which causes me to roll my eyes.

"Why are you always here?" I ask sharply. "Don't you have some dance routine to learn or something?"

She laughs sarcastically. "Wow, good one. Maybe you should've been a comedian with all the jokes you have."

"Perhaps it's time for you two to pay rent since you're here basically every day," I throw back at her, glancing at Sophie, who's scowling at me. I notice how she's chewing on the side of her cheek, probably so she doesn't tell my ass off, but considering the way I'm treating them, I deserve it.

I expect them to make a smartass comment about how I give them whiplash with my mood swings, but neither of them do.

They'd be right, of course. Being so close to Sophie, smelling her in my house long after she's gone, fucks with my head. I'm constantly reminding myself that she doesn't deserve my wrath, so I purposely keep my distance. It's for her own good.

"Maybe I should move in, considering your third bedroom is available now that your mysterious roommate has moved out," Maddie singsongs. The girl is relentless.

"I'd move out before either of you could move in." I take a swig of my beer and try to ignore them.

"What the hell is your problem?" Liam barks. I can tell he's pissed by the way I'm acting, but I kind of don't give two shits about it. Instead of arguing with him, I finish my beer, then go grab another one. While I'm twisting the top, I overhear Maddie chatting with Sophie.

"Have you gotten any more messages on your dating app?"

The question freezes me in my tracks. Why the fuck is she on a dating app? Sophie doesn't need that. Nothing but perverts and players hang out on those. I toss the cap in the trash and then pull the bottle of tequila from the cabinet. Without bothering to pour it in a shot glass, I take a swig. This day just keeps getting better.

"I haven't been paying attention to it, honestly. Most of them are weird as hell," she admits, and it makes me grin. How fucking selfish am I?

A part of me feels as if I've pushed her to this because I refused to give her a chance although it's for her own benefit. If only I could look outside my own bullshit, but I don't like me very much, so why would I expect her to? Sophie needs a man who doesn't have issues—someone who can love her unconditionally, wholeheartedly—and right now, I can't be that man. I don't know if I'll ever be.

Once the alcohol swarms through me, I walk back to the living room and try not to pay attention to anything they're saying about dates and guys. I focus on the TV I can't hear because they're being way too loud. Though I have questions, I keep them to myself, not wanting to act like a jealous ex or something.

Maddie's voice lowers. "I think you should go for it. You're hot as hell." Her voice grows louder as she continues. "There's bound to be someone out there for you who isn't afraid to commit."

That's a direct jab toward me, which I more than deserve. Sophie promised she'd keep what happened between us, but I often wonder if her sisters know. Especially by the way Maddie's staring at me right now.

"I'm sorry, what did you say?" I ask because I wasn't paying attention. I'd zoned out again.

"I asked if you were on a dating app too?" Maddie smirks, knowing damn well I'm not.

A roar of laughter escapes from Liam, and all I can do is flip him off.

I narrow my eyes and scoff. "Too many people are serial daters on those apps. Don't have time for that."

A blush hits Sophie's cheeks, and I wish I could tell her about the way I've felt since the moment I laid eyes on her. I wish I could speak candidly and put it all out on the line, but in the end, I know I'd just hurt her. It's who I am, and she deserves better. She sure as fuck deserves better than some dude on Tinder too. I drink my beer, feeling the alcohol flow through my veins while the ceiling seems to close in on me.

I stand and go to the kitchen to grab another drink. When I turn around, Sophie stands with her hands on her hips, not allowing me to avoid her this time.

"What's your deal?" she asks boldly.

I glare at her, studying her chestnut eyes while her mouth purses in a firm line.

"Nothing," I say.

"Nothing," she whisper-hisses. "Nothing? You've obviously got an issue with me being here or perhaps just me in general."

Her frustration causes me to chuckle.

"I don't have an issue with you, Soph."

"Then Maddie?"

I shake my head and lean against the counter. "I've had a shitty day."

She helps herself to the fridge and pops open a can of soda, then starts drinking it. "So I guess every day I'm around, it's a shitty day then? Because that's what it seems like."

I can see her pulse ticking rapidly in her neck and can only imagine how much courage it took for her to confront me. Though she's sassy as sin and usually speaks her mind, this is a bolder side she's showing. One I really like. When it comes to me, she typically holds back. One day, I wish she'd just give it to me—tell me off and say how much she hates me—so then I can bury these dangerous emotions I've kept at bay, forget about her, and forget about what happened.

Though I'd never be able to forget her.

"No," I croak out. "Not exactly." Sophie is like a ray of sunshine on my dark, stormy days, and she has no idea I use my asshole ways to hide behind my true feelings.

With pursed lips, she tilts her head at me, giving me a chance to explain myself, but I don't.

"Are we done here?" I ask. "Kinda tired of the interrogation."

"Wow. You really are an asshole," she barks as I walk past her, not wanting to be alone with her any longer. I go back to the living room, and Maddie's looking at me with a big ass grin.

"Did you just kiss my sister?" she whisper-shouts.

Liam chuckles, which only annoys me further.

"What, why? Did you two make out while we were gone?" I snap back.

Maddie's smile fades, and she stiffens. I look back and forth between them with a cocked eyebrow and neither finds it funny.

"That's what I thought." Just as I'm getting ready to add fuel to the fire, Sophie returns, and I can tell she's pissed. I know I'm to blame, but I tell myself it's better this way. I've said it so many times over the past two years that even I'm beginning to believe it.

The thoughts of her being with someone else consume me. Closing my eyes, I envision her kissing or sleeping with another man, and it frustrates the fuck out of me. Liam turns on a movie, some stupid chick flick, and though I don't understand why he subjects himself to this shit, I'm grateful for the distraction. He's not dating either one of them and, as far as I know, doesn't plan on it. Typically, movies like this are date movies where you get laid after, but that isn't happening for anyone in this room.

When another cheesy line is said, I let out a groan, and Maddie jerks her head in my direction with a scoff. You'd think I told her dancing was stupid by the way she's acting. The truth is, we should be watching explosions and gun fights, not this romantic comedy shit. Finally, I can't take it anymore and leave.

Once I'm in my room, I shut the door behind me and sit on the edge of my bed. I scrub my hands over my face, trying to get a hold of myself because my control seems to be slipping, and I know they're all annoyed by me and my asshole attitude.

After a few deep breaths, I walk to my closet and pull out a shoebox I keep tucked in the back. It's been a few years since I've opened the box full of memories—some good and some bad. Even looking inside is torturous, but I have to, especially after today.

I set it on the nightstand next to my bed and pry off the lid. Instantly all the old thoughts come rushing back, nearly paralyzing me where I sit. With an erratic heartbeat, I grab a photo of Emma and me when we were happy. One of those genuine moments when everything was right in the world. There's another photo of us on Valentine's Day along with a few movie tickets and doodles she drew me. I can't seem to take my eyes off the picture of us, laughing and smiling. I stare until my eyes cross. With blurred vision, I place the top on the box and put it back. Looking inside that box brings an old familiar weight on my chest, and I'm nearly gasping for air.

When I close my eyes, the only person I see is Sophie. Just knowing she's downstairs has me wanting to get out of bed so I can talk to her, open myself up and let my emotions bleed out with no consequences, but it would be pointless. Maybe looking for love on one of those stupid apps would be the best thing for her, after all. I'm gonna have to accept that she'll meet guys, and not interfere, regardless of how I feel.

CHAPTER EIGHT
SOPHIE

SIX MONTHS EARLIER

It's hard to believe Lennon could basically go into labor anytime now. I'm over-the-moon excited to be an aunt for the first time and can't wait to hold that sweet precious miracle. The days aren't passing fast enough, and Lennon agrees. She's ready to burst and complains daily about how she's sick of being pregnant.

My phone buzzes and pulls me away from my thoughts as I pack up my violin. This weekend is the last performance of the Christmas program, and we'll be playing all the classics. Most members of the orchestra are busy during this time of year, so our director agreed to change rehearsals to twice a week instead of our typical schedule. Pulling my phone from my pocket, I unlock it and smirk when I find a text from Liam.

LIAM

Any luck on that stupid dating app?

I chuckle, knowing he's used the same one in the past. He's been ragging me ever since I downloaded it, but I blame Maddie.

SOPHIE

Hardly. Every date I've been on has sucked. If
you can even call them dates.

LIAM

Thinking about trying it again. Might help me
expand my pussy portfolio.

SOPHIE

You're disgusting.

I can imagine the smug look on his face and shake my head. Honestly, I'm ready to give up on this app and dating in general, but I'm trying. Maddie forced me to give it a chance because it's more than obvious Mason isn't interested. Instead of continuing to get my hopes up, I knew it was time to move on. I've been on a few awkward dates, a couple of shitty ones, and some that made me want to fall asleep from boredom. I'm not hopeful, but at this point, I have nothing to lose—except maybe my will to live. I'm not getting any younger, and I don't want to be single forever, which is inevitable if I don't put myself out there. I wish there was a singles app for musicians, but until then, I'll stay on this one and weed through the weirdos.

LIAM

Wanna hang out tonight? I'm off tomorrow.

SOPHIE

Nah. I'm exhausted from playing so many shows
and want to go to sleep early. I'm ready to crash,
and I have more performances this weekend.

LIAM

Fine! Guess I'll hang out all by myself.

I grab my violin and walk to my car. As I cross the parking lot, I find it hilarious he's trying to guilt trip me, but I really am exhausted. All I want to do is eat dinner, shower, and lock myself in my room away from Maria and Carter.

Liam's great company, but I'm not sure I would be. If we

watched a movie, I'd fall asleep. If we had dinner, I wouldn't be any fun. Right now, I want to decompress and not socialize. After I get inside the car and crank it, I text Liam back.

SOPHIE

I'm sure there's someone you can hang out with in your long list of contacts. Start at the letter A and work your way down

LIAM

You're right. Maybe we can get together next weekend?

SOPHIE

I might be able to squeeze you into my schedule!

I tuck my phone away, then drive home. I think Liam's noticed how I've tried to create distance by not going over to their house as much. Each time I've been there, Mason has treated me like shit anyway. Plus, I'm trying the whole "out of sight, out of mind" trick, hoping it will allow me to forget Mason and our past once and for all. Though it feels as if it's all burned into my memory. Liam hasn't called me out on it yet, but he knows my real feelings. How can he not after all this time?

I'm hungry and tired, so I stop at a restaurant and grab a chicken salad to go. It doesn't take long before my food is ready, and I'm on my way to the apartment. When I arrive home, Carter's car is parked in Maria's spot and I'm half-tempted to run my key down the driver's side. I suck in a deep breath and try to get rid of the scowl before I walk inside, but it's no use.

His socks and shoes lie in the middle of the floor as he sits on the couch with his feet propped up on the coffee table. The TV is so damn loud. If he's not hard of hearing, he will be. Carter gives me one of those douchey head nods, but I ignore him. It's gotten to where I can't pretend to make small talk anymore, though he doesn't know how to take a hint. I go to my room so I can eat in peace and quiet. Well, *try* to anyway.

It's not even seven yet, but I'm ready to fall asleep. After I take a shower and am comfortable in my bed, I scroll through my email on my phone, but before I set it down, I notice a few notifications on the dating app. Curious, I open it to see what perv has messaged me this time and consider taking a screenshot to send to Maddie so she can at least be entertained by my pathetic love life. As expected, the dirty-talking douchebags have filled my inbox, but then I see another message that's shockingly normal. His name is Weston, he's 29, and by his profile picture alone, he looks decent and charming.

WESTON

Hi, Sophie! It's nice to virtually "meet" you. I see you're in Sacramento as well, so we're close. I'm probably being forward, but I can tell there's something special about you just from your profile picture. Chat soon?

I go to his profile and scroll through his photos. The man has his shit together, that much is certain. Seeing he's still online, I go back to my inbox and reply.

SOPHIE

Hi! Thanks for the note ☺ It's nice to virtually "meet" you too. Honestly, it's refreshing not to get a message from a creeper.

WESTON

I can only imagine what kind of messages you've gotten. So tell me about you, Sophie. You play violin professionally? That's incredible.

SOPHIE

I've been playing since I was a teenager, and I love it. Music is everything to me. What do you do for a living?

WESTON

I'm a correctional officer at the prison. Love my job and don't mind most of my co-workers. Ha-ha. Plus, I wouldn't be a homeowner without it.

I like how he conveniently threw that in there, and I find myself smiling as I chat with him.

SOPHIE

Wow, how awesome!

WESTON

Yeah, thanks! Random, maybe, but…do you like
to eat?

I chuckle, hoping this conversation isn't about to turn weird by him having some strange fetish with food or something.

SOPHIE

Who doesn't love to eat? My favorite is breakfast
food!

WESTON

Great! I know a great place that serves the best
breakfast I've ever eaten. We should do brunch.
I'd love to chat with you in person. See your
smile. Hear your laughter. Get to know you
better.

I'm genuinely grinning at how candid he's being right now. My past few dates have sucked, but so far he seems different—I don't get the urge to block him like the others. Also, he hasn't asked to see my nipples yet, so that's always a good sign.

I think about meeting him before replying, and at this point, I have nothing to lose. I grin and send him a message back.

SOPHIE

That sounds awesome 😊 When?

WESTON

Are you available next weekend?

A smile touches my lips, a real one, and I look forward to meeting him. I know I told Liam we could possibly hang out, but he'd choose a date over me any day, so I don't feel too bad about it.

SOPHIE

Yeah, let's do it.

I'm taking a risk. This could go one of two ways—good or bad —and if he's weird, like all the other men I've met from this app, I swear, I'm deleting my account and becoming a nun.

"I'm nervous as hell," I tell Maddie, brushing my fingers through my hair. She called me on her way to practice as I was getting ready for my brunch date with Weston.

"He's cute. Just be yourself. You're a catch. Any man would be lucky to have you, sis." I can hear the smile in her voice.

"And that's why you're my favorite sister," I taunt, deciding to pull my hair half-up. I want to look put together but not like I'm trying too hard. We've been chatting over the last week, getting to know more about each other and finding out what we have in common. He's been normal and still hasn't asked for any nudes, so I'm hopeful at this point.

"Just don't do him on the first date. You gotta make guys work for it," Maddie coaches me, then snickers. The irony isn't lost on me, considering her sacred virgin status, though I have a feeling she'd toss it for a hot guy.

As I grab my keys, she continues talking about dance and her instructor, and my mind reluctantly goes to thoughts of Mason. Maybe I'm an idiot for sleeping with him so quickly, but I don't regret it. I'm just disappointed it never led to anything more.

When I climb into the car, I end the call and try to push my thoughts of Mason away. The man is more infuriating than rush hour traffic on a Friday afternoon. Over the past year, he's continued to frustrate me by consistently pulling me in, then pushing me away, usually within the same conversation. It's as if he's afraid to get too close, and the moment he feels that shift, he pulls back. I hate when he does that and wish he'd let me in, even as just friends.

I have to remind myself why I'm dating in the first place—*to move on*. I'm tempted to call Lennon, but she's so focused on the baby coming that I don't want to bother her with my lame drama. Instead, I turn on the radio and blast the music until I'm at the restaurant.

Glancing down at the clock, I realize I'm nearly twenty minutes early. I take the extra time to try to get a hold of my nerves. I wait ten minutes and see a message from Weston. If he's not a creep, I plan to exchange numbers with him so we don't have to go back and forth on the app. I've learned to never give my number until after we meet. At this point, I should give up violin and write a book on how *not* to online date. *The Unsuccessful Adventures of Online Dating* by #1 Single Girl Forever, undoubtedly bound to be a bestseller.

Cracking up at my own pathetic joke, I walk toward the front of the restaurant when I see him heading toward me. Tall with dark hair and a sharp jaw. Damn, his picture didn't do him justice. He smiles when his eyes meet mine and my cheeks heat. Weston is as sexy as sin in a dark blue polo shirt and jeans, and I worry I didn't dress up enough.

"Hi," he rasps.

"Hello," I reply shyly.

He opens the door for me and gestures for me to walk through ahead of him. A gentleman from the start. I already like where this is going, considering the last guy I agreed to meet up with barely peeled his eyes off my chest long enough to hold a conversation.

"You look great, Sophie." He shoots me a wink, which causes me to blush.

"Thanks, you too." And I mean it, allowing my eyes to linger over his large biceps.

Weston places his hand on the small of my back as the waitress leads us to a table. Before we sit, Weston pulls out my chair for me. I've never had a man be so effortlessly polite, and I'm honestly impressed. She hands us some menus, and we look over them while she grabs our coffee. I can't help but glance at Weston and notice his strong jawline and plump, kissable lips. Once our mugs are delivered, the waitress takes our order.

"I'd like the blueberry pancakes with sausage," I tell her.

"I'll have the same thing." He shoots me a wink.

As I add cream and sugar to my coffee, Weston takes a sip of his without anything in it.

"So where do you see yourself in five years?" he asks.

"Hmm." I tap my finger across my lips. "I hope to be married and starting a family, but at the very least, living in my own place."

Weston's kind eyes meet mine. "So you have a roommate?"

"Yeah, my friend Maria, well, and her boyfriend too. He's a new addition, though." I try not to seem annoyed by him, but I think Weston notices. Anytime I think about Carter, curse words ensue soon after, but I'm trying to be on my best behavior. First impressions and all.

"Uh-oh." He chuckles, noticing the change in my demeanor.

"I'm particular and don't care for change, but he's shaken things up around the apartment and is a slob."

I realize I'm rambling and try to wrap up this topic. "But I'm easy to get along with otherwise. It's small things that irk me, like mustard smeared on the counter or a sip of milk being left in the carton."

Weston chuckles at that last bit. "Yeah, that'd irk me too for sure. Probably one of the main reasons I live alone. I'm saving my space for the woman I'm gonna spend the rest of my life with. Just waiting to find her. Maybe I have."

The butterflies in my stomach flutter again. He knows exactly what to say, and I'm all smiles as our food arrives. We eat and chat about everything, and the conversation doesn't seem to drop once. Being with him already feels so natural. It's as if I've known him a lifetime.

"Do you like playing professionally? Or is it one of those things that turned your passion into a chore? I hear that happens sometimes with creative professions."

I appreciate that he's more interested in asking me questions than talking only about himself, which is different from the other guys I've met from the app. Weston listens as I chat about violin and how it essentially changed my life.

"It's my escape," I admit. "Music is deeply ingrained inside me, and it does something to my soul. Nothing in my life has ever affected me the same way violin has."

"Wow," he whispers. "I've never met anyone quite like you, Sophie. You're beautiful, intelligent, talented." He leans forward, resting his arms on the table in front of him and flashes a panty-dropping smirk. "So when do you want to get married?" He winks before leaning back to take a sip of his coffee, and I nearly choke from his words.

"Tomorrow?" I taunt. "I mean, Vegas is only a few hours away."

"Don't tempt me, sweetheart." His voice is velvety sweet, and though we're finished eating, I don't want this day to end. By the way he's looking at me, I think he feels the same. Or at least I hope.

The waitress brings the check, and Weston quickly hands her his card.

"I can take care of mine," I insist.

"Now, it wouldn't be a date if you paid, and that's *exactly* what this is," he explains, grinning. I know our time together is coming to an end when the waitress asks us several times if we need anything else after Weston pays. We take the hint and decide to leave.

Weston politely walks me to my car and pulls me into a hug before we part ways. It feels nice, comforting to be in his strong arms.

"Can I see you again?" he asks, opening my door for me.

"Absolutely," I say without hesitation. Weston leans down and presses his lips to my cheek.

"I'll call you soon to set something up." He smirks before crossing the parking lot. As he walks away, I let out a shaky, excited breath. I can't wait to see him again.

Before I drive home, I text Maddie and let her know how it went.

MADDIE

OMG! That's SOOO exciting! Wait, so why aren't you doing him right now if it went well?

I roll my eyes. She always has sex on the brain.

SOPHIE

Because I want to get to know him first! Geez. I didn't get the app for booty calls.

MADDIE

Okay, fair. When are you seeing him again?

SOPHIE

We agreed to set something up soon. Also, can you keep this between me and you? Lennon is ready to pop any day now, and if this doesn't work out, I don't want to hear it.

MADDIE

Secret's safe with me.

SOPHIE

And that's why you're my favorite 😉

We say our goodbyes, and I drive home with a goofy smile on my face. Maybe I won't give up on dating after all. A few hours with Weston has changed my mind and maybe I won't be single forever.

For the past week, I've spoken to Weston every single day on the phone, and I'm almost scared of how easy it feels.

After I head to the rehearsal hall for a quick meeting, I get a text from him, asking me over for a movie and dinner this weekend. I nearly squeal and can't type my response fast enough.

I'm on cloud nine the rest of the day and text Lennon before I go to bed to tell her the news, since I plan on seeing Weston again. Lately, she's been busy preparing for the arrival of the baby and stressed out about our parents not talking to her that my relationship woes seem so childish to mention. I send her a picture of him, then share all the details, and how we're going out again this weekend. Thankfully, she's supportive and excited for me, but I feel bad for not telling her right away.

Everything in my life seems to be working out, and for the first time in a while, all the pieces of my life are falling together. Before I go to bed, I text Weston good night. He's working the night shift, so I'm surprised when I get a response.

WESTON

Good night, sweetie. Can't wait to see you soon.

SOPHIE

Same! I can't wait either.

A smile touches my lips before I fall asleep.

When I wake up the following morning, I check my phone and read several messages from Lennon. I squeal when I find out she's in labor.

It takes me less than five minutes to get dressed as I try to contact her or Hunter. Maddie calls me as I head across town to pick her up at her dorm.

"I'm on the way," I say in a rushed tone, hoping we don't miss the arrival of the baby.

"Okay, hurry up! But be careful! Oh my God! We're gonna be aunts!" Maddie squeals.

Becoming an aunt, finding a man I adore, kicking ass at violin…I'm on top of the world at the moment, and it feels fucking amazing.

After I get Maddie, we chat about how much we're going to spoil our niece on the way to the hospital. Lennon calls to check on our location and tell us she's not delivering yet, but I don't think she realizes we wouldn't miss this for a million dollars. It takes no time to make it there, and I have to tell Maddie to bring her excitement down a few notches before seeing Lennon, but she doesn't listen to me, or anyone, ever.

As soon as we walk into the room, Maddie startles, which makes me chuckle.

"Whew, no baby yet," she says as soon as she sees Lennon.

"Where's loverboy?" I tease with a shit-eating grin when I notice Hunter isn't around. Lennon filled us in on everything that's happened since they returned from Utah back in July and the details of our mother showing up two months ago. It's been rocky since she found out she was pregnant with her dead boyfriend's baby. She's been slowly letting Hunter into her life, though she struggles emotionally with it, which is why I've been trying to give her space and time to adjust.

When Hunter returns, we chat about baby prep and different facts he's learned about pregnancies. It's obvious how much he cares about Lennon and the baby, and I'm happy she has Hunter. Although they hated each other in the beginning, it's clear they've formed a close relationship now. Grieving the loss of Brandon together has brought them closer. I'm happy she has him, and that he's been so willing to do anything for her, even if she doesn't quite see what the rest of us do. He's so in love with her, and a part of me wonders how long it will be until she realizes it too.

Soon, Lennon has dilated enough to push. Seeing how much

Hunter protects, comforts, and loves her through it all makes me respect him on a totally different level.

When I meet my niece for the first time, happy tears form in my eyes. Watching the birth of my niece quickly becomes one of the highlights of my life. We snap pictures, saving the memories that'll last a lifetime. Maddie and I refuse to leave Lennon's side until she's rolled into the recovery room.

"You were taking photos?" she asks, yawning through her words. "Will you send me some?"

Maddie instantly begins to airdrop the two hundred photos she took to Lennon, and I send the few I captured too. I'm sure she's texting a picture to our mother because that's how she is, even after our mom hurt her. When she announced the baby's name, Alison—after the singer who sang Lennon's favorite song, "Baby Mine"—my emotions begin to take over.

She holds Alison so tight to her body as if she'll never let her go. After the baby is fed, we decide to give Lennon some alone time and promise to come back later. Maddie and I are still riding the high of the new baby when we leave the hospital. The happiness I feel for Lennon is indescribable.

Once I've dropped Maddie off, I go to the apartment and practice the rest of the day until I return to the hospital that evening.

Seeing Lennon become a mother and watching Hunter right by her side give me hope that maybe one day I'll have that too—a family.

It's been a few days since the baby was born, and I've spoken to Lennon every day. I've gone to their apartment because I can't get enough of my niece. I'm trying not to be the overbearing aunt, but I can't help it. Alison is adorable, and I love her so much.

I spent most of the day rehearsing with my quartet because we have to perform at a wedding toward the beginning of the year. It's one of the things I do to make extra cash on top of playing in the orchestra and teaching kids during the school year. Once we've practiced until we can't go any longer, I head home and take a shower because I'm supposed to meet Weston tonight. As soon as I walk inside and set my violin down, I get a text.

WESTON

Thinking about you, beautiful.

A blush covers my cheeks.

SOPHIE

Me too. Excited about tonight.

WESTON

Same. It's so weird how we haven't known each
other for that long, but it feels like I've known
you for a lifetime.

I've thought the same thing since the first time we met. Things were so easygoing between us with no downtime or awkwardness.

SOPHIE

I feel the same way.

WESTON

Can't wait to see you 😊 I'm gonna start dinner
soon.

Dating and being with a nice guy are all new territory for me. In my past, I've dated nothing but douchebags, and I can tell Weston's different. He's proven that to me each day we've spoken and even more since we met for brunch.

After I get out of the shower, blow-dry my hair, and put on some makeup, I slip on some jeans and a sweater because it's chilly outside. I check the time and realize I need to get going. Weston offered to pick me up, but I'd much rather drive myself so I can leave when I want to leave, which I doubt will happen. Things are too easy with Weston.

Before I leave, I send a text to let him know I'm on the way, then I call Lennon.

"I'm leaving for my date!" Excitement coats my tone.

"Oh, awesome. Going somewhere special?" She's talking low, and I'm sure it's because she doesn't want to wake Allie.

"To his house. He made dinner, and we're watching a movie," I explain, feeling my nerves bubble to the surface.

"You're gonna have fun, Soph. I'm excited for you. Let me know how it goes, 'kay?"

We chat about Allie, then I let her go as I turn on Weston's street. I slow down, searching for his house in a quiet and quaint neighborhood with perfectly trimmed lawns and bushes.

When I arrive, I pull into his driveway. His house is adorable and looks well taken care of.

Weston meets me on the sidewalk with a dishrag in his hand and a smile on his face. As soon as I get close enough to smell his cologne, he wraps his arms around me and pulls me into a hug. I look up into his eyes, and an electric current swirls between us.

"Dinner is ready. Can't wait for you to try it out." He grabs my hand and leads me inside his home. Everything is pristine and clean, and I can't stop looking around as he guides me to the kitchen where food is waiting on the stovetop.

"Wine?" he asks, and I nod as he pours us both a glass. Weston places generous portions of chicken fettuccine alfredo on two plates with garlic bread. The table is dressed up with candles and a fancy tablecloth. Looking at how much effort he put into tonight causes me to grin as he sets our plates on the table. I sit beside him and can't stop looking at this gorgeous man over the rim of my glass.

"This is amazing," I compliment, trying to soak in the moment. I can't remember the last time a man cooked for me. Hell, I can't remember the last time anyone has treated me the way Weston does—as if he cares.

"Wait until you taste it." He winks as I finish my glass of wine.

I pick up my fork, and he waits as I take a bite. The delicious flavors fill my mouth, and I'm impressed he cooked this. "Wow."

It doesn't take either of us long to clean our plates. The last time I ate was breakfast earlier today, so I was starved. I got so busy I forgot to stop for lunch.

Weston refills our glasses, and he leads me to the living room and hands me the remote. "I'm gonna let you choose what we watch."

He sits on the couch, and I plop down next to him. Our bodies are so close I can feel the warmth of him against my skin. I click on an older romcom. "This okay?"

"As long as I'm watching it with you, I don't care what it is."

I giggle and press play. Weston's fingers trail on my arm, and though we're close to one another, it's not enough. I finish my second glass of wine, and he asks me if I want another, but I refuse. When his eyes meet mine, the urge to kiss him takes over. He stands to get himself another drink and a bottle of water for me, but when he returns and sets his glass down on the table, I pull him closer to me.

Our mouths crash together in a wave of passion and desire.

"Soph," he whispers as his body hovers over mine. "We should take it slow. I don't want to rush this with you."

Gently, he brushes my hair from my face as I lift my lips back to his.

"When it feels right, it's right," I tell him matter-of-factly.

"You're sure?" he asks.

I nod, my body and heart knowing, guiding, urging me forward. Weston pulls away, stands, and holds out his hand.

When I take it, he leads me to the bedroom. I have zero doubts about this man, about how much I want and need him, and about how he's the one for me. Weston doesn't rush. He kisses me as we undress and then makes love to me.

The next morning, I wake up in his bed and am almost shocked I'm still here. He's not lying next to me, and I pull the sheets from my naked body. I dig in the top drawer of his dresser and slip on a T-shirt, then walk through the house where he's cooking breakfast for us.

"Good morning, beautiful." He smirks. I lean against the doorway and admire the muscles that ripple down his back. Weston is gorgeous as hell with his six-pack and sexy V that goes all the way down to his wonderful package.

He scoops some eggs and bacon on two plates, then leans forward and kisses me when he comes close, and I'm ready for my second helping of *him*.

As we're eating, we share stolen glances and knowing smirks.

"You know you're mine now, Soph," he tells me sweetly. "I don't want any other man to have you."

"I just want you, Weston. I can tell you that," I say, confidently.

Looking at him, our future flashes before my eyes, and it's so damn beautiful. Me and him, little feet pitter-pattering on the hardwood floor, and a dog. All that's missing is the white picket fence.

"What're you doing on New Year's Eve?" I ask nervously.

"Nothing yet. I don't have any plans."

"Want to go to a party with me? I want you to meet everyone."

"I'd love to join you, sweetheart."

It's the next step in our relationship, for him to meet the people I care about the most. And God, I hope they like him as much as I do.

CHAPTER NINE
MASON

FIVE MONTHS EARLIER

I FINISH STOCKING the cases of beer and wine I bought for the party in the fridge. Tonight, we decided to relive our college days and throw a huge New Year's Eve party. Liam and I invited every person we know, and I expect a house full. It's been a while since we've let loose and hung out with our friends. Though lately, it's been a bit difficult.

Since Lennon had her baby a few weeks ago, Hunter's been helping her in any way he can. He's been by her side since the day Brandon died. Their relationship has formed into more, though neither will admit it.

Lennon's gonna make a great mom, and Alison's going to be spoiled rotten, especially if Liam, Sophie, Maddie, and I have anything to do with it.

It hasn't been easy on any of them. We're all still grieving the loss of Brandon, and not a day goes by when we don't think about him. But out of all of us, Hunter has had it the worst. It's obvious how much he loves Lennon, how much he's always loved her, and though he was an asshole to her in the beginning, we know he'd do anything for her now. He's stepped up to fill the shoes of his best friend, which is more than admirable.

I texted him a few days ago and invited him to the party, but he refused to leave Lennon at home with the baby, which is understandable since it's only been a couple of weeks. Lennon still needs help, and he won't leave her side. If it were me, I'd do the same thing.

"Did you get champagne?" Liam asks from behind, pulling me from my thoughts.

"Damn. I knew I was forgetting something."

"We can't toast at midnight unless there's champagne," he argues.

It takes everything in me not to burst out into laughter. Ever since I've known him, he's always had a soft spot for traditions.

"Don't know what to say. You go to the store. It was a madhouse. I'm surprised I made it out with everything I did. One of the frats is throwing a huge ass party, so the liquor stores have been wiped," I explain.

I open the fridge and pull out a bottle of Dom Pérignon.

"Happy?" I ask, waving my hand for him to see the expensive bottle of champagne.

"You're a dick." He smirks. "You know Sophie is bringing someone tonight, right?"

I somehow keep a straight face. "So?"

"So… He raises a brow. "Don't want you to get your panties in a knot about it."

I pull a beer from the fridge and twist it open. "Why would I care?"

He shrugs. "Okay. Whatever you say."

My heart gallops in my chest as Liam walks away laughing. Bringing someone? *Who?* It's been a while since I've seen or spoken to her, but she's been busy with performances because of the holiday season. It's always a hectic time for her plus with the arrival of the baby. Hunter's randomly thrown it into our text convos that she's been at the apartment.

Part of me feels blindsided by Sophie dating, but I shouldn't.

I'm sure it's because of that stupid ass app that Maddie was so fucking pushy about.

I finish my beer and open another. Hopefully, by the time she arrives, I'll have had so much I won't even care that she's here with someone else.

An hour passes and the house is full of people from all different times of Liam's and my life. Work and college friends, some of the neighbors, and a few people I don't know. I continue to drink my worries away and am relieved when Sophie isn't on time. I halfway wonder if she decided to stay away and won't show. I'd rather that because I'm not sure I could handle seeing her with another man, though it's my own damn fault. I can't expect her to wait around for me forever because that's how long it may take me to get over my own bullshit.

Ellie, one of the girls who works with Liam, has been eyeing me all night. She walks over to me and strikes up a conversation, talking about her job, but I'm hardly listening.

The door opens, and Sophie walks in. I zone out by how gorgeous she looks with classic red lips and her hair pulled up halfway, showing the softness of her neck I once tasted. She takes a few steps, and that's when I see her date. There's nothing special about him—tall, dark hair, wearing a stupid polo shirt and khakis. His eyes stay focused on Sophie as if she gets out of his sight, he'll strike like a snake ready to attack.

Immediately, I hate him.

Sophie introduces Mr. Douche to Liam, and I try to focus back on Ellie even though she's already realized I'm not paying attention. Her eyes follow my gaze, and she spots Sophie.

"You like her or something?" she asks, and it's the first time anyone has ever thrown that question at me. Do I like her? Fuck, if I could, I'd love her. But I keep that to myself.

I look at Ellie, giving her my full attention. "No. She's a friend. Really good friends with Liam."

She. "Oh, so *he* likes her?"

Shaking my head, I laugh, then take a sip of my beer, placing my back toward Sophie. It's better I don't see her right now, not when she's looking so deliciously distracting.

"No. Liam is like the Grinch. His heart is three sizes too small."

This causes her to laugh, which makes me chuckle. Ellie is a nice girl, and she keeps throwing me those "let's fuck" vibes, but I can't go there with her. Ever since Sophie, I haven't been with another woman. I've tried, but I'm pretty sure she broke my dick that night in the bathroom. She's the only woman I want, but my head and heart are too damn stubborn to give in. It's the only way I can protect her from me and the black cloud that follows me around.

Sophie giggles in the corner and that guy's hands all over her, touching her, pulling her closer to him until they kiss. My jaw clenches, and I excuse myself. Walking away from Ellie, I go to the kitchen, needing to be alone. As I place my hands on the counter and suck in a deep breath, Liam enters.

"You mad, bro?" When he chuckles, I want to punch him right in the throat.

"Shut the fuck up." I let out a breath, one that feels as if it were smothering me from the inside out.

"Listen. You had plenty of chances to be with her. And I knew, I fucking knew you seeing her with someone was gonna do this, so that's why I warned you."

He's right, of course, but I'd never admit it out loud. I can't.

Moving closer, he places his hand on my shoulder and squeezes. "I understand how hard it's been since Emma, and I also know what trying to move on means and that you might not be ready for that yet. Regardless, I'm here for you, always. You know that."

Liam's words are sincere, and all I can do is thank him. Only a few people in my life know what happened, and Liam was there for me through the heartache.

"Thanks. Wanna do a shot?"

I don't give him the chance to respond. I grab two shot glasses from the cabinet and fill them full of Jack. We take them down in one gulp, and when he walks away, I take another. For some reason, I only drink this much when I'm around Sophie—as if I'm trying to drink her and the memories of us away, but it never works.

Eventually, I go back into the crowded living room, and that's when I spot Maddie. Of course she's stealing the spotlight, something she's great at. Most of the single guys are paying attention to her as she talks about dancing professionally, but I have a feeling they think she's a stripper, which makes me laugh. She's got the moves, that much is sure. I stand off to the side and chat with a few of my fraternity brothers and our neighbor, Kilan. I try to ignore Sophie and halfway succeed. That is, until she moves across the room toward me, pulling her date behind her.

"Mason! There you are!" When she looks at me, she's smiling with a twinkle in her eye. I force out a smile, but it fades when she introduces me to Weston, her *boyfriend*. Well, that escalated quickly.

I shake his hand, *hard*, and he returns the pressure. There's nothing like a solid handshake, but he takes it to a level it shouldn't have gone, almost as a warning to stay away from his woman.

"Nice to meet you," I lazily say.

He places his arm around her, and she leans into him, the way couples do. "Babe, you need another drink?" Weston asks her sincerely.

"I'm okay right now." The way she looks at him makes my stomach turn.

"So how'd you two lovebirds meet?" I finally ask, already knowing the answer to the question but want them both to confirm.

Weston begins the story as he holds Sophie tight against him, not letting her go. "From the moment I saw her picture online, I knew she was the one. I messaged her, and she instantly responded, and we've been inseparable ever since. If I could spend the rest of my life with her, I would." He leans over and places a kiss on her lips, and she melts into him. It's fucking hard to watch.

"You *will*," she whispers, and it drives a knife straight through my heart. My vision blurs as I try to focus on something else and chug the rest of my beer.

"Well, congrats. Hope you two are happy together," I finally say, wanting Sophie to have all the happiness in the world even if it can't be with me. But I don't have a good feeling about this dickwad. I need another drink, so I walk away, letting them have their moment. I'm gonna pay for it tomorrow with a massive hangover but fuck it. I don't want any memory of seeing her with another guy.

Liam set up beer pong on the pool table, just like old times, and a group of guys are in the back room whooping and hollering with each ball that's sunk in a cup. I stand close by and watch, but I'm really keeping an eye on Sophie and her boyfriend.

There's something about him I can't seem to put my finger on, but I don't trust him. They move closer to the beer pong table, and I can almost hear their conversation. Sophie laughs before excusing herself to go to the restroom. Weston checks out other girls as he finishes his beer, then grabs two out of a random cooler, double fisting them. I walk over to him, wanting to chat without Sophie around.

"Having a good time?" I ask, glancing over as he watches the girls dance in the middle of the living room.

He points his beer at Maddie. "You think that one's legal?" He chuckles, not realizing that's Sophie's sister. "I'd like to show her a good time."

My pulse quickens, and I'm two seconds from laying him down flat, but somehow, I restrain. He's gonna feel stupid when Sophie introduces them, or maybe not. The guy is a dirtbag, that much is obvious.

"Damn," he says as Ellie passes by, checking out her ass in that mini skirt. Weston chuckles. "Wonder if she'd be down for a threesome. I'd fuck her and let Sophie watch."

I tighten my fist as he laughs, and I can't find the strength to pretend it's funny. Sophie returns, standing on her tiptoes to give Weston a kiss.

"Missed you baby," he tells her, and I try not to roll my eyes or call bullshit on him.

"I wasn't gone that long." Sophie's smile drops when she takes in my firm expression.

"Long enough for me to notice." He grabs her ass, claiming her as his in front of everyone.

"Fuckface," I whisper and force myself to walk away.

He didn't notice anything but the other girls in the room while she was gone. I don't say anything else and move toward the patio door and stand on the back porch, staring out at the dead grass. The stars twinkle up above, and I'm so fucking frustrated I can barely control myself. It's official, Sophie is dating a goddamn creeper.

After a second, the patio door swings open, and Sophie walks out.

"What the fuck was that?" she snaps. "I heard you muttering under your breath and so did Weston."

I step toward her. "Was what? Me not standing there and watching you hang all over that prick?"

"You were rude as hell, Mason, and I don't appreciate it." She places her hands on her hips. "I've been nothing but nice to you and respected your wishes by keeping us a secret. Even when you still act like a dick to me, I'm always nice in return. Would it kill you to give me the same respect?" I can see the hurt on her face, but she has no idea how much it's killed me to stay away.

I take a few steps forward, erasing the space between us and moving her away from the patio door so no one can see us. She's breathing hard, her chest rising and falling with every breath she takes. My face is mere inches from her. Her tongue flicks out and swipes across her lips that look so fucking kissable right now.

"He's fucking bad news, Sophie. The moment you left for the bathroom, he was gawking at every other chick in there and making crude comments about Maddie. Whoever he's pretending to be for you is not who he really is when you're not around. I don't want you to get hurt. I realize the irony of the statement, coming from me, but you have to believe me when I tell you I get a bad vibe."

She sucks in a tense breath and pushes her index finger hard into my chest. "That's rich coming from you, Mason. You don't want me to get hurt, huh? Well, let me tell you something. You have zero right to say anything about Weston. You don't know him at all, Mason. At all. How am I supposed to believe you after the shit you've put me through these past couple of years? You don't want me, but you don't want anyone else to have me, is that right?" She's so heated, and I blow out a breath of frustration, brushing a hand through my hair as I realize she's not going to believe a word I say.

"Soph, please." She goes to walk away, but I grab her hand to keep her planted but pull a little too hard and she crashes into my chest. With big brown eyes, she looks up at me, and her breath hitches. "Shit, sorry. For the record, I care about your happiness more than anything."

"Good, then maybe you should let me be and stop trying to find the worst in people. I'm trying to move on and maybe you should too. It's what you wanted anyway."

I open my mouth to tell her the truth of how I still feel, but no words come out. It's too late anyway. She slips away from me, not looking back, and slams the door shut when she enters the house. I sit in the patio chair and listen to the laughter coming from inside the house, knowing I should be in there having a good time with everyone. Though I try, I can't seem to shake the way Weston acted and how Sophie is so easy to dismiss it. She's blinded by what she thinks is love and who she thinks that guy is, but that doesn't mean I'm going to sit on the sidelines and be forced to watch him hurt her.

Time and time again, Sophie has proven to be so fucking sweet and trusting. I hate that she can't see through this guy's performance, but nothing I say or do will change that. If he hurts her, cheats on her, or any of the above, I will lose my shit.

"Auld Lang Syne" plays over the stereo inside. I stay out here by myself, hoping this year will be different but knowing better.

There will be no "New Year, New Me." Instead, it will be more days of being unable to move on with my life, but I'll be damned if some man from a dating app ruins Sophie's. Especially one who wears a mask around her.

I finish my beer and prop my feet up when Liam comes outside.

He takes a seat next to me. "You okay?"

"Yeah, I'm good."

We both stare out at the grass.

He breaks the silence. "Sophie was pissed, you know."

"Did you get a weird vibe from her boyfriend?"

Liam doesn't hesitate with his response. "Yeah, he's a twat. Looks like a creeper, too."

I clap my hands together and point my finger. "I knew it. I fucking knew it! I tried to warn her about him."

After sucking in a deep breath, Liam speaks. "She's not gonna listen to us. She's too blinded by new love and needs to make her own mistakes."

"I get that, but what if he hurts her?"

Liam sets his beer down on the table, and his eyes meet mine. "If he does, I'll kill him."

That makes two of us.

CHAPTER TEN

SOPHIE

THREE MONTHS EARLIER

I STILL CAN'T BELIEVE Weston asked me to move in with him so soon. Although I've lived with Maria since moving to Sacramento, I knew it was time to go. She's talked about starting a family, and it was either move out or be left with an apartment I couldn't afford. When Weston asked me, I felt like he was proposing. It's a big step for both of us and a step toward our forever. I've fallen in love with him quickly—hard and fast—and I can't imagine him not being in my life.

I've only been living with him for two weeks, but so far, waking up in his arms has been amazing. I didn't realize a relationship could be like this, but I knew it was possible. Sometimes, I think about Weston and me and wonder if we'll have the same unconditional love Lennon and Hunter have. While he gets frustrated with me sometimes, I know it's normal during this adjustment phase. He hasn't lived with a woman before, and I haven't lived with a boyfriend, so it's a change for both of us. But honestly, I'd rather deal with him than Carter any day.

After rehearsal, I surprise Weston and pick up something for dinner before heading home. I'm so used to only worrying about myself that it's nice to have another person to think about. Weston has filled a hole in my heart I didn't realize was there. I pull into the driveway and notice he's not home yet, so I grab the food and bring it inside.

While I wait for him, I clean up the kitchen and wipe down the counters. Weston's particular about his house and doesn't like anything to be out of place. I learned that the hard way after I first moved in. Every item needs to be put back where it was, and he can't stand a mess, which I can appreciate after living with Carter, who was a complete slob.

This morning, I drank a cup of coffee and left my cup in the sink, so I want to wash it before he comes home. I don't want to be the annoying roommate like Maria and Carter were for me. I'm not walking on eggshells, but I'm trying not to disrupt his habits either. The last thing I want is for him to regret asking me to move in.

I check the time and begin to worry slightly. He typically works from five to five, and it's nearly six thirty, so I send him a text. Sometimes, he has to stay later if another one of the correctional officers is late, but that rarely happens.

SOPHIE

Hey baby! I picked up dinner for us. How much longer will you be?

I pace the kitchen, and after ten minutes, finally get a response.

WESTON

Already ate. Having a drink with the guys. Won't be home until later.

I let out a long, frustrated sigh. If he had communicated this earlier, I would've only bought food for myself and not waited on him. Instead of voicing my frustration, though, I send a quick message back and slide my phone across the table as I eat a piece of chicken and some potatoes.

Over the past few days, he's been drinking more than usual, and I've tried not to say anything about it, but it's been enough to notice. I haven't told a soul either, not even my sisters. After I put my leftovers in the fridge, I go to the living room and watch TV, trying to occupy my mind. Hours pass as I mindlessly watch different shows. A yawn escapes me, and I look at the clock and see it's nearly eleven.

Ever since Brandon died, I've had anxiety when people don't show up when they're supposed to. I know how much it affected Lennon, and my mind seems to always go to the worst-case scenario. I contemplate texting him again when the door swings open, slamming against the wall. As soon as he walks in, he complains how it's dark in the house, so I turn on the lights for him.

He's so drunk he can barely walk.

"Did you drive like that?" I ask, concerned as hell.

"Why do you care?" he throws back at me.

"Weston. Why didn't you call me? I would've picked you up."

"I don't need you mothering me."

"I'm not. I just worry about you and don't want anything terrible to happen." I try to explain, but he's not hearing me, which only pisses me off. Instead, he rolls his eyes and stumbles into the kitchen, but this conversation isn't over. The last thing I need is to lose the love of my life after I've found him, but he doesn't seem to understand that at all.

Weston opens the cabinet and pulls out a bottle of whiskey and begins to drink more. When I try to pull it from his hands, he transforms into a different person. A monster. His hard fist connects with my face as he rips the bottle from my hand and slams it on the counter.

He. Hit. Me.

I'm in shock and might be seeing stars. My mouth falls open when I put a hand over my cheek, too shocked to speak. He grabs my arms as hard as he can and pulls me forward, close to him. He doesn't seem to notice he hit me. He doesn't seem to care. My face is pounding, but I can barely focus on it with his tight grasp on me.

"Don't you *ever* fucking do that again," he demands.

His fingers dig deeper into my skin and pain courses through me. "You're hurting me, Weston."

He tightens his grip like a vise on my arm and jerks me forward. I nearly gag from the smell of alcohol and stale cigarettes drifting from him. For the first time since we met, I'm scared when I see the dangerous look in his eyes.

"Do you understand me? Do you understand you don't fucking control me? I do what I want, and as long as you live under my roof, you do what I want too. Got it?"

His words rock through me, shaking me to the core. He doesn't mean it. He can't.

"Let go of me," I say between gritted teeth as tears being to spill down my cheeks.

As if the tears woke him from his drunken stupor, he looks at me with sad eyes and releases his hold on me. "Oh my God, Soph." He blinks, then scrubs a hand down his face.

Night and day.

I pull my arms back and rub the area where he held on to me, but I can already see it's going to bruise. The tears continue to fall, and I walk away from him, but he follows me.

"Sophie, I'm sorry. Baby, don't leave," he begs. "Please."

I look at him but can't find the right words. I don't want to upset him further because he's been drinking so much, but I can't have him thinking it's okay to put his hands on me.

"That can never happen again," I tell him flatly.

He closes the gap between us, opens his arms, then pulls me into them. "I'm so sorry. I don't know what came over me." He holds me against his chest. "I had a bad day and didn't mean to take it out on you. I'd never do anything to hurt you, sweetheart. I'm so fucking sorry." As we release our embrace, he leans down and kisses me and apologizes again. I *want* to believe him. I have to.

Before we go to bed, I walk into the bathroom. When I see what he's done, it causes me to cry even more. Never, in my life, did I think he'd do this. I've seen him in a new light. I try to let my emotions out quietly, but eventually, he knocks on the door.

"You okay in there?" His soft voice sounds like the guy I've fallen for and not the monster I saw tonight.

I quickly wipe my tears away and turn on the water to splash my face. "Yep, almost done."

By the time I enter the bedroom, he's already passed out, still fully dressed, and snoring. I undress him so he'll sleep comfortably, though, at this point, I'm not sure if he deserves to. After he's down to his boxer briefs, I pull the blankets over him and crawl into bed. It takes a while for me to fall asleep, but eventually, I do, with sadness in my heart.

The next few days are awkward between us, but I've been trying to forget it as he shows me how sorry he is for what happened.

A few mornings later, I stir awake to Weston kissing my cheek and telling me goodbye. It's early, but he makes sure to wake me anyway. He's been trying, as much as he can, and I appreciate his effort.

"I love you so damn much, Sophie. I'm sorry again for what I did," he softly says before placing a sweet, lingering kiss on my lips. He's apologized every day since it happened.

"I love you too," I whisper. "Don't forget tonight is my sister's secret proposal," I remind him. "You're still coming with me, aren't you?"

"Absolutely. I wouldn't miss it for the world." He winks. "Love you."

I repeat his words before he stands to leave for his day. After falling back asleep, I wake up around eight to a text message from Hunter, but I'm not too alarmed by it because he's been texting me lately to discuss his plans.

HUNTER

You awake?

SOPHIE

Sure am. I've not had coffee yet, though, so tread lightly.

I get out of bed and make a pot because I need all the caffeine I can get right now after not sleeping very well.

HUNTER

You think you can distract Lennon today? Ask her to go grocery shopping or something? I need her out of the apartment. I didn't think about how I'd get everything set up if she's coming directly home after work.

SOPHIE

You got it, bro. Is it weird to call you bro?

HUNTER

Ha-ha. Yeah. Don't do that. Weirdo.

I snort and pour myself a cup, then add my favorite creamer. I nearly orgasm when I take my first sip because it's so damn good.

SOPHIE

Yep. I got you. I'll text her in a while, so then it's not so suspicious. I need to go to the grocery store anyway.

HUNTER

Thanks! I seriously owe you one.

SOPHIE

At this point, you owe me two.

HUNTER

Deal 😊

I sit at the table and finish my coffee. Glancing at my arm, I notice the bruises are darker and let out a deep breath. My upper cheek looks slightly discolored too, but it's nothing I can't hide with concealer. I don't know how I'd explain what happened to anyone, considering I'm still in shock.

Instead of continuing to think about it, I lose myself in music as I typically do when I'm frustrated or upset. Since Weston's house is three bedrooms, he's allowed me to set up an area in a spare room. I grab my violin, pull the music stand from the corner, and begin to play the songs in my heart. It's not surprising when Robert Schumann comes out. A tortured soul like most of us musicians.

After I've played for an hour straight, I take a quick break, then go back to it. For the past few years, I've taught piano on the side, but after I moved in with Weston, I put my lessons on hold. Considering the mood I've been in, I'm thankful for the space from other people, though I could use the money.

Hours pass and my stomach begins to growl, so I eat a banana. I try to push the thoughts about Weston out of my head and decide I'm going to keep this to myself and give him the benefit of the doubt. He's been stressed, and I understand how that can affect everything. Add alcohol to the mix and it's a recipe for disaster, but I never thought I'd be on the receiving end. Though I wasn't trying to tell him what to do, I understand how it looked from his point of view. It's the last thing I wanted, and I wish I could take it back.

I have no appetite, but I force myself to finish, then decide to text Lennon to make sure she can meet me. If she says no, I'm not sure what I'll do other than beg because Hunter needs her out of the house for his master plan to work.

He has a cute scavenger hunt planned at a park based on fairy tales and bought her a dress to wear that matches the whole theme. A smile hits my lips as I text her, knowing what's in store for her later.

Since dating Weston, I haven't hung out with Maddie or Lennon as much as usual, which is my fault. I love them dearly, but I've been focused on my relationship lately. Weston doesn't want them to know our personal business and has made several comments about how much I tell my sisters. So I try to keep everything as private as possible, but it's hard as hell because I'm so used to sharing every little detail about my life with them. But out of respect for him, I don't.

When Lennon messages me back, agreeing to meet me, I text Hunter and tell him the plan to get her out of the house worked, but stupid me, I only gave myself fifteen minutes. So I hurry and get dressed, then head to our favorite grocery store.

I have to remind myself not to mention anything about tonight, so I tuck it away deep inside. With one look, Lennon can tell I'm lying because I suck at it, so as long as I steer the conversation away from unrelated things, I'll be fine. I'll keep the focus on school, since she's back to teaching again, and my adorable niece.

I'm nervous to meet up with Lennon, considering how strained things have been lately and all the changes happening in our lives. She hasn't been unsupportive of Weston's and my relationship, but she worries about me. I understand because I worry about her too, especially after Brandon's unexpected death, everything going on with our parents, and Hunter.

By the time I make it there, she's already waiting for me by the entrance. As soon as I see her, I smile, and she starts talking as we walk in. I grab a cart, and we head straight to the veggies. I need to keep her here as long as possible to give Hunter enough time to do this thing.

"So how's school been?" I ask, not making eye contact with her as I push the sleeves up on my sweater and reach for some bell peppers.

"It's been great. Getting ready for the spring concert next week," she tells me. A moment later, Lennon grabs my arm and pulls me closer to her. When I look into her eyes, I jerk my arm from her grasp.

She lowers her voice, worry blanketing her tone. This is the last thing I wanted to happen, especially here and when I'm still dealing with my own feelings over it.

"What happened, Soph?" She goes quiet, and I can tell she's concerned. I feel myself begin to break, so I push my emotions back, not wanting to cry in front of Lennon. I'm stronger than that.

I let out a laugh. "It's nothing."

As suspected, she doesn't buy it. "That's *not* nothing."

Lennon places her hands on her hips and waits for me to explain, but I don't know where to begin. I can't tell her how I truly feel about it, so I suck in a slow breath and give her a brief summary. It sounds so stupid coming from my mouth in the middle of a grocery store.

"Did he hit you?" Her eyes scan across my face, and I realize I didn't add more foundation before I left.

"It was an accident, Lennon," I say between gritted teeth, trying to push down my embarrassment.

She shakes her head, angry and obviously upset. "You don't drink too much, then accidentally hit someone. This is not okay."

I want to change the subject and talk about something else. Anything but this.

"He promised me it would never happen again, okay?" I snap, wanting her to drop it right now. I think about Weston and everything he's done over the last few days to make it up to me. I have to believe it was an accident. A man I love would never do anything to hurt me. Up until that night, he's made me extremely happy, and what we have is special. My anger rises as I continue, "He loves me, Lennon. I know that's hard for you to believe because no one is allowed to be happy except for you." As soon as the words leave my lips, I wince at myself. I shouldn't have said that.

"Are you serious right now? I want nothing but the best for you and Maddie. That's total bullshit you'd say that to me." Lennon turns to leave without looking back at me.

Guilt streams through me along with a handful of other emotions. I chase after her, not wanting her to leave but knowing she can't. I refuse to be the reason Hunter's plans fall through, and I don't want my sister mad at me for eternity. Not when today is going to be one of the happiest days of her life.

"Lennon, wait. I'm sorry. I don't want to argue with you." She ignores me, not making eye contact because I pushed her too far. "I didn't mean to say that. I have a lot going on right now and shouldn't have taken it out on you. You only want the best for me." Tears well in my eyes, but I try to keep them at bay. There's so much I want to tell her but can't. If Weston found out, he'd be pissed, and if Lennon knew how scared I was that night, she'd tell me to leave him.

"You need to be careful, Sophie. It's not okay for someone to lay their hands on you, no matter what, and I'm worried about you. I already don't care for the dickface, but then this happens."

It's the first time she's admitted she doesn't like him although I already suspected as much. None of my friends do, but I wish they'd give him a fair chance. Liam and Mason hate him. Hunter and Maddie don't seem to care for him either.

"I know," I finally say. "He promised, though, and I believe him." I'm not lying when I say those words.

After knowing him for months, I've never seen him act that way. Alcohol makes people do stupid things and so does stress. His boss has been riding him, and although it doesn't excuse his behavior, I want to believe he'll change. Lennon continues but eventually drops it. I can tell it's in the forefront of her thoughts, but I'm relieved all the same. I chat about Allie and Hunter, about work, and about anything other than myself.

Once I've grabbed a few things for lunch and dinner, we check out, and Lennon helps me load my groceries in the car. Before I leave, she pulls me into a big hug, and I feel something more behind it than usual. "Please take care of yourself and call me if something happens or if you need to get out because he's drunk again. *Promise* me."

I look at her, noticing a tinge of fear for me in her eyes. I smile to appease her. "I promise. But you have to promise me something too."

"What's that?"

"You won't mention this to anyone. Not even Hunter. Please," I beg. The last thing I need is Hunter acting like a big brother and kicking Weston's ass. And if Lennon tells him, Mason and Liam will find out too. It would be a bad situation and put me in a terrible position. I want to keep this all to myself, and if she hadn't seen the bruises herself, she wouldn't know either.

She narrows her eyes. "I will this time. But if I see even the tiniest of marks again, I'm not staying quiet," she warns. "I will call the cops on him."

And she went there. The last thing I need is the cops involved in my business too. Lennon's blowing things out of proportion, but I don't dare say that to her. I explained how he's been stressed, and I swear to her I'll let her know if something else happens. We exchange one last hug before parting ways.

On the way home, I think about what Lennon said, and while I agree with her, she doesn't know Weston. She doesn't know how much we love each other. The man would rope the moon for me if I asked. It was a one-time thing, and we'll work through this and be better for it in the end.

I park and put away the groceries, then jump in the shower to get ready for Lennon's secret proposal tonight. I'm so damn excited about it that I can hardly stand it.

After I've fixed my hair, I make sure I've covered the slight bruising on my face and add some foundation down my neck to blend it in.

Glancing over, I see the time on my phone and realize Weston should've been home already. Though I'm nervous because of what happened, I find the courage to text and ask where he is. He promised to join me. My parents are in town, and many of our friends will be there, so it's important for him to attend because I want to introduce him. Weston could make an amazing first impression with my folks, and who knows, maybe he'll get some ideas for our engagement too.

We need to leave in the next thirty minutes if we're going to make it on time. Considering it's a surprise engagement, we can't be late.

SOPHIE

Hey, baby. You almost home? We need to leave
soon for Hunter and Lennon's thing.

WESTON

Ah, babe. Sorry. I got held up at work because
someone called in sick. Won't be able to make it.

My entire mood shifts, and I'm upset he won't be coming. Instead of replying, I grab my keys and leave. It's better for me not to say anything at all than to text my emotions, especially since things are rocky at the moment.

Before I put the car in reverse, I text Maddie to see if she needs a ride. Thankfully, she does, so I won't have to walk in all alone. When I pick her up, she's her happy-go-lucky self, and I'm glad one of us is a giant ray of sunshine. The girl knows how to make me smile when I don't feel like it.

"Where's Weston?" she asks.

"He's still at work and couldn't make it."

"That sucks. Mom and Dad wanted to meet him. They were talking about it at breakfast this morning."

"I know." It's all I can say because no one is more disappointed by it than I am. Maddie changes the subject and talks about a ballet number she's learning at the moment. Though she loves jazz, toe, and lyrical, she's amazing at pointe too. I think about her life and how beautiful it is that she's living her dream. It's hard not to feel a tinge of envy by how innocent she is. I want her to stay this way forever.

Eventually, we arrive at the park, and Maddie wraps her arm around me as we walk in. She makes me feel young and free again, regardless that I'm five years older than her with a stack of responsibilities on my shoulders. As soon as we enter the Mother Goose concert area and say hello to everyone, an announcement is made to keep quiet because Lennon's arrived.

Excitement ripples through everyone, and Maddie tries to hold in her squeals by covering her mouth. When Lennon walks on stage, blindfolded, I nearly begin to cry because I'm so damn happy for her and Hunter. My musician friends begin playing, and soon, Hunter is down on one knee asking her to marry him. I get choked up and so does Maddie because they've waited so long for this and deserve a lifetime of happiness. A love like theirs is special, and they're both so damn lucky. I think about Weston and know we'll eventually get there, or at least, I hope. The thought of him not being here with me, experiencing this special moment, stings.

After the proposal, we eagerly wait for Lennon and Hunter to join us. From the corner of my eye, I see Mason and Liam. I freeze and try to focus on Lennon, pretending I don't see them. To this day, Mason still causes a thunderstorm of emotions inside me. He's like lightning, and I've been waiting for him to strike again. If only he hadn't been so damn stubborn.

Trying to keep my attention on the happy couple and Allie, I suggest they take more pictures together. This moment needs to be documented and remembered forever. Maddie grabs Lennon's phone and gets to work posing them. If dance doesn't work out for her, she should be a professional photographer. I stand back and watch in awe. Once they're done, Hunter tilts his head at me.

"Where's your boyfriend?"

Heat hits my cheeks. I should've been more prepared for this question. "Oh, he couldn't make it. Got caught up at work."

Lennon frowns when our eyes meet. I try to silently tell her everything is fine, but I'm not sure she's buying it.

"Right," Mason says behind me.

Glaring at him, I roll my eyes, but it doesn't seem to faze him in the least. Maddie lights up when she sees Liam. Her reaction to him causes me to hold back my laughter.

As soon as Lennon and Hunter are pulled away, Mason pulls me off to the side. It's the first time we've been alone together since the intense conversation we had on the patio New Year's Eve. I've avoided him like a flesh-eating bacteria ever since.

"What the hell is going on with you, Sophie? Something isn't right." He has that same look in his eyes as Lennon did earlier as he studies my face.

I grit my teeth. "You're out of line, Mason. Worry about yourself. It's what you're good at."

"You're acting like the boogeyman is gonna pop up at any moment. Like something's wrong. I know the signs. I've seen them before. You've not been yourself, and no number of lies will change that."

I glare at him, pissed that he can see straight through me and angry because he never gave me a chance. Now that I've moved on, he wants to play the hero.

"Where's Weston really at? Funny how he always has something come up when there's a group of people involved. Please tell me you aren't that dense, Soph. I'm worried about you." His voice is hushed.

"You haven't earned the right to worry about me, Mason. For years, you've done nothing but ignore me, pretend I don't exist, and pretend we never happened as if you wish it hadn't. And you know what? I wish it hadn't *either*."

I glance at Mason one last time before I push away from him and walk toward Maddie. He winces as if I've slapped him, his jaw tight and his body tense. Perhaps that was a mean thing to say, but he pushed me too far this time questioning my decisions when he's been absent from my life for months.

Today has been a clusterfuck of emotions, and I'm ready to get the hell away from him. I'm ready to be alone because I'm too emotionally unstable to be around people.

Maddie finishes her conversation, and we meet with our parents. After Lennon and Hunter leave, I tell Maddie I'm tired, and we make our way to the car.

"You okay?" she asks as we walk down the path through the magical park full of fairy tales and nursery rhyme characters.

"I'm fine." But I don't know if I am. The only thing on my mind right now is the sincerity and concern in Mason's eyes when he looked at me. Something I haven't seen in a long time.

The first time Mason met Weston, it was obvious he hated him. I was too inside my head and heart to listen when Mason told me to be careful.

I go home and climb into bed, not waiting up for Weston. Sleep finds me before he gets home, which is good, because I'm not sure what I would've said to him otherwise, and I'm sure he's been drinking again.

CHAPTER ELEVEN

MASON

ONE MONTH EARLIER

It's gotten to a point where I can't stop thinking about Sophie. Every morning when I wake up and every night before I go to sleep, she's on my mind. I'm worried as fuck, and Liam is too because she's avoiding us. Me, I understand, but him? They were good friends and hung out all the time, but it slowed down the moment she started dating Weston and then abruptly stopped when she moved in with him.

As I'm sitting at my desk eating another shitty microwave meal, I decide I'm not going to let this sit. I can't seem to shake the bad feeling I have about this guy.

Now that I'm playing secretary at the DA's office until a forensics position opens in the fall when Jack retires, it'll make getting information much easier. Just being Michael Holt's son gives me an advantage. Though I curse it most of the time, this time it comes in handy. Considering Sophie could be in more danger than any of us realizes, I'm not afraid to use it to get what I need.

As I walk across the building to Jerad's office, I shoot a text to Liam and ask him to call me when he goes on break. I've known

Jerad since my first internship right after college. Back then, he was a nobody here, but now he oversees an entire department of criminal investigators and has access to information I can't get on my own. I have no doubt he'll help me, but I can't just pick up the phone or shoot off an email with this request. It'll probably require an explanation of sorts, which I'm ready to give. There's a lot of risk asking for an off-the-record background check, but I don't think I'll be able to sleep at night if I don't find out everything I can about this prick.

When I step inside Jerad's office, he's busy flipping through a folder of images while eating lunch. When I glance down, I see a horrific crime scene, and I can't believe he's able to chew his food while looking at it.

"Dude…" I groan. "You're fucking weird."

He shrugs. "To what do I owe the pleasure?"

I take a seat in front of him. "I have a big favor to ask."

"Daddy couldn't help?" He smirks, already knowing about my relationship with my father. It wasn't something I could keep secret years ago when I assisted him in the department. Instead of talking shit, I keep my comments to myself about that, but he sure knows how to press my buttons, as most do.

"No. I don't want him involved in my business," I reply curtly.

This causes Jerad to let out a hearty laugh. "Your business *is* your father's business, Holt. You already know this. Why do you think you're here in the big DA's office doing bitch work?"

I should've known he'd give me a hard time. Although I don't see him that often, this is typical. "You done yet?" I arch a brow, seemingly bored with his antics.

"Eh. I could probably keep going." He chuckles. "But I'll spare you. What's going on? Must be serious if you need my help."

I sit on the edge of my seat. "You still have access to run in-depth off-record background checks, right? Or can easily get them?"

"Yes," he draws out, eyeing me curiously.

"I'm concerned my friend is dating a dangerous man, and I need to get some info about him. Can you help?"

He pops an eyebrow. "Might cost ya."

"Oh, shut the hell up." I stand, ready to walk out because I won't beg.

"Sit. You know I don't like all those dramatics. What is with the Holt family always making a damn scene?"

I sit back down, relieved since I didn't have a plan B.

"You better remember me when you're sitting on your father's throne, okay? What's the dickhead's name?" Jerad asks.

The last question causes me to laugh. "Weston Westbrook."

He narrows his eyes. "Is he a fuckin' cartoon?"

I snort. "He looks as ridiculous as his name sounds too. Has one of those haircuts I had when I was five."

Jerad grins. "You must have a thing for this girl."

I can't deny it. "I'm worried about her. She's showing all the signs of abuse, and the way this guy acts…I can't place it. He has that overbearing narcissist vibe to him, and I swear he's manipulating her emotionally. I'm seeing the signs: avoidance, seclusion, denial, and excusing the behavior. The last time I saw her, she looked terrible. Stressed, worried, upset. The woman who stood in front of me wasn't the woman I've known for years, and I'm concerned about what he's capable of doing. What he's already done."

Jerad lets out a calm breath. "I'll take care of it. He's from Sacramento?"

"Honestly, I don't know much about him other than he lives here and has a correctional officer job or something."

"Did you search the system for him? See if he's really a correctional officer? He'd work for the state, and we'd have records on file."

My eyes go wide. "No. I didn't even think about it."

Jerad shakes his head. "And you want to investigate crime scenes."

"I want to do forensics. It's different," I remind him, nearly jumping out of my seat to go back to my desk to search for Weston's name in the public directory.

"I'll keep you updated with what I find. Also, don't tell

anyone. I don't want to risk anything by helping you stalk this guy. Got it?"

I nod. "I owe you big time. Thank you."

"Should have something for you by tomorrow, maybe earlier," he tells me as I make my way out of the room.

Once I'm back at my desk, I go to the public directory where all the state employees are listed and search for Weston's name, but nothing comes up. I try to convince myself that something is wrong, or I'm not searching the correct place, so I call the prison and ask for him. If he answers, I'll hang up. I'm put on hold, and when the woman comes back on the line, she seems annoyed.

"No one by that name works here."

I sit silent for a moment. "Sorry, I must've called the wrong place. Thanks."

I hang up, my mind reeling. He doesn't work at the county jail because I know every person there. But if he doesn't work at the prison, that means he's a fucking liar, and who knows what else he's lying about. I'm seething and seeing red, but thankfully, my cell ringing pulls me away. When I see it's Liam, I pick up the phone and walk to a secluded place where I can have some privacy.

"What do you need?"

"Before you tell me to mind my own damn business, I've been doing some digging on Weston."

"Mason…" Liam warns.

"He doesn't work at the prison," I blurt before Liam can say another word.

"What?"

"He's not in the state directory. He's not a correctional officer."

"Goddammit. We need to follow him," Liam suggests. "We need to learn as much as we can about this bastard before we confront him."

I snort. "And all this time, I thought you were gonna tell me to let it rest."

"It's obvious there's an issue. I'll be home late tonight, but I'm off tomorrow. I think Sophie said he leaves early in the morning.

We can follow him and see where the fuck he's going." I'm happy Liam is suggesting this because I would've otherwise.

"You know where they live?" I ask.

"I know *everything*."

Snarky asshole.

"Okay, it's a plan then." I let out a breath, and we make plans for tomorrow morning before ending the call.

I can't seem to focus on anything for the rest of the day. My mind is in overdrive as I think about Sophie and Weston and what she must be going through. She'd never tell us. On the way home, I call Maddie and am shocked when she picks up after the first ring.

"Hello, loverboy," she purrs, which only makes me laugh.

"You're ridiculous," I blurt. "But I do have some questions for you. And you can't say shit to Lennon or Sophie."

"You think I'm *not* good at keeping secrets or something?"

"I know how you are with your sisters, but this is serious, Mads. Real serious."

"Okay, what is it?"

"What can you tell me about Weston?" I ask, pulling into the driveway. The call stays silent as I walk inside the house and grab a bottle of water. "Maddie?"

"Yeah, sorry. You kinda blindsided me. I don't know much about him, honestly, other than he doesn't want Sophie to hang around anyone but him. She's cut off Lennon and me, which is fucked up if you ask me. We only get her attention when Weston isn't around." I can tell she doesn't like him very much either, which says a lot. Out of the three of them, she's the most outgoing and easiest to get along with.

"I'm worried about her, Mason," she says.

I release a deep breath. "Trust me, I am too."

"What're you up to?"

"I'm doing some research. Something isn't right about her boyfriend, and I'm worried as fuck that he's not who he says he is."

"Good." She sighs. "Thank you. I've had a bad feeling about

him for a while, but she avoids talking about him. I've asked her to join me for lunch so many times over the past month, and she's given me an excuse every single time. Honestly, I miss my sister and the way things used to be."

"I know. Thanks, Mads. Please don't tell anyone we talked about this." I look at my phone and see I'm getting another call from Jerad. "Gotta let you go. I'll keep you updated. If you think of anything, even if it's something weird or awkward, please let me know, okay?"

"No problem."

Part of me feels relieved to know it's not just Liam and me who are concerned. I'm not acting out in jealousy, so to hell with anyone who claims it as so.

I flip over to the other line, hoping he's still there. "Hey."

"Damn. Took you long enough." Seriousness coats his tone. "So. I did some digging, pulled some strings, and got the info much quicker than I thought I would."

My heart is racing, and it feels as if time stands still as I wait for him to tell me what the fuck he found.

"He has a history of abuse. When he was a teenager, he stabbed another kid, who lived, but it was a close call. He got out of it by claiming self-defense. He resisted arrest and assaulted a police officer. Was put on probation, then spent some time in juvie for another assault charge. But the records were sealed because of his age at the time of the incident. There was also a domestic abuse call about four years ago, but my guess is the woman left or he beat her into silence because there hasn't been anything since."

"Fuck," I say, running my fingers through my hair, knowing I need to fill Liam in as soon as possible. "Motherfucker," I repeat over and over.

"Also…" Jerad continues. "He doesn't work at the prison. I knew that as soon as I realized he had a criminal history because he'd never be eligible. Still, I checked, and there's no record of him ever working for the state."

I blow out a long breath. "Yeah, I called, and they told me they didn't know who I was talking about. Shit, shit, shit."

"What're you gonna do, Mason? I can tell you're up to something when you ask for favors like this."

I stare at the whitewashed wall. "Not sure yet. This is bad, and she won't believe me without proof."

"Let me say this. I think people can change. He was young when the first shit happened, but the domestic abuse is from adulthood, which means his behavior has only escalated. So I think whatever you're planning, you need to be careful and watch your back."

"I will." My mind is running a million miles per hour as I think back to the first night I met the bastard. He was a master of disguise, maintaining a façade in Sophie's presence. After another warning from Jerad, I end the call and text Liam everything that I learned. He's just as pissed off as I am, and we're determined to figure out Weston's secrets together.

For Sophie. For her safety. Because we don't give a damn whether she likes it or not.

After I eat some questionable leftovers, I shower and try to sleep. At four in the morning, my bedroom door swings open, and a wide-awake Liam stands in my doorway.

"Get the fuck up. It's time to go," he tells me, flicking on the light.

"Have you slept?" I ask, running my hand over my face, my eyes trying to adjust to the brightness.

"No, I don't have time for that. My flight ran late as usual. But if Weston's working the early shift, we need to be in their neighborhood now," Liam explains. Considering he's a bounty hunter, he's experienced in doing this sort of thing, so I couldn't have chosen a better person to help with this. He's literally experienced in stalking people.

I get dressed, and by the time I put on my shoes, Liam's already brewed a pot of coffee. He hands me a to-go cup and sips out of his. His truck's still running, and as soon I climb inside, he speeds across town. Every turn we take, I try to memorize where we are. I've not been invited to Weston's, and I'm almost certain Liam hasn't either, but I don't ask how he knows where they live.

Once we're in a normal-looking neighborhood, Liam turns off the truck lights, then we sit and wait.

"It's that house right there." He points in the distance. Sophie's car parked next to the bastard's. Liam pulls out a pair of binoculars and puts them to his face. "Here he comes."

My jaw locks the moment I see Weston.

"He's wearing some kind of uniform. Why would he go through all the trouble to lie?" Liam asks.

As the car backs out of the driveway, Liam waits a moment before turning on his lights and following. We maintain a distance, but we're close enough to keep up with him.

"Where the fuck is he going?" I ask, confused because we're on the other side of town. We've been following him for nearly thirty minutes, and I'm almost concerned he realizes we're behind him because of the way he's braking and randomly speeding up.

"I don't know, but he's driving erratically like he's drunk or something." Liam grabs the steering wheel with white knuckles but trails far away enough not to look suspicious.

Glancing around, I realize we're in the industrial district. We're on the opposite side of the city, not even close to the prison at all. The car pulls into a warehouse. Liam slows at the end of the street and turns off his lights. We wait until Weston gets out of the car and walks inside.

"This is weird as fuck," I whisper.

Liam watches the building like it might disappear as I research the address of what the hell this place is. I ask Liam for his binoculars and barely make out a sign that says something about storage. Going back to my phone, I add the word to my search and eventually come across a listing for a security guard position that was posted a year ago.

"It's a storage warehouse," I tell Liam. "He's a goddamn security guard."

Liam glances at me. "If he's lied about this, what else is he hiding?"

"That's what concerns me the most," I admit. *What's his motivation for lying?* Frustration and annoyance take over when

Weston steps outside. When I get out of the truck and slam the door, Liam calls out my name and follows me.

"Mason, you're gonna blow our cover."

"I don't give a fuck," I hiss.

"Alrighty, I guess we're doing this." Liam cracks his knuckles. "Gonna fuck him up then?"

I snort. "Well, no. But I have a few words for him."

When Liam and I round the corner, Weston glances up from his phone and narrows his eyes when he sees us. Normal people would say something, but Weston isn't normal. He instantly balls his hands into fists.

"What the fuck do you want?" he asks.

Liam takes the lead and pushes Weston with all his strength, knocking him off balance. Weston stumbles back, losing his footing, and I can smell the alcohol permeating from him. The motherfucker is drunk, so that means he either started early or woke up still trashed from the night before. As Weston picks himself up from the ground, Liam places his foot on his chest, knocking him back down. It's not fair because Liam is double Weston's size, and he could easily squish him like a bug.

"Now, we have a few things we need to discuss," Liam tells him.

I move closer and recognition finally flashes across Weston's face. "Wait. I know you two fucks. Sophie's friends, right?"

Liam adds more pressure, keeping him pinned on the ground. "Exactly. Her *friends*. Now, explain to us why everyone thinks you're a correctional officer when you're nothing more than a fuckin' security guard?"

In a split second, Liam loses his balance as Weston struggles against him and is then standing on his feet. He marches closer, getting into our faces. "I'm gonna call the cops on you both for assault and get you arrested. You have no fucking business following me here." He pulls a Taser from his belt and points it at Liam, who rushes him and fights for it, ripping it from his hand.

With adrenaline pumping, I take a few steps forward, then bring my fist back and connect with Weston's jaw. He falls to the ground, and I go to him, fist dawn, but Liam holds me back before I can connect with his face again, which is probably for the best since I'm two seconds from destroying him. Anger and frustration, my old friends, encourage me as Weston glares with rage in his eyes. Just like at New Year's, he flips a switch as if he's emulating human behavior, and the motherfucker smiles.

"You're such a goddamn pussy." He spits out blood.

"This isn't over," I grit. "You touch her, hurt a single hair on her head, and you'll be seeing us both again." It's not a threat, it's a promise, and I'm not sure he realizes I'm not joking.

Weston lets out a laugh. "You have no idea who you're fuckin' messing with. And if you tell her anything about this, trust me when I say she'll be the one to pay."

I see red, but Liam grabs me and pulls me away before I can do anything else.

"If anything happens to her, you'll be fucking sorry," I shout.

Liam's stronger than me, and although I'm heated, leaving is for the best. The last thing I need is an assault charge.

"So that went over well," Liam tells me as we get in his truck. "Fantastic."

All I can think about is what he said. "Do you think he'll hurt her?" I shake my hand, knowing it's going to sting even more in a couple of hours.

Cranking the truck, Liam releases a sharp breath. "He better not, but I'm not sure what he's capable of. Did you see the look in his eyes?"

"What look?"

"Exactly. It was like nothing was there. No emotion. Like he doesn't have a soul or something."

I nod. "Yeah. He seems off. Sophie isn't safe. I'm convinced. We need to warn her, Liam."

We ride in silence, both lost in our thoughts.

"You hungry?" he eventually asks.

I look at the time on my phone and see it's barely past five. "Sure."

Before going home, we stop at a twenty-four-hour diner. We

order coffee and the daily breakfast special. I'm half-tempted to call Sophie right now and tell her she needs to leave Weston, but it's as if Liam can read my thoughts because he shakes his head.

"Sophie isn't gonna listen to us. You know that, right?" He sips his coffee, peering over the rim of the cup.

"Maybe she'll listen to me." I'd like to think she'd be reasonable, but after her reaction at Hunter and Lennon's proposal, I'm not sure. Things have been awkward between us since then. More awkward than normal.

Roaring laughter rips through the quiet diner. "Doubtful. You're the last person on the planet Sophie is gonna listen to."

I arch an eyebrow at him. "You're not a tad dramatic."

Liam shrugs. "No, just realistic. She's pissed at you. She's been pissed at you."

"For what? I didn't do shit. I've always had her best interests in mind."

I want to smack the shit-eating grin off his face. "Does she know that, though?"

A frustrated groan released. "She *should*."

"Let me see. You've had a thing for her for years and refuse to do anything about it, which, I understand why. But then she finally starts dating someone, and you've got nothing but negative things to say about it. Again, I get why but—"

"He's a creep," I interject.

"Right. But your timing is shit. So it makes you look like the jealous guy who never stepped up, and that's how she views all of this. I don't think you could say anything to fix that either."

When our breakfast arrives, Liam eats as if he hasn't seen food for a month. Considering he worked all day yesterday and got home late, there's no telling when he ate last, especially when he's on special assignments.

"Do you think we could get her to the house?" I ask. "Maybe she'd listen to you if she won't give me the time of day?"

"Possibly, but she's been avoiding me too." Liam shrugs. "I can text her and see if she'll come over. If not, you're gonna have to go to her. I think she has a right to know, but you need to be the one to tell her. If I know Sophie as well as I think I do, she's gonna have a fuckton of questions and want an explanation."

He's right, but a part of me doesn't know where to start. If she already thinks I'm the jealous guy who wouldn't make a move, then I'm doomed from the start, but I have to try. The last thing I want is for something to happen to her while knowing all of this and not tell her. I'm already living with impossible guilt from my past. I don't need to add more to it.

"You're right. If you can get her to the house, I'll make sure she gets the message."

"It's gonna be hard as hell, but I know what's at risk here. I'll make it happen, even if I have to call Lennon and Maddie and get them involved too. I hate being the bastard who makes it a family matter, but that's where we're at with this."

"I agree. That's exactly where we're at."

"Hell, I'll carry her to the house caveman style if I have to," he adds.

"Kicking and screaming?" I mock.

He snorts. "Wouldn't be my first time."

"And in case she refuses to listen to me, plan B is you intervene and tell her he has a record, so she knows our concerns are valid. You didn't break her heart, so perhaps she'll give you more than five seconds to explain."

We finish eating and go home. Liam goes to his room, and I rush to get ready for work and somehow make it on time. The day drags by, and Liam texts me in the afternoon and lets me know Sophie agreed to meet him for dinner tomorrow at the house, but she was vocal about me not being there. This might be a lot harder than I originally thought.

MASON

Fine. I'll make myself "unavailable" for an hour, then I'm coming home, and we're having an unavoidable chat.

LIAM

She's gonna hate me as much as she hates you for this.

MASON

Then you can join the club.

I've been on edge all day thinking about seeing Sophie tonight. After Liam told me how pissed Sophie is at me, it's bothered the fuck out of me, but I deserve it. I wish I could be the man for her, the one who makes her happy and gives her what she needs and wants. And there's no fuckin' way that Weston gives her that. It's more than obvious he's a placeholder, which makes me sick to my stomach.

Instead of going straight home from work, I stay late, trying to keep my mind busy as I go through files and organize them into the electronic system. What I'm doing is nothing more than bitch work, but it's a foot in the door until the fall. Eventually, all the internships and experience I've gained over the years will come in handy. Though my dad will take credit for it all, as he somehow manages with everything I accomplish, regardless if he agrees with my career choices or not. People in the department will think I got the job because of him as well. I have so damn much to prove either way.

I check the time and realize I need to get going. She's been at the house for nearly thirty minutes, and I don't want Liam to have to stall her. My nerves get the best of me as I head home. When I see her car in the driveway, I park behind her, knowing if she gets pissed and tries to leave, she won't be able to. It's a dick move, but I'm gonna make sure she listens to me.

When I walk into the house, Liam's laughing as Sophie tells him something. She glares at me, giving me her perfected *go to hell* look. I smile, but she rolls her eyes and turns away. If that's any indication of how annoyed she is I'm here, I can only imagine the daggers she's throwing at Liam right now.

Instead of starting the conversation now, I go take a shower, giving them time to chat since she's not going anywhere.

Once I'm done, I go to the kitchen and make myself a plate of food. Sophie and Liam are on the back porch, but it doesn't look like they're talking.

Just as I finish eating, Liam comes in and drops a beer bottle in the trash. "You should go out there now."

"How is she?" I ask.

He shakes his head.

I place my plate in the sink, then walk outside. When I sit, Sophie looks at me. It's a stare down until I break the silence.

"How've you been?"

She bites the inside of her cheek and looks stressed.

"How do you think I've been?"

"Good, I hope."

"What do you want, Mason?"

Sucking in a deep breath, I study her. Though I'm sure she'd deny it, the chemistry between us is still there. Regardless that she's with Weston now, the underlying electrical current that's always streamed between us still pulls us together.

"Soph, your boyfriend—"

"Don't you dare start that again," she warns.

"He's not who you think he is," I blurt, ignoring her.

A sarcastic laugh escapes her. "How do you know anything about our relationship? Oh wait, you don't."

I'm trying to stay calm for her sake. "He's not a correctional officer, Soph. He doesn't work at the prison and never has. I checked."

Sophie shakes her head, her lips in a firm line. Standing in front of me, she points a finger in my face. "How dare you go behind my back and snoop on him? How fucking dare you, Mason. Your audacity is mind-boggling."

Standing, I grab her elbow, trying to calm her down, but she pushes me away.

I release her, but I don't let her get far. "I'm trying to help you."

She snaps her gaze to mine with fire boiling in her eyes. "Listen to me and listen to me very carefully, Mason. For years of my life, I waited around for you. Seriously waited for you. It was *your* choice for us not to have a relationship, for us not to progress any further, though I made it clear what I wanted. I tried being your friend, but your behavior toward me didn't merit my friendship. Now that I've found someone, you feel threatened, but this jealousy bullshit has to stop. You need to butt out of my relationship and mind your own damn business."

Her words drive through me like a rusted knife, ripping and tearing flesh, leaving a deep wound exposed. "Sophie." My chest deflates. "I'm not the only one who's worried—"

"No, Mason. I'm done," she cuts me off, then slides the patio door open and walks inside the house. I stand for a moment, looking at the pink and purple sky, wishing things were different. I wish I hadn't pushed her away for so long so she'd trust me now, but I did and I don't know if this is fixable.

The patio door slides open. "Sophie needs you to move your truck, ya bastard," Liam tells me with a smirk.

"What happened to plan B?" I ask him.

"I tried, man. She stormed in cussing your name, and I started to explain that we had good reason for looking into him, that we found out some bad shit that made us worried, but she wasn't having it. Said I had no room to talk and mocked my wealth of knowledge on relationships, then marched out."

I shake my head. "I might just make her wait out there all night."

"You've always been stubborn. She might murder you, though."

The door closes, and I take another minute to myself before walking through the house to meet her in the front.

She's standing by her car, but instead of doing what she demands, I stalk toward her. Sophie steps back, pressing her body against her car, and sucks in a sharp breath. Although she doesn't want to listen to me, I'm determined to make her.

"Real cute parking behind me. It's as if you both had this planned the entire time," she says with venom in her voice.

Staring into her brown eyes, I shrug, wishing I could read her thoughts. "I'm sorry for hurting you. I never wanted to fucking hurt you, which is why I only wanted to stay friends. Maybe you don't understand that, but I wouldn't expect you to. But as your friend, I'm so damn worried about you. About the way you're acting. The seclusion. How you've put a wall up between all of us, even your sisters. I don't know what's going on with you, Sophie, but this didn't happen until you started dating him. So I have my reasons for checking him out."

She tries to open her mouth and speak, but I place a finger over her soft lips to silence her.

"The foundation of your relationship was built on a lie, unless you knew that already. Did you?"

She doesn't answer me, but there's a flicker of sadness in her eyes.

"You didn't. And I know I can't make you happy. I can't give you what you want, but I'll be damned if someone like him has you in ways I can only dream of and then disrespects you while forcing you away from everyone who loves you. Over my goddamn dead body. So if you hate me for that, then so be it. Hate me. But trust me when I say I've only had your best interests in mind, and I only want you to be safe. Weston is dangerous."

Tears form in her eyes, and I want nothing more than to lean over and kiss them all away, but there's a wall between us, one I can't climb.

"Let me leave," she says in a cracked voice.

I nod, then walk to my truck, and back out of the driveway. As Sophie's car rounds the corner, all I can do is hope I got through to her before it's too late.

CHAPTER TWELVE

SOPHIE

PRESENT DAY

Things have been rocky with Weston, and I wish our relationship could go back to how it was in the beginning. Carefree and happy.

Since he lost his job a couple of days ago, he's been drinking nonstop. His temper has flared on more than one occasion, and he makes me feel like I'm a burden. Things have escalated to the point where my feelings for him have faded, and I wonder if I was in love with him at all or just the idea of it. He changed after I let him in and knew how to use my compassion against me.

There are times when I try to be on my best behavior because I don't want to upset him, knowing it might set him off. Moving in with him was obviously a mistake. I would leave if I had money and somewhere else to go, but I'm afraid he'd come after me.

I'm scared he won't let me leave without a fight.

Living with him has become unbearable. For every good day we have, there are a handful of bad ones. This man is destroying me from the inside out. He manipulates my emotions every chance he gets, and now that I'm aware of it, I notice it each time. Although I promised Lennon I would tell her if he hit me again, I haven't found the courage to say anything to anyone.

I want to break up with him and get out of this fucking house. I tried to call it off a few weeks ago after Mason and Liam tricked me into coming over for what I imagine was an intervention of sorts. As soon as the words left my mouth, Weston slammed me against the wall and held his hand to my throat. He promised me if I ever left him, he'd kill me.

I haven't been able to shake those words or the look in his eyes when he said it.

He really is a monster.

Learning that he lied about his job plus having a record was a hard pill to swallow. I didn't want to admit I was wrong about Weston, especially to Liam and Mason, who've disliked him since the beginning. I'm embarrassed and want my life back.

Leaving won't be easy. I've been trying to plan, doing and saying what he expects to stay under his radar. It's safer that way.

The last time we were intimate, I told him I was too tired, but he ignored me and pushed for it anyway. He reminded me if I ever left, he'd find me and make sure I'd regret it. It was another threat, one I don't doubt he'd follow through with, which is why I haven't figured out how to get out from under his power.

Living in this house and being tormented by him is a prison.

Regardless, I push the thoughts to the back of my mind and am taking it one day at a time, hoping it will be a decent one. Hoping I can get the courage to walk away for good. Hoping I'll survive him.

This evening will be the first time we've left the house together in weeks. We're going to Hunter's brother's wedding reception, and I can't wait to see everyone. I've felt trapped, and Weston has made it very clear he doesn't want me around anyone but him. For the past few days, he's done nothing but drink nonstop, and I've tried to stay out of his way and let him do what he wants. It's easier. Every response I've given him has been a supportive one, and I agree to whatever he says.

I roll over and see he's still sleeping, so I sneak out of bed to make us breakfast. When I look at the clock, it's barely past nine, and I'm shocked we slept so late—well, shocked I did.

He passes out from the alcohol he's consumed, and some days, he doesn't wake up until noon. I've asked him to speak to a counselor and get help instead of drinking his worries away, but he refuses. He insists he doesn't have a problem, and the only issue he has is when I bitch about it.

After I brush my teeth and pull my hair into a ponytail, I head to the kitchen, then make some coffee and grab the ingredients for breakfast from the fridge. It doesn't take long before the meal is ready, and I'm placing bacon and eggs on two plates.

Weston stumbles from the bedroom and plops down at the table, his eyes barely open. He looks like absolute shit, and nothing like the man I met six months ago or the man I'd fallen in love with. I set a mug in front of him, knowing he's still drunk from the night before.

"Hungry?" I ask with a smile, handing him a plate.

He shrugs but starts eating right away without a thank you or any sort of appreciation. Though I'm not the least bit surprised anymore. He's an ungrateful bastard, to say the least.

For a while, we eat in silence. When our plates are empty, I clear the table, then refill our coffees. I'm happy he's drinking something other than whiskey for now.

"I saw a security guard position at the mall on a job board when I was scrolling online yesterday. Offered good hours and benefits, too," I mention as I begin rinsing our plates. My cheeks heat in fear because I realize my slipup. Mason was the one who found out he lied about his job and wasn't a correctional officer. I hadn't said anything to Weston, knowing he'd be livid. While I was angry at the time, Mason was right about one thing. I do need to be careful.

Weston's eyes lock onto mine. "What do you mean? A *security guard*?"

I shrug nonchalantly. "Just something I saw in passing. It's the same thing as what you were doing, isn't it?" I ask, playing stupid so he doesn't see through my lie.

He pounds his fist on the table, making me jump. "What? You don't trust me? Don't trust that I'm looking for a fucking job? It's only been a couple of days, for fuck's sake. I don't need you job hunting for me, Sophie." The venom in his tone slices right through me.

Though my heart beats rapidly in my chest, I suck in a deep breath and try to stay calm. "Sorry, I just thought I'd pass on the information I saw."

Narrowing his eyes, Weston watches me like I'm his prey. "You know damn well it's not the same thing, don't you?"

I've always been a bad liar and wish I wasn't so transparent. "Okay, yeah, I did. I know you were a security officer, but it's not a big deal, Weston," I quickly rush out with a sincere look. "We'd just met, and I'm sure you accidentally misspoke about your job or were trying to impress me." I push off the kitchen counter and walk toward him, hoping to dissolve his anger brewing. "Baby, it doesn't matter to me. You could shovel shit for all I care."

"It was that guy, wasn't it? Mason. Is that his fucking name? What else did he tell you about me?" He stands from the chair so fast it falls to the floor.

"No." My eyes go wide, and my adrenaline spikes as I step back.

"You're fucking lying!" Weston screams and takes his mug and slams it against the floor, shattering the porcelain into a hundred pieces. He takes a step closer but trips over the table leg, causing everything on top to go crashing over. "You're a fucking lying cunt!" he shouts in my face as I cower backward.

He's losing it, and I don't know how to calm him down when he gets like this. He picks up a chair and throws it across the room. It slams into the wall, causing a clock to fall and break.

"Weston, please," I beg, trying to steady my voice and reason with him. I suck in a steady breath, not wanting him to see how scared I am, but it's useless the louder he gets. My body shakes, and I'm cursing myself for bringing up jobs because I knew better. Weston throws his fists around, breaking through the drywall, then kicks the back door so hard, he leaves a dent in it. His knuckles drip with blood, and I want him to stop so he doesn't hurt himself further—*or me.*

I step closer, gently reaching for him. He rears back in his blinded rage and then all I see is his fist. It happens so fast I don't have time to react before it hits my face. At the moment, everything goes black, and I'm blinded by pain. I'm dazed, confused, and hurt…again. I fall to my knees, holding my cheek. There's nothing I can do but cry and leave the room, so I do both. I stand, stumbling on my feet, unable to focus and rush to my purse to grab my keys.

Weston realizes what I'm doing and stalks after me, yanking my arm until I fall on the ground. He's too strong for me to fight and throws me around like a rag doll. My knees hit the carpet, and when I look up at him, he's smiling maniacally.

"Where the fuck do you think you're going?" he hisses.

I don't say anything, but if my daggers could kill, his ass would be laid out right now. Too bad he's twice my size.

"So, Sophie," he says, twirling my keys around his finger. "Did you fuck him? I bet you did. Probably fucked his loser friend, too. You're the town whore, aren't you?"

"*What*? What're you talking about?" I cry, still holding a hand over my eye, tears streaming down my cheeks.

Weston manically laughs. "You know exactly who I'm talking about. Mason, that little bitch of a friend you have. You fucked him, didn't you? Why else would he come after me to defend your honor?"

I swallow, keeping my tone flat as I wipe my face, honestly having no idea what he's talking about. All Mason told me was that he dug up information on him, not that he confronted him. "No."

Weston towers over me, then leans down and wraps his hand around my throat, nearly choking me as he slowly rises with my life in his grip. "How many times are you gonna fucking lie to me today?"

I gasp for air, crying as I try to pull his hand off me. I've never been so scared for my life as I am right now. "Please," I choke out. "Please, stop."

He releases me, and I crash back down to the floor, sobbing.

Weston walks away, placing my keys on top of a bookshelf I won't be able to reach. I've never felt so helpless in my goddamn life as I do right now. Somehow, I pick myself up off the floor, feeling broken and not sure what I'm going to do.

I go to the kitchen and grab a bag of peas from the freezer as Weston sits at the table chugging whiskey straight from the bottle.

"Soph," he says, meekly. "I'm sorry. I didn't mean—"

"Don't," I tell him between gritted teeth, glaring and letting him get a good look at what he's done to me.

My arm is killing me because I landed on it, my throat hurts, and my face is throbbing. He could've broken my damn arm, too —my livelihood depends on being able to play violin, and if he or any man tries to take that away from me, I don't want to think about what would happen.

I sit on the couch, placing the bag on my eye, hoping it's not swollen and won't bruise but knowing better. If I don't show up to that reception tonight, Lennon will come looking for me, and if I do show up, it will be more than obvious what happened. I could get an Uber, but Weston is too unpredictable for me to decide what to do. One wrong move and he could end me for good.

Weston follows me from the kitchen and sits on the couch next to me. "Please, Sophie." Tears well in his eyes, and I'm not sure if his emotions are real or if this is another one of his acts.

If anyone should be crying right now, it's me, because the man I thought I loved isn't the man who hurt me. The thought of what that means is frightening. There are times when Weston is so damn sweet and others when he's a monster. Though he's been the latter longer than I care to admit.

"I'm sorry. It'll never happen again," he says as if he's rehearsed it. "I promise to get help. I promise to go to counseling like you asked. I can't lose you, baby. You're all I've got left in my life." His voice cracks as if he's truly sincere, but I've heard it all before.

He's playing to my emotions. I don't know what to do at this point because his mood swings give me whiplash. I wanted him to get help so we can go back to how things were before, but he's burned that bridge now. I wish I didn't have to second-guess him, but it's his fault I have those thoughts in the first place. He says he'll get help, but after all this, I know it'll only be to pacify me so I'll stay.

I should call the cops on his ass and get him thrown in jail, but the justice system doesn't usually work in the victim's favor. The second he gets out, he'll be out for blood. *My* blood.

How the hell did I get myself into this situation? Because I wanted to be loved and have someone to love. How sad is that?

I close my eyes, letting the ice-cold bag rest on my eye until it's numb. I tell Weston I'm tired and I'm going to take a shower. Once I'm done sobbing under the stream of water, I lie in bed, exhausted from the morning, though it's not even noon yet. He doesn't follow me, which I'm grateful for. I'm not sure I could stand to look at him.

After staring at the ceiling for nearly an hour crying, I somehow drift to sleep. When I wake, there's a huge hole in my chest where my heart should be, and my body still hurts from this morning's shitshow.

I glance at the clock and it's nearly five p.m. I can't be late to the reception, so I get dressed.

When I walk into the bathroom, I'm horrified by how awful I look. I barely recognize myself with my disheveled hair, puffy face, and swollen eye. There's no way I'm going to be able to cover up the bruising and no amount of lying will convince Lennon otherwise.

But maybe, if I'm smart, they can save me tonight.

It might be my only way to get out of this house and away from Weston for good. Maybe things would be different if we didn't live together. Maybe we rushed into this, and things moved too quickly. Regardless, his abusive, manipulative nature isn't a fluke or a one-time thing. This is who he is. Since I moved in, his physical and mental abuse has only gotten worse.

As I'm getting ready, Weston comes into the bedroom and stands in the doorway with bloodshot eyes. He must've been drinking the entire time I was asleep.

"Where do you think you're going?"

"To the reception, remember?" I say in the reflection before turning around and facing him. "You should get dressed, honey. We don't want to be late." I'm walking on thin ice, hoping it doesn't crack and I fall through.

"We're not going anywhere," he spits out.

Instead of showing my cards and getting upset, I swallow it down and give one of the best performances of my life.

"Baby, they're expecting us," I remind him as I walk toward him, hoping he buys my act. "If we don't show up, Lennon will get worried, and we don't want any extra attention on us. Just me and you, remember? Just me and you. It will be fun to get out of the house together." I smile wide.

He seems to buy it, wrapping his large hand around the nape of my neck, then smashing his alcohol-soaked lips against mine. I force myself to kiss him even though I hate every fucking second. His hands move down my body, and as he squeezes my breast, he moans in my mouth. I'm disgusted by his touch and have to fight back a gag.

He moves his sloppy kiss down my jawline, ruining my makeup in the process, then sucks on my neck. He sucks hard, causing me to wince and pull back. That'll leave a mark.

Weston's eyes meet mine, his flaring with control. "I want to show every person there that you're mine. You're fucking *mine*, Sophie."

"Of course. They all need to know," I lie through my teeth.

"Even Mason, your little fuck boy," he hisses, narrowing his eyes as if he's studying me.

I nod. "He knows, baby. He knows I belong to you. I'm yours, Weston." I tell him what he wants to hear, and this seems to please him. He rubs his body against mine, and he's hard as a rock. I swallow back the bile begging to come up.

Just as he's convinced, my phone vibrates in my pocket, but I ignore it, not wanting to lose his attention. I want to keep his focus on me and my words.

He runs his fingers through my hair and wads my strands in

his fist. As he forces me to look into his eyes, pain rushes from my scalp straight to my heart.

"If you ever leave me, I'll end you, Soph. If I can't have you, no one can. *Ever.*"

I swallow hard and force a smile, though I'm trembling down to the bone.

"I'm not going anywhere, Weston. I'm with you for life." The words fall out of my mouth like poison, and all I know is that I have to get the fuck out of here, out of his grasp as soon as possible, because I don't doubt him or his words.

One thing's for certain—when it comes to his possession of me, he's not a liar.

CHAPTER THIRTEEN

I CHECK the text from Lennon and ignore it, but I won't be able to stall all evening. When she told me she'd call the cops, I knew she would do it. Having them show up here with the way that he is and after his admission would only make things worse for me. I need a solid plan without all of that.

After I put on a dress, I go to the bathroom and try to figure out what I'm going to do. I apply enough heavy makeup so it's not as noticeable, but if anyone stares too long, I'll have to figure out what to say, especially since Weston will be with me and he's not going to let me out of his sight.

After I apply heavy makeup and fix my hair, I walk into the living room where he's sitting with the bottle in his grasp.

"I can't go to this alone, babe. I want you there by my side," I plead, knowing damn well he won't let me leave without him.

"Fine," he huffs, slamming the bottle on the coffee table, swaying as he walks past me toward the bedroom.

Weston returns dressed, dangling his keys in one hand and mine in the other. There is no way in hell I'm getting in a car with him in this state, but he probably won't let me drive my car either. He'll kill us both and possibly someone else too.

"Sorry about your keys," he says, handing them over. He sounds genuine, but from experience, it'll be short-lived.

"Honey, you should let me drive." I try to reach for his keys, but Weston jerks his hand away.

"No. You aren't driving my truck." His booming voice sends an uneasy shiver down my spine.

"I'll drive my car," I quickly say.

"No, I'm driving mine." His gaze burns into me, letting me know he won't budge.

Instead of arguing with him, I try to reason with him. "Okay. Let's have some coffee then. It'll help you sober up a bit before we leave."

He hesitates, but then thankfully agrees. After an hour of waiting, his eyes don't seem nearly as glassy. I check the time again, and when I notice Lennon called, I know I have to respond before she gets even more worried.

SOPHIE

Sorry, running late. On our way now.

LENNON

Okay, I'll meet you in the hallway. I have big news!

She seems overly excited and I fear I'll rain on her parade with how shitty things are going with Weston.

As I follow him to his truck, I have a bad feeling that maybe we shouldn't go and almost ask if we can cancel. But staying here with him in his current mindset could be even more dangerous. I need to tell Lennon and Maddie the truth, though it'll be obvious as soon as they see me. Nothing gets past them—surely, another black eye won't—and they won't let it slide this time.

After I buckle in, Weston speeds down the road. I want to ask him to slow down but don't want to risk setting him off again. He grabs my hand and forcefully interlocks his fingers with mine, holding me so tight it hurts.

"You're mine, Sophie. You'll *always* be mine," he says with a threatening grin that sends a chill up my spine.

"I know." It's all I can say as he speeds recklessly down the highway in a vehicle that could easily be used as a weapon.

When the reception hall comes into view, I release a sigh of relief. He zooms into the parking lot and nearly hits a pedestrian. I cover my mouth with my hand to hold back my scream, and he laughs while veering around the old man trying to enter the hall.

"Weston," I whisper-hiss.

"He'll learn to get the fuck out of the way, won't he?"

Fear builds in the pit of my stomach, and I force it down as he parks. Weston looks at me. "Be on your best behavior in front of your little boy toy, Sophie. He better stay the fuck away from you…or else."

"I don't have a boy toy, Weston. You're all I need," I say, knowing my lip service will feed his ego.

He palms my cheeks and roughly pulls my face until our lips collide. "I better be. Best behavior, or you'll regret it."

"Okay," I whisper.

When I step out of the car and see Lennon crossing the parking lot toward me, I've never been so thankful to see her. Weston's a dick, but in front of my sisters, he puts on a show, displaying just how charming he is when he wants to be.

"Hey!" Lennon says and pulls me into a big hug. I smile, happy to see her and to be alive after the drive over here. "Everything okay?"

She studies my face, and I turn my head toward Weston, who's walking fast behind me and making sure to keep me in line. "Yeah, totally. We lost track of time."

He catches up to me and grabs my arm like I'm a child to pull me away from Lennon.

"I need a beer. Let's go," he barks, walking past Hunter and guiding me inside. We go to the bar, and he gives me a dirty look when he orders two beers as if he knows I'm going to say something about him drinking. It's the last thing he needs to do because he doesn't know his limits. I keep my focus on the floor and try not to make eye contact with anyone because I'm worried they'll see how swollen my face is. I wish I could disappear right now.

As if Lennon can read my thoughts, she walks up and pulls me away. Before capturing me, she gives Weston the sweetest expression. "I gotta run to the bathroom and change Alison. Wanna come with me, Soph?"

"Sure," I say, knowing Weston won't say no to Lennon, who then waves Maddie over too. Lennon grabs the diaper bag, and Weston gives me a silent warning, causing a knot of fear to form in the pit of my stomach.

Once we're in the bathroom, Lennon locks the door and grabs me, turning me toward her. "Please tell me you're not trying to cover up a black eye, Soph. I swear to God, I will murder him."

"It's not what you think," I say out of habit, though it's no use. He doesn't deserve the excuses anymore. He doesn't deserve me.

Maddie is a ball of fire, pissed to the extreme. "Did he hit you?"

As I try to explain, my bottom lip trembles, and my emotions begin to pour out. The questions continue one by one, and I answer them truthfully. I explain about his drinking and driving, and why we were so late, and then Lennon's words bring me back to reality.

"You can't honestly keep making excuses for him, Soph. He's a drunk, and he's hit and hurt you on more than one occasion," she tells me firmly. "Please leave him. I'm scared for you."

I swallow hard, feeling my heart in my throat and feeling my entire world crash around me as the truth of why I can't leave falls out. "I don't have anywhere else to go. I don't have money to get my own place, and I can't go back to my old apartment. What am I supposed to do, Lennon?" I'm so fucking scared, and I know my sisters see it in my expression and hear it in my voice.

I've thought about my options over and over the past couple of weeks. My only choice is to quit my dream job—resign from the symphony—and move back to Utah with my parents, ultimately ending my career as a professional musician, which can't happen. I won't let it. She offers for me to stay with her, and while it's generous, that's not my only concern.

"It's not just that," I meekly say. "He won't let me break up with him and leave."

Both of their eyes go wide, and the questions keep coming. I explain how I tried to end it a few weeks ago and he slammed me into the wall. And then I tell them what he said. "He told me if I left him, he'd kill me."

Lennon urges me to go to the police and get a restraining order.

"I'm scared, Lennon," I say as tears glide down my cheeks. They pull me into a hug, and when I'm with them, I feel safe. Leaving the reception tonight is going to be difficult, especially if he's drinking again.

"I know, Soph. We love you and will protect you, okay? Hunter, Mason, and Liam are all on your side too."

The thought of them coming to my rescue makes my heart swell, but I don't think Lennon realizes how dangerous Weston is. She hasn't seen the side of him that I have. He threatened to kill me, and if they get involved, he'll retaliate against them too.

"Don't say anything yet, okay? I'd rather move my stuff out when he's sober, tell him it's over, and then if he doesn't take it well, we'll get the cops involved." I wipe away the tears, knowing I need to stop crying, or my makeup will fade away, revealing all my secrets. I wish I could leave him tonight, but it's best not to do anything abrupt with him or make a scene in public.

"You aren't doing it alone, though," she tells me, and I agree although it's dangerous as hell.

After a moment, I'm grateful when Lennon changes the subject. Just as she's about to announce her big news, police sirens echo in the distance.

"What the hell is that?" Maddie asks, unlocking the door, and we see people rushing down the hallway, almost as if the place is on fire. Maddie steps out, following the crowd, and we stay close behind her. Tons of people are by the door, and we somehow make our way through them until I finally see Hunter and Liam. They look terrible, and I'm fearful that something's gone wrong.

"What happened?" Lennon asks as we make our way to them. The look on their faces isn't like anything I've ever seen before. Police fill the parking lot and yellow caution tape is being drawn. I look around—trying to spot Weston, trying to find Mason, and trying to put all the pieces together—but nothing is making sense.

The only thing that pulls me away from my panic is Liam. "Your boyfriend," he snaps, his jaw twitching with anger.

Everything happens in a blur. Lennon says something about Mason going to jail. Weston's name is muttered. Then something about a fight.

"Where's Weston? Is he getting arrested too?" Glancing around, I'm worried as hell although a night in jail might be good for him. It would give him a chance to sober up and me the opportunity to pack my stuff and leave him for good.

I continue searching for him through the crowd.

"Do you see Weston?" I ask Lennon.

"Maybe they're cleaning him up in one of the ambulances," she suggests, trying to calm my growing hysteria.

"No." Hunter's voice rings in my ear as he steps closer to me. "Soph, he's…" He sucks in a deep breath. "They tried to resuscitate him, but—"

"What?" I gasp at the same time Maddie does too.

Everything goes black as I hold on to Lennon like a life preserver. Before he can continue, an officer walks up and tells the guys they better get Mason a good lawyer, and when Lennon asks for what, I nearly drop to my knees when I hear the word *murder*.

I'm gasping for breath and cling to Lennon in horror at the realization of what happened, still trying to understand the few details I've been given, but nothing makes sense. I sit on the sidewalk, placing my head between my knees, and wish I'd wake up from this nightmare. I never wanted anything horrible to happen to Weston. I wanted to escape him, and knowing Mason's responsible tears me apart.

Liam helps me up, being as gentle as he can while shock soars through me. I can't help feeling like this is all my fault. Every bit of it.

He takes me into the reception hall and sits me down on one of the chairs against the wall, then falls to his knees in front of me.

"You look like shit, Soph," he tells me with a small smile. Looking over my face, he notices my black eye but doesn't mention it.

"I feel like shit too." My head is pounding. I'm slowly falling into the darkness, a place I don't want to be mentally. I begin to shake, the adrenaline wearing off as my body tries to process everything that's happened today.

"Listen…" His voice is calm as if he's treading lightly. "Weston had a gun. Did you know he brought one?"

My eyes widen at the realization.

A gun.

The realization makes bile rise up my throat, and I have to stop myself from releasing it.

"No," I finally say. "I had no idea he owned a gun." I'm not surprised, though.

Tears fall, blurring my vision. With all the threats Weston threw my way today, does that mean I was his original target? Was he planning to kill me after the reception after he told me to be on my best behavior? I honestly believe he would've tried or shoved it in my face to prove a point.

My mind spirals out of control, and Liam places his hand on my knee.

"What about Mason? This is all my fault." I cover my face, not able to look at Liam.

"It's not, but the officers will need statements from everyone, and I think you need to be truthful." He glances at my eye again. The makeup doesn't fool him. Placing his thumb under my chin, he moves my face where he can get a better look at it. Gently grabbing my arms, he inspects the bruises left there too. Liam is pissed.

"You have to be honest about the abuse, about how he's

treated you and what he's said to you. All of it. I don't know everything that's happened, but I've dealt with some bad people, Soph. I've seen women who've been abused by men just like Weston, and unfortunately, it didn't end well for them. I've had to track down murderers, psychopaths, drug dealers, you name it, and I have no doubt Weston would've continued hurting you. Now is the time to come clean with the police and not sugarcoat it or lie like you've done to the people who love and care for you. It won't be easy, but it's for your benefit, and honestly, it's for Mason's too."

I suck in a shallow breath and nod. "I'll tell them everything. I promise."

"I think you should stay at my house tonight. It would probably be best if you didn't go home right now, not with everything that's happened."

I agree, thankful for his friendship, for everything. "Trust me. That's the last place I want to be right now anyway," I admit.

Liam gives me a sad look. One I can't seem to shake. The pity in his eyes is the same look all of them have given me at some point over the past few months. I'm a fucking fool.

He pats my leg and stands.

"I need to make a phone call quickly. Stay here." Before walking away, he gives me a small smile, one I don't return.

As I'm lost in my head, I overhear Liam talking to someone about Mason. When my thoughts go to Weston and all the horrible things he's said to me today, Liam's voice pulls me back.

"Okay, are you ready to go back out there? We're probably gonna get bombarded."

He holds out his hand, and I take it. I feel safe for the first time in months.

Once we're outside, I notice Hunter talking to the police. Maddie is next to Lennon and Allie, and when I catch sight of Savannah and Hayden, I feel horrible. It's my fault their special day has been ruined. All of this is my fault. I burst into tears again, and my sisters come over, not leaving me alone.

Liam goes to the police officer and waves to join him. I suck in a deep breath, look at Lennon and Maddie, then follow him.

The truth will be out there today. No more lies. No more excuses. I promised Liam I'd give a statement, and I will. After it's all said and done, I hope I'll be okay one day and be able to live with myself because right now, I don't feel like that's a possibility.

CHAPTER FOURTEEN

MASON

Being booked into jail is uneventful, though it doesn't help that every person I pass knows my dad. I am fucked. I've been sitting on a bench in a stark white cell for the past three hours. My fists and face hurt, and when I'm finally granted my one phone call, I dial Liam.

"How's jail?" he answers after the first ring.

"Already watched a dude piss all over the floor."

"You'll be out soon. We each gave our statements. Sophie was truthful. Talked about the verbal and physical abuse. They took pictures of her bruises, and she put it all out there. It was bad, Mason. You were right. If you wouldn't have killed him, I would've after finding out everything that he was doing to her. On top of that, verbal and mental abuse, too."

The seriousness in his tone feeds my rage even more.

I knew something wasn't right. *I fucking knew it.*

All that matters now is that she's okay. I can't blame her for being scared of him, considering how out of control he was with three men fighting back his same size.

"Where is she now? How is she?" I'm more concerned about her well-being because I can only imagine how she feels and what emotional state she's in.

"I made Sophie come home with me and told her she was sleeping here. She's a fucking wreck and blames herself for it all," he tells me. "She was worried about you too," he adds, and it makes my heart jolt forward, but I don't address it.

"I'm glad she's there. And Serena?"

"She's on her way to you. She said she'd leave as soon as possible."

"Fuck," I mumble.

"If you need to get bonded out sooner, let me know. I can call someone," he offers.

"That's okay. I'll wait for Serena and let you know. Thanks, man. Thanks for being my best friend through all the bullshit."

"You're not gonna get all sentimental on me now, are you, and confess your undying love for me?" Liam snickers.

"You wish, you bastard," I barely get out when the officer tells me my time is up. I let Liam go and am escorted back to my jail cell with a piss-covered floor. I'm thrown inside like a criminal, like a murderer. Without a doubt, word has already gotten around town that the district attorney's son killed a guy and is sitting in jail. I need Serena to get her ass here as soon as possible.

Another hour passes, and I'm relieved when the door swings open. An officer lets me know I've been released, and I'm so thankful Serena came through. She's going to lay into me, no doubt. As I grab my shit and walk through the door, I'm shocked when I look at my father. The color drains from my face when I realize how livid he is. Behind him, Serena looks half terrified and half pissed off.

"What're you doing here?" I bark out, not wanting him to come to my rescue because he'll hold it over me for the rest of my life as he does everything else.

"You think my son, my only son, gets arrested for murder and no one tells me? If so, you're stupider than you look right now."

"Ahh. Almost forgot everyone was on your payroll." I nearly bite my tongue off trying to keep the rest of my heated words to myself. Though it pains me, it's for the best, considering we have an audience.

"You're set to be on the docket first thing Monday morning. More strings I was forced to pull for you." He glances at Serena. "Since your lawyer is present, I assume you don't need me anymore." The agitation is prevalent as he glares at me.

"I didn't need you in the first place," I spit out, wishing he wouldn't have come.

My words cause my father to let out a hearty, sarcastic laugh. "That'll be the day."

"Try not to kill anyone else while you're out, got it? Your tallies are adding up," he snaps before leaving.

I'm two seconds away from telling him to go fuck himself when Serena grabs my arm and squeezes. "It's not worth it."

I suck in a deep breath, trying to calm down. "You're right. But damn, sometimes he's intolerable."

She snorts. "I think he means well. He doesn't want you sitting in jail and rotting. That's not a life for you."

I let out a steady breath, though I'm pissed the hell off. "He's more concerned about himself and how it will affect his reputation if I sit in a cell, not the fact that I'm there."

"You look good," I tell her as we walk outside. It's nearly midnight, and I've had a hell of a day. I want to go home and sleep in my bed because, for a moment, I thought I'd be sleeping on a cold bench.

She smiles. "Thanks."

Her heels click on the pavement as we walk across the parking lot toward her BMW. After she unlocks it, I slip inside. The car is an upgrade from what she was driving while in law school. When she gets in, she bends over to remove her six-inch heels and throw them in the back seat. It causes me to laugh.

"You could kill someone with those heels," I tease.

She laughs. "They're my secret weapon."

I wouldn't put it past her if she felt threatened.

I'd trust Serena with my life. She knows the legal system like the back of her hand, and she's an up-and-coming lawyer in Sacramento. Serena's worked her ass off to get where she is in her profession. She's one of the best criminal defense attorneys in this city, and I'd almost be willing to bet in the state. Hard-ass is her middle name, and she doesn't take no for an answer. Not from anyone, not even my father. The girl is a genius but also has street smarts too—a lethal combination. And damn, I'm happy she's on my side and has been for years, even before she could legally practice law in California.

"So tell me what happened," she says as she backs out of the parking lot.

"Is this on the record or off?" I quip, and she playfully rolls her eyes as she takes the ramp to the highway.

"Start from the very beginning. If you want me to represent you and get your ass off for murder, then I need to know it all, know what I'm up against. I'll put on the record what needs to be there. The rest is between us." She smiles.

I try to think back to when this all started, and I know I need to be open with Serena. Not only is she representing me, but she's my friend too. I tell her about Sophie and how Weston got into the picture of all of this, and why I looked into Weston's past.

"Does anyone know you did that?"

"Liam and Jerad. Liam isn't gonna say shit. Jerad won't either, considering he wasn't supposed to do it in the first place. I trust him, and he's holding a position for me in his department, if I didn't ruin my chances," I continue, explaining how I tried to warn Sophie about Weston being dangerous.

"But she didn't take your advice, obviously."

If she would've, maybe none of this would've happened, or maybe she'd be dead. There's no way to predict what could've happened. "No." It's all I can say as I temporarily get lost in my thoughts, but Serena quickly pulls me out of my head.

"So what happened tonight?"

I think back to the evening's events, and everything seems like a weird blur. Maybe it's because I'm somewhat in shock. There was a point when my friends and I could've died. Being held at gunpoint is scary as fuck, and nothing could've prepared us for that. I try to replay it all, from the confrontation to the parking lot fight when he pulled out the gun. Serena listens carefully, and I know she'll probably remember this conversation word for word because that's how she is.

"Well, considering there's no open carry in the state of California, we'll have that on our side. Not to mention, he pulled it out with intention to threaten and kill. That's essentially assault with a deadly weapon. Doubt it was registered to him, considering he had a record. Either way, you acted in self-defense since he pulled it out and threatened you and your two friends with it. Hopefully between the witness statements and him breaking the law, this'll be an open and shut case without contest. Of course, we'll see what we're up against at your plea hearing on Monday."

"You think it'll be easy to prove self-defense?"

She grins as she takes the exit toward my house. "Absolutely. Considering who your daddy is, I'm sure it will be no issue."

"Oh, shut the hell up." I groan. "It's gross when you call him my daddy."

She snorts. "Your father is probably gonna be there. He already mentioned as much when we were waiting for you to get released. Lay low for the rest of the weekend. Considering who you are, people will be talking. The rumors are gonna go wild if they aren't already. I'm surprised the news station wasn't waiting for you when you were released, considering how high profile your father is."

"Anything for a scandal." I groan, rolling my eyes.

Serena turns on my street, then pulls into the driveway.

"You okay?" Her voice softens.

"Yeah, I'll be fine. I'm exhausted and need to decompress."

A small smile touches her lips. "Also, I know how you feel about your dad being in your business, but you may want to thank him. He literally saved your ass quicker than I could've. No one cares about an attorney, but when the DA walks in, shit moves a little faster. It's kinda magical."

"If I didn't know better, I'd say you were a fan. You in line to be the third Mrs. Holt?" I tease, and she makes a gagging sound. Sometimes, it's too easy to give her shit.

"You know it's complicated. I don't want to owe him anything because he holds it over me. I promise you, the only reason he was there was to beat the reporters. Any longer and he'd have a fire to put out, and he's worried about appearances. Always has been. That much hasn't changed and never will."

She leans her head against the seat. "He's a hard-ass, but I don't think he's a bad guy. I do believe he cares about you, but I'll stop now. I'm not a therapist, just a lawyer."

I chuckle. "Thanks. So how've you been?"

"Good, Mason. Real good. Working a lot, living that lawyer hustle life. How about you? Landed that dream job yet?"

A lump the size of a golf ball forms in my throat. "Depending on how all this goes will ultimately determine that. There's a guy retiring in forensics in the fall, and I've pretty much been guaranteed his position, but I don't know anymore."

Serena grabs my hand and squeezes but then pulls away. "It's all gonna work out. It always does."

"Yeah, I hope."

We sit, listening to the hum of the engine, both lost in our thoughts. So much has happened over the past few years. I've worked so damn hard to earn that promotion, and this one night could ruin my entire career. But if that's what it ultimately took to make sure Sophie was okay, then I'd sacrifice it all a hundred times over.

Serena breaks the silence. "I'll pick you up on Monday at seven thirty. That way I know your ass will be on time," she says, snickering. "Also, I might need to chat with Sophie. If the case isn't thrown out, we may need her to testify as a character witness."

"I'm sure she'll do whatever you need." Talking about Sophie with Serena is awkward, and I'm glad she hasn't asked me anything personal.

"Well, get some rest and try to stay out of trouble for the next forty-eight hours, alright?" she teases. "No more excitement for a long while."

"Trust me when I say I've had enough for a lifetime. Thanks for everything," I tell her as I reach for the handle.

"You're welcome. Call me if you need anything, even if it's to talk," she says.

"I will." I open the door and stand in the driveway. She waves, and I watch her car until the taillights fade in the distance. I pull my phone from my pocket and realize how late it is and how exhausted I am. I'm ready to hit my bed as soon as I see it.

When I walk into the house, I notice how eerily quiet it is but can see a lump of a body on the couch. I take a few steps forward and hear Liam snoring, which means Sophie is in his bed. Though he can be a prick, he loves Sophie like a sister, and most likely refused to let her sleep on the couch, which makes me smile.

I climb the stairs and grab some clothes, then go to the shower. As the hot water streams over my body, I can't stop thinking about the gun, then Sophie's sweet face comes to mind, along with the makeup she used to cover the bruises that fucker left.

While I hate that a life was lost today, I think Weston was capable of causing irreparable damage to Sophie, if he hasn't already. The thought of his mental and physical abuse has me seeing red again, but it's over, and all I can hope is that she'll be able to heal.

Hopefully, Liam told her the details of today, but if she wants to know, I'll explain it the best I can. My heart still aches for her and everything she's been through. I wish she would've listened, but I'm convinced he wouldn't have let her go so easily.

The water runs cold, and I take that as my cue to get out. I grab a towel and dry off, then get dressed. Instead of going to my room, I go to Liam's and crack open the door. Moonlight splashes across the floor, and I can hear her steady breathing.

My sweet Sophie, I think to myself, stepping inside and going toward her.

I hate to wake her, but after everything, I need to see her, even if it's to say I'm here for her.

And I always have been.

CHAPTER FIFTEEN

SOPHIE

"I THINK we should take a break, Weston. Until things settle down for you. Some time apart might do us good," I say after he stumbled in drunk again. I can't continue to live like this. He seems to love drinking more than he loves me.

"What the fuck did you just say?" His harsh tone echoes through the room. "Are you breaking up with me?"

I shake my head, his booming voice scaring the shit out of me. "No. Not at all, but…"

He takes two steps forward, running his fingers through my hair, then holding it tightly in his fist before slamming me against the wall with every bit of strength he has. A picture falls to the floor, and the glass shatters. The pain is excruciating, but he doesn't seem to care.

"Weston, please," I beg with tears in my eyes.

His strong hand wraps around my throat, and when I gasp for air, he adds more pressure. I try to stay calm, not wanting to panic because he seems to get off on my fear. I claw at his fingers, but it's no use.

"If you ever leave me, I'll fucking kill you. You're mine, and I'm not letting you go. Ever. Only death will separate us. Got it, baby?"

I nod, unable to speak as he holds me hostage. With a disgusted expression, he finally releases me. He watches with zero emotion as my *body slides down the wall. I tuck my head between my knees and cry. Is he capable of killing me? Hell, he's proven he is.*

A hand on my arm startles me awake, and I shriek into the darkness.

"Shh, shh, Soph. It's me," Mason says softly, clicking on the lamp on the nightstand beside the bed. I look around the room, uncertain of where I am until the day all comes flooding back. I'm in Liam's room.

I wrap my arms around Mason's neck, and the tears begin to rapidly fall. "I'm so sorry, Mason. I'm so sorry."

It's the only thing I can say. It's the only thing I feel. Everything that happened tonight is my fault. I knew Weston was dangerous, but I never thought he'd have a gun.

Mason wraps his arms around me, and we stay in each other's arms for a while. It's comforting to have him hold me like this. He doesn't need to say anything at all because our bodies speak for us. Either one of us could've been on the other side of that bullet, and I'm so damn thankful we weren't. I'm so thankful for him.

Mason slowly pulls away and focuses on me. The lamp barely brightens the room, but it gives me enough light to see his dripping wet hair. The smell of soap fills the room.

Bringing his thumb to my cheeks, he gently wipes away my tears. "You okay?" I don't know if he's referring to the nightmare he woke me from or this entire night, but whether or not I'm okay is yet to be determined. I'm alive, but is that really the same thing?

Mason studies my face, then glances at my black eye and throat. He clenches his jaw, and I know he has questions. With flared nostrils, his mouth transforms into a straight line. Anger is written all over him as he tenses. I lower my eyes, not wanting him to see me like this—to see me at my worst—but it's far too late for that now.

Slowly, Mason places his hands on top of mine, and the warmth of him is comforting. "Sophie. I'm so fucking sorry."

My heart races. "Don't you dare apologize, Mason." More tears begin to well on the brims of my eyes until they fall. I'm not sure how I still have anything left inside me after the day I've had.

"If anyone should be doing that right now, it's me. I fucked up and treated you like shit and didn't listen to you. I was so damn stubborn and thought I had things under control. I have so many regrets over the past six months. All of this could've been avoided. All of this." Deep, heart-wrenching sobs escape me.

He gives me a sad smile and shakes his head. "You didn't know."

I scowl at him for making excuses for my actions. "You warned me over and over again. And maybe…" My voice begins to crack. "If I had listened, none of this would've happened."

Mason doesn't take his eyes from mine, his voice so soft, steady, and calm. "Don't blame yourself for what happened. For his decisions. This isn't your fault. You didn't bring a loaded gun to a wedding with the intent to use it. You didn't do anything wrong."

Not able to look at him any longer, I cover my face with my hands and let it all out. Just the thought that Weston could've killed him sends me into hysterics.

Mason rests his hand on my back and tries to comfort me. He eventually pulls me back into his arms, but it's no use. My body trembles as I think about everything, my mind spiraling and battling between what could've happened and what did. Weston, his threats, and the fact he's no longer here. Maybe if I would've pushed harder for him to get help, to stop drinking, it wouldn't have escalated to this. The root cause of everything is me. I forced him to go to the reception when he clearly didn't want to go.

I cry against his strong chest until I feel like I have nothing left, until I feel like a hollow shell of myself. He doesn't say anything as I use his shirt to dry my tears. Eventually, I pull away and look at him. Knowing I look like absolute shit, but I feel so damn pathetic.

"You're gonna get through this, and so am I. We're gonna get through this together, Soph. You're one of the fiercest women I've ever known. We'll survive this." Mason is so damn calm and sweet, and I don't deserve it after the way I pushed him away. "I'm always here for you, okay? I haven't been the greatest friend to you over the years, and maybe if I would've been nicer, you would've trusted me when I told you about him. You're not the only one at fault here. I'm sorry for treating you that way. I hope we can move forward. Start over." He winks.

A small smile plays on my lips, and I nod. "I'd like that."

"Good. I'm glad you're staying here."

"Wish I would've made Liam change his sheets first, though," I say, chuckling.

"Well, if it makes you feel better, he's hardly home anymore." Mason shrugs, and the silence wears on.

"What happened today, Mason? Will you tell me?"

His voice softens. "Soph."

"Please," I beg. "I only managed to get bits and pieces, and it doesn't help that my shock made it hard to comprehend anything. I was so worried about you. It was overwhelming, almost too much to handle at that moment, but I have to know, Mason. I want to hear it from you."

Mason runs his fingers through his hair and hesitates. He chews on his bottom lip before rubbing his hand over his jaw. "I don't even know where to start," he admits, blowing out a breath.

I patiently wait, not forcing him to speak.

"There was an exchange of words, and I didn't like the way he was talking about you. I followed him outside with Liam and Hunter behind me. All I wanted was for him to know hitting you wasn't okay. I warned him to stay away from you and what would happen if he touched you again." He places his hand on my knee. "It's not okay that he hurt you. The moment I saw you today, I knew he had punched you, and I wanted him to get the hell out. It was clear you were scared."

I try to swallow down the lump lodged in my throat.

"But I didn't want *this* to happen. I just wanted him to know we knew and weren't gonna put up with it. I told him to fight someone his own size and let him get in my face to prove my point. Once he threw the first punch, I knew that was my opening to take him down and hurt him the way he's hurt you. My fist connected with his face, and I was sure that'd be enough to get him to leave. It should've knocked him out, but he barely stumbled and got right back in my face." Mason glances down at his knuckles, and I notice how cut up they are.

"Then he pulled out the gun…" I whisper, and Mason nods.

"Fully loaded. He held Hunter, Liam, and me at gunpoint. Even shot off some warning rounds to show us he was serious. At that moment, I thought one of us was gonna die. But I wasn't gonna allow that to happen. I wasn't gonna let that bastard win. We'd already lost Brandon, and I kept thinking that this couldn't be the way our lives ended. I thought about you and your sisters. With the gun pointed at us, my adrenaline spiked, and it all happened so fast. I charged toward him, and we fought for the gun. When it went off, I thought I was shot," he admits.

I release a ragged breath. "He would've killed you."

Mason's eyes meet mine. "He would've killed *you*, Sophie."

I nod and tuck my bottom lip into my mouth. My body's on the verge of shutting down from the emotional roller coaster I've ridden today as Weston's threats from before we left for the reception echo in my head. I could've easily been on the receiving end of that gun because of his anger and his need for control and power. I can't help but think those bullets were meant for me if I had tried to leave.

The revelation of it all confuses me, and I'm not sure how I should feel.

Grateful I'm still alive?

Guilty Weston's dead?

Mason's voice pulls me out of my head. "Did you love him?"

My heart races as I look at the man I wish would've given me a chance all those years ago. Right now, I don't have the strength to put up a wall and hide behind it in front of him.

"I did," I admit. "I loved the man I thought he was, not the man who hit me."

His expression doesn't change, but I can see his pulse ticking rapidly in his neck.

"So now what? What're the next steps?" I ask.

"Now, I go in front of a judge Monday morning and hope my

lawyer can save my ass. But I'll sleep a lot better tonight knowing you're safe, and that's all that matters."

Mason pulls me into another hug, and I inhale his scent. Before he leaves, he tells me good night and turns off the lamp. I close my eyes and try to fall back asleep, thankful my friends are safe. If something would've happened to any of them, I'm not sure I would've been able to live with myself.

We're all okay, even if I don't feel like I am.

But I have to believe that I will be eventually.

CHAPTER SIXTEEN

MASON

Fuck my life.

It's the first thing on my mind Monday morning when Serena texts me to let me know she's on her way to pick me up. Thanks to my dad for bailing me out, I didn't have to spend the past two nights in jail, but knowing he's going to be in court and give me grief for getting into trouble *again*, I'd almost wish I did. It pisses me off that he was able to pull his title to get me in front of a judge this morning. I don't want special treatment from anyone.

"Looking sharp," Serena says the moment I get inside her car and buckle up. "Minus the dark circles under your eyes."

I turn and glare at her.

"It's gonna be fine," she tries to reassure me, but it doesn't work. I haven't been this anxious since the last time I was dragged into court five years ago.

"Sure, it is," I mutter. "Especially when I have a big X on my name already."

"Look, you know the truth. If it goes to trial, you have two witnesses to help persuade the jury. Not to mention Weston's criminal and abusive history and the fact he was carrying a gun illegally."

I stare out the window. "Yeah, it looks good from that perspective, but the judge is gonna dig up my history too."

"You weren't charged with anything back then either. Rightfully."

Serena leans over and pats my leg when we hit a red light. "I've got your back, Mason. Always have."

I turn and give her a grateful smile. "I know."

We arrive at the courthouse for my arraignment where the charges will be explained and I'll be asked to enter a plea. If the prosecutor decides to try the case, the judge will schedule a trial date and ask for discoveries to prove guilt or innocence. I have no idea what to expect although I should, but my stomach is so damn twisted I can't think or breathe.

Once my case number is called, Serena ushers me inside, and we stand at the podium. There are a few people in the pews, but I am quite shocked when I don't see my father. I told Hunter and Liam not to come until it was crucial for them to get involved. They'd already given their witness statements, so anything more would be done in depositions.

We watch as the judge takes his seat, calling out the case number once he's done, and he asks the prosecutor to start. Once they give the information of the potential charges, the judge faces me.

"How does your client plead?"

I speak up with Serena to my side. "Not guilty, your Honor," I respond, my voice shaky though I'm trying to sound confident.

We wait as he looks over the information in front of him. He has all the police files thus far as well as the statements. After the judge breaks down the events of that night, Serena explains that I reacted in self-defense. Then the prosecutor makes a smartass comment about how the victim *once again* isn't here to give his side.

And my last name strikes again.

He knows damn well I'm the DA's son, and my father isn't the most liked man either. Those involved in public service are all shady fucks. Too many innocent people are locked up while too many criminals get a slap on the wrist.

As soon as the thought hits me, the courtroom doors swing open, causing us all to turn and look.

"Son of a bitch," I mutter, and Serena shushes me.

"He's probably here to support you," she says, and we both know that's a bold face lie. My father is never anywhere unless it's to benefit himself.

"Attorney Holt," the judge chides. "Your interruption—"

"I apologize, Judge Harris, but as the defendant's alternate lawyer, I have been informed of a video that will show Mason was acting in self-defense and thought you should see it right away."

Alternate lawyer? I snort to myself, which makes Serena jab me in the ribs.

The judge waves him up and gives him a look like *this better not waste my time.* The way they whisper to each other, it's obvious they have some kind of work relationship. The judge says something about using his title to my advantage, which makes me grind my teeth in anger.

"Officer, can you get a screen in here so we can present the discovery?" the judge directs his order.

A few minutes pass all while my dad refuses to look at me, and I wonder what the hell kind of video he could possibly have or where he got it from. If me being here didn't drag his name through the mud, he wouldn't go through the trouble.

My dad inserts the thumb drive and surveillance footage appears. Though it's in black and white and a little grainy, it's obvious it's from an outside camera near the reception hall. I can see Weston's back as he waves his gun at the three of us, and I plead with him to put the weapon down. Though there isn't any sound, everyone can see he threatened us with it, held us at gun point, and I tried to get it out of his grip in self-defense. He blew two warning shots off before I charged him.

Relief floods through me the minute the video ends, and the judge calls my father back up. He's asking him how he obtained it, and he's claiming the gas station owner sought him out and gave it to him.

Serena and I look at each other, knowing it's a bold face lie. I wouldn't put it past my father to go looking for such a video and *demanding* it. Legally, he'd need a warrant to obtain it, but my father's practices aren't always known to be legal.

The prosecutor then tries to argue that the video could've been tampered with to make the DA's son look innocent. My father glares over his shoulder, daring him to push his limits.

If I weren't the one being accused, I'd almost believe my dad would go to the necessary means to tamper with such evidence, but considering what happened, I'm tempted to shoot a glare at him myself. Though it goes to show by the prosecutor's accusation that corruption and bribes and anything else aren't too far-fetched in this situation.

"Your Honor, I would not have had the time nor risk my ethics as the district attorney to do such a thing," my father says loud and clear. "The prosecutor is free to analyze the video themselves if that would untwist their testicles."

Serena's eyes nearly fall out of her head at my father's bold words. He has balls of steel, that's for sure. I, on the other hand, am not one bit shocked that he'll do or say whatever it takes to win a case.

"That's enough, Attorney Holt," the judge snaps. My father raises his hands up in mock surrender with a small smirk playing on his lips.

"My apologies," my father chastises the prosecutor.

"Due to direct evidence of the incident, it's clear the defendant was acting in self-defense to protect himself and his two friends. The victim's weapon was brought out illegally, and even after the defendant tried to surrender, the victim continued to make threats to his life. This case is dismissed. You're free to go."

My heart fucking drops.

Holy shit.

Serena turns toward me, but I stand frozen in shock. "Mason! Oh my God." She wraps her arms around me, but I can't move. I was so damn certain I was going to be preparing for a trial to prove my innocence in front of a jury.

She escorts me out of the courtroom, my head spinning as I wrap my mind around it. I knew Serena told me not to worry, but I know firsthand how our justice system can screw innocent people. I wrestled a man with a gun, and it went off and killed him.

In some people's eyes, I'm sure they'd think justice wasn't served at all. But I know the truth of what happened that night.

Once we're out in the parking lot, I meet up with my father by his Range Rover. He's not parked in his usual spot, which means he came today just for me. Well not *me*, but to make sure I didn't make him look bad again.

"Mason," he says curtly with his hands in his pockets.

"Dad," I respond, mimicking his stance.

"Mr. Holt," Serena says behind me. "Thank you for providing the evidence on such short notice. Saved me a lot of work…" Then she smirks. "Less billable hours." She winks because we both know she'd never charge me.

"Just doing my job," he states, though we both know it's a load of shit.

"Right." She flicks her gaze to me. "I'll meet you at the car. Good to see you again," she tells my father before walking away, leaving us in an awkward silence.

"You look like shit," he begins.

"Thanks for noticing." I grunt.

"You been sleeping?"

I shake my head. "Not really."

"You wanna tell me what provoked that fight in the first place?" He crosses his arms over his chest, straightening his stance. He stands well over six feet, his body large and demanding. "Or tell me how you got yourself into that situation?"

There's judgment in his tone. His questions aren't borne out of sincerity or genuine concern.

"A friend of mine was dating him. He'd been hitting her, and he showed up that night shit-faced. My friend arrived with a black eye, and we were chasing him out of the reception hall before he started a scene at the wedding."

"There was history there previously," he says, not asking. "I could tell."

"Yeah, we threw some words and punches before the first time I suspected he was hurting her."

"This girl sounds like an idiot if she stayed after he hit her once," he blurts, making me see red.

"She's not," I grit between my teeth. "She's a victim, and if I hadn't confronted him that night, I have no doubt he would've killed her. He had threatened it more than once."

Just saying that aloud causes my heart to pound.

"Yeah, I read the police reports," he says gruffly, his lips in a firm line. "Still don't understand why you had to get involved."

I narrow my eyes at him, trying to see the hollow part of his chest where his heart should be. "Because she's a friend and it's important to me."

"Yeah, well, remember the last time you had an important girl in your life."

"That's not the same thing and you know it!" I shout as I step closer to him, daring him to push me right now. I don't fucking care who he is or where we are, I'm so goddamn tired of him bringing up my past and throwing it in my face anytime it suits him.

"Mason…" Serena calls my name in the distance, her heels clicking on the pavement behind me. "We should go." She tugs on my arm.

"You're welcome, by the way." His snarky tone makes my blood boil. "You'd spent the weekend in jail and would be going through weeks of court shit without my evidence today."

"Go to hell," I spit, seething as I give him an earful of what he deserves. "That wasn't for me, and we both know it. You moved on and got yourself a new cookie-cutter family. You can't stand that I didn't follow in your footsteps, and trust me when I say, it'll be a cold day in hell when I do. Just once can't you be proud of me for me?"

"Mason..." Serena warns, squeezing my arm.

"It's okay," my dad says way too calmly, holding up a hand toward her. "Mason's always had a temper, so I'm used to his wrath."

I have the opposite of a temper until someone pushes me too goddamn far, and he's been pushing me for the past five years.

"Why don't you and this girl you spoke about come over for family dinner on Sunday?"

The only thing I can do is laugh in his face. He's lost his damn mind if he thinks I'd ever do that. "No, thanks. Gonna be busy."

I take a step around him, walking toward Serena's car with her next to me.

"Mason, wait." I pause but don't look at him. "You need to lay low while the media covers the story. Just because you're walking away doesn't mean you're off the hook entirely. You're on leave until further notice."

If Serena wasn't next to me, piercing me with her eyes to stand down, I'd be clawing at his throat for bringing my job into this. He knows I'm at his mercy, considering I work in one of the departments his position oversees.

Finally, I face him. "For how long?"

He shrugs, grinning. "I'll let you know. Stay out of trouble and it won't be too long."

I anxiously shake my leg as Serena drives me back home. My father knows what buttons to press, and if he didn't hold my future in his hands, I would've told him to fuck off or worse. Hell, I don't know, but I can't stand his shit anymore. Though there's not a damn thing I can do about it as long as he's the DA.

"You alright?" Serena asks when she parks in my driveway and kills the engine.

"Well, I've been better," I say sarcastically. "On one hand, I'm happy I didn't get charged, but on the other—" I don't finish my colorful thoughts about my father, but I don't need to because she understands.

"I know, Mase. He's not an easy man to love, but whether you like it or not, he *is* your father. He came today, got your ass off a potential homicide charge, and you walked out a free man. I mean, I'm good, but I'm not *that* good."

"You would've eventually gotten the charges dropped in discovery," I tell her with a small grin.

"Well, obviously. I kick ass in the courtroom," she gloats, and we both laugh. "So, do I get to meet her?"

I furrow my brows, confused. "Who?"

"The infamous Sophie," she teases. "I think I should meet the woman you killed a man for."

"Really?" I deadpan.

"Oh c'mon, you know I'm giving you a hard time. It's been five years, Mason. You haven't been dating."

I glare at her accusation. "And how would you know, hotshot? You basically live in that new fancy office of yours."

"Liam gives me a weekly update."

I snort. "He does not."

"Okay, maybe not, but I see your social media pages, and I do talk to Liam at least once a month. He says you've been after this woman for a while."

Rolling my eyes, I groan and make a mental note to punch Liam later for gossiping about my nonexistent love life. "And I suppose he tells you all about his traveling adventures and dozens of one-night stands?"

"Oh totally. We talk all about them over brunch. I'm starting to get concerned his dick is gonna fall off soon, though."

"Starting to?" I chuckle. "I'm surprised there isn't a line down the block to get to him."

"According to him, there's a girl named Maddie who's been quite relentless."

I smirk, nodding. "Yeah, that's Sophie's little sister. She's a handful."

"How young are we talking? Legal, I hope?"

"Like Liam would ever touch someone underage? She's twenty, but she's innocent, though she doesn't always act like it. She enjoys tormenting him as much as she can."

She nods, smirking. "Good. He needs to be kept on his toes."

"No shit." I grab the door handle and step out of her car. "Well, come on."

Serena follows me into the house, cackling. "Wow, love what you guys have done with the place," she teases. It's been a year since she's been inside, but it hasn't changed a damn bit.

It's only after nine a.m., and I'm surprised to see Sophie isn't on the couch. "Soph?" I call out as I walk through the house.

"Mason?" she shouts, rushing out of the kitchen and charging right at me. "Oh my God, you aren't in jail!" She wraps her arms around me and squeezes hard.

I hold her to my chest, inhaling the top of her head that smells like sweet strawberries. Chuckling, I shake my head. "Nope."

Sophie pulls back, looking into my eyes. "What happened? How'd it go?"

Before I can respond, she blinks and notices Serena behind me. "Oh, sorry. I didn't realize you had company."

Serena steps closer and smiles. "I'm Serena, his lawyer. It's very nice to meet you." She holds out her hand, and Sophie's eyes light up.

"Wow, you're very pretty." Sophie smacks a hand over her mouth as she uses her other to shake Serena's. "Sorry, that was a weird thing to say."

"Definitely not the worst thing to hear on a Monday morning," Serena teases. "Thank you." They drop hands. "How are you doing, by the way?"

"I've been better, but I literally owe my life to Mason, so I'm damn grateful too." Sophie looks as if I hung the moon, and by the smirk on Serena's face, she sees it too.

"Well, you'll be glad to know Mason's case got dismissed, and he's a free man," Serena explains. "There was video evidence plus the witness statements. Yours helped too, Sophie. Thanks for being so honest."

Sophie lunges for me again, and this time, I don't care that Serena is watching and will give me shit for it. Once we pull back, I wipe away the tears on her cheeks.

"I was so nervous you were gonna get locked up or something.

All these crazy scenarios were running through my mind, and I wouldn't have been able to live with myself if you were punished for something that was my fault."

"It wasn't your fault," I remind her. "But you don't have to worry. Things will eventually go back to normal."

"What do you mean?" she asks, studying my features. "Did something else happen?"

"I have to take a leave from work." I shrug. "My dad thinks the press is gonna be on his ass, which means I need to lay low for a while."

"Oh, Mason. I'm sorry."

Before I can respond, Serena chimes in. "Perhaps he can use his time off to liven up the place." She winks. "Help him redecorate or something."

"Hey, it's my bachelor pad," I defend.

"Smells like one too," she retorts.

Sophie giggles, and after a moment, I walk Serena out of the living room and tell her I'll be in touch. She gives me shit but understands why I'm smitten with Sophie. She's ragging me so hard, I nearly kick her ass out the door. But she laughs all the way to her car.

Once I shut the door, I lean against it and sigh. It's already been a hectic day, and it's far from over.

"Soph," I say after we eat breakfast and finish off a pot of coffee.

She looks up at me, her eyes so damn sad and tired. "Yeah?"

"We should probably get your things from the house. I assume at some point his family is gonna have to go through everything there, and you won't get the chance then."

She nods as if she'd been thinking the same thing. "Will you come with me?"

"Is that seriously even a question?" I'm not letting her out of my damn sight again.

CHAPTER SEVENTEEN

BEING HERE IS SURREAL. Everything about the past three days has felt like a dream or, rather, a nightmare. Mason getting arrested for Weston's murder scared the crap out of me, but knowing all charges have been dropped eases my anxiety some. Still, I worry about him and what this means for his career and future. He's been put on temporary leave until who knows when. The only thing he's told me is that his dad suggested it until things "calm down." Whatever the hell that means.

After his court hearing on Monday, we went to Weston's house to grab my things, and I could see the pain and anger written all over Mason's face as he took in the scene. Shit's knocked over from our fight that morning, holes are in the walls, and the kitchen remains a fucking mess. He didn't say anything, but I caught him shaking his head and watched his hands ball into fists several times.

Once I had everything I needed, I left that house once and for all. I breathed the biggest sigh of relief. One I'd been holding in for six months.

Back at Mason's house, I informed the director of the symphony what had happened, and he told me to take all the time I need. I take the week off or at least until I can think straight again. Music soothes me, and although I could use it right now, the thought of picking up my violin and playing brings me to tears. My heart isn't in it. Hell, not even super glue could put my shattered heart back together right now.

I still don't know how I feel about what happened or the fact that Weston is gone. My heart and head are conflicted, torn between losing the man I had fallen in love with and a man who was nothing like the man I first met. With his witty personality and sweet charm, he lured me into his web. Once I was addicted to him, he ripped the rug out from under me and revealed the monster he truly was. I thought I knew him and thought I loved him. Hell, I thought he loved me too. But you don't hit and hurt the person you love. He revealed his demons to me on a gold platter the moment I moved in with him.

I should've left sooner. Fear and the hope that things would change kept me a prisoner in his home.

He could've killed me.

He had a gun.

A gun I didn't know existed.

Would he have used it on me? The next fight? The next time I pushed his buttons too far? The next time he drank?

Questions flood my thoughts as I squeeze my eyes shut and try to push them away. I can't think of the what-ifs because it'll send me spiraling again, and I won't let him win. He doesn't get to control me anymore. I'm free.

"Soph?" I feel a hand on my shoulder, and I relax at Mason's soothing voice.

I open my eyes to my savior, the man who saved my life, after falling asleep on the couch after breakfast. He's dressed in slacks and a button-up shirt, and I make sure my gaze doesn't linger on him for too long.

My feelings for him have always been there, even when I forced myself to pretend they weren't and pushed them away in hopes they'd disappear. Knowing he only saw me as a friend made it possible to ignore them, and for years now, I did. From the moment I started dating Weston, things were strained between

Mason and me, but it didn't mean I stopped caring about him. Mason tried to warn me, to protect me, and wanted me to understand the concerns he had about the man I was sharing a bed with every night. Bitterness that he didn't give us a shot three years ago and my pride kept me from listening. He's always looked out for me, and I know that now.

Blinking up at him, I take in his features. Still gorgeous, built, and tan, every inch of him is pure perfection.

"You okay?"

I inhale a deep breath, then exhale slowly. "Yeah, I'm fine. Just thinking about all the unpacking I should be doing. But at least I managed to finish a load of laundry so I can hang up my clothes."

He takes a seat next to me on the couch. The couch I've been sleeping on the past two nights because I didn't want to be an inconvenience to Liam and take over his bed again. We argued about it, but I insisted, and he eventually caved since he barely fit. The cushions are comfortable for a little bit, but after a few hours, the springs were killing me. I stretch my arms above my head, tilting my head until a crack sounds.

Mason furrows his brows and frowns. "Your back hurts?"

I sigh, slumping my arms down to my sides. "Everything hurts."

"Let's find something to binge since we'll be stuck in this house for a while." Mason grabs the remote and clicks on the Netflix app. "Might as well be on house arrest since I've been *ordered* to stay hidden until further notice."

His dad told him to keep a low profile and not talk to the media about anything. Being the DA's son and not being in jail already has people making assumptions about the whole situation.

"Sure, might as well. I haven't watched TV in so long I don't know what's good," I admit, reaching for a blanket.

Mason grins.

"What?" I ask, then pat down my hair, wondering if it's sticking up in a rat's nest. "Do I have something on my face?"

He shakes his head and chuckles. "No, nothing like that. I'm glad you're safe, Soph. I feel a lot better with you being here."

"Really? Because I feel like I'm intruding on you guys," I admit. I hate being an inconvenience.

"Uh, no. Not at all. I'd be going stir-crazy if you were anywhere else. Well, *crazier.*" He flashes me a boyish grin as if admitting that made him more vulnerable. This side of Mason makes being *just friends* hard as hell. It's difficult not to feel something for him when he's like this.

"Does this mean I'm finally off your shit list?" I tease, needing to lighten the mood before my heart reads deeper into his words and creates something I know isn't really there.

He turns back to the TV, scrolling through shows and movies. "Oh, sweet Sophie. You've never been on my shit list. Not even for a second." My cheeks heat, and when he glances at me, then winks, I'm quite sure my heart stops beating altogether.

The next day as I sprawl out on the couch with a book and wait for my food delivery, Mason plops down by my feet and places them in his lap. I smell his body wash and glance over and see his hair is still wet. Stifling a groan, I force my eyes away from the view and back to the pages.

He reaches over and tilts the hardcover to get a better look at the cover. "That's a good one. Second one was slow, though."

"You've read it?" I ask, surprised as hell as I place the book flat against my chest. "Wait. You read?"

He quirks a brow. "Don't sound so surprised, geez. I read it when it first came out."

"I'm not *surprised.* I didn't know you were into adult fantasy books."

He shrugs, reaching for the remote. "Used to be. Didn't finish the series."

"What?" I gasp. "It only gets better!"

Mason furrows his brows at me. "You've read the entire series already? Why are you reading book one then?"

"You've never re-read a book or series before?" I ask defensively.

Mason shrugs. "I had to read a lot in college and it didn't leave much time for leisure reading."

"I bet you'd like Teddy Leigh. I binged his last series. So damn good." I release a dreamy sigh. "Plus, he's hot too."

Mason glares at me. "Yeah, now I really want to read it and think about his hotness."

I roll my eyes. "No one said you had to think about how he looks, though why wouldn't you want to? Beyond intelligent, sexy, plus he's funny! I stalk, *er*, follow him on social media."

Grabbing for my phone, I click on the app and look up his handle. Before I can say another word, Mason scoops it out of my fingers. "Hey!"

"Let me see this guy. I bet he's an old fart."

I laugh at his tone. "Nope. Early thirties."

"He looks like any other guy with dark hair and a beard." Mason hands my phone back.

"To you, maybe." I chuckle, wondering if I detect a hint of jealousy in his voice. "Anyway, his books are amazing so you should read them solely because of that fact."

"I'll get right on it," he deadpans.

"I have his books in hardcover if you want to borrow them. But you need to treat them nicely. They're all signed."

Mason leans back with a groan, but I see the smile he tries to hide. "Of course, they are."

We spend the day like this, bantering about anything and everything. We started watching *Lucifer* on Netflix yesterday, and we're already on season two. I half-listen as I continue reading my book, and we actively avoid the elephant in the room as my feet remain in his lap. It's the only way I can keep my emotions down about the reality of our situation. Mason's charges might've been dropped, but it's the aftermath of it all that I'm most concerned about. The promotion he's supposed to get in the fall, his relationship with his father, and our friendship are all still up in the air, but when it's just the two of us hanging out, it's easy to pretend at least for a little while that everything's fine.

By Thursday morning, Lennon and Maddie are on the doorstep demanding I give them more than two-word text responses. They've been messaging me nonstop, but I haven't been in the mood for conversation, considering what they're going to force me to talk about.

"You can't deny your niece. Let us in," Lennon demands, holding Allie on her hip.

"You can't use her as bait." I chuckle, reaching out to grab her. She's six months now, and her little personality is starting to show. "Come here, baby girl. You're welcome anytime." I smile, holding her against my chest.

"Are the boys here?" Maddie asks, and I roll my eyes.

"Just Mason."

We retreat to the living room where I was folding laundry since I'm living out of my suitcases. They look at the mess and help me pile it on the coffee table so they can take a seat on the couch.

"How's it going?" Lennon asks.

"Good. Trying to organize my shit." I grab my books one-handed and set them in a pile.

"Soph." Lennon's tone has me turning to look at her. "How is it *really* going? You okay? You haven't been too responsive to my texts."

I sigh, taking a seat. Before I can respond, Maddie strolls in from the kitchen with a popsicle in her hand. I didn't realize she snuck in there.

"What? There are more if you want one." She plops down on the end of the couch, then holds her arms out for Allie. I hand her over, then swipe the popsicle out of her grip. "Hey!"

"Those are mine, thank you. Mason bought them for *me*," I taunt.

"So you can't share?" Maddie gives me a pointed stare.

"Ugh, fine." I toss it back at her with a grin and see Lennon staring at me. She knows I'm avoiding the conversation at hand.

"Are you going to his funeral?" she asks.

I frown, then shrug. "His mom reached out to me yesterday and gave me the details. If I don't go, she'll wonder why her son's girlfriend isn't there. She just lost him, and I don't want to cause any more pain or stress by explaining to her why I won't be attending. He might've been a monster to me, but that shouldn't be his mother's last memory of him. She didn't do anything wrong."

"Yeah, that's a tricky situation, Soph. I'm sorry." Lennon frowns.

"We should all go," Maddie chimes in. "That way you don't have to do it alone, and we can pull you away if things get weird."

"Yeah, we'll go with you," Lennon agrees.

"You guys would do that for me?" I ask, stunned. They hate Weston almost as much as Mason does, so this won't be easy for them either.

"Of course," Lennon says. "Make an appearance and then we can get the hell out of there."

"Thank you." I wrap my sister in a hug and hold back the tears threatening to fall. I've tried so damn hard to keep them under control when I'm around other people. Only in the shower will I let them fall, mixing with the water, but as soon as I'm done, I straighten my spine and push them back again.

I'm not crying for him. I won't.

"So how has it been living here?" Maddie asks. "I imagine lots of women, beer, and porn on the regular."

I furrow my brows as Lennon snorts. "Mads!" I scold, narrowing my gaze on Allie.

"She doesn't know what I'm saying anyway." She shrugs, then lifts Allie higher on her lap. "Do you, baby girl? No, you don't," she says in a high-pitched voice.

"See what you're leaving me with?" Lennon holds out her hand, which causes me to laugh.

"I babysat her last year, so it's your turn," I retort, and we both chuckle. Lennon went through hell after Brandon's death, and we gave her space to deal with it but only because Hunter was looking after her. Hmm…is Mason my Hunter?

Could he be? Or better yet, does he want to be?

"Is it weird?" Maddie asks.

"Is what weird?"

"Living here with Mason and Liam."

"No, actually. Aside from the fact that I feel guilty as hell about this whole situation. It's my fault this happened. I brought Weston into my life, into our lives, and am the reason we're all in this mess." I haphazardly rub my arm where one of the bruises is still sore from when he grabbed me hard. "As soon as I can afford it, I'll find a place and move because the last thing I want is to be a burden when I already feel like I'm to blame for everything."

"Like hell you are." Mason's booming voice comes from behind us as he walks into the living room.

"Jesus, you scared me," Maddie scolds. He scared the shit out of me too.

Mason ignores her as he approaches me. He leans over the back of the couch, towering over me. "You have nothing to feel guilty about, you hear me? He's the one who made the choice to bring a gun, to lie about his past and job, and treat you like a human punching bag. I'm not one hundred percent innocent in the events that took place on Saturday, but I'd go to prison for the rest of my life before I'd let you take the blame for any of this."

His words hit me like a ton of bricks, and I'm left speechless. The intensity in his eyes pin me in place, and I want to reach out and hug him.

"Mason's right," Lennon blurts after the silence gets awkward. "You were the victim, Soph. You can't continue to blame yourself for any of this."

My eyes shoot to her, and I hate the look of pity she gives me. I swallow and break my gaze before glancing back at Mason.

"Thank you," I say softly. "And maybe we should blame Maddie," I say teasingly, hoping the intense moment between Mason and me fades away.

"What the heck?" she screeches. "How so?"

Playfully, I point a finger at her. "Who made me get that stupid dating app to start?"

She rolls her eyes. "I picked some good ones on there for you, and if my memory serves me correct, you had something to say about all of them," she says matter-of-factly, flicking her attention to Mason. I panic for a second, worried she's going to rat me out on why I didn't pursue them.

"Okay, fine. You're off the hook," I quickly say, wanting this conversation to end.

"I'm gonna hop in the shower," Mason says, touching my shoulder and giving it a light squeeze. He went to the gym a couple of hours ago, and now that I'm looking, I notice his shirt is covered in sweat. He likes to work out and box, but now that he's not at his day job, he spends more time there.

"Was that not the sweetest, most alpha male thing to say?" Maddie blurts the second Mason heads upstairs.

Oh my God.

I hope he didn't hear that.

"If you don't have his babies, then I'm gonna," Maddie continues.

"Just when we thought it was safe to bring you back into the conversation," I tease, blushing.

"Seriously, I think my ovaries burst," Lennon adds, and I narrow my eyes at her.

I groan. "Shut up. Both of you."

"Speaking of babies and ovaries," Lennon says. "I never got to tell you guys on Saturday."

My eyes widen as I study her expression. "Are you pregnant?"

When she smiles with a nod, I open my arms and lunge at her. "I can't believe it!"

Maddie charges for her next, handing me Allie. "Dude, no wonder you made us stop at Taco Bell earlier."

We laugh, and this was just the news I needed to hear.

"When did you find out? Do you know how far along?" I ask, bouncing my niece on my knee.

"Probably five or six weeks. I see the doctor next week to confirm. I found out last week and told Hunter on Saturday morning before the wedding, which is why I didn't get the chance to tell you guys sooner."

"You're gonna be a big sister, Allie Kat," I say, kissing her chubby cheeks. "Two kids under two. Oh my God." I laugh.

"Yes, I know." Lennon smiles, but it's one of pure joy. She and Hunter deserve it, and I'm so happy for them.

We talk and play with Allie for another hour. I avoid bringing up Weston for as long as possible, though they're both concerned. They've already agreed to come to the funeral with me this weekend, and once it's over, I'll have closure for good.

Allie starts to get fussy, and Lennon says she's ready for a nap. As Maddie changes the baby, Lennon pulls me to the side and gives me a concerned look. "Listen, I know this is hard for you, and you just want to push it away for now. I'm not going to tell you how to deal with this, considering the way things happened, but I do think you should talk to someone so you don't bottle it up. I was doing some research and found these grieving groups. It's like group therapy where people who lost someone close to them can chat openly about it. Even if you aren't grieving *him*, you're grieving the life you thought you'd have. You did love him at one point, and you're grieving a loss regardless. It might be something to consider."

It wasn't because I'm actively trying not to think about any of it. But I know my sister and how much she loves me, so I give her an appreciative smile. "I'll think about it. Thanks."

Do I want to talk about it? Would it help? Or would it open wounds I'm not ready to dissect?

We say our goodbyes, and soon they're off, leaving me in a quiet house. Mason is in his room, obviously wanting to give us privacy down here. Considering this is his home, I think that's super nice.

I wake up the next day, sore as hell. As appreciative as I am for being able to stay here, this couch is killing me. I toss and turn all night, unable to get comfortable for too long before I'm forced to find a new position.

Mason strolls down the stairs in nothing but gray sweatpants. I swallow down the lump lodged in my throat at seeing him this early in the morning with messy hair, sleepy hooded eyes, and shirtless with his body on display.

Jesus.

Is this my punishment? Getting to look and not touch?

Fucking brutal.

"Morning," he says with a deep throaty voice. "You're up early."

"Couldn't sleep," I say, darting my attention away and pretending to focus on the very interesting coffee table in front of me. "What're you doing up?"

"Taking you shopping. We leave in an hour."

My head pops up as he walks through the living room and into the kitchen. His back muscles are a very welcome distraction.

Wait, *what*?

"Shopping for what?" I ask, following him.

"Enough is enough, Soph."

He turns on the coffeemaker, then digs around in the cabinet. "You want some?" he asks, grabbing two mugs before I even respond.

"Sure, yeah. Wait. What're you talking about?" I ask, going to the fridge for creamer because I need to keep my hands busy before I do something stupid like reach out and touch him.

"You need a bed," he says, turning to face me, and I blink. "We have the third room, so you might as well use it. We'll get a bed, nightstand, and dresser, a bookcase for all your books, and whatever else you need. No use sleeping on that shitty couch because it's not that comfortable. I've spent a few drunken nights on it myself."

"Mason," I say softly, placing the creamer on the counter next to him. "I appreciate you giving me the third room, I really do, but I can't afford all that. I'm already gonna be stretching my budget to pay my portion of the rent, so—"

"Who said you had to pay rent?" he snaps, narrowing his eyes on me.

"Well, no one, but I'm not gonna live here rent free."

"You are," he says, his blunt tone leaving no room for argument, but I push anyway.

"Mason, please don't treat me like a sick puppy."

"Soph, I wasn't." His voice is genuine, but his expression drops.

"I know you didn't mean to, but I don't want anyone's pity. You're already being way too nice, so yes, I will pay rent to live here. I'm not a freeloader and want to pay my share. I'll take on a few extra students to tutor and save up for a bed."

"Let me buy you a bed, Soph. Please." Mason takes me by surprise, and I gasp when he steps toward me and grabs my hand. He wraps both of his palms over my fist, then rests it on his chest over his heart. "Let me do this for you."

"This isn't picking up a dinner tab, Mason. This is a bed and furniture."

"Well, it's my house, and that room needs to be furnished." He shrugs, knowing I can't argue that, and flashes a victorious grin.

My shoulders drop as I officially give up the fight. He has a point.

"Fine." I groan. "But nothing fancy. Super cheap. We'll go to a thrift store or something."

The coffee maker beeps as he closes the gap between us, then kisses my forehead. I allow my eyes to close for the briefest moment as I lean into his touch. Then he drops our hands, which I immediately miss.

"Sure, Soph. Cheap," he deadpans. "Then we'll get you some sheets, blankets, a lamp, and some décor. You can set it up however you want. Just please, no pictures of babies in flowerpots."

I snort and laugh. "No babies? Afraid they'll give you nightmares or something?" I tease.

"It's not because of me," he says with a knowing smirk. "Liam."

This makes me laugh harder. "Why? He thinks it'll be contagious, and he'll suddenly have one of his own?"

His smirk deepens. "Exactly. His biggest fear is commitment, and babies have commitment written *all* over them."

"Bless the woman who manages to tame him one day," I tease.

Smiling, he nods while pouring coffee into our mugs, then adds cream and sugar into mine. Butterflies swarm in my stomach because he knows how I like it. I've only been here for six days, but it already feels like home.

Mason is home.

CHAPTER EIGHTEEN
MASON

BEING this close to Sophie is dangerous.

I know it, but now that she's here, in my house, drinking my coffee and sitting on my couch, I don't want her to leave. There's been a huge shift in our friendship over the past year when she first started dating Weston, and this is another one—one I'm growing damn fond of.

Although we don't do anything when we hang out, I look forward to it every day when I wake up. Given the shitstorm that is now my life, Sophie is safe, and that bastard will never hurt her again.

The fact that I'm not working pisses me off, but I know the reasons behind it, so although I worked my ass off to get where I am, I can't fight it. That promotion to be a forensic investigator, even though it's a rookie position, is mine, and I'm not going to let it slip between my fingers after being at the grunt level for years. If it wasn't for Sophie being here with me, I'd probably be drinking way too many beers and self-destructing as I replay the memory of that gun being pointed at me and my friends.

But truthfully, I don't regret a damn thing. I'd follow him out of that reception hall again and again if it meant making sure he'd leave Sophie alone for good. The fact he acted like he was cracked out on coke and clearly drunk wasn't something I anticipated. He should've gone down the first time I decked him, and we would've all walked away.

Blinking, I clear that night out of my head. It's been on repeat since the moment it happened although I've been trying to push out the thoughts, memories, and horrific aftermath.

Waking up to Sophie in my house for the past several days has shifted my mood when the demons threatened to pull me under. This nightmare feels like a repeat of what I went through years ago, and although the circumstances are different, the anxiety is the same.

Spending time with Sophie keeps me preoccupied, and I'll forever be grateful for her company. But now that she's here and staying, she deserves more than a shitty couch to sleep on.

"Mason, it's too much," Sophie repeats for the third time.

I saw the way her eyes lit up at the upholstered bedframe with built-in storage underneath. She rushed over to touch the dark gray pattern. Then her eyes bugged out as soon as she found the price tag.

"Let's find you a mattress set now. What size do you want? Queen?" I walk toward them when Sophie's hand brushes mine.

"Wait." She attempts to pull me back, but instead, I thread my fingers through hers and pull her with me. "Mason…a full would be fine."

I drink her in, noticing the sparkle she had pre-Weston is coming back. Her long brown hair is pulled up into a half ponytail with waves flowing down her back. Though she wears a touch of makeup to cover her bruised eye, she doesn't need it either way. Sophie always looks stunning.

"A queen for a queen." I wink, but my attempt to reassure her that she deserves this bed doesn't work. She groans, knowing damn well she won't win this argument.

After I've tracked down the salesman, ordered the frame and mattresses, and paid an assload for same-day delivery, I drive us to the next store.

"Really?" she asks, laughing. "You want to shop here?"

I park my truck and kill the engine. "Sure, why not? Is it for a secret society only or something?"

"Okay. It's your funeral." She shrugs.

And I drove myself right to it.

Once we're inside, Sophie's eyes light up like a kid in a candy store. This place is insane.

"Well?" she asks, looking up with a knowing smirk.

"I'm regretting every decision I made that's brought me here." I deadpan, glancing at the aisles that never seem to end.

"Liar," she says. "You guys could use some new shit in your house anyway."

"Why do I have a feeling we're about to go on a fat ass shopping spree?" We walk farther into the store, then grab two carts.

Sophie giggles, and I follow her lead.

We head to the bedding first, and the options are overwhelming, to say the least. Sophie looks through them all, taking her time, but her eyes widen when she checks the prices. "Soph, stop stalling."

"I'm not," she says without looking at me.

"What about this one?" I ask, pointing at a solid gray comforter set. "Matches the headboard of the bed."

She squints at it, pursing her lips left and right. "It has no personality."

"Okay then." I chuckle. "What kind of personality does your bed need?"

Sophie glances over her shoulder and glares. "I meant *my* personality. Your bedroom should reflect you and your happy place. When things in your life are shit, you should find solace in your room, surrounded by the belongings that bring you peace. That's what I want my bedroom to be. Somewhere I feel safe and comfortable."

Safe and comfortable. That's exactly what I want for her. *With me.*

"So not the gray?" I tease, needing to lighten the mood before I choke on the tension between us.

She steps closer and smacks my arm. "You're such a guy."

After searching for another ten minutes, Sophie squeals when she finds a pattern with Eiffel Towers surrounded by Paris written in pink script. The cream-colored background is pretty, but I don't tell her that.

"Is that the one?" I ask, eager to move to the next section of the store so we can get the hell out of here.

"Yes! I love Paris! Well, the idea of it. I've never been. But it's my dream destination vacation."

I grab the handle of the bag and haul it into my cart. "Perfect."

Sophie bites down on her lower lip, then meets my gaze. I know she hates that she needs help and didn't ask, but I'm offering anyway. "What's next?" I question, hoping to snap her out of her overactive thoughts.

"I need some pillows," she says.

"Lead the way."

An hour later and after a lot of convincing, Sophie has new pillows, a lamp with an Eiffel Tower as the base, and a few décor items. Then she forced me over to the kitchen area. As long as we weren't shopping for her specifically, she was all about it. Now, I'm the proud owner of a twelve-piece set of dinner plates with four ceramic mugs to match, a paper towel holder that apparently suits the counters better, and some kind of silverware organizer contraption. After all that, Sophie dragged me to the bathroom section and picked out a set of oversized super soft bath towels. When I spotted an Eiffel Tower shower curtain, I threw it into the cart too, which made her grin ear to ear.

Just as we push our two carts toward the checkout, I see my aunt out of the corner of my eye rushing toward me. I inhale a sharp breath, knowing I'm about to get hounded.

"Mason!" she squeals, then pulls me in a hug. She's my dad's sister, which should be awkward, considering how my relationship with my father, but she gives him enough shit for me to know she doesn't always like him either. "It's been a while, kiddo. How've you been? You doing okay?"

She gives me a look that tells me she knows what's been going on behind the scenes. She might not always get along with her brother, but she works in politics too, and they all talk.

"I'm fine." I give her a reassuring smile so she doesn't say what's really on her mind. "This is my aunt Sylvia."

My aunt grins.

"This is Sophie, my—"

"Roommate," Sophie quickly clarifies.

She's much more than that. More than my friend even. But how the hell do you introduce someone as your one-time bathroom quickie fling that you've friend-zoned, killed her boyfriend, and who now lives with you?

Roommate it is.

"It's so lovely to meet you." Aunt Sylvia wraps her up in a tight hug. Yep, she definitely knows Sophie is much more than a roommate.

"Oh, you too."

"Since Mason hasn't visited his favorite aunt in a long time, I'd love to invite you both for dinner some night."

Sophie glances over at me, and I quickly intervene.

"She's just getting settled into the house and has a busy work schedule, so maybe in a couple of months," I offer so she doesn't push.

"Sure, that'd be great." Aunt Sylvia winks at me, and I muffle a groan. "You two kids have fun shopping." Then she turns her attention toward Sophie. "If he starts acting anything less than a gentleman, remind him that I have an entire baby album of him with lots of bath time pictures, and I'll gladly show them off."

Kill. Me. Now.

Sophie giggles, her cheeks turning bright red. "He's been very respectful, don't worry. This whole trip was his idea. In fact, he *insisted*," she reassures her.

Aunt Sylvia smiles proudly at me. "That's my boy. But I might show her anyway because you were *so* darn cute," she says in a high-pitched voice, patting my cheek.

"I would *definitely* love to see those pictures," Sophie adds.

"Sure, fine," I say as if it wouldn't bother me. "I was a cute kid, though. You might not be able to resist me once you see them." I shoot Sophie a wink.

"Well, you call me when you kids are available for dinner, and we'll make it happen. I better go find your uncle Frank before he wanders off." She waves and rushes to the other side of the store as fast as she came barreling over.

"Baby bath pictures, huh?" Sophie teases as we push our carts to the front to check out.

"Shut up," I mutter, earning a playful laugh in return.

Once I've paid and we've loaded up the truck, I drive to IKEA. "What're we doing here?" Sophie asks, unbuckling her seat belt.

"Well, you need a dresser and nightstand, right?"

She shrugs.

"You do. Let's go."

"I don't need both," she insists as we walk inside. "I already feel like you've done too much."

I frown.

"At least let me buy something so I feel like less of a freeloader!" She groans, pushing the cart we grabbed on the way in.

"Fine. You can buy the burritos."

"Huh?" She furrows her brows.

"For lunch. You like burritos, don't you?"

"Uh, yeah. Who doesn't?"

"Good. Then it's settled. You choose what you want, and you can buy us lunch."

Sophie snorts as she follows me down an aisle. "Hardly seems fair."

"Oh, I don't know. I have a pretty big appetite," I muse, patting my stomach. "I might do some real damage."

"Now you're just trying to amuse me."

I smirk. "Is it working?"

"No!" she says, but she's full-on laughing.

Thirty minutes later, we're back in the truck with both pieces of furniture. It didn't take nearly as long since both of our stomachs were growling at the mention of food. By the evening, her bed has been delivered and set up. I put her dresser and nightstand together while she washed her new bed set and decorated the room. She ended up finding a bookcase she wanted online instead, so I help her arrange the area to make sure there's a spot for it once it's delivered. Sophie folded her clothes and unpacked some of her bags, making the room her own.

"I like it. Looks awesome," I tell her, collapsing on the bed.

"Hey! I just made that!" she playfully scolds.

"And you're about to sleep in it," I tease. "What do you think, Soph? An okay place to live for a while?"

She gives me a somber look, the corner of her lips tilting up slightly. "I think it's more than okay." Sophie takes a seat next to me and rests her head on my shoulder. "I don't know how to thank you, Mason. You both for letting me stay here. For helping me. For…protecting me." She starts to choke up, and I know she doesn't want to say the words.

I tilt her chin so her eyes meet mine. "And I'd do it all over again if it meant keeping you safe. No matter what."

Sophie studies my lips, and I swallow hard. Then as if she realizes she's staring at them, she jerks to her feet and clears her throat. "Well, I think I'm gonna go to bed."

"Yeah, me too." I push myself up. "Someone dragged me all over town today."

"Oh my God." She laughs, swatting at my chest.

We stand mere inches apart, and I can't help myself. I need her closer. I wrap my arms around her shoulders and pull her to my chest. "Sleep well in your new room." Then I lean back, kiss her forehead, and walk away.

"Good night," she calls out weakly.

Today is a day neither of us have been looking forward to, but I understand Sophie's reasons for going to that motherfucker's funeral. She's too kind to tell his mother the truth, but I'm relieved that Maddie and Lennon are joining her at least.

I make us coffee while she showers and wait for her in the living room. Once she's dressed and comes downstairs, I hand her the mug with just the right amount of cream and sugar. Her voice is low and soft as she thanks me.

"Soph, you don't have to go if you're not up to it. You can say no," I tell her gently.

It's going to be a weird and emotionally draining day for her.

She sips her coffee and lowers her gaze. She shrugs before finally meeting my eyes. "I just want to get it over with and move the hell on for good. I feel like this makes it final."

"Closure," I confirm, and she nods. "Okay, I get it." Hell, I get it *too* much, but I don't tell her that.

"My sisters will be there, and we won't stay longer than needed," she reassures me. "I told his mother I'd give her the key so they could go into his house and clean it out. After that, I'm putting these last six months of my life in the past for good."

I look at her, noticing how much makeup she's wearing on her face. I hate that she has to cover up marks that asshole gave her. They're almost gone now, but I almost wish she'd bare it all so his family can see what a real piece of shit he was.

"You will, Soph. I'll make sure of it." I wink, needing to see her smile so I can stomach the idea of her going there. She rewards me with a grin, and that's enough.

Maddie charges through the front door without knocking and goes to Sophie's side.

"Well, come on in," I tease.

"Where's Lennon?" Sophie asks.

"Her pregnant ass couldn't keep up."

"I heard that!" she shouts from the front door before shutting it. "Hey!" She gives us a wave before storming past us. "Gotta pee, hold on."

Before either of us can say another word, Liam walks down the stairs in only his boxer briefs, and for a split second, I consider giving him a warning that we're not alone but fuck it. Let fate handle his ass instead.

I study Maddie as she tenses, and her spine goes straight. She's watching Liam's every step as he rounds the banister with half-opened eyes. His hair is messy as hell, which is his norm. It's only tamed after a shower and he finger-combs it. We've been friends and roommates for way too long for me not to know his routine. Maddie is gawking and possibly drooling at the fact that he's built like a linebacker, and his shorts aren't concealing much.

Sophie blinks, shifting her eyes from him, and I wonder if she's blushing because of how he looks or because we all saw more than we bargained for.

"We aren't alone, dude," I tell him, chuckling. He's halfway to the kitchen when he pauses and glances over his shoulder, finally realizing Sophie and Maddie are on the couch next to me. As if his luck would have it, Lennon comes out of the bathroom at the same time and runs into him.

"Oh my God!" She pushes his chest. "Put some clothes on, Liam!" Lennon covers her eyes as she walks around him.

I laugh, knowing Lennon is one hundred percent devoted to Hunter and will more than likely tell him about this later.

"Yeah, Liam," I mock. "Your booty shorts are a bit revealing."

"Last I checked, I live here!" he shouts, flipping me the bird over his head as he continues walking toward the kitchen, no doubt about to snag a cup of coffee.

"Oh my God. I must be dreaming," Maddie mutters, her body still frozen in place.

Lennon comes over and pinches her arm.

"Hey, what the heck?" Maddie rubs a hand over the spot.

"Just confirming you're not dreaming and still virginal." Lennon shrugs with a knowing grin. "Let's go."

"That was uncalled for!" Maddie whines, standing up and following Lennon.

I stand with Sophie and walk her to the door. "You've got this."

She nods and pinches her lips together into a small smile. "Thanks. We shouldn't be too long."

Wrapping one arm around her shoulders, I pull her into my side, then kiss her forehead. "See ya soon."

Lennon drives off with Sophie in the front next to her. Maddie's in the back, leaning forward to be closer to them. I wave to them, and then they're gone.

"What happened to getting our boys-only crib back?" Liam complains the second I sit on the couch next to him.

I snort at his choice of words. "Sorry, man. Back to pants you go." Narrowing my eyes at him, I add, "And not only for her sake but also for mine. Did you shrink your clothes or something?" I ask, laughing.

"Dude, shut the fuck up. I was on the road and needed some new ones. These were the closest to my size I could find at the time."

"You might want to retire them then." I lean over and grab my mug from the coffee table. "If you bend over, they're gonna rip right down the middle." I can't stop laughing as I try to take a sip, and without another word, Liam stands up, pulls his boxer briefs down to his feet, then kicks them off before sitting back down.

"Better?" He faces me with a shit-eating grin.

I fly off the couch, nearly spilling the hot liquid on myself, and glare. "Pretty sure I've had a chick on that couch at one point," I tell him as I head to the kitchen for food.

"Pretty sure I did too," he calls out.

"Jesus fuck. I'm done with you."

An hour later, Hunter comes over, and Liam finally gets dressed. I refuse to sit by him in case he decides to do another strip show. Hunter can get that surprise instead.

"So where's Allie?" I ask when I notice Hunter carrying two six-packs of beer instead of a car seat.

"Mrs. Locke wanted her for the day, which means I'm getting shitty. It's been way too damn long," he explains, grabbing a bottle and twisting it open. They're lucky to have Brandon's mother in their lives to give them little breaks.

"It's not even noon." I can't help laughing, knowing how exhausted he's been with their six-month-old. Now that Lennon is pregnant again, Hunter's probably taking more of the diaper duties at night. He's been fiercely protective of her ever since she got pregnant the first time.

"It's five o'clock somewhere." Hunter chugs his beer until it's nearly half gone.

"Been rough or what?" I ask, deciding to grab one too.

"Lennon has been sick all week, even worse than the first time she was pregnant. She didn't have morning sickness then, but certain smells would make her nauseous. Now she's puking her guts out all day long, so on top of taking care of her, I take the baby at night so she can get some rest."

Hunter's a damn saint and loves her more than anything. He has put Lennon's and then Allie's needs in front of his own since the day Brandon died, and I'm so proud to call him one of my closest friends.

"So you gonna catch me up? What's going on with you and Sophie?" Hunter asks after his second beer. "You two getting closer?"

"We're just friends," I say as if I've rehearsed it. Sucking down my beer, I want to change the subject, but I know Liam's going to be no damn help.

"Who bought her an entire bedroom set..." Liam adds.

Yep. *Asshole.*

Hunter raises his brows, smirking. "Have you learned nothing from my experience?"

I roll my eyes. "Not the same thing."

"Not too far off really," Hunter states. "You two already hooked up, so—"

"What the hell? How do you know that?" I ask, glaring at Liam.

"I didn't, but I do now." Hunter throws his head back, cackling when he sees my expression.

"Nice one." Liam fist-bumps him.

"I hate you both." I finish my drink, then slam it down on the table. "Neither of you are supposed to know that."

"Well, then you shouldn't be so damn obvious," Hunter muses. "Isn't that what you told me not too long ago? Oh, the irony."

I roll my eyes. "Fuck off."

"Okay, seriously," Hunter says. "Don't sit around and wait for her, man. You almost lost her once to that asshat. Want to watch her fall in love with another guy? You were almost too late last time, but this is your second chance. Don't waste it."

My jaw clenches at the mention of Sophie moving on. That's the last thing I want, but the baggage I carry is too much.

"It's not that easy," I say. "I haven't been able to settle down with anyone since Emma. She deserves better than a guy who's weighted down with the guilt of his past."

"Have you considered telling Sophie? Opening up and exposing those demons you feel are too much for her and letting *her* decide?" Hunter says so damn confidently as I glare at him.

"When did you become the love doctor?" I snicker, grabbing another bottle.

"You two want to be alone? Jesus." Liam groans. "Gonna trade recipes next?"

"Oh, sorry. Forgot Mr. Jaded and Anti-Love was here." Hunter nudges his shoulder. "And if you must know, I found a badass beer cheese dip recipe that's fucking delicious."

"What the hell is that?" Liam asks.

I snort, shaking my head.

Hunter meets my gaze again and arches a brow. "I think you'd be surprised by Sophie's reaction if you told her."

Swallowing, I look down and shrug before leaning back against the couch. "You guys know how fucked up I was after that. I drank myself stupid for days, didn't work, was failing my classes, and not living or coping. Then my dad being mixed up in it didn't help matters. Still doesn't. He loves throwing that shit in my face, especially now. There's a damn black cloud following me, and I don't want that for her."

"You gotta stop blaming yourself," Hunter says and not for the first time either. "At the end of the day, it was *her* choice. If it didn't happen that night, it would've eventually. She was determined and having the last word to blast you was her way of placing blame on anyone and anything besides herself. I know you loved her, but she made that choice, Mason. Not you."

If only I could believe him, I might be able to put that part of my life behind me for good. Until then, it haunts me, and I'm afraid it will for the rest of my life.

CHAPTER NINETEEN

SOPHIE

I DIDN'T CRY for him. *I won't.*

I've already done enough of that while he was alive.

Weston's mother is beyond distraught, hysterical even, and while I feel bad that she lost her son, the relief that he'll never be able to hurt me, or anyone else again, overrides those feelings of guilt.

Throughout the service I'm numb, almost in shock, as people share stories about Weston. The entire room believes he was a good, loving man, and it makes me sick to know so many people are celebrating an abusive manipulator. As the pastor continues, I'm torn between the guilt of his death and the happiness knowing I'm free from him.

He tried to kill Mason.

He would've killed me.

And if I would've escaped him, whoever he trapped next would've been the new target. Weston was an emotionless monster who didn't understand compassion on the most basic level. I'm still not sure how I ever fell for a man like him.

As soon as the funeral service is over, Lennon and Maddie escort me out of the building, and we leave. Part of me wants visual confirmation that he's actually gone, never capable of ruining my life again, but I don't stay for the burial. Sadness weighs heavy on my chest, but I refuse to feel sorry for him or give him any power. I don't want to feel bitter or angry because that's still allowing him to affect me from the grave.

It's over now. It's really over.

The healing can finally begin, hopefully.

Once we're back in the car, we're all silent, and it takes a few minutes to realize Lennon isn't driving us back to the house.

"You need a drink and some food," Lennon says as if she read my mind. "Then I'll take you home." She finally looks at me. "Plus, we need sister time."

"Yes!" Maddie adds from the back seat, though she wedges herself between us as much as she can. "Did you guys see the package on Liam? How did that *thing* not impale you and get you pregnant?" she asks Lennon.

"Oh my God…" I laugh, pushing Maddie's hand off my seat. "She's already pregnant, for one."

"Why do you think I pushed him away?" Lennon snickers. "He's a…beast. To say the least." I watch her expression and am almost certain I see her blush.

"So since I'm not well experienced in the area of penis size—"

"Maddie!" I shout.

"Would you rather I google it?" she retorts. "You're my big sisters. You're supposed to tell me these things!"

"Fine," Lennon says, giving me a look and shrugging. "Liam is definitely…well-endowed. Let's just say that."

"And can we talk about that man's ass? I could bounce a quarter off that thing," Maddie adds.

"Does Hunter know you check out other men's penises?" I taunt, batting my eyelashes at her.

Lennon glares and her nostrils flare. "Don't make me turn this car around and tell Mason you want to jump his bones and lock you two into a bedroom until you finally fuck it out. Because I will."

"Her hormones are crazy, Soph. She'll do it," Maddie says matter-of-factly.

I roll my eyes at her threats. "Wouldn't matter anyway. He's made it perfectly clear we're only friends. Roommates. Thinks of me like a sister. And now probably a damsel in distress he has to save. In fact, he probably pities me. It doesn't mean Mason *wants* me. He's had the chance to say something for years."

"So give him a second one," Maddie says confidently. "You live in the same house now."

"It's too soon, Mads," I tell her genuinely. "As much as I wanted Mason before, the timing is all wrong. In fact, that seems to be the story of our lives."

Lennon parks the car, and I didn't realize we were at a Mexican restaurant. "What do you mean?" She gives me a puzzled look as if she's studying my face, then her eyes widen. "Did something already happen between you two? Like before? Before Weston? When? Recently?"

She's rambling off so many questions that my head spins. Knowing I can't push this conversation off any longer, I suck in a deep breath before releasing it.

"I'm gonna need a couple of drinks in my system before we talk about this."

An hour later, I'm three drinks in, and Maddie and Lennon are looking as if they're about to wring my neck for keeping this secret from them.

"Oh my God!" Lennon's outburst nearly has me spewing my drink all over her. She's been staring with her mouth open, shocked as hell when I confess the real story of how Mason and I first met that night.

"In the bathroom? How does that even work?" Maddie asks.

"Like…you want a play by play?"

"I know how sex works, but in a bathroom? Ew!"

"I'm with Mads on this one." Lennon snickers.

"It wasn't *ew*!" I laugh, my cheeks burning with heat. "It was hot and spontaneous and probably should've never happened, but it did. It's made things weird for sure, but I think we're finally over that. I think of Mason as one of my closest friends now. I know it's only been a week since the incident, but it's as if we've been able to pick up where we left off years ago. Before all the awkwardness, even before Weston and I met."

Just saying his name aloud makes me want to vomit.

"You two are gonna do it again," Maddie says casually before taking a sip of her soda. "I'm calling it."

"Oh, I'd put money on that bet." Lennon nods. "I had a feeling about him. The way he tried to pretend you didn't exist and purposely gave you short answers. It was as if he was trying to shield himself from falling for you. But *why*?"

"Yes, why?" Maddie says in a mocking tone, pursing her lips together. "Let's dissect this and figure out what Mason's deep issues are and why he won't fuck you again."

"God, Maddie." I nudge her. "Can we talk about your sex life instead? Oh wait…" I taunt, knowing that'll get her off this subject.

"Ugh." She groans. "I think I'm gonna sell it off. I mean, why not get paid for something so many men want to experience? Deflowering a virgin, that's gotta be worth a few grand at least! Plus, I could use the money and maybe buy myself a damn car."

"You are not selling your V-card!" I scold, though I'm happy that they're done talking about my life for once.

"There are websites and apps for it! I'm so doing it!" she threatens, unlocking her phone, but I'm quick to grab it out of her hands.

"Do I need to call our parents and let them know their youngest daughter, their baby, is looking not only to have sex before marriage but also *sell* herself to a man? You want to have that conversation?"

Maddie rolls her eyes and relaxes her shoulders as if she doesn't give a shit. "Why don't you send them a picture of my tattoo while you're at it too? Give them a stroke for sure."

I slam her phone down on the table in front of her. "Someone dropped you as a child, didn't they?"

Lennon chuckles, then excuses herself for the third time to go pee.

"I'm keeping my eyes on you," I half-threaten when the three of us walk back to the car. "I'll hire Liam to be your personal security if I have to."

"Oh no, don't do that…" she deadpans. "Don't have the big, burly, and well-endowed man follow me around at all hours of the day!" She puts her hands up in a mock prayer.

"I'm done with you," I say, pushing her away.

"You had that coming," Lennon tells me. "She'd probably climb Liam like a tree and give him a run for his money."

"Let us all pray for his safety instead then."

Later that night as I lie in my new bed and look around my new room, I find my mind circling with thoughts I can't seem to sort out. Lennon's words from earlier in the week about finding a grieving support group weigh on my shoulders. Maybe she's right, and I should look for a way to cope with my emotions and how this really affects me.

Instead of rolling over to go to sleep, I grab my phone and search for local groups, and after a few minutes, I find a grief circle at a church that isn't far. I read about what it is, who it's for and how it can help, and decide to give it a chance. If it's not for me, then at least I tried and won't go back.

With my mind decided, I lock my phone and bury my head in my pillow to drift off to sleep.

The next morning, I'm woken up by a knock, and when I peel my eyes half open, I find Mason in the doorway with two mugs.

A girl could get used to waking up like this every day.

"Morning, sleepyhead." He smirks, walking all the way in. My eyes scan down his body, enjoying the view as my gaze shoots back up to meet his expression with one brow arched.

"Uh, hi," I croak, then clear my throat.

Sitting up, I blink a few times until my eyes adjust to the lights, then lie against the headboard. Mason sets my coffee on the nightstand before coming to sit near my feet.

"Your bookcase arrived this morning," he says, then takes a sip. "I put it together for you, so I just need to bring it in here."

My eyes widen in shock. "Wait, what? How?" That one-day shipping wasn't a joke.

I grab my phone and look at the time. "It's noon! Oh my God, why didn't you wake me sooner? I could've helped you."

"Seemed like you needed to catch up on sleep, so I let you rest." Mason shrugs as if it wasn't a big deal.

He's not wrong. It's been one of the hardest weeks of my life, and I wouldn't have been able to get through it without him and my sisters.

Mason's been going out of his way for me, and I can't help but wonder if it's because he's trying to make up for pretending I didn't exist for the past three years or because he feels guilty for what happened between us in that bar bathroom.

I sure as hell hope it's not the latter.

"Seriously, thank you." I reach over and place my hand over his. "I appreciate it. Everything. I appreciate this all so much."

"You're welcome, Soph. I'll do whatever I can to help. I woke up early anyway. I'm going a little stir-crazy not working."

I don't miss the frustrated groan that leaves his lips, and I feel awful that he's been put on leave. "I know, it's weird not running around with my head cut off. But I think I'm going to visit a grief support group. Lennon mentioned it and going might help me work through my emotions. Maybe I'll be able to heal quicker and can put it all in my past where it belongs."

"A grief support group? Like where you talk about missing a loved one?" His tone is edgier than before, and I don't miss the way his jaw tightens.

"Basically, yeah. Talk about a death that impacted you and how you're dealing with it," I try to explain, but when his brows crease, and he tilts his head, I know he's still confused about why I would go to something like that. "I'm not grieving *him*. But I do need to work out how I feel. I thought I was in love with him. I saw a future with him. I thought we were planning our forever together—as stupid as it makes me feel now. When things went from bad to worse, I became a shell of the person I used to be, and I recognized that. I wanted out. I wanted to leave, but I was scared of what he would do if I did. I feel foolish when I say it aloud—"

"Soph, no," Mason interrupts harshly, reaching over to grab my hand. "You were a victim, and he brainwashed and manipulated you. Don't continue to give him that power over you. You have no reason to feel stupid. It's easy to turn a blind eye to issues when you love someone. I wish I would've done something sooner, but I messed up when I thought keeping you at a distance was best for both of us."

"There wasn't anything you could've done, Mason," I reassure him. "I didn't want help. I thought I had it under control. If I said the right things, did what he asked, didn't get in his way, didn't push his buttons. As long as I didn't piss him off, I believed he would love me. I don't know why or how I became that person. Looking back now, that woman wasn't me. I was trapped under his spell, and if it wasn't for you, I have no doubt he would've done something to me. Something much worse than a black eye and bruised limbs. Those I can cover up and heal from, but the emotional and mental—the invisible pain—that's what I need to work through."

"I get it," he says with a small smile. "If you want me to go with you, I will."

"Thanks, I appreciate it. But this is something I need to do on my own."

Mason nods and stands. "Well, let's get your bookcase in here so you can organize all your books because I know you're dying to," he tells me with a soft chuckle.

I shrug with a smirk. "Maybe. But how? Should I do by spine color? Genre? Author?"

Mason reaches for me and pulls me out of bed. With his arms wrapped around me, I melt into his hard chest and inhale his fresh just-out-of-the-shower scent. "Oh, sweet Sophie. What am I gonna do with you?"

My insides nearly burst when he calls me that. It brings back every single memory of that night together, and my stomach flutters just thinking about it.

Then he kisses my forehead, letting his lips linger for a moment longer than necessary before he pulls away and leads me out of the room with our hands still joined.

It feels weird being around people grieving those they love and miss. I don't plan to reveal my whole story or the truth of why I'm here. There's no easy explanation, and these people are strangers to me, which makes me feel slightly uncomfortable.

The moment I enter, my guard goes up, and I'm not sure I can do this. With my head down, I walk to the snack table and grab a cookie. I realized it's stale and grab a Styrofoam cup for coffee instead.

"Unless you have a death wish, I wouldn't drink that," a deep voice next to me says. The rasp of it commands my attention, and goose bumps surface across my arms. Rough and low. A slight accent, I think. The moment I look at him, I realize how much it doesn't match his physical appearance. He flashes a warm smile with straight white teeth, and it takes a minute to realize he's waiting for me to respond.

"Is that so? Think someone poisoned it?" I smirk, putting the cup back to be safe.

He rewards me with a nice-sounding chuckle, his eyes sparkling under the lights. "Might as well be…" Then he leans in close—almost too close. "But I'm pretty sure it's decade-old instant coffee. The elder church ladies here don't let anything go to waste."

"Ah…" I say, putting the pieces together. "So what you're saying is I should've brought my own?" I eye the paper cup in his hand.

He holds it up proudly. "Yep. I got here early and made the mistake of trying it, nearly choking to death. So I made a quick trip across the street to the cafe."

I smile, the weight of my anxiety slowly releasing from my chest.

"I'm Caleb, by the way," he says, holding out his free hand. "It's nice to meet you."

"Sophie." I shake it. "You too. Oh, and thanks for the warning. I appreciate it. My roommate usually makes the coffee in the morning, but I was running late."

"My pleasure." Caleb's bright blue eyes meet mine as a wide grin splits his face. "Well, I think we're about to start, but I'll give you my number afterward so if you're running late next time, I'll grab an extra coffee for you."

My eyes widen, my insides fluttering with confusion.

"Sorry, that came out a bit too strong, huh?" He frowns, placing a hand over his chest. "I only meant that as a friend. Surprisingly, I'm not very good at socializing."

"Could've fooled me," I quip. "And no, it's fine. My guard is a little up."

"Totally understand." Caleb flashes another warm smile that has me breathing easier now that I realize he's not hitting on me.

The minister from the church announces for us to find our seats. The chairs are in a circle, and it seems so formal. I follow Caleb and sit next to him.

A woman sits beside me in the empty chair. "First time?"

I nod. "That obvious?"

She shrugs. "Yeah, but don't worry. Everyone is very kind and supportive here. They've become like my second family."

"That's good to know." I hold my hand out toward her, trying to come out of my shell a little and participate as much as I'm capable of. "I'm Sophie."

"Dacia." She takes my hand with an assertive nod. "Nice to meet ya."

The room goes silent as the minister stands, introduces himself, and welcomes everyone. Pastor Jude is probably in his fifties, soft spoken, and has a kind smile. He mentions how happy he is to see a few new faces, directing his gaze at Caleb and me.

I learn so much in the one-hour discussion. Dacia lost her twin brother unexpectedly six months ago to a drug overdose and blames herself. It's heartbreaking to hear her talk about her grief and the struggle she has accepting she couldn't help him. I catch myself tearing up a few times, oddly grateful I'm not suffering in that capacity.

I've decided not to share too much and dip my toe in just enough to participate. Mostly because I don't know how to explain what I'm feeling to strangers, but I also don't want to get too personal, especially if I don't plan on returning.

Caleb lost his wife only a few months ago, which makes me feel like scum when I thought he was flirting with me earlier. I can tell he's distraught over her and talks so warmly about his late wife, Sarah, who tragically died in a car accident.

The others share and talk about their stories too. So many others. Parents. Siblings. Spouses. One woman lost her child only a month ago.

The tears in my eyes aren't for Weston, though. They're for everyone here who lost someone they truly loved and cared for, and that brings a whole new perspective to what I'm going through.

I walk out with Caleb and decide to give him my number anyway. It might be nice to have a friend who doesn't look at me with pity and sadness.

"You remind me of someone," I tell him once we've reached the parking lot. "You must have one of those faces."

Caleb chuckles, then brushes his hand over his jaw that's

covered with a few days of old stubble. "I've heard that a time or two."

"Well, you do kind of have that tall, dark, and charming vibe so—"

He arches a brow, and I cringe as soon as the words spew out of my mouth. "Oh my God. That came out all wrong."

"It's okay. My wife used to make comments all the time about being the cliché of a romance hero in one of her books. Then she'd say I wasn't allowed to leave the house looking like one."

There's a glimmer of sadness in his eyes as he talks about her, and my heart squeezes at how much pain he must be in.

"I'm so sorry to hear about your wife. I can tell you love her a lot."

"I won't lie and say it hasn't been hard. My friend is the one who told me to come to one of these meetings and give it a try…" He shrugs casually. "So here I am."

"Yeah, my sister suggested it to me as well. I'm not sure if I'll come back, though."

"No?"

My shoulders rise and fall, my mind going through a range of thoughts. "I haven't decided yet."

"Fair enough."

Before I can get into my car, Dacia walks up. "Anyone else drink that coffee in there?"

Caleb and I look at each other and break out into laughter.

"I swear, it was like a million days old! There's a cafe across the street. Would you guys want to go? Or if you have plans, don't worry about it." Dacia glances between us.

She's in her late twenties or early thirties and has long legs and skinny hips. Honestly, she's gorgeous with jet black hair and light-colored eyes, and the fact she's sweet and kind only adds to her appeal.

Before I can respond, Caleb answers. "Sure, I have a few minutes to spare."

"Yeah, me too," I reply.

We ended up sitting at the cafe for almost two hours. I haven't laughed that much in so long. Part of me felt guilty about it, considering we were at a grieving circle talking about death and the emotional roller coaster it brings. However, Dacia explained how she overcame the dark days. She talks to her brother and believes he's listening and watching over her. It's what brings the light back into her life.

I thought it was super sweet, but I have no urge to talk about Weston. It's hard to explain how I'm not missing *him*, but I nod along so I don't look like a crazy person who's glad her boyfriend is gone so he can't hurt her ever again.

Before we leave, the three of us exchange numbers, and I agree to see them at the next meeting, though part of me still isn't sure I want to return. If anything, it's been nice to meet some new people who I might eventually feel comfortable opening up to. Perhaps one day, when I'm not anxious about what their reactions might be, I can share my story about Weston's and my relationship.

"How'd it go?" Mason asks as soon as I walk into the kitchen. "You were gone for a while."

He digs through the fridge and pulls out random things, which makes me wonder what the hell he's doing.

"I ended up meeting a couple of people, and we went to the cafe across the street to chat. It was okay, I guess. Weird. I didn't go into too many details." I shrug, reaching for the packet of shredded cheese he tossed on the counter. "What're you doing?"

"Making a taco salad. Want some?" he asks, reaching for the can of diced tomatoes to open it.

"You're cooking?" I chuckle. "Since when?"

Narrowing his eyes, he swipes the cheese from my fingers. "I cook. I just haven't been in the mood, but I'm starving and can only eat so much takeout before I feel like shit."

"Good point." I smile, grabbing the lettuce. "I'll chop this."

We work side by side, making easy conversation while I mix the greens with tomatoes, cheese, and olives, per his request. Mason cooks the meat while I crush a bag of Doritos and add it in with sour cream. Once we're done, we toss everything together with some taco sauce and scoop it into two bowls before we sit in the living room.

"It's so good," I moan around my first forkful.

"What is that?" Liam asks, walking down the stairs and putting on a shirt. As soon as he takes the last step, his nose scrunches as he sniffs our salads. "I smell something delicious."

Mason and I both snort. "Did you only come out of your cave because you smelled food?"

"Actually, I was sleeping, and it woke me up. Now where is it? What is it? I want some."

"You're such a man-child." I snicker. "Taco salad. Kitchen."

Mason clicks to Netflix, and we eat while watching *Lucifer*. Things between us have become so comfortable, and any awkwardness that lingered before the incident is long gone. I love hanging out with them, even if the circumstances aren't ideal.

"Dude, you guys are way behind on this show," Liam says, plopping down on the couch, and it makes me bounce a little.

"No spoilers!" I point my fork at him.

"Don't worry. I'm on a new show anyway," Liam says, taking a gigantic bite. He acts like he hasn't eaten in a week, which I find hilarious since he eats nonstop.

"Which one?"

"I'm not telling you."

"What?" I squeal. "Why not? What I'd do?"

Mason laughs, and I look at him confused. "He's probably embarrassed to admit he's watching a chick show."

"Aww…Hulk. Don't be," I tease, using the nickname Maddie sometimes calls him, which I think he secretly likes.

"Don't call me that. And I'm not embarrassed, but I don't need to hear your judgments." He keeps his focus on his food and the TV. He tenses anytime Maddie is around, but who knew calling him that would have the same effect? *This is good to know.*

"I think it's a cute nickname," I say, setting my bowl down on the coffee table, then moving closer to him so I can wrap my arm around his shoulders. "C'mon, tell me!" I beg, sticking out my lower lip and giving him my best puppy dog face. "I swear I won't tease you. Maybe it'll be one I want to watch with you?"

Liam groans, making a point not to look at me. "Fine. But you can't give me any shit. Got it?"

I smile, giddy. "I'd never."

"*Hart of Dixie,*" he murmurs, lowering his face to shove another large bite into his mouth as if that'll cover up what he said.

"Oh my God! I love that show!" I squeeze his arm and give him a side hug. "Now we can watch it together!"

Mason's laughter tears my gaze toward him as he shakes his head with a goofy grin on his face.

"Shut up, fucker," Liam snaps.

"Time to turn in your man card, dude."

I shuffle back to my spot on the couch, then grab my bowl of food. "Don't be so mean!" I playfully smack his arm. "It *is* a good show."

Liam extends his arm toward Mason and flips him the bird. "I swear, you two are toddlers."

"But I'm your favorite, right, Sophie?" Liam goads with a smug smirk.

"Of course. My favorite shit-stirrer," I tease.

CHAPTER TWENTY

MASON

I KNOW Liam and Sophie are just friends, and their friendship has been solid since they met, but I'm still jealous as hell of it.

I pushed her away all that time, pretending our bathroom quickie never happened, and have been kicking my own ass for it. Seeing them hang out and grow closer makes me wonder if that's where our friendship is leading too. Though I'm the reason it never turned into anything more, I'd be a liar if I said I wasn't tired of fighting my feelings for her, especially after everything we've been through.

After we finish our food and an episode of *Lucifer*, Sophie steals the remote and turns on Liam's chick show. I pretend to be annoyed with it, but after the first episode, I'm actually interested. But I'm not admitting that to either of them.

Hell, Rachel Bilson rocks a pair of short shorts and high heels like it's nobody's business.

Yep, that's what I'm going with. Just in case either of them asks or makes a comment about why I watched it with them all damn night long.

Sophie's up early the next morning for her first day back to work, and when I see her zombie-walk into the kitchen toward the coffeemaker, I smile at how cute she looks after rolling out of bed.

"Morning," I say, leaning against the counter with my own cup. I'm so used to being up early for work, and since I plan to go back as soon as fucking possible, I'm not about to eff up that schedule by sleeping all day. Whenever my dad decides to lift my ridiculous "leave" and says I'm in the clear.

"Hey." Her voice is gruff.

"You okay?" I arch a brow.

She blinks and nods before pouring a large cup of coffee. I shuffle around her and grab her creamer from the fridge.

"Thanks. And yeah, I'm just tired."

"Stayed up too late? Reading?" I probe, wondering what kept her up. We all stopped watching TV around eleven then crashed.

"No, Caleb texted me shortly after I went to my room, and we ended up talking for two hours. Then I couldn't fall asleep right away."

I don't hide my disapproval as my brows shoot up. "Caleb? Who's that?"

"Oh, he's one of the people I met at the grieving circle I told you about. We went to the cafe afterward."

I rack my brain, scratching the back of my head as I try to recall her mentioning one of those people was a guy. "Oh. Didn't realize you were on texting terms already."

Sophie tilts her head as if she's trying to read my thoughts. Shit. I straighten my spine and give her a look of indifference. "I mean…well, you just met. Seems quick, that's all."

She shrugs as she takes her first sip. "Yeah, I guess. He lost his wife a few months ago, and I think he needs an ear to listen. It was his first meeting, too."

Well, now I feel like a piece of shit for making assumptions.

"Oh. That's sad. How old is he?" I ask, shuffling around the kitchen so she can't see my face. Maybe he's eighty, and I'm worrying for nothing.

"Early thirties, I'd guess."

Fuck. Or not.

Sophie digs into the fridge and sets a carton of eggs, milk, and shredded cheese to the counter. "I'm gonna make some scrambled eggs. Want some?" she asks casually, grabbing a glass bowl and a whisk from the drawer.

"Uh, no thanks. I'm gonna work out first." I finish the rest of my coffee before setting the cup in the sink.

"I was thinking, if you guys wouldn't mind, maybe we could have a little dinner party here sometime?" Sophie asks as she cracks an egg, keeping her focus in front of her.

Standing close, I lean against the counter while she mixes her ingredients together. "A dinner party?"

Sophie finally meets my eyes and shrugs. "Yeah, like where I make food and people come over to eat." She smirks.

I snort, shaking my head. "I know what a dinner party is. But why?"

"Well, I'd like to invite Caleb and Dacia, the girl I met there too, and thought it'd be nice to introduce everyone. Dacia lost her twin brother, and Caleb lost his wife. They'd probably like to hang out with people outside the grieving circle."

"You just met them," I say accusingly. "They could be serial killers for all we know."

Sophie glares at me, then rolls her eyes. "Your job has made you jaded."

"No, I've always been jaded," I quip to cover up the fact that it's true. Jaded since I found my girlfriend unconscious five years ago.

"They're both very nice, and after talking to Caleb last night, I got the impression he's lonely and could use some friends."

"Sounds like he wants to get in your pants," I blurt without thinking and am immediately awarded with the Sophie death glare.

"Seriously? Why can't a guy and a girl be friends without the expectation of sex?" She starts whisking with a little rage. "Oh wait…" She glances with a sneer.

"C'mon, you know that's not what I meant. I don't want you to be taken advantage of because…well, you're nice, Soph, and sweet and kind. And guys who are *lonely* will use that to get close to you. I don't want you to get hurt again," I tell her sincerely.

"It's only a dinner party," she tells me, reaching for a pan and pushing me aside so she can reach the stovetop. "Plus, I'll invite Hunter and my sisters, and you guys can all see for yourselves that he's harmless."

"Alright, fine." I give in because she'll win anyway.

"Yay!" she squeals. "Thank you. Tell Liam he's coming too."

Sophie returns to work the week of July Fourth and performs at the park like previous years. We all go and watch, and although I'm supposed to be keeping a low profile, I refuse to miss it. I study her as she plays her violin, and it's captivating as always. The way her body moves and works the instrument, the intense way she concentrates as her eyes read over the music, it's addictive to watch, and I'm mesmerized by her.

When she's gone, I find myself missing her. She works during the day and gives violin lessons a couple of nights a week, plus she's been going to her grieving circle and meeting up with Caleb and Dacia. Sophie's keeping herself occupied, and I hope she's giving herself time to work through her issues.

Two weeks after the incident, I'm allowed to go back to work and can keep my mind busy instead of having my dark thoughts consume me. Between that, being forced to stay home, and thinking about Sophie, it's good to finally have something to do. Though after a long day, I enjoy coming home and seeing her as much as I can. We watch Netflix, make food or order dinner, and then end up hanging out until we're both ready to crash for the night. Liam is home sometimes, but he's been gone for work a lot lately, especially this time of year. Sometimes Maddie swings by, and then the four of us end up in some weird group non-date.

On nights when it's just the two of us, sometimes she reads on the couch, and I have to actively concentrate on not getting a hard-on while her feet rest in my lap. It's not her feet, but how she allows me to glide my fingers across her cute toes. She made a comment once about her feet aching, so I offered to rub them, and now I find it hard to keep my hands away. Even if it's as *friends*, a part of me can't help those feelings of wanting *more*. If we crossed those lines, we'd never be able to return to being friends like this. As both of us are still dealing with our demons, it's not the right time. The timing is always wrong, but damn, how I wish it were right.

It's one of those nights when Liam is out and Maddie has dance class, so Sophie and I will be alone. I have no desire to go out like before. I like knowing where Sophie is, and that she's safe. She probably thinks I have no life outside these walls, but I don't want that life anymore. Hustling at work to make sure that promotion stays mine and protecting Sophie are my priorities now.

After work, I head to the gym for an hour, and then I come home to shower. The moment I walk in and hear Sophie sniffling in the living room, my heart pounds with concern.

"Soph?" I ask, dropping my workout bag and walking toward her. She has a book propped up on her knees as she lounges back on the cushions, and I hear her suck in a deep breath as she cries harder. "Hey." I shake her shoulder a bit, and she startles, whipping her book as she jumps.

I put both hands up in surrender, stepping back. "It's just me."

She yanks out her earbuds I didn't realize she was wearing and scowls. "You scared me to death!"

"Is that why you threw your ten-pound book at me?" I snicker, then reach down to grab it off the floor.

"It was a knee-jerk reaction," she says defensively. When I hand it back, she wipes her tears away. Her eyes are red and cheeks flushed.

Stepping closer, I cup her face and study her. "Are you okay? Were you crying?"

Sophie's eyes flutter before her head leans into my palm. But then as if an alarm went off, she snaps back into place and pulls away. "I was reading and listening to music, and the combo made me emotional."

She sets her book down and then rounds the coffee table and walks toward the kitchen. "How was your day? And your workout? I should've known you were home. You smell sweaty."

She's rambling, which usually means she's nervous. The thought makes me smile because, after all this time, I'd assume she wouldn't be. Especially if she only saw me as a friend.

I follow her and respond. "All good. Glad to be back although we're dealing with some intense cases. Gives me good fuel for my boxing, though." I reach into the fridge for a bottle of water, then suck it down. "How was your day? Anything exciting?"

Sophie walks around me, grabbing items out of the fridge as she speaks. "It was fine. We're working on some new music, so that's always fun. Found a new client for some tutoring lessons and that starts in a week, which is nice. Otherwise, same ole, same ole. Lennon and Maddie met me for lunch, I went to grief circle and then had coffee with Caleb. Oh, that reminds me—"

Checking the time on my phone, it's close to eight and I didn't realize it was so late. She sure kept busy, though.

"Would you mind if we did the dinner party this Saturday night? I cleared it with everyone else's schedule, so if you're free, I'll make it official and get started on the menu."

"The menu? How fancy are we talking here?" I lean against the counter as she sets a pan on the stovetop and starts cooking the meat. There's cheese, lettuce, sour cream, and tomatoes on the counter, which means she's making tacos, my favorite.

"I have the main course narrowed down to three items, so I'm still deciding, but I'm thinking formal wear. Not suit and tie fancy, but please take ten minutes to shower…"

As she continues talking about appetizers and side dishes, a part of me is worried she's drowning herself to avoid her true feelings. She's talked about it some, but it's been a while since she's mentioned it. She goes to her grief circle, but I don't know how much she opens up there. It's been a month since the incident, and I wonder if she's blocked it out of her mind entirely. Hopefully, the meetings she's attending are helping, especially since it's essentially become a weekly routine for her.

I've done enough schooling to know this is a common occurrence for trauma victims. They go into shock or block it out, which is an avoidance tactic. The shit that asshole put her through was enough to traumatize anyone. Considering how things ended, I wouldn't be surprised if she deals with it without *actually* dealing with it.

After she finishes cooking, she sets everything out and hands me a plate of two tacos, made the way I like them.

"Thank you, Sophie." I reach for her wrist so she'll stop moving for a second. She's hell-bent on racing a million miles per hour. "You didn't have to cook for me, but I appreciate it, especially since you made tacos."

"Well, I was starving waiting for you and contemplated eating without you." She grins, and it makes my heart pound harder.

"You didn't have to wait for me," I say, releasing her. "Now I feel bad."

"Nah, don't. I was caught up in my book anyway." She waves me off, but I don't miss the hint of blush on her cheeks. It's as if being caught doing something nice has given her true feelings away.

We take our plates and drinks to the living room and settle on the couch.

"So what book are you reading anyway? And why did it make you cry?" I ask before taking a massive bite.

"Don't make fun. I was reading a romance novel, and the main characters can't be together, which makes my chest ache. The angst and tension are intense." I study her as she talks about them as if they're real people. "And before you say anything, yes, I know it's just fiction."

I chuckle when she rolls her eyes. "Damn, you reading my mind now?"

"I've learned a lot about you this past month." She smirks.

"Then I was reading it while listening to a sad song, and my heart shredded."

Once we finish eating, I clean up since she cooked, then get in the shower. Considering I'm living the plot of her damn romance novel, constantly fighting my feelings because I can't be with *her*, my showers last until the water runs cold. I pump my cock over and over until I release all over the wall and curse myself for feeling this way about her. Pissed I missed my damn chance. The more time we spend together, the harder it gets to fight my heart.

By the time I'm done, it's almost ten o'clock, and I'm exhausted, but I don't want to miss the opportunity to watch one of our shows before bed. It's become tradition, and no matter how tired I am, I'll stay up with her.

I'm surprised to see she isn't in the living room when I come down, and when I peek into her bedroom, I notice she's fallen asleep with her book. Walking inside, I click her lamp on and place her book on the nightstand. Then I grab an extra blanket and cover her body since she's lying on top of her comforter. She looks exhausted, too. Before walking away, I brush a hand over her face and kiss her forehead.

"Good night, sweet Sophie."

I close her door halfway before walking out.

I should go to bed too, but now my thoughts are running all over, so I sit on the couch and turn on the TV. She'll kill me if I watch *Lucifer* without her, so I click on Liam's stupid show and watch all the Southern drama on the screen.

My eyelids are heavy, and when I can't fight it any longer, I eventually lie down. Only a moment passes before I can no longer hear the TV, and I'm drifting off to sleep. I don't know how much time has passed when I hear wailing and nearly fly off the couch. I rub my eyes and blink until I can read the time on my phone. It's after three in the morning, and when I hear the noise again, I realize it's coming from Sophie's room.

She's groaning and grinding her teeth. I push open the door and step inside, the light from her lamp shining on her face that's scrunched and moving from side to side.

Fuck, she's having a nightmare.

Rushing to her side, I bend down and carefully shake her shoulders while whispering her name. I try to prepare for her to head butt me or claw at me, so I don't get too close right away.

"Sophie, baby. Wake up," I say a little louder, adding more pressure to her shoulder. "You're dreaming."

She blinks her eyes open, looking all around and then focusing on me. Her chest is rising and falling rapidly, and her forehead is covered in sweat.

"Are you okay?" I ask softly.

Her breathing is shallow, and I place my hand over her cheek to reassure her that she's safe.

"Yeah, I think so," she finally responds, pushing her palms into her eyes. "Just an intense dream that felt way too real."

"Sorry if I woke you."

"Nothing to be sorry for, Soph. I'll grab you a bottle of water, hold on," I tell her as she sits up and nods.

Once I'm back, she takes it and sucks half of it before setting it down. "Thank you."

"Do you want to talk about it?" I ask, cautiously.

She sucks in her lower lip, not meeting my gaze. "It was about Weston," she answers. "When he'd drink a lot and—"

I grit my teeth, my jaw locking tight at the thought of his hands on her. "I'm so sorry, Soph. I wish so many times I would've intervened sooner."

She shrugs, finally looking at me. "I doubt it would've helped. I didn't see what was right in front of me, and by the time I did, it was too late. I felt trapped and knew getting out would be hard, impossible even. I pushed everyone away because I was ashamed and afraid he'd hurt you all too."

"None of it was your fault," I reassure her. "I'm sorry it's haunting you in your sleep."

"It started last week, which is weird because they didn't start right away. But this one felt a little too real. Makes me feel like he'll show up and finish the job of what he wanted to do to me and you."

There's a tear that she tries to wipe away, but I cup her face with both hands, then kiss her forehead. "I'm here. He's never gonna hurt you again."

She nods, then takes me by surprise when she wraps her arms around me and pulls me close. "I'm so thankful for you, Mason." Sophie hugs me as if I'll disappear the minute she lets go.

Fuck, I want to say so much to her right now. Tell her how sorry I am for treating her the way I did before, for not seeing how amazing she is, for not being strong enough to work through my own shit back then so I could give us a proper chance. All the what-ifs, the could've-beens that I'm constantly pushing away.

"I'm here, Soph. Always," I tell her when she releases me. "Move over." I nod my head toward her bed so she understands what I'm doing. Maybe it's selfish, but it's for her too.

Sophie scoots to the far side of the bed, and I slide in behind her. I wrap my arms around her as she rests her head on my chest, and I hold her as though we're more than just friends.

After a half an hour, I still can't sleep. My mind is way too alert that Sophie is tucked into my body. She's flipped over so my chest is to her back, and we're spooning. I haven't done this in years… since Emma. It brings a lot of emotions to the surface, but these are different. I like how it feels to hold Sophie. To touch her. My hand on her stomach rubs against her bare skin from where her shirt slid up. She's so soft and smooth, and my heart pounds at the intimacy of it all. I should stop, get out of her bed, and go to my own room now that she's sound asleep again, but I don't.

I reluctantly leave before her alarm goes off and take another long shower before I go to work. I'm dead ass tired but regret nothing. Holding her for hours was as much for her as it was for me. I wanted to give her more time after Weston's death and the shitstorm relationship he caused, but my willpower is ready to snap as I keep my feelings tucked away. I can no longer pretend, no longer hold back the feelings screaming to come out, and can no longer pretend I don't deserve her anymore.

But I'm not sure she's ready to hear my truths.

CHAPTER TWENTY-ONE

MASON

SOPHIE'S BEEN RUNNING around the house all day, cleaning, cooking, and stressing over all these tiny details. I can't tell if it's nerves or if it's a coping mechanism. I've asked if I can help with anything a dozen times, and she gives me stupid little tasks such as making sure my room is clean. When I asked her why it mattered, I got some half-ass reasoning as she waved me away.

It's to a point where I'm a little worried so I go against my better judgment and text her sisters in case I should be concerned or if this is something she does.

MASON

> Your sister is cleaning like a mad woman. Is this her normal nervous behavior?

LENNON

> What kind of cleaning are we talking here?

MADDIE

> Well, she does live with two guys. I'd be cleaning like a crazy person too.

I roll my eyes at her jab.

MASON

Well, she's currently mopping the ceiling…

MADDIE

Oh shit.

MASON

What?

LENNON

That's level red.

MASON

Meaning what?

LENNON

She's gone manic.

MADDIE

Without even having to take the good stuff.

MASON

What the fuck are you two talking about?
English, please!

LENNON

You know when a person takes Adderall who
doesn't need it so instead of it calming them
down, it does the opposite effect? That's Sophie
without having to take meds.

I'm growing more uneasy with each text they send back.

MASON

What triggers it? Nerves?

LENNON

Stress, anxiety, emotional breakdown.

MADDIE

It's happened a few times before.

MASON

WTF? So what am I supposed to do? How do I
help her?

LENNON

Honestly, you're better off leaving her alone and
letting it run its course. She pretends to be
strong for so long before her emotions bubble
over and she's forced to deal with it.

I'm not sure I should tell them about the nightmare she had a
few nights ago, so to avoid getting on Sophie's shit list, I keep it to
myself. Honestly, they may already know anyway.

MASON

Well, I'm concerned because she's running
around with her earbuds in, and I don't think
she's stopped moving in three hours.

MADDIE

Get her to drink some OJ or some kind of juice.
It'll level out her blood sugars.

MASON

Okay. Anything else?

LENNON

If you can calm her without freaking her out, that
might work to settle her nerves.

MADDIE

Banging her up against a door might work.

LENNON

Maddie!

MADDIE

It's a valid suggestion!

MASON

Jesus Christ.

LENNON

Ignore her.

MADDIE

Rude!

MASON

Thanks for all your help…

LENNON

She'll be okay. Just be there for her.

I lock my phone and tuck it into my pocket. Fuck, I don't know what to do.

After hearing rattling in the kitchen, I jump off the couch and head toward her. With shaking hands, she grabs the dinner plates from the cabinet. Since I tower over her, I grab them from behind her before she drops them on the floor.

"Oh, thanks. They were a little higher up than I could reach. Can you grab those glasses for me too? I've polished the silverware, so those are good to go. Now I need to find a nice serving tray and—" She's rambling so fast I can barely keep up with what she's saying. Once I set the plates down on the counter, I grab Sophie's shoulders and turn her around so she's forced to face me. Her eyes widen at the sudden movement as I steady her.

"Soph, slow down," I firmly tell her. "You're running in circles around the place and—"

"I'm fine. I don't have time to slow down. The party starts in a few hours, and I have a million more things to do and—"

Thinking about what her sisters said, I say to hell with it and improvise. Before she can speak another word, I cup her face and slant my mouth over hers, fusing our lips together. After a couple of seconds, her body relaxes against mine as if she's giving me permission to continue.

Knowing I can't let this go much longer, as much as I fucking want it to, I reluctantly pull away. Tasting Sophie again after all this time might be the death of me.

I stare down as she catches her breath, and I wonder if she's going to slap me. When she finally blinks up at me, confusion is written all over her face.

"What was that for?" she asks softly, bringing a finger up to her lips.

"You were starting to lose it and clearly needed to be brought back down to earth," I tell her, hoping the excuse is valid enough for her to believe. "You're stressing out, Soph."

"So…kissing me was to shock me or something?" she asks, and I can't tell if she's offended or relieved I snapped her out of it.

Swallowing, I release my hold on her and brush a hand through my hair. I'm not sure how I'm supposed to answer or if I should reveal what her sisters told me.

"You were freaking me out. Sorry, I shouldn't have done that. I wanted you to slow down before you—"

"No, I got it. It's fine," she says, her voice sharp. "*I'm fine.*"

"Let me help. Please."

Sophie nods, and her chest is still rapidly moving. That kiss was maybe ten seconds, but it was the best one I've had in a long time. Since the last time I kissed her three years ago.

"You can set the table, and I'll finish prepping the food."

"Deal."

When the doorbell rings a few hours later, Sophie is mostly back to her normal self. I can tell she's a bit anxious, but it's better than before. I answer the door to greet Hunter, Lennon, Allie, and Maddie.

"Hey, man. Hey, there's my favorite little lady." I reach over and kiss Allie's cheek.

"What am I? Chopped liver?" Maddie steps in around me, scoffing.

"Don't mind her. She's sexually frustrated." Lennon snickers, handing Allie off to Hunter. I usher them into the living room where Liam is already waiting with a case of beer. He wasn't too excited about this formal dinner either, but I reminded him it was for Sophie, so he caved.

"Soph, your sisters are here," I call up the stairs. She's been in the bathroom for almost an hour.

"Coming!"

"She doing better?" Lennon leans over and whispers.

I take two beers and hand one to Hunter before twisting the cap off mine. "Yeah, I did what Maddie suggested, and she's all good now."

Hunter nearly chokes on his beer, looking up at me. By his reaction, my guess is Lennon read him our text messages.

"Really?" Maddie squeals, and Lennon scowls at her for being so loud.

"No!" I narrow my eyes.

"Pussy," Maddie whispers.

"You've got quite the foul mouth," I taunt, then glance at Liam, who's purposely avoiding the conversation.

"So, Hulk. You ready to make a woman out of me yet?"

Maddie has balls, I'll definitely give her that. She's young, probably too young for Liam, but she doesn't let that deter her from hitting on him as often as she can.

"I don't mess around with jailbait," he throws out before taking a long swig of his beer.

"I'm twenty!" she argues. "Do I need to show y'all my driver's license? I'm not a kid."

Lennon chuckles, and I shake my head. Poor Liam doesn't know what to do with a woman like Maddie. Though he should be used to girls throwing themselves at him, Maddie isn't just some girl. She's in our inner circle, and she's not the hit-it-and-quit-it kind. He's smart to keep his distance even if Maddie is a hell of a catch.

Before any of us can answer her, Sophie comes downstairs, happily greeting her sisters and niece. I look at her, nearly choking on the air around me as I take in how gorgeous she is. Her long, dark hair is curled in waves with a long braid wrapped around the crown of her head to look like a headband. I've only ever seen her hair like that once since we've known each other—the night we met. She's wearing a pink dress that settles above her knees and hugs her waist, pushing her breasts high. It must be new because I didn't see it in her closet when I helped her unpack. Her face is done with makeup, which she doesn't wear that often either. And her lips. Red, smooth kissable lips.

She's *stunning*.

Her eyes catch mine, and I don't even care that she caught me staring. Sophie watches as I study her, wanting to memorize every curve. I linger on her face for a moment, then scan down her body and back up again. "You look beautiful," I mouth and smile when she blushes.

Before I can walk toward her, the doorbell rings again. Sophie rushes to the door, but I don't follow her. Fuck, her guests are here.

Just get through this one night, I remind myself. I can do it for Sophie.

I hear a man's voice followed by Sophie's laughter. My guard rises, and I wait impatiently for her to walk him in here.

"Where's Dacia?" she asks. I don't hear his response, but then Sophie speaks again. "Oh, too bad. I hope she feels better soon."

Piecing it together the moment I see only him, I realize Dacia isn't coming.

"Hey guys, this is Caleb Royce," she announces the moment they come into view.

I look up and see a man who is way too close to Sophie, being too friendly, and smiling way too wide at her. A man who doesn't look like he's just lost his wife.

Everyone around me greets him, but my jaw is locked tight, and I freeze as I study him.

"These are my roommates, Liam and Mason. My sisters, Lennon and Maddie. My future brother-in-law, Hunter and my adorable niece, Allie."

"Wow, it's nice to meet you all."

Caleb stands tall, about my height. He's broad like me, too, and I can tell he's older, by five years at least. We're all standing, but I don't like how close he is to her and see red the second he wraps an arm around Sophie's waist and leans in to whisper something into her ear.

"Dude, you need to chill," Liam whispers loud enough for

only me to hear. "I can see you're tense as fuck, and if Sophie notices, she's gonna get anxious again."

I unlock my jaw and try to shake it off, knowing Liam's right. "I don't have a good feeling. Haven't since the day she's mentioned him."

"Give him a chance at least before you start throwing punches." He snickers.

I roll my eyes and jab my elbow into his ribs. "Funny."

Sophie tells us to come sit at the table because she has appetizers and the main course will be ready in ten minutes. Following them, I wait until we're all in the dining room before I plan to offer to help her bring stuff in. Before I can say anything, Caleb is at Sophie's side, telling her he'll assist her.

I sit across from Lennon, who pierces me with her hard gaze. Apparently, I'm more transparent than I thought I was. Sophie's laughter from the kitchen echoes, and Caleb's follows, driving the knife in my gut deeper.

Less than fifteen minutes later, we're all sitting and eating Sophie's delicious meal. I relax slightly when she takes the seat next to me, but Caleb is on her other side, and I have to lean forward to keep my eye on him.

Between Lennon and Maddie, the conversation flows. Caleb opens up about his late wife, and when Liam glares at me, I know he thinks I'm overreacting. But after the shit that went down with Weston, I'm always on high alert when it comes to Sophie and her safety. Hell, if Liam wasn't a longtime friend, I wouldn't trust him around her either.

"Babe, I forgot the diaper bag in the truck," Lennon tells Hunter.

"Gimme the keys and I'll go grab it." I stand before either of them can protest.

"Sure. Thanks," Hunter says, reaching into his pocket and handing them over. "It's in the back seat."

I head outside without suspicion and can look at this guy's car for any clues whether he's an actual decent guy. Once I grab the bag from their truck, I walk to the street where he parked and laugh when I find a Ford Taurus. An old ass one too.

Grabbing my phone from my pocket, I quickly snap a pic of his license plates, then I peek into his windows. There are a couple of duffle bags in the back, a pair of shoes on the floor, and some empty takeout containers.

Is this guy living in his car?

Shaking my head, I head back inside and deliver Allie's bag. After we're finished eating and the table is cleared, Lennon excuses herself and asks Sophie if she can use her bedroom. All the girls follow. Apparently, it takes three of them to change a diaper, which leaves the guys together in the living room.

"Sorry to hear about your wife," Hunter offers. "I lost my best friend last year. I know it's not the same, but—"

"Yeah, thanks." Caleb scrubs his hands over his jeans and nods. "It was quite sudden."

"Can I ask how?" Hunter says.

"Car accident. She was on her way to work in the morning, and I was already at my job. I didn't find out until five hours later when they tracked me down."

"Man, I'm sorry to hear that."

"How about your friend?" Caleb asks.

"Motorcycle accident."

The room goes silent.

Brandon dying changed everything.

"Okay, all clean…" Lennon returns.

"How far along are you?" Caleb asks Lennon when she takes a seat on the couch next to Hunter. "Sophie told me you're expecting again."

"I am!" she beams. "Only two months. We were shocked it happened so fast after Allie," she admits. "But we couldn't be happier." She smiles up at Hunter who cups her face and presses his lips to hers.

"And now you know how she got pregnant so soon," Maddie cracks. "They never have their hands off each other."

"I think it's sweet," Sophie chimes in. "At least one of you men knows how to handle a Corrigan woman." She smirks at Liam who, in return, rolls his eyes.

"Sorry, Soph. You're not my type," he retorts, making all of us laugh, considering we know who she's really talking about. But hell, if that confirmation doesn't send relief through me.

"Why's that funny?" Caleb asks.

"Long story," Hunter says. "That's a story for over a round of beers."

My whole body tenses. I hate that Hunter is being so nice to this asshole.

Sophie excuses herself to check on the dessert. A moment later, she shouts from the kitchen, and I fly off the couch to see if she needs help. She returns before I can and puts on a sad, pitiful face.

"My dessert burned. I forgot to turn the oven temp down after the casserole." Her shoulders slump, and I feel bad, considering how much work she put into tonight.

"Oh, Soph. That's okay," Lennon says, waving her off.

"No, it's not," Sophie retorts. "I'll grab something quick. Stay here, and I'll be right back."

Allie starts to fuss, and Lennon says it's getting close to her feeding and bedtime so they're going to go. Sophie protests but understands the fussier Allie becomes. It gives me hope that this night will come to an end, but as soon as Hunter, Lennon, and Maddie leave, Sophie announces she's going to grab a pie from the store.

"I'll come with you," Caleb offers, and before I can come up with an excuse as to why that's a horrible fucking idea, they're both out the door.

"I hate that guy," I grit between my teeth to Liam. He's on his third beer and shakes his head at me. He thinks it's because I'm jealous, but it's much more than that. "I don't have a good feeling about him. I think he's living in his car."

"He's a widow who's probably connected with Sophie on a different level." He shrugs, but I don't care what he thinks. My gut tells me this guy is bad news.

Once they return, Sophie serves us warm apple pie with New

York vanilla ice cream. I'd say it was delicious if I wasn't so annoyed with Caleb being here too.

"So Caleb, where did you say you worked?"

"I didn't, but I'm a broker at First Financial."

"How long have you been there?"

"About eight years," he replies. "A year after I graduated college."

"Where'd your wife work?"

"Mason!" Sophie shouts, her eyes narrowing in disapproval.

"It's okay," Caleb reassures her, placing his hand on her knee, and it takes all the control I have in the fucking world not to rip his hand off her. "I don't mind talking about her. She was an elementary teacher at St. Mary's. Taught second grade for four years."

"How long were you guys married?" Liam asks.

I give him a mental high five for coming to my side.

"Seven years this fall."

"I think that's *enough*," Sophie says between tight lips.

Once we're finished with dessert, Sophie says she's going to make a pot of coffee, and of course, Caleb follows her like a damn puppy. I'm more than ready to get this night over with, but I'm not leaving him alone with her.

They return with a tray of coffee, and when I realize she forgot her creamer, I head to the fridge and grab it. She's sitting on the couch with Caleb to her right, so I lean over on her left and pour the creamer into her cup. Sophie looks up with a grateful smile and thanks me. I rest my hand on her shoulder and throw her a wink.

As soon as I sit next to her, Caleb turns until their knees are touching and talks about Dacia and another member of their circle, knowing damn well I can't contribute. This guy is pissing me off.

"So, Sophie hasn't told me much about you two," Caleb directs at Liam and me. "What do you do for a living?" he asks, and the condescending tone about how she hasn't mentioned us is crystal clear in his voice.

"Mason works in forensics, or something." She looks and scrunches her nose with an apologetic expression. "What's the technical term?"

"I'm on my way to becoming a forensics investigator. Finished my internships and working at the DA's office until the position opens this fall," I clarify, and the way Caleb's spine straightens has me grinning.

"Wow. That's quite the accomplishment. What do you do at the DA's office?" he asks.

"Mostly bitch work," I say, keeping it as vague as possible. "My dad's the DA."

Caleb swallows.

"And Liam's a bounty hunter." Sophie waves her hands toward him.

"Fugitive recovery agent," he corrects like always, which has us all laughing. "I travel a lot and get to put people back in jail. It's the best job ever." He flashes a shit-eating smirk.

"He thinks it's permission to do whatever he wants." Sophie cackles. "Yet I've never seen you lose your temper since I've known you."

"Because I know how to contain myself. Good restraint and willpower," Liam responds. "Until the situation calls for something else."

Sophie snorts. "Liam thinks smacking guys around on the job—"

"Only if they throw the first punch," he interrupts. "Or they resist."

"Neither of you have been married?" Caleb abruptly changes the subject, and I want him out of my damn house.

"No," Sophie answers with a laugh before either of us can. "The only woman I've ever heard of being in this house is their mysterious third roommate who I've never met."

Liam nudges me with a smirk. "You gonna tell her?"

I shrug. "Didn't know it was a huge secret."

"Tell me what?"

"Who it was," Liam answers.

"Were one of you sleeping with her?" Sophie asks.

Neither of us responds.

"Or both of you?" Her attention goes from me to Liam and then back to me. "Never mind, I don't want to know." She looks away, finishing her coffee.

Moments later, Sophie tells Caleb that she's exhausted from cleaning and cooking all day and ushers him to the door. When she thanks him, I peek into the entryway when he leans in and hugs her, then kisses her cheek before walking away. I release a breath when she shuts the door and that dickwad is finally gone.

I quickly sit back on the couch with the remote before she stalks back and stands in front of the TV with both hands on her hips.

"What?" I play dumb.

She scoffs, then rolls her eyes. Grabbing the coffee mugs from the table, she stomps to the kitchen, and I quickly follow behind her.

"You gonna tell me what your problem is or risk breaking all the new china?" I flash her a smug grin, knowing she picked out our dishes and would never throw them. Leaning against the island, I watch as she moves around the kitchen with a scowl.

"Could you two have been ruder to my guest?" she finally snaps.

"Rude? How?" I ask, my voice growing louder.

"I didn't do anything!" Liam says in defense, walking in and grabbing a beer from the fridge. "I was on my best behavior. Mason's the one who thinks he's a serial killer."

I glare at him. "Oh sure, if he doesn't have a warrant out for his arrest, you don't care."

"That's not true," he says, pointing with his unopened beer. "I'd care if he were a sniper."

"You're useless," I mutter, yanking the beer from his hand and walking back to the living room.

A few minutes later, Sophie joins us, her frown still etched on her beautiful face. "You bombarded him with questions about his late wife and personal life. I told you he was still grieving, and you had to bring it up!"

"I was making conversation!" I stand, setting my beer on the table and walking toward her. "You told me to make him feel welcome. Were we supposed to ignore the elephant in the room and talk about the weather?" I wave my arm out, frustrated as fuck that she's upset with *me* over this Caleb douche. "Or maybe why he's living in his car? Why he's touching your knee and leaning into you? Should I have talked about *that*?"

Sophie blinks, takes a step back, then pins me with a glare. "What're you talking about? He wasn't doing those things. Wait. Were you snooping in his car? What the hell is wrong with you?"

Liam chuckles before sneaking around her and going upstairs, leaving me alone with a pissed-off Sophie. *Asshole.*

"Fine, you want to do this now?" I take another step toward her. "He's into you, Sophie. He painted this sob story about his late wife, but I'd bet money he's a fucking liar. You don't check out another woman's ass, find ways to touch them, or get that close to a person you met a few weeks ago after your wife died only three months ago. He'd still be struggling to get out of bed, he'd be drinking himself stupid, he'd be *grieving* the love of his life! You can try to say he's hiding his pain but trust me when I tell you the only thing he's hiding is the truth."

My voice is loud and deep, no longer able to contain my anger from this whole situation. Sophie looks like I've lost my damn mind, and maybe I have, but she means more to me than I've ever admitted.

"Mason…" Sophie croaks. "I think you're misreading him because I don't see any of that. He started at the grieving circle the same day I did because he needed to talk about his feelings and be around people who understood what he's going through."

"How can you not see through his bullshit, Soph? Especially you."

"What's that mean?" She furrows her brows, crossing her arms over her chest.

"You saw firsthand what losing Brandon did to your sister.

What it did to Hunter. If they didn't have each other, they would've been worse. Lennon fought for months about her feelings because she was still in love with Brandon. She tried pushing Hunter away to avoid the guilt of moving on. I wasn't around them that much while they were going through all that shit, yet I could see their pain and struggles."

"Their story is different…"

I arch a brow, daring her to challenge me on that.

"And what would Caleb's motive be then?" she pushes.

"He probably goes from grieving circle to grieving circle to find women like you who lost someone and are vulnerable. How can't you see the way he was looking at you?"

"And why does it matter to you so much how he was looking at me? You've made it crystal clear that we're only friends, so let's say he is lying and wants to get me into bed. Would that be a problem?"

My eyes narrow into slits as I close the gap between us. Sophie steps back until her back touches the wall and we're chest to chest. "You're much more than a side piece, Sophie. More than a quickie in a bar bathroom. So fucking more than some asshole's game."

Sophie inhales sharply, keeping her gaze on me as the tension heightens between us. "You're overthinking this. Everyone grieves differently. It doesn't mean he should stop living his life."

Taking a step back, I suck in a deep breath, and brush both hands through my hair. I clench my jaw, my blood boiling with frustration and anger, and the need to prove my point to her becomes overwhelming.

Can't she see I'm trying to protect her? After Weston, her guard should be up. She shouldn't be letting anyone near her, especially not some guy she met weeks ago. Sophie is too goddamn sweet for her own good. She wants to see the positive in every situation and person, but misses what's right in front of her. I'd be pissed about it if it wasn't one of her best qualities and why I was drawn to her in the first place.

"Sophie." I place my hand on the wall behind her and lean down so we're only inches apart. "The point I'm making is that the fucking last thing you're thinking of when you lose a loved one is how to get another woman into bed with you. Throwing shit, punching walls, contemplating how to take your own life because nothing makes sense—those are things I'd expect to see or hear. The pain, the insufferable guilt that it was her and not you, the dark thoughts that evade your mind. Those first few months after death are intolerable. You'd rather suffer in silence than admit how much pain you're in, but I can guarantee you with every fiber of my being that touching another woman would be the last thing on my mind. Losing your wife should feel like losing half of your own soul. That guy, no matter how good of a front you say he's putting on, did not lose a spouse."

Sophie's chest rises and falls rapidly as if she can't catch her own breath. Her gaze is locked on mine, and her stare is intense as if she's trying to read my mind.

"How do you know that stuff?" she finally asks. "How would a man act after losing his wife?"

I swallow, knowing I can't lie to her. She deserves the truth.

Inhaling a deep breath, I try to mentally prepare myself for a conversation I've never had with anyone, not even the guys because they were around during this time and knew as soon as it all happened. "My girlfriend committed suicide, and it was my fault. I found her, but it was too late. She was already gone." My chest deflates, the words feeling heavy as if they'll smoother me.

Her breath hitches as a hand flies up to cover her mouth. "Mason."

"Even if he's saying his wife died in an accident, trust me when I tell you the grief never goes away. The pain, the guilt, the ache—it lives on eternally."

CHAPTER TWENTY-TWO

ALL THE AIR leaves my lungs as Mason's intense stare sends shivers down my entire body. His revelation has my heart racing as I try to wrap my mind around his words.

"Mason…" I whisper his name again. "I had no idea."

He shakes his head as if he can't believe he shared that part of himself, but I'm glad he did. I want to know everything about him. Mason steps back, putting space between us as he inhales a deep breath.

"Will you tell me about her?" I suck in my lower lip, knowing I'm stepping in unknown territory.

Mason nods as he takes a seat on the couch, and I follow, sitting next to him.

"Her name was Emma. We'd been dating for almost two years, and I was madly in love with her at the time. She was outgoing, unpredictable, spunky."

His voice sounds so broken as he says her name aloud, as if it causes him physical pain to say.

"Things were great until they weren't. She was spiraling before she overdosed, but I was only twenty and thought she was stressing out about school. I was in a frat, partying and rebelling against everything my dad stood for. Without even telling people, they knew who I was because of my last name. At the time, it felt like I had a point to prove, and it wasn't always a good one. I enjoyed getting on my father's nerves. When he'd call, I wouldn't answer, and after a dozen missed calls, he'd show up to check on me. Wanted to make sure his money was going to good use. Then he'd talk to my professors and the dean and send in a donation check to make sure I stayed on the straight and narrow. He barged into my life every damn chance he could, which made me hate him more. I wanted to live my life without him hovering, and at that age, I did whatever it took to piss him off."

I nod, understanding his reasoning although his college experience was different from mine. Though if I had gone to a college closer to home, I can't say my father wouldn't have forced his way into my business either.

"I met Emma in English class my first semester and we were inseparable. She was a wild girl, which is what I liked most about her. I knew it'd drive my dad crazy, so in my head, she was perfect. At the beginning of our sophomore year, she took pills to stay awake longer. That evolved into opioids. She claimed she was only taking them for back pain from sitting because she was studying so much. That should've been a red flag right there because she didn't study nearly as much as she led on. We were together all the time when I wasn't in class or doing my own thing. I noticed how high she was getting from them and told her she needed to stop, but she reassured me it was to get through midterms and then again for finals. She seemed to be in control of her habit, so I stopped pressing the issue, and we stopped fighting.

"A few times, she'd call me in tears, saying she was going to kill herself. I'd rush over and calm her down, stay with her all night until her high wore off. It was happening every couple of weeks, and after a while, I stopped believing her wolf cries and didn't rush over. Each time I'd get there, she'd be rambling about something else, but after a while, I stopped believing she'd take her own life. I didn't know why she would in the first place. I hadn't suspected she was depressed, but afterward, I found out there was a lot I hadn't known about her.

"I begged her to stop taking them, to get help, told her I'd take her to narcotics anonymous—*anything*. I even found her dealer and threatened him with bodily harm if he didn't stop selling to her. It only pissed her off and then found another dealer. I threatened to go to her parents, and she mentioned again how she'd kill herself if I did. I was juggling so much with school, my father, and the stress from trying to keep up. Whatever love Emma and I had for each other was dissolving. She wasn't the girl I had fallen for, and I didn't know how to help her.

"Finally, I reached out to her sister and begged her to help me help her. She was able to get through to her in a way I hadn't, and we'd grown closer while trying to help Emma."

"So she got clean for a while?" I ask, trying to wrap my head around everything he's said.

"No, she got better at disguising it. I tried to be there for her, but everything had put a strain on our relationship. It was the end of our sophomore year when my frat house was having their last party before the summer. She didn't want to go, but I had to, and after a few hours, I was drunk. The year had taken a toll on me, and I went for the beer and alcohol hard. By the time I checked my phone that night, I had six missed calls from her, three missed calls from her sister, eight text messages, and three voicemails."

"Jesus. What happened?" I curl my feet under my body, inching closer to him.

"She texted that she was done, couldn't go on living like this, and wanted to put both of us out of our misery. Claimed I didn't love her anymore so what was the point of living. It was stuff she had said before when she was doped up, so my first reaction was that she was losing her shit again. Her sister left me a voice message to go check on her since she wasn't in town. I reassured her that I would, but then a fight broke out at the party. I got distracted for half an hour trying to break them up and clean up their mess.

"By the time I listened to Emma's earlier voice message, it was an hour later, and it didn't sound like the usual messages she left me when she had been high like before. I texted her that I was coming over, but she never texted back. I couldn't drive for shit, so I stole someone's bicycle and raced over there as fast as I could. I wasn't sure if she was sleeping it off, but my gut told me something was wrong."

I blink away the tears in my eyes. I've never seen Mason like this before. His shoulders slumped, his eyes sad, and his hands in fists.

Swallowing hard, I brace myself for what's coming next.

"I found her in her room, unconscious and unresponsive. Her eyes were half open, her body stiff. I knew CPR, so I started compressions right away and tried to revive her, but I knew I was too late. As soon as I saw an empty baggie on the nightstand, I knew she'd taken a crap ton of pills." Mason keeps his head and eyes lowered, and I can tell how painful this is for him to repeat.

"You don't have to continue, Mason…" I tell him softly.

He finally meets my gaze. "I want to share her story with you. I've kept it inside for so long."

"Okay." I nod.

"I called 911, but it didn't matter because she had stopped breathing long before I arrived. They pronounced her dead at four fifteen in the morning, and once the autopsy results came in, we learned she had overdosed on so many pills, her heart stopped within twenty minutes. She had taken more than her usual opioids too. When she left the voice messages on my phone, she'd already swallowed them all. She'd called her sister to tell her she loved her, but it was the letter they found a week later that destroyed me for good."

I can't even begin to imagine the pain he went through, so I don't say anything as he takes a break.

"She blamed me, said I didn't want her anymore, believed I had fallen out of love with her and was seeing someone else. She popped pills to relieve the pain I was causing her when they were what caused the wedge between us in the first place. I begged her…I fucking *begged* her to stop."

Mason's face falls in his hands as his voice strains, and I can no longer keep my distance. I wrap my arm over his hunched back and lean my head on his shoulder, trying to offer comfort anyway I can.

"She was an addict," I tell him softly. "You tried, Mason." I squeeze his arm.

He shakes his head and slowly sits up. "Not hard enough. Her sister took her to NA, called her every single day to check on her, and thought she was fighting the addiction. I believed she was too or, rather, wanted to believe she was. But she was sneaking around behind our backs, and I became desensitized to her cries for help. It was my fault. No matter what anyone says, I will always blame myself for not staying home that night, for not checking my phone sooner, or at least for not forcing her to join me. I should've protected her from herself, kept her within reach, but instead, I made her fight alone."

I nod, knowing I can't argue with his logic although I don't believe he could've done much for her at that point. He was only twenty, and that's a lot of stress and responsibility for anyone to deal with, nevertheless a college kid.

"I know there's nothing I can say that will change what happened or how you feel, but I appreciate you sharing your past with me. I hate how this haunts you, and you're forced to live with the pain of losing someone you loved. I'm sorry you feel guilty and blame yourself. I'm so, so sorry, Mason." It's all I can offer him at this point, and it doesn't feel like enough.

Vulnerability coats his voice. I notice how his body shakes as he talks, and how distraught he still is five years later.

"I was a fucking mess, Soph. The aftermath of her death changed everything for me." He locks his eyes with mine when we both sit upright on the couch, only inches apart. "Destroyed everything in my path. I nearly flunked out the following year and wanted to take my own damn life. The pain, it was unbearable. If it weren't for Brandon, Hunter, and Liam, I'm quite certain I wouldn't be here right now."

His words hit me hard in the chest. "What happened?"

"Emma's family threatened to sue me. They claimed I drove her to popping pills and then did nothing about it. Wanted to use Emma's suicide note in court to prove I was the reason. Her sister knew the whole truth, though, and tried to get them to stop, but with their own grief, they wanted justice and for me to pay. Of course, my dad stepped in as the DA and paid an assload of money as "compensation." My dad didn't do it for my sake, though. Nothing ever is. It was all to keep my name out of the news and his name out of any bad press. He's held it over my head ever since."

"Oh God," I mutter, pinching the bridge of my nose. "And then Weston…"

"Yep." He nods. "Daddy to the rescue but, again, not for *my* sake. Another thing he can taunt me with, though. The son who keeps getting in trouble, who's at the center of another death."

"Weston wasn't your fault, and neither was Emma's, even if you think differently," I say carefully. "Have you heard from Emma's family since? Or was the money all they were after?"

"They said justice would someday get me, and that's the last I heard from her parents. Her sister, Serena, was my saving grace, though."

My eyes widen. "Wait. Serena? Your lawyer friend?"

"Yeah, actually…" He scrubs a hand over his face and takes a shallow breath. "She moved in here with us that summer."

"*She* was the third roommate?" My jaw drops.

He nods, confirming.

"Wow." I blink, hadn't expected that. "So she didn't hold a grudge like her parents?"

"No. She knew the truth, but she hadn't wanted to tell her parents everything to tarnish the memory of their daughter, so I agreed that it was best not to share the whole story with them. It wouldn't fix anything or bring her back, so once my dad paid them off, that was it."

"How did Serena end up here then?" I ask because I'm nosy and want to know if there's more to it than he's telling. I only met

Serena once but could tell she was obviously someone important in his life.

"Well, I was a mess, and she worried about me. I dodged her calls, didn't answer the door when she came barging over, and ignored her and everyone else for weeks. Emma's death happened at the end of the semester, so I was spending the entire summer in the house. Liam tried to help me, but he still had to work and couldn't *watch* me all the time. I was drinking nonstop to numb the pain and hitting anything or anyone who got in my way. When I say I was a mess, I didn't recognize myself anymore. It got that bad. One day, I woke up to Serena moving in boxes of her shit. She said she wasn't gonna let me grieve alone, and since I refused to call her back, Liam said she could move in."

"Wow…" I say. "That's why she jumped to help you right away with Weston."

"Yeah, she's a lawyer now. She's a few years older than us and was going into law school when she moved in."

"Why didn't you guys ever talk about her before?"

"I guess because I knew it'd circle around to Emma, and I wasn't ready to talk about her to you or anyone. Talking about her is still hard. I live with it every day, and it's not something I like putting on someone else." He finally lifts his eyes to mine. "Just like you don't want pity looks and people to walk on eggshells around you, I felt that tenfold. Every day. My close friends knew, but I wasn't ready for anyone else new in my life to know. It's a lot of emotional baggage and—"

"I think everyone has some kind of emotional baggage," I tell him truthfully. "Is that why you stopped dating altogether?" For the past three years, I've never seen Mason with another woman, but whether or not that was because he only slept with them and didn't date them, I don't ask.

"At eighteen, Emma was my first…everything. My first real relationship. My first love. My first heartache." I see the shame and remorse in his expression. "I shut down after that. Knew my past was too much to put on someone else. Didn't ever want to go through that again. Kept everyone at a distance so nothing more could come from it."

It clicks then when he looks at me, his eyes soft and his lips in a firm line. He hasn't been in a serious relationship since her because not only does he blame himself for everything but he also refuses to let himself be happy again.

"You can't keep punishing yourself, Mason. You probably don't want to hear it, but you have a lot to offer someone. Even if you don't believe me, Emma was responsible for her own life, too. You can't keep all the burden on your shoulders."

"Well, it's fucking hard not to. Especially when I relive that night over and over again in my mind, all the things I didn't do, all the things I could've done differently, all the things I should've said that might've stopped her. It's so goddamn hard to think I deserve anything less than living with the guilt for the rest of my life."

His words are sharp, but arguing with him isn't going to change the way he feels. And on some fucked-up level, I understand.

I take his hand and place his palm on his chest. He furrows his brows, and I tilt my head, hoping he can hear the sincerity in my voice. "You have the best heart, Mason Holt. Even if you shield it, even when you push people away, and even if you think otherwise. You go out of your way for the people you care for, and I do understand because I feel a different kind of guilt when it comes to what happened to Weston and how it involved you. I hate that I let him into my life and essentially yours. But what's done is done. You have to forgive yourself for what happened to Emma because, ultimately, it was *her* choice. You tried to help her. Serena tried to help her, and even if you think you could've done more, it might not have mattered. If it hadn't happened that night, it could've happened another night. She was sick, she was addicted to drugs, and she was using you as her excuse."

Mason stares at me, expressionless, as his throat tightens.

"Forgive yourself, Mason, and live your life again. You deserve it." I release my hand from his. "It's because of you that I'm here, alive and safe."

He drops his hand, letting it smack down on his thigh. "And I want to keep you that way," he says in a rough voice, a vein in his forehead throbbing. "I don't trust Caleb."

"I know your guard is up, but you have to understand that even if he were interested in me, the feelings aren't mutual," I tell him honestly. "Caleb's a nice guy. He's been a shoulder to lean on, and I've tried my best to listen when he's needed it, but that's all we'll ever be in my eyes. If he wants more, he's gonna be sadly disappointed."

"I want to trust your judgment, Soph. But after Weston and what I've seen in the past few years with criminal cases, it's hard not to feel skeptical of a guy like Caleb," he says earnestly.

"Okay, how about this? I will only see him at the grieving circle from now on. Perhaps I'm giving him the wrong idea by being so nice, and if I back off a little, he'll get the hint," I tell him because the last thing I want to do is give Caleb the wrong idea. I was trying to be there for him as a friend, but nothing more is ever going to happen.

"If that's the only offer I'm gonna get, then okay, I'll take it," he says with a smirk. "Just promise me you'll be careful, okay?"

"Of course." I return the smile.

We both stand, exhausted from the night, and I'm ready to pass out. The memory of his kiss from earlier hits me as we stand chest to chest, and I wonder what it'd be like to kiss him again. For real this time.

"Your dinner was amazing, by the way. Sorry I made things weird." He nervously fidgets with his shirt and then brushes a hand through his hair. I've learned over time that's one of his nervous tics.

"Thank you, and it's fine. Maybe inviting him over wasn't the best idea, after all, but I'll make sure he understands that I'm not interested in anything more than a friendship," I say, wondering if that's what he's really concerned about. "Sorry for snapping at you," I add.

Mason surprises me when he steps closer and brings a hand to my face. Then he brushes my hair behind my ear with a tender look. "Never apologize to me for being angry. I'd rather you not hide it anyway."

"I think at this point, we're beyond hiding stuff from each other." I smile when he flashes me one of his deep grins. "Thank you for telling me about her. I know it wasn't easy for you." I wrap my arms around his waist and hug him tightly. "I hope you know how much I appreciate your openness."

His body stiffens for a second before relaxing around me and closing his arms around my back. I feel his mouth on the top of my head as he gives me a small kiss. "You're something special, Soph. I guess I can see why Caleb finds it easy to talk to you."

I pull back slightly. "I like to think it's because I was the oldest kid, and someone was always crying over something." I chuckle, knowing my sisters would most likely agree.

"Probably. You have a good heart too. It's hard not to feel comfortable around you." Then he gives me a sweet, lingering kiss on the forehead as always. "Good night, sweet Sophie." When he pulls back, he winks, and everything I've tried not to feel for him hits me in full force.

Knowing he pushed me away three years ago and after all this time because of his past makes me wonder if things would've ever worked out between us if he'd let himself be happy. If he'd opened up to me then or if he had never gone through it at all, would there have been a chance for us after all?

Mason walks around the sofa and toward the staircase, and before he takes a step, I stop him.

"Mason, wait."

I swallow, my breaths coming out quicker, and when he pauses and turns toward me, I decide it's now or never. He kissed me earlier today, and even though he says it was to calm me down, I believe there was much more to it. There's no way he didn't feel what I felt.

"Yeah?"

I stalk toward him and launch myself into his arms, wrapping my hands around his neck and pressing my mouth to his. He doesn't hesitate and holds me in place as our lips devour each other. Mason's hands slide down my body, then he palms my ass cheeks and lifts me until my legs wrap around his waist.

Turning us around until my back hits the wall, he holds me up with his hips. Large hands cup my face as he slants his greedy mouth over mine and teases my tongue with his. Tingles travel down my spine as he kisses me, heating my body from within, and it's definitely one for the books. Mason kisses me with so much passion and desperation, I never want him to let me go.

Tightening my hold around him, he presses into me harder, letting me feel how aroused he is. I grind my hips against him, and then he pulls back with a growl, pressing our foreheads together.

"Soph…" He breathes out. "Fuck, you better stop that."

My breaths come out as pants as I try to form words. "You kissed me back."

"You kissed me back this afternoon," he retorts, and then we both laugh.

"Were you just trying to calm me down earlier?"

"Yes, but I also wanted an excuse to kiss you." The vulnerability in his tone makes me smile.

Mason sets me down on my feet, so I have to look up his large frame to meet his eyes. "Why?" I ask, eager to hear him say it. Say he feels what I feel. "Why did you need an excuse?"

"Because you're not mine to kiss," he says softly.

I swallow, the weight of his eyes pin me in place, and my entire body shivers with anticipation. I suck in a shallow breath as I choose my next words. "So make me yours."

CHAPTER TWENTY-THREE

MASON

Spilling all my truths about my past to Sophie wasn't as painful or hard as I anticipated. It was intense and a little emotional, but it's not difficult to open up to someone like her. She's so damn easy to talk to and trust. She always has been, and I'd been fighting getting closer to her for years, but I can't hold back anymore. The moment she leaped into my arms, there was no going back. Sophie Corrigan brought me back to life, breathed meaning into my soul, and gave me hope for the first time since Emma died.

"So make me yours."

Goddamn, the way she bites her bottom lip has me fighting my restraint. Leaning in, I cup her cheek and study her expression. Her swollen lips, so damn soft and inviting. Her dark eyes, intense and begging me to kiss her again. Her body, arching into my touch as if she'll combust without it.

Kissing her earlier was spontaneous, something I'd been fantasizing about since the first time I kissed her, but I don't regret it. Hell, I wanted her mouth on mine again as soon as I walked away.

Then I remembered the incident was only a month ago, and it was too soon. Even though I've been burying my feelings for the past three years, I forced a smile and told myself it was to calm her down. Only half a lie.

But fuck it. She was never Weston's. Won't ever be Caleb's.

Sophie is *mine*.

"Are you sure about this?" I ask, keeping focused on her. "Because if I kiss you again, I won't have enough strength to walk away from you this time."

When I see the tears in her eyes, I'm taken aback and worried I said something wrong. Then she smiles wide and nods frantically. "If you have feelings for me the way I have feelings for you, then please tell me. Tell me so I can stop second-guessing." Her tone is pleading, and I hate to think I've caused her any pain in thinking her feelings were one-sided.

I step closer, pressing my forehead to hers as I cup her soft cheeks. Our breathing is the only sound in the room, except maybe the beats of our pounding hearts.

"I've felt something since the moment I met you. I acted on them, foolishly thinking I'd be able to walk away, but instead, I've been lying to myself. I knew being friends with you would be next to impossible, which is why I pushed you away the majority of the time. I didn't want to hurt you, the pain I felt was my own doing, and I suffered knowing you didn't deserve the burden of my past. When we met, it'd only been a couple of years since Emma's death, and I was still dealing with it, but I knew then you weren't just another girl. You made me think I could have happiness again, *deserved* happiness again. But then the realization hit that you were Lennon's sister, and Brandon was my best friend, and I convinced myself that crossing that line would only end badly. I only ever wanted you to be happy, which is why I tried to walk away. You deserved someone who could give you so much more than what I could at the time. Someone who was emotionally available to love you the way you should be loved."

"I wish you would've given me the chance to show you that you were enough, *are* enough, have always been enough for me." She pushes against my chest slightly so our eyes lock. "You stood up for me in a way that nearly got you killed. I can't imagine a better man for me."

Her chest rises and falls as her words repeat in my mind. So goddamn beautiful. Inside and out.

"Kiss me, Mason."

Sophie's demand has me pressing our lips together in a white-hot kiss. My hands greedily explore her body as she moans into my mouth, our tongues twisting together in a dance of want and desire. My fingers find the curve of her breast as I growl against her lips, remembering every touch I felt from the very first time I tasted her. Everything about her feels perfect against me, and when her hand sneaks under my shirt, trying to lift it, I pull away and push her to arm's length.

"Soph, wait…"

She meets my eyes, her mouth agape.

"I want to do this right with you. No frantic quickies on a bathroom sink," I tell her.

"Well, that made it quite memorable for me, I must say," she admits with a light chuckle as she smooths down her hair. "But you're right. We should take this slow. Not jump into bed together. No sex. For a while. Like a long time. A year."

My eyes widen. "Okay, I didn't say that."

Sophie rewards me with one of her sweet laughs, and her head falling back before meeting my gaze again. "I'm messing with you. But I like the idea of not rushing. We did things backward, and I want us to give this a real shot. If that's what you were thinking…"

I close the gap between us, cupping her jaw as I slowly bring our lips together. "Dear God, please give me the restraint."

She chuckles. "You know my father is a pastor, right? You might not want to be praying to God about having the willpower not to sleep with me."

"Jesus Christ," I mutter. "Go to bed, woman. Before I change my mind entirely." I press a kiss to her forehead.

Sophie blushes, then laughs as she walks around me while I

hold in a groan. Fuck, my dick is hard, and if it could, I'm sure it'd be cursing too.

"Good night," she singsongs, looking over her shoulder as she licks her lips.

I smirk, knowing damn well she felt how aroused I was. Catching her eyes on my groin, I purposely adjust myself while she watches. "Good night, sweet Sophie."

The day after Sophie's dinner party, I kissed her good morning for the first time. It was Sunday, and it was just us the whole day. At first, I worried things would be weird or awkward, but nothing is with her. We watched Liam's show and then laughed when we knew he'd be pissed we were continuing it without him. I made coffee and added in her creamer like always. Later in the afternoon, she snuggled up on the couch and read her book while I rubbed her feet. Then that evening, she left for a grieving circle meeting, saying that it was her last one. She was ready to put the past behind her, and I wanted to support her in whatever decision she made.

That same morning, Liam left for a four-day trip, and I hadn't bothered to tell him about Sophie's and my newfound relationship. I hadn't mentioned it to Hunter either, but he knew within a couple of days thanks to Sophie telling her sisters and of course, Lennon telling him. Not that I care, though. I'm ready to let the world know because after confessing my feelings to her and sharing my past, I've realized life is too short not to tell the important people in your life how much you care about them.

We spent the weekend and most of the week alone, meeting up for breakfast and coffee before work, then hunkering down together in the evenings. It's complete bliss, being in our own little world. It hardly feels real because Sophie was always within my reach when we'd watch Netflix and talk about books, but she was never mine to touch.

There were moments when I held back even when the timing felt right, but I knew having secrets and not giving her my whole self wouldn't be fair. I also tried to be considerate of her just being in a relationship, albeit a bad one, so I didn't know if she'd want to date again. It wasn't until she asked me to admit my true feelings that everything changed.

And every day I'm so damn thankful she did. It lit something inside me that made me realize I didn't want to go back to only being friends with Sophie. I've waited long enough.

"Holy fucking shit!"

Sophie nearly jumps out of her skin when we hear Liam's booming voice from behind us. I'm leaning against the kitchen counter with my arms wrapped tightly around her while she stands between my legs. I had my face in her neck, kissing the soft spot below her ear when his loud ass came barreling in.

It's Thursday morning, and I hadn't anticipated seeing him until tonight.

"You two. Fucking finally!" He charges in, dropping his bag on the floor. He surprises us both when he wraps his long arms around us in a group hug. "I was getting blue balls from your lack of fucking."

"Christ, Evans," I mutter, pushing him away.

Sophie turns around as my arms fall to her waist. "Liam! We're not jumping back into bed together, so calm the hell down."

Liam chuckles as he helps himself to some coffee. "Good, Sophie. Make the fucker wait it out for being a pussy and putting you in the friend-zone the past few years."

I roll my eyes and groan, but Sophie laughs. "Not a bad idea."

"Funny. Both of you." I release my hold on Sophie. "Why don't you tell Liam how *Hart of Dixie* season two ends?"

"What? You assholes watched my show without me!" Liam shouts, nearly spewing his coffee all over.

"Mason!" Sophie scolds with her hands on her hips.

"Gotta shower and get ready for work…" I rush toward the stairs. "Unless you feel like joining me…"

"Sorry, big guy. I don't swing that way," Liam quips. "But I'll come soap you up if you want!" His loud footsteps come closer as Sophie's laughter echoes.

"Stay away from me, asshole!" I call out, taking the steps two at a time in a hurry to the bathroom.

I finish my workday early, glad to be able to come home to Sophie and spend extra time together. The guys at work have been giving me shit all week for the extra pep in my step, but I don't give a fuck. Sophie being mine has been years in the making, and I'm going to do everything in my power not to fuck it up this time. I can't. She's way too important to me and building a real relationship with her is my number one priority.

The moment I enter the house, I hear a sweet melody coming from a violin. She's taken on a new student, and I never get tired of hearing her play or seeing the way her face lights up when she's talking about music.

I quietly walk into the living room, trying not to disturb them, but as soon as I round the corner, I trip on a pair of shoes and nearly tumble into the couch, making noise along the way.

"Shit, sorry." I straighten myself.

Sophie's eyes widen, and the little girl she's teaching starts to giggle.

"*Crap*. I meant crap. Sorry." I hold up my hands, walking backward. "Sorry."

"Is that your boyfriend?" the girl asks, and I notice the blush on Sophie's cheeks.

"Uh…" Sophie stammers, blinking. "Why don't we start from the top, okay? Your mom will be here soon."

I arch a brow, smirking. She rolls her eyes at me, and I walk into the kitchen chuckling.

Twenty minutes later, Sophie wraps her arms around my waist from behind once her student leaves. "Any chance you're cooking dinner for two? Because it smells good."

"Hmm…that depends." I place one hand over hers that are locked against my torso.

"Oh yeah? On what?" she asks.

I put the lid on the pan, then turn around to face her, keeping her arms wrapped around me. Tilting her chin, I smirk and look into her eyes. "On what your answer to her question was."

Sophie's eyes narrow. "Really? You're gonna hold an eight-year-old's question against me?"

"I mean, I'd rather be holding something else against you, but now that the question is out there…" I grin, wondering if she'll dodge it or not. Though I'm only messing with her, I enjoy watching her squirm.

"Let's see how good this meal is first. Can't be locked into anything with someone who can't cook."

I laugh at her attempt to get out of answering. "Well, fuck am I glad I made one of my best dishes."

Sophie steps back then grabs two plates and starts setting the table. "Am I setting one for Liam?"

"I only know how to cook for two, so that fucker is on his own from now on."

She snickers, then swats my chest.

After we eat together and talk about our day, we settle on the couch for our nightly routine of Netflix. Sophie decides to read and rests her feet in my lap. Halfway through an episode of *Lucifer*, she wiggles her feet against my groin, purposely rubbing against my dick.

"You better stop that," I warn.

She works her feet on either side of my cock, stroking it and teasing me. After a minute, I grab her ankle and squeeze. "Soph… you better not start something you don't plan on finishing."

Keeping her eyes on the pages, she sits up and inches next to me. With one hand on her book, she reaches into my lap and starts stroking me with the other.

My head falls back with a groan. "Are you seriously reading while touching me?" Her eyes are glued to her paperback.

"What? Never heard of multi-tasking before?" Then she one-handedly turns the page.

How the hell did she do that?

Her hand slides up my torso until she reaches the band of my shorts and dips her hand inside. With her palm over the fabric of my boxer briefs, she wraps her delicate fingers around my cock and moves her hand up and down my length.

"You aren't playing fair," I growl, throwing my hands behind my head. Sophie touching me is something I've been dreaming about since the moment I met her. "Sophie."

"Hmm?"

Unable to take it any longer, I pull her hand out and leap on top of her, tossing her book aside in the process.

"Hey!" she says before I cover her mouth with mine.

I settle between her legs as she wraps her arms around me, and I cup her face. "Do you feel like reading now?" I ask, grinning and looking down at her.

"Well, I was at a really good part…"

I press my forehead to hers, groaning. "Why do you enjoy torturing me?" I ask, sliding my hand up her body and palming her breast.

She bites her bottom lip, releasing a groan. "After hearing Liam say that I should make you wait for putting me in the friend-zone, I was thinking it wasn't such a bad plan."

"Oh really?" I slide my lips down her jawline and latch onto her neck. "You're taking advice from a self-proclaimed bachelor who's never had a relationship longer than the length of a movie?"

Sophie snickers, wiggling her body beneath me. "But I bet he gets a lotta ass with that knowledge."

"More ass than a pair of jeans," I confirm.

Sophie's head tilts back, giving me further access to her soft flesh. I suck and lick, grinding my body against hers.

"Maybe Liam's theory isn't as great as I thought…" She moans, arching her hips toward me.

"Christ, you're killing me, woman." I slide off her so we're aligned on the couch, my hand roaming down her body until it cups her ass. She wraps one leg around my hip, feeling how aroused I am for her. I'm not sure if she's testing me or not, but I want everything she's giving me.

My fingers explore her stomach as my other hand stays wrapped around her head. Sophie kisses me with a hot fervor, and it's like the past few nights where we get lost in each other's mouths, though I've been careful knowing she doesn't want us to rush.

"Touch me, Mason," she whispers, then drags my hand between her legs.

Like an overeager teenager, I happily oblige and bring my fingers to the button of her shorts, undoing them as fast as I can. Sliding my hand in slowly, her breath hitches as I rub the pad of my thumb along the lace of her panties.

"Mmm…Sophie. Are you—"

The ringing doorbell startles me, but I choose to ignore it. Slipping inside her underwear, I slide down her slit, her back arching as soon as I press into her. Her pussy coats my finger, and we moan in anticipation.

"Sweet, sweet Sophie. Jesus, you're already wet for me."

The doorbell rings again. Twice.

"I'm gonna punch whoever's at the damn door," I say, groaning when it rings again.

"You better answer it in case it's an emergency," she tells me, and we sit up. I grind my teeth together, annoyed and frustrated that whoever it is has given me severe blue balls.

"Don't go anywhere," I tell her with a kiss.

I adjust myself as I walk to the door, ready to curse whoever the hell it is. Once I open it, I'm nearly shocked and rooted to the spot when I see my father.

Motherfucker.

"What're you doing here?" I deadpan.

"We need to talk."

"It's not a good time." I hold my stance, arms crossed over my chest.

"Make time, Mason. It's about your case."

I narrow my eyes. "I thought it was over?"

"It is, but there's more to it than that. You gonna let me in or not?"

I sigh a deep breath, shrugging and opening the door for him to come inside.

He follows me to the living room where Sophie is sitting, her cheeks still flushed from our hot make-out session.

"Dad, this is Sophie." I wave my arm as she stands and steps closer. "Sophie, this is my dad," I tell her slowly, feeling the awkward tension of this situation. Her hair is tousled from messing around, and he notices.

"Nice meeting you, Mr. Holt."

"It's a pleasure," my father says, taking her hand in his.

"I'll leave you two to some privacy," she says quickly, and I feel awful that he's cutting into our time.

I walk toward her, reaching out with an apology, but she smiles and shakes her head. "It's okay. I should go to bed anyway."

I'm not letting my dad make her feel uncomfortable, so I tell him to give me a minute and walk Sophie to her room.

"Sorry, I have no idea why he's here," I say as soon as I close her bedroom door behind us.

"Don't be. It's fine. Take your time." She wraps her arms around my waist as I bend down to kiss her swollen lips.

Blowing out a slow breath, I try to prepare myself for whatever reason he's here.

An hour later, he finally leaves, and I'm left with a million thoughts. I won't be able to sleep, so I check if Sophie is passed out yet. She left her bedroom lamp on, and whether or not it was for me, I step inside her room and shut the door.

Sliding into bed behind her, I wrap my arm around her waist and pull her against my chest. I bury my nose in her hair and inhale the scent of her sweet shampoo. Then I press a kiss below her ear and feel her shiver.

"Are you awake?" I whisper.

"No."

I chuckle, pressing kisses along her jawline. "No? So I shouldn't ask you out on a date for this Saturday?"

"Mmm…" she hums. "What kind of date?"

Smirking, I slide my hand into her sleep shorts and wait to see if she stops me or not. When she doesn't, I explore further until I realize she's not wearing panties.

"Did you lose an item of clothing?" I taunt, moving my hand down lower.

"Figured I'd help you out…"

I smile, bringing my lips over her ear as my finger slowly slides inside her, feeling how wet and smooth she is. "Goddamn, woman. You've been waiting for me?"

"Would it be cringy to say I've been waiting for the last three years?" She finally lifts her eyes and glances over her shoulder.

"Yes, but I'd love it just the same." I slant my mouth over hers and lose myself for a moment. "So about that date. What do you say?"

Sophie's breathing rapidly against me as I wait for her response. "I suppose I could squeeze you into my schedule."

"Oh, well thank you," I quip. "But I only take girlfriends on dates, so…"

"Really?" Her eyes widen as she bites down on her lower lip. I sink a second finger inside her, and she gasps. "You want to have this conversation right now?" Her head falls back against my shoulder as I increase my pace, rocking in and out of her tight pussy.

"I think I do," I tell her matter-of-factly. "Unless you'd rather I'd introduce you in the same category as Liam? Even though you're a much hotter roommate."

"So what're you saying? You want to make it *official*?"

I chuckle at her condescending tone, sinking deeper inside her as I bring the pad of my thumb to her clit and rub circles. "I'm saying, I want you to be *mine*, Sophie. I know we're taking things slow, but you've been the game changer in my life longer than I want to admit. I might've taken a long ass time to finally get here, but fuck, baby. I don't want to let you go now. I want you all to myself and want the fucking world to know it."

Sophie's pants while I bring her closer to the edge. As she bites down on her lip, I listen to her uneven breaths as she rides out her climax. Her lips part, eyes squeeze tight, and she moans through the pleasure. After she's come down from her high, Sophie turns toward me, and I slide my fingers between my lips.

"Still so goddamn sweet."

Sophie plants her palms against my cheek and brings our mouths together for a searing kiss. When she pulls back, she stares at me. "You're kind of a softy under all those layers of concrete."

"I am *not* concrete," I defend. "Wait, I'm not a softy either."

She chuckles. "Yes. I'll go on a date with you."

CHAPTER TWENTY-FOUR

SOPHIE

SEEING this side of Mason is something I never thought would happen. I've hoped, dreamed, and fantasized about it, but I never thought it'd become a reality. From the moment he kissed me last weekend after confessing his demons about his past, I've somehow managed to fall even harder for Mason Holt.

When he asked me out on a date and implied he only takes his girlfriends out, I thought I was going to pass out. I might be in my mid-twenties, but he made my heart flutter like a fourteen-year-old girl at a boy band concert.

"So how was your baby appointment?" I ask Lennon once we find seats at Panera. She was dying for their broccoli cheese soup, and I only had a half day of rehearsals. Unfortunately, Maddie had classes.

"It was awesome!" She beams, putting some roll pieces in front of Allie in her highchair. "Weighed and measured me, all the usual checkup stuff, but we'll go back in a couple of weeks to get an ultrasound and the official estimated due date."

"Oh yay! Any intuition on what you think the gender is?" I ask before taking a bite of my sandwich.

"I'm leaning toward a boy because this pregnancy has felt so different from my first, but they say each time can be different no matter what the gender. So honestly, I don't know! I'll be happy either way."

"I know you will be." I smile, looking at Allie who's munching on some bread. "Are you excited to become a big sissy?" I ask Allie, and she furrows her brows at me. "Guess not."

We both laugh.

"So how did things go after we left the dinner party last weekend?" she asks. We haven't been able to catch up since then, and I haven't shared the latest news.

"Well…" I linger, swallowing down my food. "It got a little awkward with Caleb and the guys, but once he was gone, Mason took me by surprise and opened up to me about his past."

"What, really?" She arches a brow, stuffing more soup into her mouth.

I smile at the memory. "Yeah, it was pretty sweet how he trusted me enough to share. I was happy he did. It brought a lot of light to the table on why he avoided me."

"What was it exactly?" she asks, and I contemplate what to say.

"It's intense. I don't think I'd feel right repeating it. I'm sorry," I admit.

"It's fine, I understand. I asked Hunter once when it was implied something had happened, and he told me it was Mason's story to tell. He wouldn't budge about it." Lennon takes a huge bite of a grilled cheese. "I just want all the juicy details about you two." Lennon shoots me a wink.

I think about all of his admissions and everything that's happened between us. My heart nearly bursts out of my chest when I replay it all.

"You've got that look on your face." Lennon grins.

I roll my eyes and chuckle. "What look?"

With a popped eyebrow, she leans forward and whispers. "The sex look."

Though I'm typically not shy when it comes to talking about sex with my sister, my cheeks heat. "Just reliving the other night."

"Spill it. All of it. And don't leave out anything. Isn't that what you said about Hunter and me when we were at this stage of our relationship? Tell me how it *all* started…"

I chuckle at her eagerness. Teasingly, I cover Allie's ears and tell her not to listen to our grown-up talk.

"Well, he was telling me about why he doesn't do relationships and how he's always been protective of me, especially when you-know-who entered the picture. Everything he was saying came straight from the heart, and I couldn't hold back. It felt right, so I kissed him."

"You kissed *him*? Nice."

"Damn right. Well, first I charged him, leaped into his chest, and then kissed him."

"Ballsy. I like it." Lennon smirks, nodding for me to continue.

"So we're having this hot as hell make-out session when he tells me to stop, and that we shouldn't jump back into bed together.."

"Keep going…"

"And last night he asked me out on a date—" I pause and can't stop the smile that forms on my face. "As his *girlfriend*."

Lennon's eyes widen as she chews a large mouthful. "Oh my God!" She finally swallows it down. "Seriously? Shit, finally!" She slides out of the booth and comes around to hug me, squeezing me tight. "I can't believe it!"

"Me neither! I feel like I'm living in a dream and praying it never ends," I tell her as she takes her seat. "After the incident, he's been Mason again—sweet, caring, protective. We've decided to take our time, considering what's happened."

"That was over a month ago. I'd be jumping his bones if I were you."

"Like you're one to talk," I deadpan, knowing how long she and Hunter waited when they were in a weird non-relationship relationship.

"Shut up." She chuckles. "Did you tell Maddie?"

"Not yet. I was gonna after our lunch because I knew if I told her before you, she'd spill the beans before I got the chance."

Lennon smirks. "True."

We finish our food, and I enjoy our sisterly time together. I love catching up because between our schedules, life is getting busier with each passing day.

"Are you and Hunter ever gonna set a wedding date?" I ask as we walk out of the restaurant to our cars. They've been engaged since March. "It's been four months, so what're ya waiting for?"

I wait as she puts Allie in her car seat and buckles her up. "Waiting for when I'm not pregnant."

Snickering, I respond, "Well, my guess is you'll have a six-week window between the birth of baby number two and when the doctor clears you for sex afterward."

"Don't jinx me!" She rounds the car toward me.

"I don't believe in jinx," I tease. "Plus, we both know Hunter will keep you knocked up for the next five years if he has his way."

"Yeah, we're gonna need a bigger place. We've been talking about it and might start looking at houses soon."

"Oh that's exciting! Let me know if you want a house hunting buddy, and I'll go with you guys."

"Will do." She smiles, then wraps her arms around me. "Thanks for meeting us. It's always less embarrassing when I stuff my face with another adult and not just Allie who I think silently judges me."

I laugh, giving her a squeeze, then pull back to rub her little bump. "Anytime."

Mason's working late tonight, so I head home and decide to get all my laundry and cleaning done so I have something nice to wear for our date tomorrow night. Shortly after I've finished my second load, Liam comes waltzing in and heads straight for the fridge.

"I think you might have a drinking problem," I quip.

"No," he says slowly, twisting the bottle cap. "I have a hunting-down-idiots problem."

"I still think you should take me with you one of these times. Show me what kind of badass you really are." I smirk, folding my delicates on the coffee table.

He takes a seat next to me, propping up one of his feet. "Hey, careful." I grab the pile of panties and move them away from his boot.

Liam eyes me as he takes a long sip of his drink. "So you and Mason, huh?"

I inhale. I was halfway ready for him to bring it up without Mason present. "What about it?"

"I'm happy for you two. I hope you're okay, though."

I nod, knowing that he's talking about the aftermath of Weston. "I am. Going to grieving circle has helped some and being able to process it on my own terms. Having you two has helped me immensely."

"Mason said he told you about Emma."

"Yeah, he did." Nodding, I finish folding my things and set them into my laundry basket so I can put them away later. "I was shocked to say the least."

"It was a fucking rough time for him. He's not been the same since, but for what it's worth, I've never seen that side of him around another woman the way he's been around you."

I arch a brow, trying to understand what that means. "What way?"

Liam takes another long pull of his beer before responding. "Like he's wanted to try again. Like he has hope. Mason's not a hit-it-and-quit-it kind of guy, but he's thought that's all he was able to give someone. It wasn't until you that he wanted more again, but he fought it every step of the way."

"You can say that again." I snicker. "I understand, though. Losing someone, even someone you didn't love, is emotionally draining and hard. Part of me checked out of our relationship weeks before, knowing I needed to find a way out, but I was also scared as hell to leave. I felt strong until he was in front of me, screaming and telling me what a piece of shit I was. I hated feeling so weak, but it's something no one can understand until they're in that situation."

Liam closes the gap between us and wraps his arm around me,

pulling me to his chest. "I'm not sorry he's dead. I'm only sorry neither of us did something about it sooner."

"I know. Deep down, I think he would've killed me had he been given the chance."

He kisses the top of my head. "Not on our watches, babe."

Liam heads out that night to meet up with friends, leaving Mason and me alone to binge-watch TV. He doesn't get home till after eight, so we order food and have a night in.

"So any idea where you're taking me tomorrow night?" I probe, trying to get any details I can. Twisting the chop sticks in my noodles, I scoop them into my mouth and wait for his response.

"Yes, and I'm not telling you." He flashes a shit-eating smirk, reaching over to steal my eggroll.

"You're gonna pay for that," I tease. "That was my last one."

"Don't worry, baby. I'll pay." Mason winks, causing me to laugh.

My phone beeps with a message, and I set my container down to read it. Once I texted Maddie the same news I told Lennon, she nearly lost her shit. Then she sent a bunch of eggplant emojis saying she was officially the only sister without any dick.

I sent her a link to my favorite vibrator and told her Lennon and I had the same one.

That got her off my ass for a little bit anyway.

CALEB

Hey, want a ride to circle tomorrow night? I'll be in the area after meeting an out of town friend and can swing by?

I read his message twice, wondering how I'm going to break the news that I'm not going.

SOPHIE

Actually, I'm not going tomorrow night. I have plans and think the last time was my final meeting.

CALEB

Oh. Too bad, I was hoping to see you this week.

SOPHIE

I'm sorry. Is everything okay?

CALEB

Yeah, all good. Don't worry about it.

Shit, now I feel bad. His loss is much greater than mine, and he's not been dealing with it well, not that I expect him to, but he's used to leaning on his support team.

SOPHIE

What is it, Caleb? You can tell me.

CALEB

It was my anniversary this week. Just a tough time.

SOPHIE

I'm so sorry.

Fuck.

"What's wrong?" Mason asks after I release a deep sigh.

"It's Caleb," I say slowly. "He's asked me to go to circle with him tomorrow. I told him I had plans and wasn't going back, but I could tell something was wrong and finally got him to tell me. It was their anniversary this week. I feel guilty I won't be there, but I don't want to miss our date."

"What time does it start?" he asks.

"Six."

"And it's an hour, right?"

"Yeah, usually done at seven."

He shrugs, and I appreciate the fact that he's not saying anything rude about him. "That should be okay. We can have dinner when you get back and do the rest of what I have planned afterward."

"Really?" My heart lurches, and I pull him in for a kiss.

"Thank you. I'll make sure to pay you back later." Flashing him a wink, he grunts.

"Don't be a tease."

Snickering, I shake my head at his overexaggerated agony and type out a message.

SOPHIE

Okay, I moved some things around tomorrow
and can go. Pick me up at 5:45?

CALEB

I'll be there.

SOPHIE

Great, see you then!

CALEB

Thank you, Sophie. You don't know how much
this means to me.

SOPHIE

Of course. You're welcome.

We're halfway through another episode, cuddled on the couch when Mason furrows his brows.

"What?" I ask.

"Didn't Caleb say they would be married seven years this fall? So wouldn't their anniversary be at least a couple of months away?" he ponders, and I rack my brain, remembering when he mentioned that during Mason and Liam's interrogation.

"Hmm…yeah. Maybe he meant this week was their dating anniversary or something. He wasn't specific, so I'm not sure."

"Do couples keep track of their dating anniversary?" he inquires with a knowing smirk.

"Yeah, I think most do. How else do you know when to celebrate another year together?"

Mason brings me closer. "So when is ours?"

"Well, I don't think we can use the date of the first time we had sex, so…" I taunt, chuckling. "I guess, tomorrow?"

293

"Tomorrow? That's when we'll be official?" He grins with a nod. "Which means I have one more night of freedom. I better go meet up with Liam and make it worthwhile!"

I elbow him in the gut, making him groan. "You're funny." Rolling my eyes, I continue, "But if that's the case, then I better go out too. One last hurrah in the bar bathroom with a random guy."

Pushing myself off the couch, Mason's hand grips my wrist, then pulls me down on his lap. "Sit your pretty little ass down, woman. If there's a second round of bar bathroom sex, it's gonna be with me. Got it?" he says in my ear, sending shivers up my spine.

"Is that so? Think you can handle another round?" I look over my shoulder, wiggling my ass against his noticeable erection.

"Jesus Christ, you gotta stop doing that," he warns, wrapping his arm around my waist to hold me still. "I'm trying to be *nice* and keep our agreement of not rushing things, but you make it nearly impossible."

"You lasted years. I think you can last a few weeks…"

"I barely made it through last night," he growls, arching his hips so I can feel how hard he is, and I release a throaty moan remembering how good he felt inside me.

"Thinking about all the ways I wanted to take you, how badly I want to hear you scream my name, how desperate I am to feel you come around my cock. It took all the fucking willpower in the world to keep my dick in my pants."

I swallow, pushing myself off him.

"Where are you going?" he asks.

"Gonna take a cold shower with my vibrator."

He laughs all the way out of the living room.

CHAPTER TWENTY-FIVE

MASON

Saturday mornings have become my absolute favorite. Seeing Sophie first thing with her messy bed hair and zombie eyes makes me fall even harder. She doesn't try to impress me by fixing herself up before coming out or pretending to be someone she's not. She's quiet until she's had at least one cup of coffee to wake her up and is ready to shower after her third, and by noon, she's eager to face the day.

I love making her breakfast although it's nothing special like eggs and toast. Spending time with her, even if it's to do nothing more than eat together, makes me appreciative of how far we've come. We're both so busy during the workweek that it's nice to sit and enjoy each other's company.

"So Maddie wants to go shopping. I was gonna tell her no, but then I thought I could get some little things for myself for tonight." Sophie gives me a mischievous look that tells me exactly what she's talking about, and even if I don't get to rip them off her body, knowing she's wearing them is enough to make me hard.

"Are we talking naughty little things?" I arch a brow. "Because I could get on board with that."

"Perhaps. You'll have to wait and see."

I cup her cheeks before planting a deep kiss on her soft lips.

"Go. Have fun. But in case you're wondering, red's my favorite color. Has been since the moment I saw it on you." I wink, remembering her lacy red bra that first night we met.

She pulls back, snorting. "Good to know."

This past week together has been one of the best weeks of my life. I can't remember ever feeling this happy or eager to spend time with someone before. Fighting my feelings was a losing battle, and now I can't imagine not touching Sophie anytime we're together.

I hate that she's going to the grief meeting tonight, but I don't want to be one of those guys who tells her what she can and can't do. Douchebag Weston was a controlling asshole, and I refuse to have any of those qualities. I want Sophie and me to decide things together, but I also know she's a loyal friend, and if it's her last meeting, I can live with that. It'll give me more time to get things ready for our date night.

Though it doesn't mean I like Caleb. Hell, I trust him as far as I can throw him.

My friend, Jerad, who helped me dig up shit on Weston could easily help get me information on this Caleb guy. Sophie would probably yell at me for snooping, but considering her ex's two-faced ass, I can't be too safe when it comes to her.

I shoot him a text to call me when he gets the chance, then tell Sophie goodbye before she heads out to pick up Maddie. "Have fun."

"What're you gonna do while I'm gone?" she asks, wrapping her arms around my neck as I pull her body into mine.

"Well, I figure you'll be gone for a few hours, so I'll probably drink a few beers, call a couple of ladies over, and then jerk off in the shower."

"So…a regular Saturday afternoon."

"I mean, you could stay and participate in the festivities if you want…"

Sophie chuckles, leaning up on her toes for another kiss. "Nah, you have fun. I'll be back in a bit."

She walks out to the driveway and hops into her car, then

waves goodbye. My phone rings, and I pick it up when I see Jerad's name.

"Hey, Big Daddy."

"That's what your mother called me last night," he responds.

"Dude, gross. That's crossing a line." I shiver.

"Do I need to remind you of when—"

"Shut up. Whatever you're gonna say." I laugh, shaking my head and knowing he has too much shit on me for me to argue.

"So who are you spying on now, Holt?"

"No giving me shit this time. I had a right to be worried beforehand, so I'm taking some precautions. Not to mention my dad made a house visit a couple of nights ago."

"Was it bad?" he asks, knowing damn well our relationship isn't great.

"I don't know yet. He said Weston's family is pissed that the judge dropped my charges based on self-defense."

"Wait, what? There was a fucking surveillance video! How much more evidence do they need?" He asks the same questions I had for my dad when he dropped that bomb on me.

"Apparently, they want to fight that it was wrongful death, and that I provoked him to use his gun. Hell, I don't know."

"It's bullshit is what it is," he says.

"I agree. But there's not much I can do until they file with the courts or serve me papers."

"Dude, if they try to sue you, I'm gonna be outraged. You let me know if you hear from them because I'll do whatever you need, okay?"

"Yeah, thanks, man. Appreciate that."

"Alright, so tell me what you need. I'm not in my office, but I can be there in a few hours. Izzy has a dance recital this afternoon, so once that's done, I can head over."

"That'd be great. The name is Caleb Royce. I took a picture of his license plate and will send it over to you. Send me whatever you can find. Criminal record, work history, address."

"Got it. Do I dare ask why?" He chuckles.

"It's a guy in Sophie's grieving circle, and he's…I don't know, I get a weird vibe. He says he's grieving his late wife who died a few months ago, but by the way he looks at Sophie, I don't think he's grieving a damn thing. In fact, he gives me the impression he stalks women at these meetings or something."

"Like he takes advantage of their sadness and swoops in?" he asks.

"Yeah, I think. Hell, I don't know. I might be wrong, but I'd feel better knowing for sure that his story isn't complete bullshit. If his wife died, she'd have a death certificate by now."

"Any chance you know her name?"

"No, and I don't think I can ask Sophie without her being suspicious."

"I'll check it out. Look up the last name and see what I can find. See where his plates lead me," he confirms, and I release a relieved breath.

"Thanks, Jerad. I appreciate it. I owe ya one."

"You owe me big time already." He snorts.

"Yeah, yeah." I laugh. "Add it to my tab then."

After we hang up, I take a shower and get ready. I plan to take us out to eat, then putt-putt, and then we'll end the night at the Coliseum where we first met and dance, hopefully giving her some new memories of that place. It's nothing flashy like an exclusive yacht tour or anything, but spending time anywhere with Sophie is a blast. We'll have fun as long as we're together, and I think she feels the same way too.

"Well, aren't you looking quite handsome…" I glare at Maddie, who's eyeing me up and down. "Cologne, too?" She sniffs, wrinkling her nose. "Wow, you must really want to get into my sister's pants. Oh wait, you've already done that."

I bellow out a laugh. "Hi to you too, Mads."

"Madelyn! I heard that!" Sophie yells from the living room.

"Now you're in trouble," I tease, walking past her.

Maddie groans, lifting her arms up, then slapping them back down. "Oh, what else is new. You should be thanking me, mister."

"Is that so?" I ask as she follows me into my room.

"Your bedroom is clean." She pokes her head inside.

"Yeah? And?" I ask, digging into my dresser drawer for some black socks.

"I don't know. It's weird. Aren't most guys' rooms messy and gross?"

"That'd be the next room on the right."

"Oh hell no. I already know Liam is a pig. I can smell it from the front door." She leans against the doorframe with her arms crossed.

"Well, it's mostly messy. He comes home from trips, throws his dirty clothes into one pile, and then packs a new bag without doing his laundry right away."

"Well, considering he has to go shopping to buy new clothes on the road, I'd be surprised if he ever did laundry!"

"Can't argue that." I walk out of my room, and she follows me down the stairs. "Is there a reason you're following me?"

"No, came up here to distract you," she says once we reach the living room. She throws me a smirk over her shoulder.

"Distract me from what?"

"Sophie's shopping bags. I was under strict orders not to let you see what she bought until she was ready to show you." She flashes me a devilish grin, which can't be good.

"Wasn't she supposed to drop you off after shopping since she's going to her circle group?" I grab my watch from the coffee table and snap it on.

"We were running behind so she'll take me home before she goes to the meeting."

I check my watch and see it's only 5:15.

Maddie notices my confusion and continues, "She wants to get ready for your date before the meeting so you two lovebirds can leave right after it's over."

"Ooh," I say, it finally clicks.

"Which means you can't see her until later. No peeking either."

I furrow my brows. "Isn't that rule only for the wedding day?"

She shrugs. "Same principle."

Moments later, Liam comes barreling through the door with a girl under his arm.

Oh fuck.

Maddie swallows, straightening her spine. Liam obviously had no idea she'd be here tonight, but fuck did he pick the worst damn time to come home.

"What's up?" He nods. "I forgot something in my room. C'mon, Cheryl. This way."

"It's Cindy," she says, giggling.

Maddie's jaw tightens, and she pretends it doesn't faze her, but we all know her thing for Liam is more than attraction. He's an idiot for not taking notice.

Or maybe he does, and he's even more of an idiot for ignoring it.

I don't know what to say to Maddie, so I keep my mouth shut. Nothing I say will make her feel better anyway.

"Soph?" I knock on her door.

"Mason?"

She scrambles on the other side. "Hold on."

Chuckling, I put my hand on the doorknob and turn it. "I'm coming in."

"You're so impatient." Sophie giggles when I enter. She's struggling to hold her dress in place.

I stalk toward her, raising my brows at how damn delicious she looks. "Whatcha got going on here?"

"I was trying to zip up my dress, but…" She shrugs, and I motion with my finger for her to spin around and face the mirror.

Stepping behind her, I grab the zipper and slowly pull it up while locking gazes in our reflection. She inhales sharply once I get it zipped to the top. Gently placing my palms on her shoulders, I push her arms down and slide my hands down her fingers.

"Breathtaking," I whisper into her ear, burying my nose into her hair. "Are you sure you have to leave?"

"I wish I didn't…trust me."

I spin her around, taking in how stunning she is with her hair down in loose waves and her lips a perfect shade of peachy red.

"I'll be back before you know it," she says, and I can't tell if she's trying to reassure me or herself. "I wasn't sure where you were taking me, so if I'm overdressed or whatever—"

"Sophie, you look perfect," I tell her earnestly. "I can barely take my eyes off you."

I study her tight red dress and see she's wearing black stockings underneath. "Fuck, this might be an issue."

"Really? Not good?" Her bottom lip trembles with worry. "I can change if you—"

"Might be an issue because I want to fucking rip off your clothes right now," I admit, plucking the thin strap. The dress has a plunging neckline and a high banded waist that accentuates her tits to the goddamn moon. "I don't want to be one of those guys who tells you how to dress, but you shouldn't wear this to your meeting. You'll give them all heart attacks."

Sophie blushes and laughs, the sound going straight to my dick. "I'm gonna slip on my leather jacket before I leave, so don't worry. The most skin they'll see is my neck."

I groan, still not liking it. She looks so damn good—*too damn good*. Good enough to eat.

"Stop looking at me like that or we'll never get out of the house," she tells me, pushing me back slightly.

I grab her wrist and press a kiss to her knuckles. "That sounds perfect to me. Let's be on house arrest together." I wink. Sophie wraps her other arm around my neck and pulls me in for a kiss.

"I'll be home by seven fifteen at the latest."

"A minute later and I'm sending out the SWAT team." I slide my hands down her back, then cup her ass.

"Okay, Colin Farrell. Calm down." She chuckles then laughs harder at my confused facial expression. "From the movie? *S.W.A.T.?*"

I shrug.

"I'm gonna have to man you up with some Jackie Chan and Bruce Willis, too."

Grunting, I huff. "You can leave that to Liam. That's right up his alley."

"Hmm. True."

"Soph, I think our ride's here," Maddie calls out, and all the hair on the back of my neck stands.

"Wait, what?" I ask. "What ride?"

Sophie furrows her brows. "Yeah, I told you Caleb was picking me up for the meeting."

I pull back, my eyes widening. "Uh, no. You did not. Why the hell is he picking you up?"

"He offered when he asked if I was coming because he was gonna be in the neighborhood from coming back in town or something," she rambles, waving her hand around. "I swore I told you last night."

"Babe, trust me. You didn't tell me. I would remember."

"Well, what's the big deal?" She shrugs. "We'll drop off Maddie, then go to the meeting and he'll bring me back home. Then we can go on our date." She wraps her arms around my waist, pulling me closer and looking up with wide, sad eyes.

"Soph…" I warn, resting my forehead against hers. "I don't trust him. I'll drive you."

"Babe, don't be jealous," she says softly.

I grunt, pulling back. "I don't get jealous."

"Okay." She smirks. "Then it should be no problem that another guy is driving me."

"He's not just *another guy*, Sophie. He's a guy I don't trust. Considering the way I saw him look at you, I have every right not to trust him."

"I think you're seeing something that isn't there. I already told you this was my last meeting and that I don't see him as anything more than a friend. I'm gonna make that clear to him, too. Plus, he's still grieving his wife, and considering this was a rough week for him, I want to be there for him as a friend," she explains, but I don't give two shits about this guy's feelings. Sophie is mine, and I want to protect her.

"Sophie!" Maddie calls out. "We gotta go!"

"Mason, please. I don't want us to fight."

"I don't either, so don't go with him. Make up an excuse. Tell him you have somewhere to go afterward or that I'm taking you instead."

She frowns, and I can tell her mind is spinning. She hates conflict.

"He's already here and it's gonna make things awkward if I go out there and send him away…"

"Then I'll do it." I turn to walk out but she grabs my arm before I can march out there.

"Mason, please. Don't." Her voice shakes, and I see her bottom lip trembling. "I don't want to witness another fight. I've seen enough violence to last a lifetime."

Fuck. She knows how to pull at my heartstrings.

A knock pounds on the door. "Are you two doing it? I'm coming in!" Maddie announces. She walks in and stops when she sees Sophie and I. "Are you guys fighting?"

"No," I say at the same time Sophie says, "Yes."

"Well…can you two wrap it up? Caleb is waiting, and you're gonna be late." Maddie shuts the door, leaving us alone. The last thing I want is for Sophie to leave with us bickering, especially before our date tonight.

"Please don't be mad. I'll be back in an hour, okay?"

With my options limited, I exhale a deep breath and pull Sophie to my chest. "Let's not fight. I want us to have a good night."

Sophie pulls back slightly with a smile on her face. "With you, it will be."

Cupping her face, I slant my mouth over hers and kiss her, my tongue finding hers. My hands slide down her body, memorizing every inch of her perfect body.

"Don't start," she teases against my lips.

Groaning, I lean back on my shoes as my eyes scan down her

hot body. "You cannot wear those fuck-me heels." I pout as I imagine all the positions I'd have her in while wearing those damn things.

"I wore them for *you*." She winks.

Following her out, I spot Maddie with Caleb by the door. They're chatting, but as soon as they hear us coming, Caleb's eyes scan down Sophie's body. I clench my fists, wanting to take this guy out simply for checking out my girl. If he's not clear that she's mine, then I'm going to make sure it's *crystal* fucking clear. However, it's the last thing Sophie wants right now and after everything she's gone through, I don't want to bring her anymore pain.

"You ready?" Caleb asks, stuffing his hands in his front pockets.

"Hey, almost. Gotta grab my jacket."

I grab it from the hook and hold it out for her. She pushes her arms through, then fixes her hair and adjusts herself. Once she's turned toward me, I step closer and whisper in her ear, "You really do look stunning, baby. I'm gonna be hard all damn night long."

She blushes and bites her bottom lip. "Better wait for me," she teases, then walks toward Maddie and Caleb. I follow behind and see them out.

"See ya, Mads. Bye, Caleb." I grind my teeth together as I force his name off my lips. Before Sophie walks out, I lean down to cup her jaw with my hand. "Bye." I wink before pressing my mouth to hers once more.

Caleb stands like a statue with an unreadable expression. If he wasn't aware she's taken, he is now.

Sophie blows me a kiss, and then the three of them pile into Caleb's car before he drives off. Moments later, Liam's date stumbles down the stairs.

"Fuckin' asshole," she mutters, storms past me and out the door, then slams it behind her.

I snort and chuckle. "What the hell did he do this time?"

Taking the steps two at a time, I walk to his bedroom and knock on the door. "You decent?"

"Depends who's asking."

"Just me, ass face."

"Then yeah, come in."

Hesitantly, I let myself in and find him on the bed playing his PlayStation. "Uh, wanna tell me what happened?"

He shrugs. "Cheryl was expecting more than I wanted to give."

"Wasn't her name Cindy?"

"Was it? Well, whatever. I told her to leave if she wasn't happy to just hang out, and she got pissed."

"And you wonder why you're a bachelor," I tease, leaning against the doorframe.

"Pfft. I don't wonder." He laughs, keeping his eyes on the screen. "I know why, and I plan to keep it that way."

Since I have time to kill, I sit and play with him, or rather, he fucking destroys me because I never play video games. He tries to show me some things, but it's pointless because Liam kills me every damn time.

"You suck," I mutter after losing again.

"Actually, *you* suck." He cackles.

It's almost seven when Jerad calls, and I realize time has flown, and Sophie will be back soon.

"Hey, man," I answer, stepping out of Liam's room to avoid his shouting and cursing at the TV every five seconds. "You find anything yet?"

"Well, kind of. I think so. First, the license plates didn't match a Caleb Royce."

My heart sinks. "Not surprised, but what name was it listed under?"

"Well first, I wanted to ask. The last guy you asked me to look up. His name was Weston Westbrook, right?"

The cautious tone in his voice has me on edge as I walk downstairs and into the living room.

"Right, but he's dead," I remind him.

"Well, these plates are registered to a Dalton Westbrook."

"What do you mean? Who's Dalton? Weston's brother?"

"It appears that way. One brother and one sister. The sister lives in Tulsa. Dalton is a thirty-three-year-old male from Los Angeles, worked as a broker at a bank up until six weeks ago. No kids."

Blinking, I try to wrap my head around this information. "What about a wife? Is he married?"

"Actually, I found a marriage license from a few years ago to a woman named Sarah."

"Okay and?" My heart is pounding so hard I wouldn't be surprised if he could hear it over the phone.

"I also found her death certificate that was filed five months ago."

"Jesus." I brush a hand through my hair as sweat beads on my forehead.

Pacing the living room, I grab some water before I fucking faint.

"Yeah, that's not all," he warns, inhaling sharply. "The cause of death was ruled as an accidental drowning, so I dug some more into the case and found Dalton was the number one suspect, but no concrete evidence was found to accurately charge him. There had been several domestic abuse calls, and although there was bruising near her neck, they couldn't pinpoint him being home that night."

"What?" I gasp. "Where the hell did he say he was?"

"Up here in Sac with his brother, Weston, who confirmed his alibi."

"And they believed him even with a record?"

"Seems so. They didn't have any other evidence to hold him longer than forty-eight hours."

"Motherfucker." I'm seething, my blood is boiling to a dangerous level of rage at the moment, and I don't know how to calm myself. "Jerad, he's fucking with her right now. Shit, shit, shit. So, you're telling me Caleb is Dalton Westbrook, Weston's older brother?"

"Yeah, man. It's all right here. He must've figured out where you guys live and who y'all are and stalked Sophie or something."

"Or he stalked her to get to me. Perhaps what my dad said was true, except the brother didn't want to wait for the court."

"Or he heard you were another privileged guy, son of the DA, who got off on a murder charge."

"It was self-defense," I retort, but I know I don't have to explain myself to him. "This can't be happening. I need to text her, tell her to get away from him, go pick her up or something. Then what? Can I have the cops haul his ass in for something? Stalking?"

"Not without a warrant or probable cause. All he's done so far is lie about who he is, not exactly illegal."

"Alright, I gotta go. I'll call you if I need something."

"Let me know."

"I will."

"And Mason? Be careful."

I text Sophie as I run up the stairs to tell Liam.

MASON

> Baby, are you still at your meeting? I need to speak with you right away. Call me as soon as you're out. Don't leave with Caleb.

"What?" Liam nearly knocks me over once I tell him everything Jerad said. "You're shitting me, right?"

"Look at me. Do I look like I am? I need to go find her."

I call her and get sent to voicemail, so I text her again.

MASON

> Soph, listen to me. Do not get in the car with Caleb. He's not who he says he is, and I'll explain everything as soon as you call or text me back but promise me you won't leave with him!

"It's after seven. Why isn't she checking her messages?" I pace frantically around his room. "I can't just stand here. I need to go find her before he does something." I continue pacing. "Fuck! I don't know where her meetings are. She's always called it group or circle, and I never thought to ask which specific location."

"Text her sisters, they probably know," he suggests, so I do without alarming them.

While I wait for one of them to respond, I call Sophie again only to get sent to voicemail.

MASON

Baby, where are you? You should be out of your meeting by now. Call me ASAP please!!! Text me so I know you're okay. Caleb is dangerous, and you need to get the hell away from him. He's not who he says he is…trust me. GET. AWAY.

"What the fuck am I gonna do?" I'm downright panicking, bending over to rest my palms on my knees as I try to catch my breath. "Fuck it, I'm gonna google it and go to the closest one."

"I'll go with you," Liam offers, placing a hand on my back. "You can't drive like this. I'll take you."

He pushes me along, then we're both out of the house and climbing into his truck. I'm on my phone searching and the nearest meeting location is five minutes away, so we try that one first.

"Fuck, the parking lot is nearly empty. I don't see his car," I say, sticking my head out the window. Just then two people come out of the exit door, and Liam drives over.

"Hi, excuse me. Do you know if Sophie Corrigan attends your grief meetings?"

"Never heard of her," the woman says.

"Is anyone else inside?"

"No."

"Okay, thanks."

Fuck, fuck, fuck.

Before I search on my phone again, I finally get a response from one of her sisters.

LENNON

St. Luke's Church over on fifth.

I tell Liam and yell at him to book it. It takes us almost ten minutes to get over there thanks to traffic, and by the time we arrive, the parking lot is empty. It's seven thirty, and the meeting ended a half hour ago.

Jumping out of the truck and slamming the door behind me, I begin screaming her name. "Sophie!" My voice is deep and loud, a sound I've never heard come from my throat before. I yell three more times before Liam tells me to get back into the truck. I don't listen, but instead lean up against it, hoping for a damn miracle that she comes back to me.

CHAPTER TWENTY-SIX

SOPHIE

Caleb parks the car in front of the church, and we sit with it running for a moment. He looks at me with tears in his eyes. Although this week has been a sad reminder of what he's lost, I'm happy I was able to be here for him tonight, considering his current state. It's hard seeing a man so broken, especially one who obviously loved his wife very much.

"Thanks for coming with me, Sophie. This has been a hard week, and I've been struggling to even go through the motions."

"You're welcome. I'm sorry you're going through this. I get it," I tell him sincerely.

His eyes meet mine. "But do you? Do you *really* get it?" His harsh question takes me off guard, and I don't know if it's because he's having an emotional week, or if he's second-guessing my reasons for joining the group in the first place. Or maybe it's my own guilt.

I suck in a sharp breath, worried he's calling me out for how I truly feel about Weston's death, but there's no way he could know. I've been vague, hardly mentioning anything about my issues as I try to work through them. For a moment, I think about Weston, and the air in the car gets thick, the weight of it sitting heavy on my chest. I feel like a fraud because I'm not mourning the loss of a man who abused me, and maybe Caleb finally realizes that.

"I do get it. It may be on a different level, but I understand what it's like to feel a missing piece of your heart," I tell him, hoping that's enough for him to stop questioning me. Glancing down at my phone, I realize we only have a few minutes until the meeting starts. "We should probably go inside so we aren't late."

With a nod, Caleb turns off the engine, and we get out of the car. *Just one hour of this, then I can go home to Mason*, I remind myself.

"Do you miss him?" Caleb asks as he opens the door to the church and motions for me to walk in ahead of him. I look at him and think about how close I was to dying by Weston's hands. My heart beats erratically, and I try to push away the anxiety threatening to take hold, but I'm failing miserably.

"I miss the good times." I spin around and walk toward the room where our meeting is held. I'm not lying but also not offering any additional information. I've kept it bottled up, refusing to tell my secret to a room full of strangers. It's not easy to explain the emotional effects of abuse to people, and considering this is my last meeting, I don't think I need to do it here.

"You okay?" Caleb asks as I take a seat and try to focus on my breathing.

"Yeah, I'm fine." But I'm not. I'm spiraling to a dark place—a place I've tried to forget so many times in the past several weeks. It's as if Weston has come back from the grave to take hold of me. To remind me I was his, and that I will *always* be his.

The chair next to me stays empty until right before the meeting starts. An older woman named Annette sits next to me and smiles. I've seen her here before. She has a kind face and is soft-spoken, but like the rest of the people in this room, she's grief-stricken and broken.

I wait for Dacia, hoping to see her tonight since I haven't heard from her lately. She's never late and doesn't usually miss any meetings, so I find her absence odd. I pull my phone from my clutch and send her a message because I'm worried. Opening the last text I received from her, the date is from a few days before the dinner party when she confirmed she'd be coming but then didn't.

Pastor Jude walks in and greets everyone with his usual warm tone. He lets us know a couple of members are running late, so the meeting will begin shortly.

"Who are you texting?" Caleb leans over and glances at my phone.

"Dacia. Have you spoken to her lately?" I ask.

Caleb shakes his head. "Nope. Haven't heard from her since she ditched your party."

I bite the inside of my cheek, then release a concerned breath. Moments later, the meeting starts, so I tuck my phone away and try to stay focused.

My mind is in another place as people go around the circle and share their stories. I think about what losing Weston means to me. For almost two months, I've buried my feelings, though the thoughts of him and what he did to me still haunt me.

One woman lost her husband three years ago and talks like it happened yesterday. I'm tempted to ask her if he ever hit her, or threw her around, or made her feel like a piece of shit the way Weston continuously did to me. Being here tonight when all I want to do is forget him sends me spiraling into a panic. I'm realizing now that I shouldn't have come.

As heat rushes to my cheeks, I quietly tell Caleb I'll be right back, trying not to draw any attention in my direction. I need to escape as quickly as possible. The walls of the long hall feel as if they're closing in, and I take deep breaths to steady my breathing. Once I'm in the ladies' bathroom, I lean my hands against the counter, absorbing the silence. I needed to get away from the grief that blankets every person in that room.

I glance at myself in the mirror. Contoured face, perfect hair, tight party dress, and as Mason called them, fuck-me heels. It's supposed to be one of the happiest nights of my life—something I've waited to experience for years—so I won't allow the memory of Weston to take this from me. I deserve to be happy, don't I?

Instead of hiding in here for the rest of the time, I head back into my seat while the pastor's still talking and take notice of how intently Caleb's listening.

"Death affects everyone at some point in their life, and most aren't sure how to react to the loss. I think offering condolences is the polite thing to do, and you shouldn't be offended when someone wants to help you." He doesn't take his eyes off Annette as tears stream down her face and fall to her lap. Watching her rips me up inside, and I offer my condolences, patting her softly on the back.

"Would anyone else like to share how they're feeling this week?" He searches around the room.

Caleb speaks up and chats about his wife and how much he misses her, and it almost kills me to hear about his pain, but then suddenly, it's like the blinders are removed. He swallows, but he almost seems emotionless as he speaks. As if he's playing a part and has taken off the mask. I study him, wondering if Mason was right, and I never noticed his insincerity before. Though I'm seeing it now in his mannerisms and the fierce way he glances at me.

"Our anniversary was this week," he continues robotically, and I suck in a ragged breath, then check the time. Only ten more minutes, then I'll leave and go on my date with Mason. I allow that thought to whisk me away, and I grow more excited with each passing second.

Pastor Jude smiles. "What about you, Sophie?"

He's never called me out before without volunteering since most people talk freely. I look up at him, feeling like a student who doesn't know the answer to the teacher's question. The blood drains from my face.

"I don't have anything to say," I murmur. All eyes are on me, and I'm pissed he brought any attention my way. I look down at my hands, wishing I could be invisible.

An older gentleman takes his turn and talks about his daughter who he recently lost in a drunk driving accident. Losing a sibling or a significant other has to hurt, but to lose a kid? I can't imagine. The meeting continues, and I find myself watching the clock more intently.

The pastor wraps up the session a few minutes early, and I can finally breathe again. I pull my phone from my clutch and open my text messages but don't see a response from Dacia.

Caleb watches me as I frown. Concern doesn't even begin to describe how I feel.

"Ready?" I ask when everyone starts saying their goodbyes, wanting to get out of here as quickly as possible.

His jaw tenses and locks, but I'm not sure what I did to annoy him. When I follow him outside, he's standoffish, but I ignore it.

Caleb unlocks the car, and when I climb inside, I buckle up because I'm ready to get home. When he gets in, a maniacal smile spreads across his lips. He continues staring, his cold gaze piercing straight through me.

"Everything okay?" I furrow my brows, searching his face.

His eyes narrow as he grabs my cheeks in his hands, pulling me toward him. "What do you think, Sophie?"

My breathing quickens as I try to pull out of his grip. Forcefully, he presses his lips against mine, and I struggle to get away from him.

Struggle to unbuckle.

Struggle to get out of the car.

But he grabs my arm, and in a split second, I see his fist coming toward me. Before I can react, I feel a sharp pain in my face, and then everything goes black.

My eyes flutter open, having no idea where I am. It's hard to focus as I look around because the room spins, and my head feels like someone drove a hammer into my face.

With my arms secured tightly behind my back, I try wiggling around but then realize my ankles are duct-taped to a wooden chair. I inhale a sharp breath when I notice Caleb leaning against a counter. We're in a house, and I'm in a kitchen, but I'm not sure where. The walls are gray, the floor is white, and the lights are so damn bright I have to squint. I quickly look over my shoulder and see a living room behind me. There's a velvet couch, a large TV, and strange art on the walls. In the corner is a sculpture and all the curtains are drawn. Did he take me to his house?

"So Sleeping fucking Beauty is finally awake." His voice is rough and nothing like I've heard before.

I glance around, unable to speak due to the tape over my mouth.

He crosses the kitchen and harshly rips it off. I let out a gut-wrenching scream, which only causes him to laugh. Going back to where he was standing, he tosses the tape on the counter. He drinks straight from a tequila bottle.

I notice a gun on the counter next to a police scanner. The volume's so low, I can barely hear it.

"Caleb." I release an unsteady breath. "What're you doing?" I try to stay calm, but I'm struggling as the adrenaline rushes through my veins. "Let me go."

Laughter roars from his chest, and that's when I notice light reflecting off the blade of the knife in his hand. "Let you go? I don't fuckin' think so, darlin'."

He saunters toward me again, and I keep my focus on him. Caleb presses the sharp tip to my chin, forcing me to look at him. I swallow hard as I stare into his cold eyes. "Caleb, *please…*"

He adds force, digging the knife into my skin until a drop of blood drips down the blade. Pulling it back, he looks at it, satisfied.

"Let me tell you a little story, *Sophie darling*." He says my name like it's poison and steps back. Disgust is written on his face as he glances at me.

"Family is everything to me. I love my parents. I love my cousins. I *loved* my brother."

I don't dare say a word. This isn't the Caleb I met weeks ago or the man who's shared stories about his wife. I don't know who this Caleb is, and it's terrifying.

"And then one day, he died at the hands of someone else," he adds.

"I'm sorry. No one deserves to lose someone they love. Your wife, your brother…"

"Shut the fuck up, bitch!" he shouts, then walks over to the roll of duct tape on the counter. He rips off a strip, then stalks toward me and slaps it over my mouth. "Don't. Fucking. Talk."

Wincing, tears welling on the edge of my eyelids. The last time I felt this scared was when Weston lost his temper and choked me so hard I thought he was going to kill me.

"My brother's death was your fucking fault. *Your* fault. It disgusts me to look at your pathetic face."

My eyes go wide, confused. His brother? My fault?

He nods at my expression, and that crazy smile returns and recognition hits me. It begins to make sense. All of it.

"Weston," he croaks out and stabs the blade into the countertop next to the gun. I shake my head, wishing I could scream so someone knew where I was. A cell phone vibrates next to him, and when he grabs it, his smirk turns devious.

"Ahh, your boyfriend's starting to panic now." His shrill laughter sends a shiver down my spine. "See, this is the thing…"

Caleb juggles the phone between his palms.

"Earlier tonight, he figured out who I really was, and while you were busy in the bathroom, your phone kept vibrating and interrupting the meeting. So I opened your clutch to silence your phone. But then I read his messages, his warnings to get away from me, and that's when I knew I had to put my plan into action tonight. He killed my only fucking brother and then got away with it!" His voice booms against the walls, and I jump.

"And it's your fault because you're a goddamn lying, cheating whore, and you got your boy toy to get him out of the picture so you two could be together. Now, you're gonna pay. An eye for an eye. Hell, you're both gonna pay, and it will be the justice my brother and family deserve."

I try to scream, but it's so muffled from the tape there's no way anyone outside this room can hear me. I'm not sure where we are, what time it is, or if I'm still in Sacramento.

"Your boyfriend is a murderer and got away with it because of who his daddy is, so I'm taking matters into my own hands. It's a shame I have to kill you, Sophie, because you're quite pretty. I would've fucked your brains out in a heartbeat."

Disgust rolls through me as I narrow my eyes at him. Then he walks toward me and rips the tape off my face again, which hurts like a motherfucker.

"You got something to say?" He leans down, his face inches from mine.

Shaking my head, I close my eyes tight, hoping this is all a sick nightmare I haven't woken up from.

"Caleb," I plead softly when I finally look at him. He stands and paces in front of me. "Let me go, and I won't tell anyone about this. We can go our separate ways and both move on with our lives. It doesn't have to be like this."

The tears come, and I try to push away my hysteria.

He furrows his brows as if he's studying me, and what scares me the most is how insane he looks.

"Did you love him?" he asks, and when I don't answer, he repeats, "Did you love my brother?"

My eyes meet his, and I notice the resemblance between the two of them even more, though I remember recalling a familiarity about him when we met. Now it makes sense. They're both fucking crazy as hell, yet I can't figure out why Weston never mentioned having a brother. He never gave me many personal details about himself, though, and the ones I knew were all lies. It seems as if I can say the same about Caleb. Knowing I need to choose my words carefully, I try with everything I have not to set him off, but I take too long to respond. It's hard to say I loved a man who hit and nearly killed me.

"Fucking answer me!" he yells, making me jump. "And don't

you dare lie to me. Your life depends on it…" His threat has my heart racing harder.

Blinking, I swallow down the lump in my throat, hoping he can't hear the fear in my voice. "Yes, I did at one time."

"But then Mason happened," he concludes. "We've been having a little chat."

I study the device in his hand, and it looks like one of those cheap prepaid smartphones. "How'd you get his number?"

"I'm a lot smarter than you think. You don't give me enough credit, Sophie," he spews as a cruel grin spreads across his face. "I mirrored your phone, knowing he'd find a way to track it and then strategically placed it somewhere else. So he'll go looking for you in one place, but you'll be in another. By the time he figures it out, your body will be cold. And if all goes according to plan, I'll have the satisfaction of killing him too." He flashes an evil smirk, and it's scary because it's genuine.

The realization hits me that he's using me as bait to get to Mason, and I pray Mason stays away and doesn't try to be a hero. I don't want anything to happen to him or anyone else.

Weston's death is partially my fault, and I feel guilty about everything that happened. I should've left that night without him, called the cops, told Lennon the truth—any of those scenarios would've kept him alive and Mason out of trouble. If I'd never dated Weston, rushed into a relationship and introduced him to everyone, things would've been so different. Or hell, if I would've left him after the first time he hit me and reported it, maybe none of this would've happened.

"So did you fuck Mason while you were living with my brother?" He steps closer, narrowing his gaze on me like a predator hunting his prey. I can taste the bitterness in his tone as he scowls at me, and I know that nothing I say will satisfy him. My chest heaves with the anticipation of his next move, and the adrenaline rushes through me, but this time, I won't take his shit lying down. I already did that with Weston, walked on eggshells, and that got me nowhere just as fast.

"I never cheated on Weston. I was faithful," I tell him

truthfully. "I loved him until he started hitting me and choking me and then threatened to kill me." I wiggle my wrists, struggling against the tape, anger fueling my next words. "Now that I think about it, you two have *a lot* in common."

And just like that, his fist comes toward me, and everything fades to black.

CHAPTER TWENTY-SEVEN

I KNEW I shouldn't have let her leave with that crazy fuck. The moment he showed up, I should've stood my ground and took her to the meeting myself. But the last thing I wanted to do was argue with Sophie before our date.

I don't want to be the guy who tells her what to do. After the hell she went through with Weston, I don't want to mirror any of his controlling behavior. I want Sophie to be free to make her own decisions, but I'm kicking myself now for not pushing harder to keep her away from him. That's when I think about Maddie because she was with them earlier.

"Fuck," I whisper, then demand Liam call Maddie as soon as possible to make sure she's okay as I continue to call Sophie.

Back when I first met him as Caleb, I could tell he was bad news. His brother gave me the same creepy vibe. The way he looked at her and used a sob story to gain her trust were red flags from the start, and I'm so pissed because my gut was spot-on. But him being related to Weston? That was one thing that had never crossed my mind.

"She's fine. At her dorm," he tells me after a moment.

"Good," I say, relieved she's okay because this is messed up as it is. He could've taken them both, but I suspect I'm his main target in all of this. Knowing Sophie's with Dalton makes me fucking sick. We have to find her as soon as possible. Liam and I stand in the empty parking lot of the church where the grief meetings are held, and I scream her name, praying for a goddamn miracle that she can hear me.

I call her again, over and over and over, pleading for her to call me. But it's no use. She's not here.

"This can't be happening…" I whisper-shriek to Liam, struggling to catch my breath. What the hell am I gonna do? Call the cops? Call my dad? Tell Jerad to put a warrant out for his arrest?

If he has my girlfriend, and she can't respond to my messages and calls, does that qualify as kidnapping?

Holy fuck, I can't breathe, and the world seems to be spinning around me. The last time I felt this way was the night I couldn't get ahold of Emma, and she ended her life. I have zero control of the situation, and it's destroying me from the inside out.

Right before I have a full-on panic attack, my phone vibrates.

DALTON

> An eye for an eye, killer. Murdered someone I
> loved, now I'm going to kill someone you love.
> Payback's a bitch, asshole.

Attached is a picture of my sweet Sophie tied to a chair with duct tape across her mouth and unconscious as she sits there so helplessly.

"Motherfucker! I'm gonna kill him!" I howl.

Liam glances at the screen over my shoulder and gasps. I type out a response, not able to stop shaking.

MASON

> If you fucking touch her, I'm gonna kill you. And
> it won't be classified as self-defense this time.
> Let her go, Dalton, or I swear to God, this won't
> end well for you.

DALTON

> Tsk, tsk. We're not playing by your rules, Mason.
> This time…justice WILL be served. It's either
> gonna be you or her. And if you call the police,
> your father, or any of your little bitch friends,
> she'll be dead before you even find her. Your
> choice.

I'm sick to my stomach as I hand my phone to Liam. His eyes widen as I try to get a hold of myself.

"What the fuck do I do?" I ask, panting as we walk to the truck.

The wheels are turning in Liam's head, and I can see he's thinking of every possible scenario.

"He disabled her location sharing," he says, sliding his thumb over the screen.

"Motherfucker." After Sophie moved in, we shared locations with her as a precaution. Knowing Weston's family might come after me for a wrongful homicide charge, we decided it was better to be safe than sorry since we all worked long hours. Considering what Liam does for a living, we've had ours shared with each other for years. He pretends to be tough as nails, but that doesn't mean I don't worry about the types of criminals he has to be around.

"Call Jerad. See if he can track her phone number to a cell tower and or even get a specific address since it's on. If he can pinpoint her location, maybe we can find his car since we know what he drives."

A million different thoughts stream through my mind, and all I can do is hope Sophie isn't hurt and is staying strong. Though, by the photo, I know he intends to break her down physically and mentally while fucking with me. He's a goddamn psycho.

I call Jerad and explain the messages and pictures and what I need from him as we climb inside the truck. Liam instantly starts it, and we begin driving away.

"You'll have to give me some time, but I can get my guy on it ASAP. You gonna tell your dad or call the cops? Report a kidnapping? You have his license plate number? We could have people all over the city looking for this sick fucker."

Letting out a smothered breath, I ball my hand into a fist, wishing I could drive it straight into Dalton's face. "I can't. He's threatened to kill her, and after knowing about his wife, I believe him. I can't get my dad or the police involved, so I have to take matters into my own hands. But so help me God, if I find him and he's hurt her…"

"Mason," he warns. "Don't do anything stupid. I'll call you when I find out more info. Give me an hour."

"An hour? A fucking hour? She could be dead by then. That's too long, Jerad."

He sighs. "It's all I can do. Tracing shit takes time, and I have to go back to the office. It's not like I can do this from my goddamn cell phone."

"Okay, I'm sorry. But every second she's gone is another second she's in danger."

"I get it, but you need to calm down. I get you're worried, but I can't snap my fingers and make it happen."

Even in situations such as this, Jerad remains calm and collected. He's doing the best he can, but I'm frustrated as fuck. The stress of Sophie being with Weston's brother is already wearing me down and this nightmare just began.

Jerad ends the call with a promise to get back with me as soon as he knows something. As we speed down the highway, my mind spirals. Though I want the whole damn city looking for her, I don't second-guess Dalton's threats, just as I didn't doubt Weston had that gun to kill Sophie. Dalton will kill her without a second thought. They're both psychotics with zero compassion. Dalton's already gotten away with murder once—hell, maybe more for all anyone knows.

The thought of him touching Sophie sickens me, especially since I doubt she went wherever he took her willingly. She's a fighter.

Liam drives across town, and we're soon pulling into the

driveway of the house. I look at him in confusion because we need to keep looking for her.

"There's no reason for us to aimlessly roam the city searching for her when we have no idea where she is. We should wait for Jerad to call and at least give us a location. Continue to interact with Dalton so he doesn't turn off her phone."

I release a frustrated breath and nod as we walk into the house. "You're right," I admit, trying to find the strength to keep texting him. Before I can finish my thought, another message comes in.

DALTON

Wondering if I should fuck her before I kill her.
See what all the fuss is about. What do you
think?

A picture comes through of Sophie still restrained to the chair, and he's pushed her dress so far up her legs that I can see the lace panties she wore for our date. My jaw clenches so tight, I might break a damn tooth. She's unconscious, and knowing he can do whatever he wants to her creates a feeling inside me that I've never felt before.

She's *mine*. She's *fucking mine*. I don't want him touching her.

"Motherfucker." A growl comes from deep in my core. I'm so damn helpless, and he knows it.

"We're gonna find her," Liam promises, bending down and opening the duffle bag he threw on the floor earlier. "We're gonna find her and make him suffer." It's clear he means business as he pulls a Glock from the bag and loads it.

"Shit. You have a gun?" My eyes widen, and Liam nods.

Good, is what comes to mind when I think about what Liam intends to do with it.

Dalton deserves to feel pain.

I want *revenge* for taking my girl. I want him to be sorry he ever insinuated himself into our lives.

"We're gonna need backup. Call Hunter and have him meet us here. Do *not* tell him why. The last thing we need is a frantic

Lennon calling the police." Liam's coolheaded as he tucks the gun in the back of his pants. "We'll explain once he gets here."

Knowing he's probably right, I call Hunter.

"Aren't you supposed to be on your special romantic date right now?" He chuckles, but it causes my heart to drop because the time Sophie and I were supposed to spend together was stolen from us.

"Can you come to the house and help us move some furniture?" I ask, trying to keep my tone even to avoid any questions.

"Uhh…seriously?" I feel guilty for lying, but if Lennon suspects anything and calls the cops, Sophie could die.

"Yeah, we need some help, and it's really fuckin' important," I snap.

He sits silently on the phone for a moment, and I hear the noise from the TV in the background fade away. "Everything okay?"

"It's somewhat of an emergency, but I don't want you to alert Lennon to anything that's going on. It has to do with Sophie," I explain carefully.

"Gonna be honest, man. You're scaring me." Hunter's voice is low.

"It's a long story. I'll tell you as soon as you get here." Worry coats my tone, and I don't think it's lost on Hunter because he tells me he'll be here in fifteen minutes. We might need his help if we figure out where the hell Dalton's taken her. The more people on our side, the better.

My phone vibrates, and it's Sophie's phone calling. With a racing heart, I put it on speaker.

"Mason!" She yells my name, and it nearly cripples me. "It's a trap! Stay away. *Please*!" She lets out a blood-curdling scream after a loud slapping sound echoes.

"Stupid bitch." I can hear Dalton's voice in the background, and my blood boils.

"Soph!" I shout.

"Hiiiii," Dalton singsongs. "Mason. I'm gonna have so much

fun playing with your girlfriend before I kill her. Probably as much fun as you had when you killed my brother. Let's play a little game, shall we…?"

Hearing her hysterics and sobs in the background nearly brings me to my knees. "Don't you dare touch her!"

"I've already told you once before, we're not playing by your rules. You're not in control here. *I am*," he spits out. "My game is very simple. Every time you don't listen, Sophie gets hurt. It's up to you…" he taunts, and I see red.

"When I find you, I'm gonna make sure you—"

The call ends before I can finish my sentence. I slam my fist into the wall and let out a deep groan. Instantly, my knuckles throb, and I want to find him and beat the fuck out of him. I'm so livid and don't know what to do as my world spirals out of control.

DALTON

Mmm…she tastes as good as she looks. I'm
almost sad she won't be around long for me to
play with her little pussy longer.

My fingers fly over the screen as I hold my breath, afraid I'll scream and otherwise lose my shit.

MASON

Stay away from her. I mean it…

DALTON

I can't help myself…spreading her blood around
and licking it off her is just too good. Fuck, she
likes it too. She's a kinky whore.

MASON

What the fuck do you want?

I grit my teeth so hard, the shooting pain is a welcome distraction while I try to sort my thoughts.

DALTON

> Aren't you paying attention, asshole? You get to
> watch me torture her, and knowing you'll never
> find her in time to save her will be the cherry on
> top. Killing her will be revenge for killing
> someone I loved. Then you'll be next because
> justice will be served. But I might make her suffer
> for a while…it'll be fun watching your reaction as
> I describe your girlfriend's last moments
> breathing. Perhaps I'll have her mouth around
> my cock first. I'll take some pics for you.

Liam stands in the kitchen, watching me as I lose my fucking mind. "What is it?"

With shaky hands, I hand him the phone with the messages on the screen. I'm shaking so hard, and my heart races so fast it threatens to give out.

This sick asshole has my entire world and could literally end it all. Needing to chill out, I go into the bathroom, glancing at an unrecognizable version of myself, and turn on the water. I splash my face, trying to get control. Nearly ten minutes pass before I walk back into the kitchen where Liam is and grab my phone from him.

"You okay?" he asks.

Before I can speak, there's a knock on the door. When I open it, I find Hunter with concern in his eyes.

"Explain," he orders, pushing past me.

Liam meets us in the living room, and I start from the beginning when I found out who Caleb was and give him all the details of what's happening. His facial expressions go from shocked to upset to raging pissed.

"So you have no idea where she could be?" Hunter asks, pacing the room. I can see the pulse in his neck erratically beating and know it mirrors my own.

My nostrils flare when I think about how that asshole could've taken her anywhere. "Not a clue. Not until we get a location from Jerad." Pulling my phone from my pocket, I open the text messages I've received from Sophie's phone and show Hunter.

"That motherfucker," he barks after reading the thread. "He's stolen my fucking sister!"

I appreciate how protective he is of Sophie too. He's marrying her sister and has known her as long as I have. When I glance back at the picture of her tied to the chair, it makes me sick to my goddamn stomach. Her lips are busted, and her face is already bruising. When I find him, he's a dead man.

"You can see why we can't tell Lennon or Maddie right now," I say so he doesn't message them.

When Jerad calls, I put it on speaker.

"I've got some info," he says.

"Tell me."

"Okay, so I was able to track her number, and it looks like she's on the north side of town. It's picking up at the cell tower over by Glenwood Meadows. So she's got to be in that area."

"Glenwood Meadows?" Liam confirms, and I nod. He heads out the door, and Hunter and I follow him.

Jerad continues. "If you need backup or want me to put out an alert, please call me, Mason. I don't want you getting into any more trouble or, hell, hurt. It's the last thing you need right now. You need—"

"I got it," I interrupt. "If I need anything else, I'll let you know," I tell him. "And thank you, man. I appreciate your help. I'll keep you updated." I end the call before jumping into the truck.

Liam speeds out of the driveway, and my phone vibrates again with picture after picture of Sophie crying and screaming. His fucking sick messages have tears threatening to fall because I can't comprehend what she must be going through or how she's feeling. I'd give up everything to get her back, even my own life.

The images burn in my mind, but I force myself to look at them. I want the anger to fuel my every move, and I plan to make him pay for this. He'll be sorry he ever went near her, and I don't give a fuck about the consequences.

He sends a text back with a cut down the length of Sophie's arm. Blood is everywhere. It doesn't look deep, but that doesn't mean he won't go deeper next time he feels like proving a point.

"He's cut her," I wail, my heart lodging into my throat as I gasp for air. Liam steps on the gas, and we're practically flying down the highway.

"Where are we going?" Hunter asks.

"Weston's house. He lives close to Glenwood Meadows. That bastard probably took her there," I reply, kicking myself for not thinking to go there earlier, considering he's probably been staying there.

In no time at all, we're pulling onto the street. The last time I was here was when I helped Sophie pack up her shit and move her to my house. The inside was a wreck from the fight they had before the wedding reception. The same day the gun went off and killed him. The same day he could've murdered Sophie. Dalton had gotten away with killing his wife, so couldn't he do the same? I'm sure that's exactly what Weston thought too.

"We should go in through the back," Liam orders. "Don't want to look suspicious and get the cops called on us by the neighbors before we get the chance to grab her."

Liam leads the way, and Hunter and I follow as he walks around the side of the house. Liam pulls out his gun, then places his back against the brick, and whispers, "Everything sounds quiet, doesn't it?"

"That doesn't mean anything. He had her mouth duct-taped," I remind him.

Seconds later, he lifts his leg and kicks the back door in with the heel of his boot.

"Damn, dude," Hunter says, impressed, but Liam's built for shit like this. Liam keeps his arms stretched out as he points the gun in front of us and walks inside, then clears the room before walking into the kitchen. On the counter, we see Sophie's phone with a piece of paper. My heart fucking sinks when I read the note.

You think I'm that fucking stupid to let you track her number? If so, then you're the idiot. Say goodbye to your little girlfriend, killer. See you soon, motherfucker. You're next.

I gasp for air, but it doesn't help. I lose my balance and lean against the counter, nearly falling to my knees. Liam and Hunter read the note.

"This is all part of his game," Hunter says as another photo comes through my text.

Dalton has Sophie's hair wrapped around his fist with a knife to her throat, and I try to choke out words, but nothing comes out.

"He's gonna kill her," Hunter whispers.

"Not if we find and kill him first," Liam retorts as he helps me stand, and we rush out of the house.

"Are you sure we shouldn't call the cops now? If he's gonna kill her either way…" Hunter says with concern written all over his face.

"The moment he hears or sees them, he won't think twice about killing her on the spot. At least we can appease him while we look for her and shoot him first when we find them," Liam says. I want to believe we'll get there before something terrible happens to her, but with every second that passes, I fear the worst.

CHAPTER TWENTY-EIGHT

WHEN I COME TO, my entire body feels as though I was thrown off a bull. When Caleb cut my arm and I saw blood, the world faded away once again. I'm not sure how many times I've been unconscious. I was in shock, horrified that he could cut into my flesh as if I'm nothing more than a slab of meat. He found way too much satisfaction in my earth-shattering screams when he pushed the blade into my skin.

My eyes are nearly swollen shut, and my lips feel busted. My back hurts from being taped to this chair for so long. What Weston did to me doesn't compare to what his brother has done tonight.

I glance at Caleb, noticing the similarities between the two and wonder how I never noticed. I'm a fucking fool. Same cheeks, same nose, and even the same coldness behind their eyes—they're monsters cut from the same cloth.

"Finally," Caleb huffs when he notices me stirring.

He looks at me like I'm a huge inconvenience, but I didn't wish for this. All I wanted to do was support someone I thought was my friend, attend grief circle, and experience a first date with Mason. I should've known it was too good to be true. The timing is always wrong, but this is the most fucked-up way for the universe to show that. The thought nearly blinds me, but I try to push it away.

"Caleb," I croak out. The excruciating pain is causing my body to go into shock.

"Stop calling me that! My name isn't Caleb, you dumb bitch."

I swallow, not knowing what's true and what isn't anymore. At this point, I don't care what his name is. I want to get out of here alive and back to Mason, but I don't know if that'll happen. My heart races when I think about dying at the hands of this monster.

He watches me, amused.

"What should I call you then?" I ask, trying to keep him talking so maybe it'll give me more time to live. Or, rather, figure out how to get out of here before it's too late.

He snarls, then shrugs. "I guess you should know the name of your killer. It's Dalton."

I nearly choke on the thick air that fills the room. Does he really have it in him to kill me? From what I've seen already, I think he might. I don't doubt he'll follow through with his threats, just as I didn't doubt Weston. I have no reason to believe otherwise, not after he's hit and cut me. I'm losing blood and hope.

"Your boyfriend must think I'm stupid as fuck." Dalton snickers, pacing in front of me, turning up the volume on the police scanner. "If he makes a call about you missing, I'll hear it, and he'll regret it. I'm not a fucking idiot like he thinks."

I try to swallow down the lump in my throat that's quickly replaced with bile.

"No," I whisper, but my response only pleases him more. "No one thinks you're an idiot."

I nod as he twirls the knife between his fingers. "Do I scare you, Sophie?"

No matter what answer I give, it won't be good enough. It's a loaded question because if I say yes, he'll continue his sick, torturous game, and if I say no, he'll change tactics until I *am* scared. After living with Weston and being pushed to my limits emotionally and physically, I never thought I'd feel fear like this again. When he died, I thought it was over, and I'd be safe.

The way my body trembles should be enough for Dalton, but it's not.

"Fucking answer me!" he screams, then slaps me across the face.

I wince but hold back from crying out. "Yes. You do," I admit. "I thought I knew you. I thought we were friends," I say with tears streaming down my cheeks because it's the truth. I believed his whole damn story.

"And that was your downfall. Your issue is you trust too easily. You're nothing more than a little lamb who so willingly followed a tiger into the jungle," he mocks with a roar of laughter.

A chill runs up my spine when he smiles. I don't recognize him with that crazed look in his eyes.

"You know…" He takes a step closer before pacing in front of me. "My brother loved you so damn much. So. Damn. Much. A month before he was murdered, he told me he was planning to propose. When I helped my parents clean out his house, I found the engagement ring. He talked about how you saved him. Little did he know, you'd be the reason for his death."

"You're lying," I say between gritted teeth. I don't believe a fucking word he says about Weston, especially that.

He's in his element with a large ass knife tightly gripped in his hand and a gun behind him. "I have no reason to lie. Weston spoke so highly of you. He *loved* you. And you pretended to love him back so you could use him for his house."

My emotions begin to spill over. "That's *not* true."

"He told me how he felt sorry for you because of your roommate situation and mentioned how you sucked dick like a champ. So he let you move in, though it seems you had an ulterior motive." He narrows his eyes before rushing over and kicking me in my stomach with all his strength. My body and my arms feel as if they may break off as I slam against the hard floor. Although my throat is dry and everything hurts, I let out a terrifying scream.

Dalton stands over me with his arms crossed over his chest, laughing.

"I'm gonna get more satisfaction ending you than I did Dacia."

His words course through me like venom. "What?"

"I wonder if you'll scream the same way she did, or if it'll take longer before you stop breathing." He speaks as though he's talking about the weather.

"No," I whisper, forcing my eyes closed, wanting to disappear as he bends down closer to my face.

"She was getting in my way of getting to you and asking too many questions. I didn't need her warning you about me, so I did what I had to do." He gives me a wide grin. "Glad you reminded me. I need to get her body out of my trunk." He purses his lips, then continues. "In fact, I can burn all your bodies together. Hers. Yours. And Mason's. Hope none of his little friends get in my way, though, or I'll have more bodies than can fit in my trunk. Hmm… maybe I'll leave you all in here while I torch the whole fucking house." I'm not sure if he realizes he's thinking aloud, but it's terrifying.

"You're a monster," I spit out, but he smirks. At this point, I wouldn't be surprised if he has weapons hidden all over this place, considering the way he talks about taking out anyone who tries to stop him.

My gut twists as I think about my friends. I hope he's only trying to scare me, but I have a feeling he's telling the truth about Dacia. I haven't heard from her in weeks.

This can't be happening.

"Thank you." He's amused. "Want to know how I killed her? It's a lovely story."

I keep my mouth shut as he stands over me. Swiftly, he brings his foot back and kicks my stomach with his boot, knocking the breath out of me. Pain shoots through my body as he kicks me again, and I'm scared he'll break one of my ribs. After he's worn himself out, and the pain becomes my new normal, he stands over me with the cell phone and takes pictures. My dress is bunched up to my waist, and I'm regretting wearing it since I'm exposed, and he has access to any part of me he wants.

"Wonder what your boyfriend is gonna think about these? Want to smile for the camera?" He continues to take more as I lay in agony.

Dalton forcefully grabs me and yanks the chair upright. I keep my head slumped, hoping this is over soon, but beating me to a pulp won't be enough for him. Dalton grabs a fistful of my hair and jerks my head back, making me gasp as the pain.

"Dacia was smarter than you. I don't think she ever trusted me and purposely forced herself between us, but unfortunately for her, she couldn't stay out of my goddamn way. So when you invited us to dinner, she told me I needed to explain to you who I was because she'd figured out that my name wasn't Caleb." He shakes his head. "She threatened to tell you if I didn't. That was the bitch's first mistake. Don't *ever* threaten me," he spits out. "It never ends well." He flashes a satisfied grin. "For the other person, that is."

Dacia, protective Dacia. She was always so intelligent and observant. I cry for her. I cry for her mother, who already lost one child. I cry because I will have the same fate as her by the same man.

"Aww, are you sad for her?" he taunts. "Boo-fuckin'-hoo."

I squeeze my eyes tight as he continues to ramble, giving me details I don't want to hear.

"I waited outside her house, knowing she'd be leaving for work soon. When she walked to her car, I snuck up behind her. She put up a good fight, but she was too weak for me. Overpowering her was easy. Almost as easy as my wife, though Dacia didn't beg me to stop like my wife did."

"You…" I swallow, shocked that the part of him being married was true. "*Killed* your wife?"

"Threats, Sophie darling. *No one* threatens me." He emphasizes his words. "She threatened to leave me after she found out she was pregnant with another man's baby, and after the whore cheated on me, I wasn't gonna allow her to do that. She was mine. Now she'll always *only* be mine."

His sentiments echo Weston's. More tears well in my eyes, and he cracks his knuckles. He's killed two women with those hands. I'll be his third.

The phone vibrates, and he laughs when he reads the message, loving every minute of this. "Oh, your sister Maddie is texting you now. What should we tell her?" He taps the knife against his lips. "I should've taken her too, but I don't know if I could've dealt with two of you cunts at once. Maybe after I've killed you and Mason, I'll go after her too. Seems like a good fuck. Bet she'd give good head with her arms and legs tied up."

The thought of him being anywhere near Maddie makes my heart race, and I'm internally panicking because he knows where she lives now. All I've ever wanted was to protect my sisters and not bring people like Dalton into their lives. I become more frantic and uneasy, knowing he could've easily taken her too. Take me, hurt me, even kill me, but leave my sisters out of it.

"What do you want from me?"

"I've got what I want for now—you. You're what's gonna bring Mason to me, and then I'll be able to make him feel the same way I felt when I learned my brother was shot. After I knock out his teeth and tie him up, I'm gonna make him watch me strangle the life from you. Maybe I'll fuck your ass first. He can witness it all before he takes his last breath."

His words are terrifying, and what's worse is that he's convinced he's capable of doing this. Mason won't go down without a fight, and most likely, he won't come alone. I twist my arms, seeing if I can loosen the tape enough to wiggle free.

"Ooh, speaking of the motherfucking devil." He turns the phone around to show me that Mason's calling. "Should I answer?"

He presses the button before I reply, then puts the phone up to my ear.

"I'm looking for you, Dalton, and when I find you…"

"Mason," I breathe out, tears falling.

His tone instantly changes, and he speaks softly. "Sophie. Oh my God. Are you okay?"

Before I can respond, he rips the phone away and laughs.

"Hurt her? Nah, she's fine. She's tough. Can take a kick to the gut like a man. Right?" He winks, which has me swallowing bile.

My heart races as he nonchalantly walks around the kitchen listening to Mason. "You don't want to threaten me. You'll be sorry if you do. Trust me. Just ask your little *sweet* Sophie." He chuckles darkly.

To anyone else, it would seem he's chatting with an old friend. Dalton is hot one minute and cold the next. Laughing, then shouting. He's unstable and the most frightening part of it all— unpredictable.

"Touch her, you say?" His eyes bore into me. "Actually, I was thinking of fucking her first. I'd like to know what my brother had and find out what's so special about her that made you kill him." He pauses to listen to Mason, then laughs again. "Oh, foul language, Mason. No, no. Don't worry…I saw the way she looked at me the first day we met…" He continues talking shit, but I tune him out, unable to hear any more as Mason yells on the other end.

I remember the day we met like yesterday because I thought he was hitting on me. Instead of listening to my gut, I chalked it up to being jaded because of Weston. He invaded my personal space and acted too friendly. However, thinking about it now, I should've recognized the signs.

Dalton ends the call and lets out a cackle as he comes toward me. Placing his hand tightly around my throat, he digs his fingers into my skin. I gasp, struggling to breathe as he closes my airway. I try shifting my body, fighting against the duct tape and his strength, but it's no use. I'm in so much pain that I'm weak and exhausted. His smile never leaves his face as everything else fades away.

"Sophie." I hear Weston's voice. *No.* Not possible. "I warned you. I meant it when I said you were *mine* forever."

I shake my head, looking at him standing in front of me

wearing the clothes he had on the first time we met for brunch. "You're dead."

He grins and cocks an eyebrow. "No, *you're* dead."

I'm unable to focus on anything. Insufferable pain creeps over me, and my stomach starts to hurt. None of this is real. I know it's not, but it seems real. In a blink, Weston is in front of me with both of his hands around my throat, choking the life out of my body.

"Weston," I barely get out the word before fighting against him. "Weston, stop."

It's as if someone turns on the lights, and I'm brought back to my reality as Dalton towers over me. I'm so damn disoriented that Weston is haunting me from the grave. My hallucinations are merging memories of the past with my present.

"You called me Weston, you little bitch." The back of his hand smacks across my cheek. My head pounds so hard, and I wonder why he doesn't just finish the damn job and end me. Why continue with this charade? I have no more tears. They've dried up. My broken body won't be able to take much more before it shuts down and the darkness returns.

Blinking, I see his fuzzy figure in front of me, and when my eyes finally focus, I see the devil is still taunting me.

"You're such a little cock tease." I hear the smile in his voice. He's giddy as fuck knowing he holds all the power over me and can easily strangle me until I lose consciousness. I don't know how long I was out before, but my dress is ripped, and my bra is exposed. All I want to do is hide from him, but he's determined to steal every last shred of my dignity.

"Smile for the camera, sweetheart," he purrs, snapping photos of me. "Oh, speaking of, I never showed you the pictures my brother sent me of you."

Just when I think it can't get any worse, it does. Dalton grabs my hair and jerks my head back, forcing me to look. After scrolling through his photos, he turns the screen around for me to see. What I see on his phone are intimate pictures I took for Weston. Along with pictures Weston took of me when I didn't know. I'm disgusted.

"I'd be lying if I said I didn't jerk off to your picture a handful of times. That ass, Sophie. I might need to have a little taste before I end you," he says, adjusting his noticeable erection.

"You might as well kill me now then," I say, holding back the urge to vomit all over him. "You fucking disgust me!"

Dalton shakes his head. "Oh no…I've got a list of things to do to you first. Cut off your fingers, one by one. Shave your head so I can have that gorgeous dark hair as a keepsake. Can't forget knocking your teeth out. Can't risk anyone identifying you. No ID means no way to link it back to me. But I've decided to add fucking you to my list too. My dick is fucking hard and needs relief, Sophie darling. You're probably wet for me, aren't you? My cock will ruin that cunt in no time, and then I'll jerk my cum all over those perky tits."

I dry heave when his hand slips into his pants and he touches himself. My head pounds so fucking hard, and each time I gasp for air, pain radiates through me.

"Fuck you." I spit out blood.

I'm done with begging. It does no good with him anyway.

"Keep it up, and I'll cut your goddamn tongue out too." He inches closer and slides the knife down my cheek, then puts the cool blade against my lips. "After I make you suck me off, of course. Should we start now? Send your boy toy a video?"

While I'm more afraid than I've ever been in my life, I can't show it. Mentally, I begin building a wall between reality and where I wish I was right now—with Mason. I picture us on the couch, watching our Netflix shows, and laughing together. I take myself out of the nightmare I'm currently living and force myself inside my fantasy.

My eyes flutter closed as he continues rattling off the horrible things he'll do to me all the while pulling at me, touching my chest, and sliding his fingers down my stomach. I remain still, feeling numb, no longer giving him the power to control my emotions.

I think about Mason. He's already had to find one girlfriend dead. It destroys me to know what this will do to him, and I can only hope he'll be okay and can move on one day. Maddie and Lennon come to mind and Allie Cat. I'll miss my niece growing up, miss Lennon getting married and holding their new baby. The realization that I won't be around is almost too much to handle, but the quicker I come to terms with it, the quicker I will be at peace before he ends it all for good.

Dalton won't make it easy. He wants revenge for his brother's death and sending Mason pictures is only the start. He won't let me out of here alive, that much is obvious.

CHAPTER TWENTY-NINE

MASON

"Driving around isn't doing us any good," Hunter says from the back seat of the truck. "They could literally be anywhere."

Liam agrees, and I stay busy scrolling through the text messages Dalton has sent over the past hour. Learning Sophie wasn't at Weston's nearly ripped my heart from my chest. I hoped he'd be there and make it easy for us to save her, but obviously, I underestimated him.

I'm not sure what the hell to do now or where to start. I feel so fucking hopeless, but I refuse to give up. Knowing what he's done and what he's doing now, I can't risk calling my dad or the cops. He's smarter than any of us thought, and I think about how he must've orchestrated attending the grief meetings with the intention of befriending Sophie.

My thoughts wander to how he found her, and then I remember she went to Weston's funeral, but Sophie didn't even know he had a brother. But if Weston told Dalton, he could've sent him pictures or details of their relationship, for all she knows. He probably started stalking her that same weekend.

Being sweet and compassionate, she allowed him into her life without a second thought. I grit my teeth, growing angrier with every passing second, and swallow down the lump lodged in my throat.

"We should go to the house and try to figure out what the fuck to do next," Liam suggests, but I'm so lost in my head that I don't reply. I'm angry and in shock that this is really happening. I keep hoping I'll wake up from this fucking nightmare. I'd do anything to switch places with her right now, anything to take away the pain she's enduring.

When we pull into the driveway of the house, Hunter's phone rings. "It's Lennon," he says, forcing a smile as he answers.

"Hey, baby. What's going on?" he greets, putting her on speakerphone.

I hear Lennon on the other line, not suspecting a thing, not knowing how much danger her sister is in, until she asks about Sophie. Hunter grows quiet, and Lennon calls him on it. Hunter tells her not to come over while explaining what's going on. Lennon is as hysterical as I feel.

"I'm calling the cops." Her words ring out.

"No!" Hunter grows more serious. "If you call the cops, you're only putting her in more danger. We're looking for her now. We're gonna find her, and if we don't soon, then we'll get the authorities involved."

Liam gets out of the truck, and I follow him inside as Hunter lingers outside, trying to calm her down.

"You need to call Jerad," Liam tells me as he paces around the living room, brushing a frustrated hand through his hair. "See if he has any other information or what can be done. We're losing time."

I nod and do what he says. Jerad instantly answers the phone.

"Did you find her?" he asks.

"No," I say, deflated. "Not yet. Do you have any more information?"

"Nothing other than the cell phone location," he tells me, but I can hear him typing away on his computer.

"He keeps sending me pictures of her bruised and beaten, and it's destroying me. We went to Weston's house since it was close to that tower, but all I found was her cell and a note from him. Dalton cloned her phone so I'd get texts from her number, but the location took us to where the original phone was."

The line is silent.

"Jerad?"

"I don't think you're dealing with an amateur psycho here. He's smarter than we think if he's cloning phones and shit. That's high-level kidnapping shit. This isn't a game. You need to get the cops involved before something bad happens, Mason."

I let out a deep breath, and Hunter walks in, angry as fuck. Not good.

"I can't. He's already threatened her life if any report is made, and I wouldn't be surprised if he's tracking those things or has a police scanner. Hell, he probably knows I'm talking to you. Fuck, Jerad. I think he'll do it. I think he'll kill her the second there's a missing person report or anything involving Sophie being taken."

"I'll call some guys and see what we can do without an official public alert. The police need to be looking for his car to make sure he's not crossing state lines," Jerad explains. "If I find out something, I'll call you."

I shove my phone into my pocket, and just like that, we're back to where we started.

"Sorry," Hunter says, shrugging. "I couldn't lie to her. Lennon knows when I am anyway. But she said if we don't find her in an hour, she's calling the cops. She doesn't give a shit what any of us say or think," he tells me before looking at Liam.

"Fan-fuckin'-tastic." Liam deadpans. "That's the last thing we need."

Hunter releases a breath. "When it comes to her sister, she doesn't care. I asked her not to call Maddie because we don't need two hysterical Corrigan sisters."

I nod, agreeing. Thankfully, Maddie is safe at home and doesn't suspect a thing. It needs to stay that way.

"What do we know about this guy?" Liam asks. "Do we know where he works? Where he's from? Would he have taken her out of the city? Jesus fuck. She could be anywhere."

Liam's panicking is making me even more edgy because he's right. He took her somewhere between them dropping off Maddie before their meeting to when he first texted two hours later. He could've driven her out to the middle of nowhere for all we know. "Everything I know is probably lies anyway, so all we have confirmed is what Jerad's told us. He was living in LA before Weston died," I explain, clamping my hands behind my head as I try to think of more. "It's a five-hour drive, so he didn't take her there."

"And what do we know about Weston? Besides the obvious." Hunter interrupts my frantic thoughts.

I rack my brain for the small pieces Sophie's shared. "Late twenties. Had a record. Born and raised in Sacramento. They have a sister who lives in Tulsa." I'm growing more frustrated. "This is doing us no good. We're wasting time."

"Do you want me to put a hit out on him?" Liam asks.

Hunter and I both turn and look at him, and I'm not sure if he's being serious or not. When I narrow my eyes, he eventually cracks a smile, but considering his job, I wouldn't be surprised if he knows the people to do that. He probably has friends in low places with some shady contacts, so I don't ask any questions. He rolls his eyes, then finally tells us he's joking, but I'm not convinced.

I'm at a loss, so much so that I'm almost tempted to call my father and get him involved. As much as it fucking pains me to need his help, maybe he can do something. Maybe he can call out a search without it being put into the system. He *is* friends with the chief of police after all. If we can't find her in the next hour, I'm going to do what I have to do, as much as I don't want to. But I have no options left.

"What're you thinking?" Liam asks.

"I'm gonna call my dad."

Hunter shakes his head. "Are you sure that's a good idea?"

Considering his father's in politics as well, he knows how critical the situation will get if I do this.

"What other choices do we have? He has connections that

Jerad doesn't, and I'm out of ideas," I nervously admit. I'm more desperate than I've ever been in my entire life. I'll do whatever it takes to save her. If all I have to do is take my father's berating and swallow my pride to find Sophie, then it's more than worth it.

"He won't be quiet. Searching for her won't be swept under the rug. Your father will try to act like the hero and save your ass and the day, like he typically does. It's a bad fucking idea," Hunter disagrees. "And you know it."

I release a frustrated huff and run my fingers through my hair. Time's running out. Every minute she's with him is one fucking minute too long. At this point, maybe we should drive around town and search every neighborhood, back alley, and warehouse until we find his car. I pace around the living room, trying to figure out where the hell he could've taken her. There's no way they left Sacramento, not considering the amount of time it took for him to send me the first pictures of Sophie. They have to be in the city.

When I'm close to giving up all hope, Dalton sends another photo of my sweet Sophie, and I nearly hurl when I see she looks even worse than before. However, this time it's not a closeup picture. I can see more of what's behind her and notice a sculpture I've seen dozens of times before. Recognition flashes across my face.

"Holy. Shit." I breathe out as relief floods through me.

"What is it?" Liam asks.

I take my phone to him and show off the picture. "Sophie," he says, defeated, but then I tell him to look closer. Pinching the screen, he zooms into the background.

"Holy fuck!" Liam slams his hand on my back. "Is that what I think it is?"

Hunter rushes over, narrowing his eyes on the screen. "What the hell is that?"

For the first time all night, I feel hopeful.

"That's a goddamn black dildo sculpture, and it just saved the fucking day," I say.

"What does that mean?" Hunter asks, thoroughly confused.

"It means we know exactly where the fuck she is," Liam tells him, taking the gun out of his pants and chambering a round. Now that we know where she is, we have to go get her as quickly as possible.

"Dude, where?" he asks, and I can see he's growing anxious like the rest of us.

"That motherfucker is right across the street. Kilan has been trying to sell the house for the past few months and has all these weird-ass sculptures inside. It's shaped like a giant dick with a mushroom head. I've only seen that big dildo-looking sculpture once in my life, and it was in that house. It can't be a coincidence. He's probably been spying on us from there for weeks."

Hunter's eyes widen. "Seriously? She's that close?"

"Yes, and we can't waste any more time. Dalton probably has no idea the mistake he made, and we need to take advantage now," Liam instructs, grabbing another gun from his duffle bag. He tries to hand it to me, but I refuse it before he tucks it into the back of his pants, and we walk out of the back door. Now, he's double loaded.

I crack my knuckles, ready to beat in Dalton's face until he's unrecognizable.

I'm coming, Sophie. I'm on my way, baby. Just hold on a little longer.

"We need to go through the back in case he's watching the front of the house. Mason, keep messaging him so he's occupied," Liam tells us as we follow him. He leads us across our neighbors' backyards until we're six houses down. We come around the side of a house, and then Liam crosses the street.

"Shit," he whispers under his breath. "The fences."

"Let's go to the next block and cut through the yard that's connected to Kilan's backyard. We'll need a solid plan, though." I'm worried as hell that this is all going to backfire, and I know they can hear it in my voice by the expressions on their faces.

I pull out my phone and text Dalton with hopes to do nothing more than amuse and distract him. He seems to eat up the fact that I'm worried as fuck about Sophie. Having power over me and being able to control the situation is something his brother loved to do, too. It's what ultimately resulted in his death, and I wouldn't be surprised if Dalton ends up the same way.

MASON

You don't have to do this. Let her go and take me instead. I'm the one you have the real problem with anyway. She didn't do anything.

DALTON

That's where you're wrong. Now which should I cut off first? Her fingers or toes?

MASON

If you let her go, you get me. Isn't that what you wanted all along anyway? Or better yet, we can forget that any of this happened and all walk away.

DALTON

Too late. I'm having way too much fun with her... and you.

MASON

You're gonna end up like your brother if you don't give her back...in one fucking piece.

DALTON

None of this would've happened if you weren't a killer.

I want to argue with him. I want to tell him it wasn't *my* fucking gun. I wasn't the one looking for a fight by pulling the trigger, but he wouldn't believe me anyway. He wants nothing but to seek his revenge, and he went after the only person who means anything to me—Sophie.

He sends another text that has me seeing red.

DALTON

Just remember, her blood will be on YOUR hands. You'll never find her, not on time at least.

We jog down the street and find Dalton's car parked on the next block.

"Fuck," I murmur. "What's the plan?"

Liam responds by taking his gun from the back of his waistband, and without warning, he pulls the trigger and shoots out two of the tires, and that's when I realize he has a silencer on the end. My eyes widen in shock. Liam doesn't play.

"You can't be too fucking careful." He smirks. "Now, he's really not going anywhere."

We rush toward the house where Dalton has Sophie, and I'm relieved to see there isn't a fence although I'd scale it in a heartbeat if I had to. As we stand in the shadows of the tall bushes, I notice all the curtains are drawn, but it's more than obvious the lights are on inside.

"You're sure she's in there?" Hunter asks, keeping his voice low.

"There's no doubt about it. Never seen a dick like that in my life," Liam replies.

"So what're we doing? We can't just rush inside. He could kill her as soon as he hears us," I say.

As if he heard me, Dalton sends a picture of all the weapons he has. Knives of all different sizes are on the countertop along with a gun, duct tape, and rope.

Fucking hell. He's worse than Weston.

DALTON

Maybe I'll alternate fingers and toes until they're all gone. But I'm wondering how she should die. Should I let her bleed out…slow and painful?

Oh wait, I know. Gunshot. The same way you killed my brother. But it's sure been fun using all my little toys on her. Should I send you a video?

The next incoming text is a picture of a gag in Sophie's mouth with tears running down her cheeks.

"Oh my God," I hiss quietly.

A rush of second-guessing soars through me, wondering if

we're going about this all wrong and should call for help and let SWAT take his ass out instead, but then I hear an ear-piercing scream come from inside.

"Goddammit. We should call the police for backup." I'm jumpy and unsure. I can't believe this is happening right now.

"Keep it together, Holt. We're doing this. No backing down now," Liam tells me, then jerks his head as if he needs confirmation I'm good to go.

I take several deep breaths before nodding in return. Whatever happens, I'll know we did what we had to in order to get her out safely.

"By the photo, it looks like they're in the kitchen, so I think if we go in through the side door in the garage, he won't notice. Kilan mentioned that the door doesn't lock, and not too long ago, the garage door was stuck open, so asked me to watch the place," Liam explains. "He was supposed to get someone out here to fix it but apparently didn't."

I glare. "That's exactly how that bastard got in."

As if he already figured it out, he frowns. "I know. I think that's where we should enter, though," Liam suggests, and I agree.

"We have the element of surprise on our side, so when we barge in, you two need to take him down right away. I'll grab Sophie and get her the fuck out of there," I tell Liam and Hunter.

Hunter speaks up. "If Liam goes in first with his gun, I can go in behind and throw something across the room to distract him. Then you come in after and grab her." We nod in agreement. There are three of us and only one of him. He might be armed, but Liam is just as dangerous with his weapon. "Be careful, okay? Lennon will murder us if we get hurt," Hunter adds.

Liam smirks. "We'll let you handle her since you're good at it."

"Shut the hell up," Hunter snaps.

"Alright, so you two go in first, and I'll focus on getting Sophie," I confirm. We cross the yard toward the garage and keep to the side of the house. I can hear Sophie's cries from inside, and I'm tempted to say fuck it all and rush in there by myself, but I know how life-threatening this whole plan is. One wrong move could mean it ends badly for us.

Liam slips inside the garage, and Hunter and I follow him. He grabs the doorknob and looks at me.

"You love her."

There's not a doubtful bone in my body when I answer. "Yeah, I do."

He grins. "Then all you need to worry about is getting her out of here. Let Hunter and me handle him. Got it?"

I swallow and nod. Liam holds his gun out in front of him after giving his backup one to Hunter, then they both enter. My adrenaline spikes as realization hits—this is about to end, and I'll get my sweet Sophie back.

Once inside the entry, I can hear Dalton's laughter as he threatens to kill her and then kill me. No fucking way in hell is that happening.

Liam quietly walks down the hall that leads to the kitchen and living room with Hunter behind him. I trust them both with my life, but right now, I'm anxious as fuck that something is going to go horribly wrong.

As we walk farther into the house, I make sure to stay behind them, and the discussion in the kitchen becomes louder.

"I'll do anything you want if you leave everyone alone," Sophie pleads, which means he took the gag out of her mouth. Thank God. Though it was probably because he gets off on hearing her beg.

He releases a rumbling laugh. "You'll do anything I want anyway."

I clench my jaw and try to calm the rage that soars through me. My heart pounds hard in my chest as I prepare for the most important mission of my life. I suck in deep breaths, trying to remain calm and assess the situation as Liam and Hunter cut through the dining room. Standing in the hallway, I keep my back against the wall and peek around the corner into the kitchen and see the police scanner on the counter as he points a knife directly in her face.

"Your pleas are boring me," Dalton tells her, unamused, dropping the knife and picking up a gun. "About as much as your boyfriend does."

"Shut up," she spits back but winces as if speaking hurts.

He points it at Sophie, giving her an eerie grin. "Just once click. That's all it would take to end you right now. Isn't this fun?"

He twirls it around his finger before placing it against Sophie's head. My body stiffens, and I nearly lose my strength as I wait for Hunter to make a fucking move. Seeing a gun pointed at her makes me want to wrap my hands around Dalton's throat until he takes his last fucking breath. I almost can't take it anymore, and my hands ball into fists, trying to keep from making any noise.

"Please," she whispers, defeated. "*Please*, Dalton."

Before he can respond, the dildo sculpture crashes to the floor, shattering into a million pieces. Dalton turns on his heels and points the gun toward the dining room. He shouts, demanding to know who's there.

Seconds later, a round exits the silencer, then blood splatters on Sophie's face and body. She wails as she struggles against the chair. Liam shot Dalton in the shoulder, purposely not killing him. He stumbles back, drops the gun, and the metal crashes against the tile floor.

I don't wait another second to be wasted before I rush into the kitchen and slam my body into Dalton. We both fall to the ground, and I kick the gun out of his reach. Liam comes and stands over Dalton, keeping the weapon pointed at his head, but the sick fuck isn't scared or threatened. In fact, he must have a fucking death wish. Dalton struggles against me, and when I push myself off him, Liam shoots again, putting a bullet in his thigh as Hunter struggles to hold him down.

"I'm gonna fucking kill you. I'm gonna fucking kill you all," Dalton warns, wailing from the pain.

"Shut the fuck up," Liam spits, kneeling and leaning closer to him. "I should put a bullet between your eyes right now." He taps the barrel of his pistol to his forehead. "But I like seeing you suffer the way you made her. So I might not call an ambulance for a while…let you bleed out a little…*just for fun,*" he mocks the way he taunted Sophie.

Seeing that Liam and Hunter have it under control, I run over to Sophie and cup her beaten and swollen face in my hands. "I've got you, baby. It's gonna be okay," I tell her, trying to soothe both of us. She's crying hysterically, pulling against the duct tape that asshole wrapped around her wrists and ankles.

"I'm so fucking sorry." It kills me to see her like this. My Sophie looks so damn broken. "I'm getting you out, baby," I say, grabbing a knife from the counter and cutting her free from the chair. I do an assessment and see the dried blood on her arm from the earlier cut. That asshole's blood spewed on her face and hair, making both of us wince. I wrap one arm around her back and one under her legs, lifting her out of the chair.

"Get her out of here," Liam shouts when Dalton tries to pull himself up. He's clearly not going down without a fight. Fucking moron.

"Hunter, do me a favor and deck him in the face for me before you call 911," I say, walking with Sophie in my arms when he pulls out his cell. I'd do it myself but getting her out of here is more important.

"Not a fucking problem." He grins, sliding his phone back into his pocket.

Then I hug Sophie to my chest and walk us the fuck out of there.

CHAPTER THIRTY

MASON

As soon as we're back at the house, I carry Sophie's lifeless body upstairs as she clings to me. My thoughts are so scattered, I can't sort through them.

Once we're upstairs in the bathroom, I gently set her down on the countertop. She's so broken and defeated, and it takes every ounce of willpower I have left to keep my emotions inside. The last thing I want to do is fall apart in front of her when she's already shattered. Studying her body, I analyze what he did to her. Her dress is torn to shit, blood is splattered all over her, and her face is red and swollen. Thank fuck he didn't touch her fingers and toes or, worse, slice her throat. That asshole got off on other people's fear.

"Do you want me to take you to the hospital?" I cautiously ask her. "You might have some broken ribs. They won't be able to do much for it, but they could give you some good pain meds."

She shakes her head. I know her well enough that arguing right now won't help, and I wouldn't win anyway. If she needs meds, I can find some for her another way. "Okay, baby."

I turn on the shower so the water can warm up. All I want to do is wash that piece of shit off her, but she's hurting.

She'll have two shiners by morning. I can already see the red marks around her neck, making me wish I could've shot that fucking bastard myself for touching her.

"Can you lift your arms?" I ask softly, grabbing the hem of what's left of her dress. With her eyes closed, she slowly raises them. She winces but doesn't stop until I can fully remove it. "I'm so sorry, sweetheart. Fuck, I'm so sorry." I carefully cup her cheeks. "I'll be super careful."

Sophie keeps her gaze to the floor, staying silent. She's emotionally exhausted, and I can't imagine what she's thinking, if anything at all.

Wrapping my arms around her, I unstrap her bra and gently slide it off. That motherfucker's marks are on her arms.

Next, I slide her panties down her legs and toss them aside. Steam fills the room, so I strip off my clothes, and after I test the water, I lift Sophie and walk us to the shower.

Once we're inside, I set her down, close the curtain, and position us under the stream.

I brush my fingers through her strands and massage shampoo into her scalp, scrubbing out the blood and tangles. She keeps her eyes shut as I rinse her hair, but moans quietly at my touch. Sophie reaches for me and tightly grips my biceps, pulling me closer. "I'm not letting you go, baby. Never again."

Her body tenses as I gently wrap my arm around her shoulders, and I know she's about to break down. I want her to feel safe with me and give her the space to release whatever she's feeling. Cupping her face, I softly press my lips to hers before pulling back and resting my head against hers. Our breathing is the only sound that can be heard over the heavy stream.

"I love you, Sophie. I love you so goddamn much." I hope by now she knows I'd do anything for her.

She pulls back slightly, out of the water, and blinks up at me for the first time since I carried her from that house.

"I almost missed the chance to tell you, so I'm taking the opportunity now. Soph, I'm in love with you," I tell her honestly. *"I love you, I love you, I love you."*

Sophie stares with tears in her eyes, and I don't know if they're from my confession or the whole situation. Either way, I wipe my thumbs over her cheeks, then pull her back into my chest. When she manages to wrap her arms around my waist, her entire body shakes as cries echo into the air. I hate hearing her sobs, but it's what she needs to process and get through this. As terrible as it all was, I *have* to believe we'll get through this.

After a while, I grab her loofah and lather her body wash on it. Slowly, I rub over her skin, cleaning more blood off her face and neck. I want his memory off her. Sophie stands silently as I scrub over each arm, her chest and stomach, down each leg, and between her thighs. Then she turns around and allows me to repeat the process. I reposition her under the water so she's facing me and watch as it all rinses away.

"I was so scared I'd never see you again," she finally says after she steadies her breathing. "I knew you'd come looking for me, but I was certain Dalton would shoot you before you'd get to me."

"I'm sure that was his plan," I tell her honestly. "But we had a better one."

"He's a monster," she says quietly. "I'm a fool for not seeing it."

"Listen to me," I demand, cupping her jaw. "You're the sweetest, kindest, most trusting person I know. That doesn't make you a fool, and thinking otherwise isn't gonna help you in this situation."

"I should've listened to you," she states weakly, tears falling again.

"I can't say I didn't wish you did, too. But I didn't know who he was either, not until today. I thought he was after a relationship, but neither of us could've seen this coming."

"I fell for it so easily. His lies, his story, everything." She sounds so defeated.

"That's because you choose to see the best in everyone, baby. Don't let him make you second-guess who you are, you hear me? You're compassionate, and he used that to his advantage. He's a piece of shit who's going to prison for a long ass time. I'll make sure of it," I promise.

Bringing her closer, I kiss away the tears along her cheeks before bringing my mouth to hers for a tender kiss. I wish I could take all the pain away and pretend none of this happened. Losing Sophie would end me for good.

"He killed her," Sophie mutters after a while. "That's my fault."

Blinking, I pull back slightly to study her expression. "Who?"

"Dacia," she chokes out.

Shock pulses through me as I try to wrap my head around what she said. "How do you know?"

"He told me. She was getting in his way of having me all to himself. I'm the reason Dacia's dead," she says with a shaky voice.

Closing my eyes, I inhale a deep breath, trying to control myself. I'd love to get him in a ring and punch his fucking lights out. He's a suspect in the murder his wife only five months ago, and now he's killed another innocent woman. I have no doubt he would've killed me or Sophie, or both.

"No, sweetheart. Dalton's the reason she's dead," I say, trying to reassure her, but I'm sure it won't help. There's nothing anyone could've said that would've changed how I felt about Emma's death. "You couldn't have known what his plans were or how he was gonna hurt her or you. That fucker is gonna wish Liam killed him because now he's going to prison for two murders and attempted murder on top of kidnapping. He's never gonna be able to touch you again."

I cradle her in my arms, needing her as close as possible. The *what-ifs* haunted me, threatening to break down my barrier of strength. I need to be strong for her so she can get through this, knowing it won't be easy either way.

What if we hadn't gotten there on time?

What if we hadn't found her?

What if he'd shot her?

What if he'd shot Liam, Hunter, or me?

The *what-ifs* are what will suffocate and choke me for a long ass time.

"The police will be waiting for our statements," I tell her after a few minutes. "If you're not ready, I'll tell them to come back. They can wait."

And they can. I've worked dozens of cases throughout my internship where witness statements weren't collected for days or sometimes weeks. They won't push her as long as I demand they back off.

"I want to tell them everything," she says. "Make sure they find Dacia's body, make sure he goes to prison, make sure I don't forget any detail that'll keep him away from me. I'll testify against him and do whatever it takes." Her lips tremble, and that's when my own dam breaks. Hearing how strong she wants to be to get justice for her friend and herself has my vision blurring with tears. Fuck, I hate that bastard for doing this to my girl and wouldn't blink if he magically died on the way to the ER.

"Whatever you want to do, baby. I'll be here with you. I'm not going anywhere."

Sophie tries to wrap her arms around my neck, but winces before she can reach high enough. I grab her hands and hold them to my chest instead as I lean down and rest my forehead against hers.

"I know." She brings our mouths together for a deep, tender kiss, and it's exactly what I needed to feel her strength. "Will you say it again?"

Blinking, I study her face, wondering what it is she wants to hear. She pulls in her bottom lip and looks at me, and then it hits me.

Lifting the corners of my mouth, I flash a small grin. "I love you, Sophie. So. Goddamn. Much."

Then she gives me the softest, sincerest look as she repeats those very words to me. "I love you too, Mason." If two people's hearts could beat to the same rhythm, at the same pace, in the same melody—it'd be ours.

I fight back a goofy smile but hearing her say that to me is a moment I want to stamp into my memory forever. She's changed everything for me, and there's no way I'd go back to the shell of a man I was before she sparked life back into my soul.

Once we're out of the shower, I help her dry off before wrapping the towel around her body. After I finish drying myself, I carry her to my bed. She could walk, but it's painful for her. I quickly put on shorts and a T-shirt before heading downstairs to her room and grabbing the comfiest clothes I can find, then head back to my room and help her get dressed.

Checking my messages, I read the ones from Liam. Dalton's been taken to the hospital, Hunter went home to Lennon after he gave his brief statement, and he and the cops are now waiting for us in the living room. I take Sophie's hand and kiss her knuckles.

"You sure you're okay to do this?"

Sophie nods without hesitation. "I'm sure. I wanna get it over with for now." She knows this won't be the last time she has to talk about it.

Leading us downstairs, I try to mentally prepare myself for what is likely going to take a couple of hours. They'll make sure my story matches Liam's and Hunter's and ask Sophie about every detail she can recall. I don't want to relive this because it feels like déjà vu. The fact that my name is going to be involved again means it's only a matter of time before my father comes barreling through my door.

"Miss Corrigan, I'm Officer Fisher, and this is Officer Gaunt. He's gonna observe while I take notes."

"Hello." Her voice is soft as she shakes his hand. "You can call me Sophie."

"Of course." He looks at me. "Mason, I presume."

"Yes." I shake his hand next.

Yep. Déjà vu.

At least I'm not getting cuffed and thrown into the back of a cop car this time.

I sit next to Liam with Sophie on my other side. We clasp hands, and when the silence takes over, it's then I can see the blue and red lights still flashing outside. I imagine all our neighbors are out on the sidewalks, trying to figure out what happened. Kilan is going to flip when he finds out. The house he was trying to sell is now a crime scene.

"So Liam and Hunter have told us most of what happened, but I'd like to get your version." Officer Fisher directs his words toward me. "Can you start from the beginning?"

I clench my jaw, thinking back to when Sophie first mentioned Dalton. "Well, I guess I should start with how I got arrested for killing his brother."

The officer nods, clearly not fazed. He's probably heard and seen so much shit in this city that nothing is out of the ordinary.

Several minutes later, I discuss how we went looking for Sophie, and when we got the text messages. Then I talk about how I recognized the dildo statue from Kilan's house and Liam's plan to go in first since he had a gun.

"What dildo statue?" Sophie asks me quietly, her brows pinched together.

"The one that Hunter knocked over," I say. "I'll explain later," I tell her with a grin, then I direct my attention back to the officer. "Kilan was a friend of ours, and we partied together a lot, so we recognized it when I saw it in one of the pictures he sent."

"Can you tell me what you saw when you entered the house?" he asks. "Walk me through the events as you remember it."

"Dalton had his gun pointed at Sophie's head, spewing all kinds of threats at her. She was duct-taped to a chair and completely helpless. Just by looking at her, I could tell he'd hit and touched her. He'd sent pictures, so I knew she wasn't able to defend herself. I went in after Liam and Hunter, and once the statue fell, Dalton shifted and directed his gun toward the other room. That's when Liam shot his shoulder, and the gun fell from his hand. I charged forward, knocking him down, but he continued to struggle against me and reached for his gun. I tried to restrain him, but he continued to put up a fight, so Liam shot his leg. After a minute, Hunter held him down as I went to free Sophie. Liam held him at gunpoint while Hunter called 911, and I got us out of there. Then I brought her here."

Recalling everything wasn't easy, but I'm not going to let my best friends down, knowing my statement is needed to keep them out of any legal trouble. Sure, Dalton is the criminal here, but not calling the authorities as soon as we knew she'd been kidnapped could come back to bite us in the ass unless we have a solid case as to why we couldn't. I'm not sure threats will be enough although we all know what he was capable of.

"Got it, thank you," he says as he finishes writing his notes. "Now, Sophie. I know this isn't gonna be easy for you, so we'll take it as slow as you need to. According to Liam, you left the house earlier today with Maddie and Dalton. Can you tell me what happened after that?"

She swallows and nods, and it's then I realize one of us needs to fill Maddie in on what happened if Lennon hasn't already.

Sophie tells him everything. From how she met him at the meetings, to becoming friends, to how they connected in the grieving circle. She discusses how she hadn't planned on attending any more meetings, but how he talked her into joining him tonight with a sob story. Sophie explains from when he picked her up, to leaving and getting knocked out in his car. My heart pounds hard with rage, and when my fist clenches, Liam notices. He gives me a pointed look to calm my shit, knowing that getting all fired up isn't going to help anything.

"I went to the bathroom shortly before the meeting ended, and when I came back, he was acting weird. I didn't know it at the time, but he had seen my text messages from Mason, and that's when he pushed his plan to happen tonight instead. Dalton deleted the messages, along with the missed calls and voicemails, so I never got the warnings."

"And Mason, you're the one who figured out who he really was. Is that right?" Officer Fisher asks, but by the look on his face, he already knows the answer.

"Correct. I had a friend run his plates, and that's when I connected his last name to Weston's. It's how I found out his entire story was a lie, and that he had been a suspect in his wife's death this past year. I texted Sophie, hoping she'd see it before her meeting was over and not get into his car. If I'd gone to the church and picked her up myself, he would've never taken her." I lower my eyes at the realization that my messages are what put her in danger.

"You didn't know," Sophie says softly, squeezing my hand. "I should've taken my phone with me. I normally do, but I left my clutch on my chair because I wasn't gonna be gone for more than a couple of minutes."

"Well, if Mr. Westbrook intended to eventually take you, then it might've been harder to find you," the officer concludes. "He would've had more time to execute it properly, and that would've made things much worse for everyone. I understand you couldn't call for help given his threats, but all four of you could've been killed tonight." Officer Fisher gives us all a pointed look, especially me.

Fuck, I *know*.

"Well, because of me, one person *is* dead," Sophie tells him.

"What do you mean?" Officer Fisher asks.

Sophie looks down at our hands in her lap, and I rub the pad of my thumb over knuckles, giving her the encouragement and strength to continue.

"My friend Dacia. We met in group together, and when I hosted a dinner party last weekend, she didn't show up. Dalton told me she couldn't make it, but I never heard from her. I brushed it off because I knew she was going through some emotional stuff after her twin brother died. She often talked a lot about how she gets through the dark days, so I thought she needed some space. I know people aren't always as strong as they try to seem. But tonight, Dalton told me she was getting in the way of his ultimate plan, and he had to get rid of her." Sophie chokes up, and I squeeze her hand, letting her know I'm still here.

"What else did he say?" the officer asks. "Did he admit to killing her?"

"Yes," Sophie answers, tears falling down her cheeks. "He took her and then stuffed her into his trunk. Are you guys able to check? She deserves a proper burial."

She wipes her cheeks, and the officer nods. "Of course. I'll get my guys on it right away."

He talks into his radio and gives the order.

"Is there anything else you two can share or think of that would help the case?" he later asks, but we both shake our heads. "If you think of something, please don't hesitate to call me. I'll give you my card. I'm sure you'll know where to find me." He directs that last part at me.

Great. He knows exactly who I am and who my father is. Not that I should be surprised.

"Let me guess. The DA's already been called?" I sigh.

He slumps his shoulders. "Afraid so. As soon as your name was brought up."

Lovely.

"Thank you for your time and for being so thorough," he says as Liam and I stand to walk them out the door. "If she remembers anything else, she can call anytime."

"Will do," Liam says. "Oh, his car was down the block behind the house. I shot into his tires in case he got away."

"Got it, thanks. We'll search it," he reassures us. "We'll let you know what we find."

"Thanks, officers."

Liam shuts the door behind them, and we stand in ear-piercing silence.

"This is fucked up," he finally says. "Now I wish I'd shot him in the goddamn face."

I snort, agreeing. "Yeah, but then you'd be going through the same shit I did to prove self-defense. At least this way, he can go to prison, and we can let the other inmates take care of him."

Liam's grin widens. "Fuckin' right. In fact, maybe I'll make a few phone calls." He winks, which makes me chuckle. Liam knows too many people. He's on a first-name basis with guards at the jail, and I'm pretty sure he sweet-talks the receptionists to get their numbers. Liam goes there when he has to check in an inmate, and I wouldn't put it past him to know people at the prison either. He's nothing if not resourceful.

"In case I forgot to say it, thanks for having my back, man." I slap him on the shoulder, and he pulls me in for a hug. "You're a good friend to have in my corner," I say in a mocking tone. He doesn't like mushy shit.

"I'd do it again in a heartbeat," he says before walking back into the living room. I follow him, and he sits next to Sophie, pulling her into his arms. He was as worried about her as I was.

"I can't say I wasn't scared, Soph, but I held onto hope that you were staying strong," Liam tells her. "I hope you know how much I love you. I would've killed him if I knew the backlash wouldn't come back to bite me."

Sophie nods, and tears fall down her cheeks. Liam is a different guy with her, and I appreciate how good of a friend he's been to her all these years.

"Death would've been the easy way out," she says, her words sounding stronger. "He can rot in prison for the rest of his life."

"Damn straight," Liam cheers with a proud smile.

"Lucky that you were home for once," Sophie says when I come to sit on the other side of her.

"Well, I'm starting to think I can't leave you two alone."

I roll my eyes at his comeback. "How long have you had that gun anyway?" I ask.

"Long enough." He winks. "I'm licensed and trained. Don't worry."

"I wasn't," I tell him honestly. I trust Liam with my life, literally.

Sophie pulls him in for another hug. "Thank you again, Hulk. I owe ya one."

Liam chuckles at her nonchalant way of thanking him. Joking or acting strong is how Sophie deals with emotional situations, but after what she already went through with Weston, I can only hope this incident hasn't broken her for good.

CHAPTER THIRTY-ONE

SOPHIE

THE LAST TIME I stayed in bed like this was when I was sixteen and had a nasty flu virus. Everything ached, my stomach hurt, and my head pounded nonstop. It was the most miserable I'd felt in my entire life.

Until now.

Minus the throwing up, this is worse than the flu. My mind won't turn off, and I can't stop feeling like his hands are still on me. The way he intimately touched me haunts my thoughts as I think about his fingers on my chest and between my legs. The fucking sicko had the audacity to do whatever he pleased to my body, and no amount of washing feels clean enough.

Worst of all, my heart hurts.

The Monday after the incident, Mason was forced to go to work although he wanted to stay home with me. I was still too beaten and bruised to go to rehearsals, so once again, I called Mr. Tanner, my director, and explained the situation as vaguely as I could without breaking down on the phone. He told me to take as long as I needed and not to worry about anything. Truthfully, I'm so lucky he doesn't kick my ass out, but I've been with the symphony for over three years, and I'm dependable. He's also well aware of what happened with Weston and the abuse I endured.

The next evening, Officer Fisher called to confirm they found Dacia's body in Dalton's trunk, just as he'd said. I was happy Mason was with me when I learned the horrific news because I felt like I was having a nervous breakdown. The realization of what happened to her made me physically ill, but instead of vomiting, I cried uncontrollably. I suspected she was dead, but I held on to a tiny bit of hope that Dalton was lying. That he only said it to scare me and prove how powerful he was. Although deep down, I knew he was probably telling the truth, but I tried to be optimistic.

The thought that it could've been me haunts me every damn second as I mourn the loss of my friend. I've been harboring so much guilt about the fact she died because of me. She didn't have to, and that bastard could've spared her life, but when you're a heartless asshole, you don't care about anyone or anything.

Dalton is empty. I could see it in his soulless eyes. He wanted to cause me extreme pain and to take everyone down with him. I don't know what his plan was originally, but I can't help but wonder if he thought he was going to die too. Or if he wanted to.

Weston died because he tried to kill Mason, Hunter, and Liam. Without a doubt he would've killed me too if he'd had the chance. Dalton wanted revenge in the worst way.

They were both monsters, and I'm not sorry for what ultimately happened to either of them.

I'm only sorry that Dacia paid the price for trying to protect me.

Unable to keep my thoughts from unraveling, I haven't been able to sleep in days. My body passes out after hours of crying, but I'm not really sleeping. I don't wake up rested. In fact, I wake up tortured.

"Soph?" Mason's soft voice lingers in my ear. It's been a week since the incident, and I still can't get Dacia out of my head. Her family had a funeral for her yesterday, but it was a private ceremony only. They didn't know me, and I wasn't sure I could handle going anyway.

"Hmm?" I answer with my eyes closed and my cheek pressed against his chest. The swelling in my face has gone down, and my ribs don't hurt as badly, but I still ache, though I think it's more of a mental pain at this point.

"Are you hungry? You need to eat, babe." He brushes a loose strand of hair off my face. "I can make tacos."

"I don't have an appetite," I tell him honestly.

"I know, sweetheart. Could you try, though? I'm worried you're gonna get dehydrated or starve. You've barely left your room." The concern is evident in his tone, so I try to get my shit together.

"Actually…" I wipe my face and sit up, knowing I look like a hot fucking mess. Mason showered with me two days ago, and I haven't had the energy to change clothes or brush my hair since then. "I talked with my parents yesterday, and I think going to Utah for a bit would help me. I need a change of scenery."

Mason searches my face, and I know this is probably a shock to him. As weird as it sounds, this past week has felt like it's pulled us apart while at the same time bringing us together. "Do you want me to go with you? I can get off work for a few days, I'm sure."

"I think I need to do this alone. My dad has a friend who's a professional counselor that I can speak with, and I think being back home will help me get out of my own head a bit," I explain, hating the pained way he's looking at me. "I should've talked with someone after shit went down with Weston, but since I didn't, I'm carrying the weight of both on my shoulders. Admittingly, I need help to get through this, and staying here, crying in my bed, isn't what I need."

Mason swallows, and I'm sure he's trying to think of ways to keep me here, but when his expression softens, he knows I'm right. I need professional therapy to deal with the demons that threaten to take over.

"Okay, baby," he finally responds. I know he's tried to help—

he's been amazing, actually—but I need more than what he can give me right now. "If that's what you think will help you, then I'll support your decision. Do you need me to do anything? Find flights for you or anything?"

"My dad already booked one for me. It leaves tomorrow at eight a.m."

"Oh. Okay. Can I drive you to the airport at least?"

"Yeah, I'd like that." I smile at him, knowing this hasn't been easy for him either. He's getting shit from his father again, but at least he didn't have mandatory leave from work this time. I'm thankful for that because I'm not sure I could feel guilty about one more thing right now.

Later that night while I'm packing, Lennon and Maddie come over. They've been quiet, neither knowing what to say or how to comfort me. Not that I can blame them. Nothing they can say or do will change the way I feel or what's happened. Being with them like this is enough for me.

"You sure you want to go home without us?" Lennon asks, half-teasing. "I forgot how small our beds were until I went back and realized we basically slept in shoe boxes."

That has me laughing a little, mostly because it's true. Even my bed at my old apartment was bigger than the one I had at my parents' home. Of course, Mason insisted on getting me a queen bed, which is perfect, considering he hasn't left my side all week. He's laid with me every night, holding me as I cry myself to sleep. Mason's been so patient and caring, and I feel bad for leaving, but I can't be a shell of a person anymore. I need to figure out how to work through these feelings I have, and I hope being in Utah will be a good start in that direction.

"Yeah, I think it'll be good to get some fresh mountain air," I say, half-teasing. "There are a lot of memories here weighing me down." Considering it all happened across the street, it's impossible to fully get away.

"I can't tell you how scared I was when Hunter finally told me everything," Lennon admits softly. Knowing the guys risked their lives for me again is almost too much to handle. Though they tell me it was nothing, that they'd do it for any one of us, I can't help but think if something would've happened, and those thoughts weigh heavy on my chest.

Lennon hasn't said it, but I can't imagine she's happy that I've put Hunter in danger twice now. He's such a good guy that he'd never let his friends fight alone, but if anything had happened to them, I wouldn't be able to live with that. Lennon's already lost so much.

"Liam told me, and I was shaking the whole time," Maddie adds.

Mason told them both not to come over that night, knowing I wanted him to hold me, but they came over first thing the next morning. They hugged me for hours, and it felt good to have them here. But I knew they had their own lives to get back to and sitting with me wasn't going to change what happened, so I eventually had to push them out that night. They've called and texted me every day since, of course.

Déjà vu.

That's what this fucking feels like.

But this time, I'm going to get real help because that's what I need. I want to be the friend, the sister, and the girlfriend they know and love. I can't be that when I'm drowning in my own guilt, choking on my emotions, and hardly surviving.

"Do you know where Dalton is?" Lennon asks. "Has he been transferred yet?"

"As far as I know, he's still in the ICU. He developed an infection after surgery, so they had to keep him longer," I say, repeating the words Mason told me yesterday. Mason's been in contact with the officer, and he has enough friends in the department to get whatever information he wants. "I'll be satisfied when he's in prison across the country."

"Or maybe he should be six feet under," Maddie chimes in. "That'd make *me* satisfied."

She told me the day after when they came to visit that she regrets leaving me alone with him in the car. When we dropped her off before our meeting, she said her gut said not to leave me.

But she couldn't have known. None of us did, not until it was too late.

"He'll get his justice," I try to reassure her. "Someday."

"Not soon enough," Lennon mumbles.

We were all raised in a Christian household, went to church weekly, and attended Bible study classes from the moment we could read. Forgiveness was embedded into our minds since childhood, but it hasn't always been easy to do. Forgiveness isn't for the people who've hurt and betrayed you. It's for *you*. To give you a peaceful mindset and to help you let go of what you can't control.

Forgiveness isn't easy. It isn't something that can be done overnight, but it's something I can focus on to try to release the anger. Forgiving someone for their actions doesn't mean forgetting. It only means realizing what's been done can't be changed and no longer allowing it to control your every waking moment.

I want to forgive the things that cannot be changed and move on with my life once and for all, but I'll never forget. Never.

"I'll be sure to tell Mom and Dad you both said hello." I snicker, pulling myself away from those thoughts with hopes to change the subject.

The next morning as Mason drives me to the airport, he holds my hand as if it's his lifeline. I hate leaving him behind, but this is what I have to do, even if he doesn't want to let me go. He's protective and has told me every day for the past week how much he loves me, and I don't doubt it for a second. Hearing those words feels so magical, especially considering how long he's hid and tried to fight his feelings over the years. I know he means them. I mean them too. I love him so damn much.

Once we arrive, Mason pulls over into the drop-off zone, and we only have a minute to say goodbye.

"I understand why you're going, but I'm still sad you won't be home with me every day and that I can't protect you." He brushes my hair from my face as the wind picks up. Mason sets my suitcase down and cups my face. "I'm gonna miss you so damn much, baby." With our foreheads pressed together, tears fill my eyes at the pain in his voice. "Don't cry, sweetheart. I'm not going anywhere. I'll be here, waiting for you to come back home to me."

I told myself I wasn't going to cry, but I've been crying for a week straight, so why should I have expected today to be any different?

"I know," I say softly. "Thank you."

"Will you text or call me when you land, please? So I know you got there safely." We pull apart, and I nod.

"Of course. It's not a long flight. I'll text as soon as I'm there, then call you before I go to bed," I promise.

"I never got to take you on our first date, you know…" Mason says with a small smirk. "I hope we can do that once you're back."

"That'd be great," I tell him honestly. Being gone for a week isn't gonna *fix* me, but distance will help in the meantime.

"Okay, baby. I better go before they all start honking at me." Mason cups my cheeks once again and slants his mouth over mine. At first, it's slow and testing, and then he deepens it, sliding his tongue between my lips and seeking more. A moan escapes me as he presses his body into me, and it's when a car tire squeals that I remember we're not alone.

"I'll see you on Saturday. I love you," he whispers before pulling away.

Looking up into his gorgeous brown eyes, there's so much sincerity in them. Mason is my whole world, and I'd be crashing down without him. *Love* doesn't seem like a strong enough word to describe the feelings I have for him.

"I love you, too," I tell him.

He looks so damn sad, which has me tearing up.

Mason wipes away my endless tears. "Text or call me anytime during your trip, okay?"

I nod, sniffling as I wrap my arms around him for one final hug. Then I grab my suitcase with my backpack on and head toward the sliding doors. Glancing over my shoulder, I blow a final kiss to the man who holds my whole heart in the palm of his hand.

"*I love you*," he mouths.

I repeat his words, then walk into the airport with a new mindset, hoping I can start over for good this time.

An hour and a half after taking off in Sacramento, I land in Salt Lake City, and after grabbing my bag and texting Mason, I'm greeted by my parents.

"Sophie! We're so glad you're here," my mom says while squeezing the air out of my lungs, and I wince slightly at the pressure.

"Kay, you're smothering her. Let me give her a hug." My dad chuckles, pulling me away. "How're you doing, kiddo? How was the flight?"

"It was good. How I'm doing is yet to be determined," I tell him with a small grin.

"I made your favorite for dinner tonight. Meatloaf with twice baked potatoes and corn on the cob," Mom says as we walk through the parking lot. My stomach growls for the first time in days.

"That sounds amazing, Mom. Thank you." I smile, also something I haven't done in days.

I think going home was the right decision.

Walking into my childhood bedroom is like walking into a time capsule. Nothing's changed since the day I left for college. I've been home a few times since then, but it feels different this time around. I'm not here for an event or wedding. I'm here for *me*.

"All settled in, sweetie?" Mom asks from the doorway.

"Yeah, I think so." I take a seat on the bed. I unpacked a few of my toiletries but left most of my clothes in my suitcase. I changed into one of Mason's T-shirts for bed because not only is it super soft and comfortable, but it also smells like him. I already miss him terribly.

"You must be exhausted today, but hopefully we can talk tomorrow?" she asks, patting my leg as she sits next to me.

"Yeah, absolutely. There's a lot I should tell you and Dad," I admit, feeling guilty I've left so much out. The last thing I want is to keep important things from them, but it's hard to talk about it in general. Also, I didn't want to worry them with me living so many miles away.

"Well, get some sleep. I'll make breakfast for you in the morning, and then we'll go from there." She kisses my cheek.

"Thanks, Mom. Love you."

My dad stands in the doorway. "It's good to have you home, kiddo."

"I'm *just* visiting," I remind him, chuckling. "But I'm glad to be home too."

We say good night, and soon, I'm climbing into bed with the scent of Mason all around me.

SOPHIE

> I'm in bed. Gonna try to get some sleep. I
> love you.

MASON

I love you so much, Soph. Sweet dreams!

I turn my phone on silent and roll on my side. A dream catcher I made at camp one summer hangs off my old desk and grabs my attention. I used to sleep with it every single night above my bed to keep away all my nightmares. After a minute of staring at it, I get up, grab it, and hang it on my bed.

I might be in my mid-twenties, but you're never too old for dream catchers.

CHAPTER THIRTY-TWO

MASON

THIS PAST WEEK without Sophie has been lonely as hell. I know why she wanted to go and knew it'd be good for her to get away, but I've missed her like crazy. Walking into her empty room and knowing I couldn't climb into bed with her was harder than I anticipated. All I want to do is protect her from everything and everyone, and it's easier when she's close, but she's safe with her parents.

Luckily, I've had to work all week, and afterward, I spent my free time in the gym. It'd been a while since I've boxed with my trainer, and I utilized this time to kick his ass. After catching Tyler up on the latest events, he didn't even chastise me for being weaker than usual. Though, after a few sessions, I was able to finally beat him fair and square.

I've kept in contact with the officers to get updates on Dalton, but I'm still waiting for him to be transferred to the jail from the hospital. Of course my father got in my business as soon as he was informed and gave me shit for being involved in yet another scandal. Surprisingly, he hasn't blamed me for threatening his reputation like he usually does. This was obviously different from the Weston incident, but considering both are from the same family, I expected him to chew my ass.

Today I finally get to pick up Sophie from the airport, and I'm so damn excited to have her in my arms again. She texted and called every day, letting me know what she's been doing and how she talked with a professional counselor there from her father's church. I'm happy she spoke to someone and that she plans to continue when she's back home. I wish I would've suggested it after Weston so she wouldn't have the weight of it all burdening her. Knowing Sophie, though, she does things on her own terms and can't always be persuaded.

The moment I see Sophie on the escalators coming down to the baggage claim, I light up like a kid on Christmas morning. She looks ten times better than when she left, and she even smiles when she spots me.

Rushing toward her, I don't stop until I scoop her up in my arms. "Oh my God, I missed you so much," I say into her hair.

"I missed you too."

I pull back slightly, cup her face, and capture her lips. She kisses me back but then breaks away a moment later. It's then I remember we aren't alone and people are walking all around us. Leaning my forehead against hers, I breathe out a sigh of relief. "So damn happy you're back."

"Me too," she says, swallowing tightly.

I grab her hand and lead her to the carousel to grab her bag. Once we're in the car, I reach for her hand and realize she's quieter than usual.

"Everything okay, babe?" I ask as I pull onto the highway.

She nods. "Yeah, just tired."

I bring her hand to my lips and kiss her knuckles. "We'll be home soon, sweetheart.".

The moment I pull into the driveway, I know shit's about to hit the fan. Serena's car is here.

And so is my father's.

Motherfucker.

Of all days for them both to come over, they chose today.

"Why are they here?" she asks as I grab her suitcase from the back.

"That's a goddamn good question," I grit between my teeth. "I'm sorry, Soph. I know having people over is probably the last thing you wanted when you got home."

She swings her backpack on and shrugs. "It's okay. Not your fault."

I lead her into the house, open the door, and when we walk into the living room, I notice my dad and Serena sitting on the couch. When they see me, they both stand. Liam's in the recliner, looking uncomfortable as hell. I glare at him, silently thanking him for the non-heads-up.

Shrugging, he smirks and brings his attention back to the TV.

"Hey, what're you two doing here?" I ask, looking at my father. I don't mind Serena being here, who's come over a couple of nights this week to hang out, but my dad isn't one for *popping in*.

Looking at Sophie, I notice she's uncomfortable and offer to carry her stuff to her room for her.

"No, it's fine. I can do it." She takes her bag and walks to her room off the living room.

"It's about Dalton," Serena begins as soon as Sophie's through her bedroom door.

I brush a hand over my jaw, inhaling a deep breath. "What about him?" I look back and forth between them, noticing the tension.

Before Serena can respond, my father shoves his hands in his slacks pockets, and blurts, "He's dead."

Blinking, I'm too stunned to speak, and before I can open my mouth, Sophie gasps from behind me. "What?" The three of us turn toward her, and I notice the color has drained from her face.

"Soph…" I don't know what to say, so I stop myself. I hold out a hand, but she doesn't take it as she walks closer. We direct our attention back to my dad and Serena.

"Are you sure?" she asks softly.

My father and Serena both nod.

"How? What happened?" I ask.

"Does it matter?" My dad scoffs. "The bastard who tried to kill you and your friends is dead. That's all that matters."

"It matters to me," Sophie retorts. "How'd he die?"

Serena swallows hard, looking down at her shoes, and I can tell something's off. "Serena, what is it?"

"Two guards were transferring him from the hospital to take him to get processed at the jail. He was supposed to have his hearing next Monday to get officially charged. Then he would've stayed there while waiting for trial," Serena explains.

"Right…" I know how it all works. "So then what happened between leaving the hospital and going to the jail?"

"There was a struggle during the transfer," my father starts. "He reached for the guard's gun and started fighting him. The other guard tried to get control of the situation and meant to tase him."

I narrow my eyes, not buying any of this. "*Meant* to tase him?" I probe, crossing my arms over my chest.

"He was startled and grabbed his gun instead and shot him," he continues. "There wasn't anything they could do. The gunshot was right in his chest. He bled out."

Looking at Sophie, she's expressionless. I'm not sure what she's thinking and don't want to ask with other people around. I wrap my arm around her waist and pull her into my side, her breathing uneven.

"You okay?" I lean down and whisper.

Liam walks over before she can answer. "So let me guess, the Westbrooks are gonna come after the state for a wrongful death suit?"

"Possibly," my dad answers though he doesn't look the least bit worried. In fact, he looks like he's already handled it. Handled *them*.

My jaw tightens. The events surrounding Dalton's death are suspicious as fuck, and knowing my dad's connections, this no longer sounds like an accident.

"If you'll excuse me…" Sophie walks around me and goes

upstairs. As soon as the bathroom door shuts, I step closer to the monster of a man in front of me.

"What'd you do?"

"Why do you assume I had something to do with this?" He asks it so casually, and it's all the answer I need to know he's responsible.

Liam grabs Serena's attention and they both take off toward the kitchen. Things were tense between us before, but now they're about to snap.

"You called the hit, didn't you? How many prisoner transfer deaths have there been?"

"At least a dozen since I've been the DA," he responds. "It's not that uncommon. It happens."

"Quit your shit," I growl. "Why'd you do it?"

I don't need him to admit it for me to know the truth. I just want to know why.

My father leans in, clenching his jaw as he lowers his eyes at me. "You should be thanking me," he hisses, his voice low and guttural. "As long as he was alive, he'd always have the opportunity to fight for bail, parole, or take an insanity plea. Hell, you know the justice system is fucked. Why do you think I'm constantly stepping in to protect you?"

"Protect me?" I glare. "Or protect *your* reputation?"

"Both," he admits shamelessly. "Now you don't have to worry about anything. I did that for you, son."

I scoff. This man is unbelievable. "You mean you did it so there's another thing you can rub in my face, hold over my head, and use to try to control me. You should've let the system take care of him. He murdered a woman. He would've had to do his time."

"You and I both want to believe that, but there are too many people who slip through the justice system. It would've pulled you and Sophie back into court to continue fighting. Is that what you would've wanted? For *her*?" he challenges, and it causes my hands to ball into fists.

"Don't..." I warn at the mention of her name. "You might be

able to live with having blood on your hands, but I can't. Not anymore."

"And what's that mean, Mason? You have more blood on your hands than I do," he nearly spits in my face before shoving me aside and walking toward the door. My feet stay planted, not wanting to give him another glance. "Oh, and Mason?"

"What?" I answer without moving.

"His parents won't come after Liam or you. It's over."

While that should be a relief, it causes my stomach to knot. Anything my father is involved in is never good. He more than likely paid them off to stay away. I should be relieved, but nothing my father does is ever selfless. He'll want me to pay him back someday, and it won't be anything good.

"You're welcome." His final words are said before he opens the door and slams it behind him.

Just as I'm about to climb the stairs to check on Sophie, Serena and Liam come into the living room.

"So?" Liam arches a brow.

I know what he's asking without exchanging words. He wants to know if my dad was involved and confirmation that it wasn't a case of happenstance.

Inhaling a defeated breath, I nod. "Yeah."

"Well, I can't say I'm sorry he's dead. After what that bastard did, he deserved it." Liam shrugs, then takes his beer and bag of chips to the couch with him.

"So why'd you wait two days to tell me?" I ask Serena.

She lowers her eyes and sucks in air through her nose. "He asked me to wait until the incident report was filed and done."

"And you didn't find that…weird?" I cross my arms.

"Mason." She deadpans because we both know my father.

"I can't believe you're on board with this. Look, I hate the guy for what he did and prefer him dead so I never have to worry about him coming after Sophie again, but my father *once again* got involved when he didn't need to. He's so fucking shady and dirty. I can't get on board with that."

"Mason, I know…it makes for a hard situation, and I get that.

But look at it as a blessing in disguise. You and Sophie can move on for good, without any concern of him. It's over now."

"Doesn't make what he did right," I say before spinning on my heels and taking the stairs two at a time until I'm in front of the bathroom door, knocking.

"Soph, baby? You okay? Can I come in?" I ask, wanting to be close to her.

"Sure," she says.

When I walk in, I shut the door behind me, then realize she's in the bathtub. The curtain is closed so I can't see her. "You alright?"

"Yeah, just tired and wanted to clean the travel day off me," she responds, but her sniffling indicates otherwise.

I don't know how to be what she needs when I sense this wall between us. I want to hold her, touch her, give her whatever it is she needs right now. Stripping out of my clothes, I pull the curtain back enough to climb inside behind her. Sophie stays silent as she moves forward a bit to give me room. The moment my legs are on either side of her, I grab her shoulders and pull her back to my chest.

Taking the loofah, I lather soap onto it and rub it over her arms. Then her neck, shoulders, and chest. Her head falls back against me as I slowly wash her body. Sophie moans softly as I cover every inch of her exposed skin.

"What're you thinking?" I whisper in her ear. She's been so quiet since I picked her up, and I'm worried something's changed between us.

She doesn't answer right away. I can tell her mind is spinning with the information about Dalton. I pull her wet hair off her back and put it to one side, exposing her bare neck. Pressing a single kiss to the soft spot below her ear, I smile when she shivers against me.

"Does it make me a bad person that I'm happy he's dead?" she asks so quietly I almost don't hear her.

"No. He was a disturbed man who made bad choices that hurt people. Anyone who was affected by him would be glad he's not here anymore." I swallow, deciding to continue. "He put you in danger, threatened both of our lives, and killed two women—and maybe more we don't know about. He deserved what happened to him," I tell her, trying to convince myself that my father did the right thing.

"Their mother already lost one son, and now she's lost the other. I feel bad for her. Is that weird?" she asks, glancing over her shoulder.

I give her a small smile, rubbing a hand over her cheek. "No, that's who you are. Sweet, caring, empathetic. I can't imagine a mother's loss, but what happened to them isn't anyone's fault but their own. Their actions had consequences that ended their lives, and unfortunately, their mother is paying the ultimate price."

"It's weird to feel this way…" Sophie says, bowing her head. "Relieved, guilty, sad. All at once."

"I know, baby." I wrap my arms around her. "It'll get better, I promise."

Sophie's truths make me feel torn about everything. The last thing I want is for her to have any remorse for what happened to either of them. They both tried to kill us, but I know that doesn't dissipate her guilt about Dacia.

We lie in the tub for a few more minutes before she says she wants out. I help her so she doesn't slip, and she quickly covers up with a towel. There's a shift in the air, and I hate it. "I think I'm gonna get ready for bed. I'm exhausted."

"Do you want me to make you something to eat first?" I ask, wrapping a towel around my waist.

"I'm not hungry," she replies as she brushes her hair. "Thank you, though."

"Okay."

I wait until she's finished, then open the door. Grabbing her hand, I pull her closer and kiss her forehead. "I'm here, Soph," I remind her. "Let me be here for you."

Her chest deflates as she nods.

Cupping her face, I press my lips to hers, but she stills. My heart sinks, knowing my sweet Sophie is pulling away.

"I'm sorry," she says softly.

"For what?" I don't like the look on her face. In fact, it scares the shit out of me to see her like this.

"I feel like I'm toxic to you. To all of you. I've caused so much pain, and the last thing I want to do is cause more for you…" She bows her head.

"Soph, what're you talking about? You're not toxic to anyone," I reassure her, tilting her chin up. "I love you."

She blinks up at me. "I know you do, and that's why I can't jump back into our life the way it was before. Things aren't the same. We can't just continue where it left off."

I inhale a sharp breath and swallow down my heart that's lodged in my throat. "We're stronger together, Sophie." I grab her hand and cup my palms around it. "We can take things slow, but you don't have to go through this alone. If anything, my past and history make *me* toxic to you, but you're the reason I've seen life in a whole new light for the first time in years. I want to do better, *be* better for you."

The way she looks at me, I can tell she's holding back her tears. "And you're an amazing man, Mason. It's why I love you so much. But I need you to understand where I'm coming from. I can't live life pretending nothing ever happened, and that he didn't touch and hurt me, because what happened has forever changed me. I need to figure out a way to get through it so I can move forward. I want to move forward with you." Her bottom lip trembles. This isn't easy for her to say, but it definitely isn't easy to hear either.

I choke back, not wanting this to be any harder for her. "Tell me what I can do, Soph. Please." I'm close to pleading on my knees, not wanting to lose her. She's the only reason I look forward to waking up in the mornings. I rest my head against hers, our breaths mingling together. "I don't want to lose you. I can't."

"I need some time. Figure out my own emotions and clear my head so I can be what you deserve," she states, her words like cement. "I want us to be together, but I feel so broken right now."

"I'll do whatever you need, but I'm not going anywhere, okay?

I'll always be here, and I want to help you through this. So please let me do that at least?"

She nods in agreement. "I've got an appointment with my new therapist, Mary, so I can work through everything conflicting in my head. Between Weston and Dalton, I need to process it correctly. I didn't after the first incident, and I'm afraid I'll spiral downward if I push it aside again."

I know she's right. Deep down, she does need to work through it all, but I wish she wasn't pushing me away in the process.

"You do what you have to do, sweetheart. I'm here to support you in any way I can, and I'm not going anywhere. You're all I need." I press a soft kiss on her cheek, committing to memory the way she feels against me.

I'm prepared for the fight of my life to keep her, no matter the cost.

CHAPTER THIRTY-THREE

SOPHIE

I MISS Mason's touch more than anything. His scent, his kisses, the way he holds me close. His T-shirt is something I can't let go of either. When the tears threaten to come, I close my eyes and inhale a deep breath. Then I bury my face in his shirt and let them fall.

None of this was supposed to happen. Mason and I were finally on the same page, getting ready to begin our relationship, and then it imploded around us. The strength I hid behind and emotions I pushed down after Weston's death blew up in my face the moment Dalton captured me.

I'd never been so scared in my entire life. Knowing the guys would come for me, I prayed for a miracle that somehow no one would get shot. My worst fear was that someone would die trying to save me, and I'm thankful every day that didn't happen.

I'm the fool who let Dalton into my life.

Why didn't I know better? Why was my gut reaction to befriend a strange man and allow him into my life with hopes to help him instead of fearing him? I can't get the thoughts out of my mind. I should've listened to Mason and not fallen for Dalton's sob story and charm.

The internal battle keeps me awake at night until I cry myself to sleep. Then the next day comes, and the guilt returns, eating me whole as I try to push the demons away throughout the day.

"Soph? You awake?" Mason calls out, knocking on my door.

"Yeah, come in," I say without turning around. His feet softly pad against the floor as he enters.

"I brought you some coffee," he tells me, and I hear the sound of a mug being placed on my nightstand. "I made breakfast, too, if you're hungry. Thought maybe we could talk while we eat. You can catch me up on everything from this past week." His voice sounds hopeful, and I hate that I'm the reason for it.

Though we texted during my trip, I left out a lot of details. Speaking with that counselor helped me see a lot of things, but it didn't answer all of my questions. I'll continue speaking with a professional, but my biggest worry is that I'll never be at peace again. Not after an innocent woman died.

Wiping under my eyes, I turn around and sit up, letting my legs hang off the bed. "Thanks, I'm starving."

I grab my cup and follow him out of my room. He has a whole spread of fruit, eggs, and bacon set up on the kitchen table.

"Wow, you made enough for an army." I take a seat on one side. "Smells good."

"Well…I couldn't sleep. Got up and decided to make breakfast and kinda lost track of time and ended up making more than usual. I'll save whatever we don't eat for Liam, though. He's a machine."

Mason's teasing voice has me chuckling, and I nod in agreement. Liam is never not hungry.

He takes the seat across from me, and we both dig in, filling our plates full of food. I haven't eaten much and have missed his cooking and company.

"This is nice," I admit, blocking out the darkness that threatens to take over. "Sitting with you over breakfast like before. Feels normal."

He smiles and nods. "It's been a lonely week without you. Liam was moping around like a lost kitty."

"You mean *you* were, asshole…" Liam chimes in at the perfect time, stalking into the kitchen in only his boxer briefs. Yep, nothing's changed around here.

"You didn't miss me, Hulk?" I taunt, wondering if he'll deny it or call me out for using that nickname he hates.

"Of course I did," he finally responds after grabbing a plate. He winks, then starts piling food on his plate. "I just didn't act like a middle schooler nursing their first heartbreak."

"Hey, Sheila LeBlanc told me I could sit by her at lunch and then changed her mind in fifth period. I was devastated," Mason retorts, throwing a piece of bacon at Liam who picks it up and eats it. "She was my first girlfriend," Mason explains.

"Sounded serious."

"Best three days of my life." He smirks.

"Three days? You were basically pussy-whipped by then," Liam mocks, grabbing the milk from the fridge, then chugging it right from the jug.

"That's gross, Liam!" I scold. "This is why you're single…"

"Oh, the types of girls he's had parading around here in our college days wouldn't blink twice at that. They weren't exactly after his…manners."

Then Liam puts it away, faces us, and pats his six-pack abs. "They were definitely after something else."

"Your one-of-a-kind personality?" I quip before shoving a forkful of eggs into my mouth.

Mason snorts when Liam glares. "Women are all the same. Only see me as a piece of meat. Relationships are so overrated."

"Ironic when you're putting a pound of bacon on your plate…" I snicker. "And maybe if you gave it an actual chance, you *could* find a woman who's after something more."

"Look, I love you like a sister, but you're kinda enough work for me as it is. Always having to get you out of trouble is my new full-time job. There's no time for relationships with you as a roommate." He winks, but it causes me to frown. I know he's joking, but underneath, there's some truth to it. "Soph. Shit, I'm sorry. I didn't mean it that way."

I lower my gaze, unable to look at either of them. I've officially become a damsel in distress who always needs saving.

"Asshole," Mason mutters. He shoulder punches Liam, then comes to my side.

"You know I'm an idiot, Sophie. Ignore me," Liam says.

When I look up, he's sticking out his lower lip in a ridiculously cute pout.

"It's fine. Seriously. I'm a mess," I say honestly, but then point my finger at him. "And you were this *way* before I needed you to save me."

Liam throws his head back and laughs. "I know, I know. I'm a mess too. But in a different way." He grins, then leans in and hugs me.

Once he leaves with half the food, Mason comes and places a sweet kiss on my forehead. "I'll junk punch him later for you."

That causes me to chuckle, knowing he'll do it for me. "That's not necessary. I'm sure there's a line of chicks he never called back who'd love to do it."

"Why do you think he hardly ever brings women here anymore? They all knew where to find him, so he started hooking up at their place or in his truck. Finally got smart," Mason says, laughing.

"Okay, so I'm never riding in his truck again."

Mason and I fall into light conversation as we eat and things feel easy for a bit. He meant what he said last night about how he isn't going to let me pull away as I drown in an ocean of guilt and pain. It means a lot that he's willing to ride this out with me, but I wish I could give him more, give him what he deserves.

The tables have turned, and I want to be the very best version of me for his sake.

We spend the day lounging in the living room, watching Netflix and talking about everything and nothing at all. Neither of us brings up the elephant in the room, though there's nothing more to say now that he knows I need some relationship distance. Mason was my friend beforehand, so it's easy to be with him without it feeling awkward. That's something I appreciate and don't dare take for granted. He gives me space and doesn't smother me, refusing to let it affect our friendship.

Liam comes and goes. He's on his phone a lot, and sometimes he looks tense while other times he's easygoing. It's a little strange, but I've come to expect that from him. Being a bounty hunter means he could get a call at any time, day or night, and have to leave town at a moment's notice.

After dinner is delivered, we eat while watching the final season of *Lucifer* until Lennon and Maddie come over. I've texted back and forth with them all week, but now that I'm back, they want to see me, which I understand. Mason gives us some privacy, but before he does, he bends down and kisses my forehead.

As soon as he's upstairs and out of view, Lennon locks her gaze with mine. "What was that?"

"What?" I furrow my brows.

"Did you friend-zone him or something?"

"Because that looked like some brotherly shit," Maddie adds.

I roll my eyes and ignore their glares. "I told him I needed a little space from the relationship thing right now, and he's respecting that."

"Oh, Soph. Why?" Lennon asks sadly. "He literally saved your life."

"We're still together," I confirm. "But I can't jump back into a full-on relationship until I work out all the chaos going on in my head."

"Look, I can't say I know exactly what you're going through, but I can tell you leaning on Hunter during those hard months really helped me," Lennon says.

"And I did lean on him after Weston, but this…" I shrug,

feeling defeated. "I need to work through it. I want to be the girlfriend he deserves. All in. Not half a person. And right now, that's how I feel."

Lennon frowns but nods as if she finally understands. "Okay, I get it. But don't let him get too far away. Don't allow him to lose hope that you'll ever come back to him. He's so good for you. You're good for him. You two are perfect for each other."

"That's the last thing I want, trust me."

"Do you have a therapy appointment this week?" Maddie asks.

"Yeah, on Wednesday. The counselor in Utah set it up for me, and then I'll make weekly appointments going forward," I explain.

"I think it'll help you a lot," Lennon says. "Being pregnant with Allie helped me cope, knowing a piece of Brandon would be left in the world, but I probably should've gone at some point to work out my emotions."

"I feel good about it already. I need to learn some tactics too so I'm not so damn trusting. It's not the worst quality to have, but it's come back to bite me in the ass twice now." I shrug, trying to make light of the situation. "Oh, Mom and Dad told me to yell at both of you for not calling enough," I add, changing the subject because I'm mentally drained from talking about me.

"They FaceTime me every day!" Lennon defends. "All they want to do is talk to Allie anyway."

"I called them two weeks ago," Maddie adds. "There's literally nothing happening in my life besides having no job, no boyfriend, and going to class."

"Oh, you poor thing," I tease. "No drama. What that must be like…"

"Pfft. There's plenty of drama with dancers. My roommate, Erin, and her frenemy Melanie, have it out weekly."

"Sounds like a reality show."

Maddie walks to the kitchen and helps herself to a diet soda before she returns. "How come no one told me college is basically high school with older, snotty girls?" She has a bag of pretzels with her too, which makes me laugh. She got lucky in the genetics department, but she works out every day. Eating a handful of those would cause me to bloat for two days.

"We wanted you to go in blind and experience college wholeheartedly," Lennon mocks, stealing a handful of pretzels.

"Yeah, thanks." Maddie groans, then shoves three salty pretzel sticks in her mouth. "Seriously, it's so stressful living in those apartments with them. First, they eat all my damn snacks…"

"Wouldn't know what that's like." I deadpan.

"And then they hog the bathroom. I constantly have to take five-minute showers so I'm not late for class. Apparently, none of them know how to clean either. They're gross."

"Grosser than living with two guys?" I arch a brow, challenging her.

"I think so. At least your man cooks, and the other, well…he's nice to look at," she says with dreamy eyes.

"You have two years left, Mads," Lennon reminds her. "It can't be that bad."

Maddie narrows her eyes. Then she stuffs another handful of pretzels into her mouth.

An hour passes before Lennon gets a text that Allie is asleep and Hunter is in their bed waiting for her.

"Please, spare us the details." Maddie mimics a gagging noise. "We all know your pregnancy hormones make you horny."

"*Hornier*…" I add.

"Oh, you just wait…" Lennon pokes her shoulder. "You'll find a man, give your heart to him, and you won't be able to get enough of each other."

Maddie rolls her eyes hard, which causes me to laugh. They were just what I needed to lift my spirits for a bit.

"Okay, you better leave before Lennon starts teaching you about the birds and the bees," I tell Maddie.

I walk them to the door where we exchange hugs, and I promise to keep them updated on my therapy sessions.

"Race you to the car," Maddie taunts Lennon, then starts

running in slow motion down the walkway. "Bet I can still win going this slow."

I burst out laughing, knowing Lennon is going to kick her ass for teasing her. She's not that far along, but she's definitely more exhausted than she was with the last pregnancy. However, that's probably from having a nine-month-old baby at home to care for at the same time.

"Good luck at work tomorrow." She goes back to teaching now that it's the middle of August. She's been struggling with having to be away from Allie all day again.

"Thanks, I'm gonna need it." She sticks out her bottom lip, weeping. "I don't want to leave her, and my students are gonna give me a run for my money, but it'll be okay. The countdown to my maternity leave has already started."

That makes me laugh. "Baby will be here before we know it.".

"She's rounding second base…" Maddie calls out. "Think she'll make it to home base before the pregnant mama can waddle her way to first?"

We look at Maddie who's running toward the car in slow motion. "I'm gonna make her ass walk home." Lennon waves over her shoulder, and when she reaches the car, she doesn't unlock Maddie's side.

"Hey! I won fair and square! Let me in!" Maddie bangs on the window, and Lennon laughs from the driver's side.

"You made your bed!" I call out to her, and she flips me the bird. "Night, little sis!" I wave, then shut and lock the door.

"You girls have fun?" I spin around and bump right into Mason.

"You scared the shit out of me!" I scold, pressing a hand to my chest as I catch my breath. "Don't do that."

Mason raises his hands. "Sorry, I thought you heard me."

"No, I was too busy watching my sisters taunt each other." I follow him into the living room but don't sit. "And yeah, it was fun. I think I'm gonna go to bed, though."

"Are you staying home from work?"

"Yeah, I think I will be for a while. It isn't in me right now," I admit, though it pains me to say. Playing the violin has always come so natural to me, but lately, it's been hard. I used to crave it. Practicing would breathe life into me as I hit the notes and made music, but not anymore.

"Take as long as you need, Soph. There's no rush," he reassures me. "I'm sure your director understands."

"He does. Thankfully."

Mason wraps his arms around me and cradles my head as he hugs me to his chest. I inhale his musky scent, the one I miss so damn much, and lose myself in it for a moment. Before putting space between us, he kisses my forehead, but his lips linger before he releases me.

"Sweet dreams, baby." He shoves his hands into his pockets and walks away. He's fighting the urge to touch me, and it makes me feel like shit for putting this space between us. But it's what I need to do until I find myself again.

"Mason, wait." I take a step, and he spins around. "Can I ask you a weird question?"

"Of course. You can ask me anything."

Inhaling a deep breath, I bite my lower lip. "Can I have your shirt?"

One brow arches as he stares at me. "My shirt?"

"Yeah. I took one with me to Utah, and well, the smell is kinda fading. So can I have the one you're wearing? It helps me sleep." I shrug, embarrassed to admit that.

Mason pulls his shirt off, then hands it to me. "You can have any shirt you want, sweetheart."

I hold it in my hands against my chest. With Mason's abs on full display, it's hard to look away. "Thank you." I suck in the smell, grinning. "I'm sorry for—"

He cuts me off before I can continue. "Don't be, Soph. You have nothing to be sorry for, okay? I'm *here*," he reminds me, cupping my face and rubbing a thumb along my cheek, so soft and sweet. "I'm not going *anywhere*."

Nodding, I smile weakly before walking to my room. It's not until I shut my door that I catch him watching me. He gives me a wink before turning to go upstairs to his bedroom. As soon as I shut my door, I sink to the floor, tears covering my cheeks as I bury my face in his shirt.

I hate that I can't fight this. This feeling of being so damn weak and ignorant. I want to lean on him, but I can't always depend on someone else to lift me up. I allowed a terrible man into our lives, and Mason may forgive me for it, but I can't forgive myself.

Not this time.

CHAPTER THIRTY-FOUR

MASON

TRYING to give Sophie the space she needs while showing her that I'm here for her no matter what is the hardest thing I've ever had to do. I want to tell her every day how much I love her, how much I want us to be together, and that we can get through this. We can get through *anything*. I want to shower her with kisses and hold her while she falls asleep.

But I can't do any of those things while she works through this, and I'm determined to respect that. But fuck me if it isn't a struggle.

It's been four days since she's been home and not hearing her play her violin has been a hard reality to swallow. When I spoke about it to Hunter, he said Lennon went through something similar after Brandon died. She used to sing in the shower daily, and then she stopped—for *months*. It broke his heart, and it's breaking mine to see Sophie's pain written all over her gorgeous face.

She goes to her first therapy session this afternoon, and I hope it can help her move forward. My words of encouragement can only help so much, and it's not enough, but the selfish part of me wished it was.

"Morning," I say when she walks into the kitchen.

Sophie's hair is a wild mess on top of her head, but it's cute as hell. For the past few days, she's met me out here for breakfast before I have to leave for work. Though I want to stay home with her all day, I know that won't help things.

"How'd you sleep?"

Sophie rubs her eyes, yawning. "Not great." When she doesn't continue, I don't push for more although I want to. If she wanted me to know, she'd tell me.

"Sorry," I say, keeping my feet planted as I lean against the counter. "Want some coffee?"

"Yes. Thanks." I pour some into the mug before handing it to her. She takes it, then finds a seat at the counter. There's never been awkward silence between us, but lately, there have been moments of not knowing what to say or how to act. I want to scoop her up into my arms and kiss her until our lips go numb. I get a little hope knowing she's sleeping with my T-shirt, and without her asking, I gave her another one last night before she went to bed.

"Happy your appointment is today?" I ask as I dig into the fridge. I don't need anything, but I need to keep my hands busy. I end up pulling out lunch meat and decide to make a sandwich for work. Someone will eat it if I don't.

"Yes and no," she says, again not adding more. "Just a heads-up, I'm meeting my sisters for dinner afterward. So I'll be home a little later."

"Okay," I say. The tension between us is so damn thick I could cut it with a knife. She doesn't want to talk to me, and I don't know what to say to her. We yo-yo between things being okay to things feeling like they'll never go back to normal again—never get back to what we once had—and that scares the living shit out of me.

"Well, I gotta head into work. Text me if you want, okay?" I tell her, leaning in and kissing her forehead. I've told her that for the past two days, and she hasn't yet, but I won't give up hope that she will eventually.

"Okay. Have a good day," she tells me.

She's all that's on my mind while I work my bitch shift. Sophie always is, but today especially since she's seeing her therapist. I want things to go well for her so she can sort through her emotions and possibly open up about it. Part of me understands the guilt she's feeling and where she's coming from, but I hate that she won't let me in so I can help her through it.

I end up leaving work at a decent time, but when I find Serena's car in the driveway, I wish I'd stayed later. She was over a lot while Sophie was gone, and I know she's checking up on me, but she doesn't need to.

"To what do I owe the pleasure of your company again?" I taunt the moment I walk into the living room. She has her feet propped up on the coffee table as she pages through a magazine. "Make yourself at home." I snort.

Serena drops the magazine with a glare. "Don't forget who bought this coffee table."

"Don't forget who hauled its heavy ass in here," I retort.

"If memory serves me right, Liam did most of the lifting." She smirks.

I toss my wallet, keys, and phone on the table before taking a seat next to her. "Memory serves you wrong."

Serena laughs, patting my knee. "How ya holding up?"

I narrow my eyes at her, searching her face. "You don't have to check on me," I tell her. "Don't you have law stuff to do? Cases to solve? Put the bad guys away?"

"Things are a little slow right now," she admits, shrugging. "And because law school sucked me dry and my boss worked me to the bone, I have no friends, no social life, and no boyfriend."

"So what you're saying is, I was your first choice to hang out with?"

"My *only* choice. I'm pathetic, I know." Groaning, she throws her head back against the couch and releases a slow breath.

"Nah. You just put your career in front of sorority parties and one-night stands." I push myself up and walk toward the kitchen. "Speaking of which, you want a beer?"

"Sure. Make it a double."

"Let's start with one."

I return with our drinks, then kick my feet up. "So tell me the real reason you're here."

"I was worried about you. After the bomb about Dalton, I wasn't sure how you'd take it. Have you spoken to your father since then?" she asks.

"Nope. Don't plan to either." I take a long swig of my beer.

"This is gonna sound weird coming from me, but he really does love you. He might not show it properly, but he's proud of you."

My face whips around as if she'd slapped me across the cheek. "Did he pay you to say that?"

"Oh my God, shut up!" She playfully punches my shoulder. "It's true. He's proud of you."

I glare, not wanting to have this argument. "Is that the only reason you came over? If so, there's the door," I tell her, jerking my head.

"Don't you dare be rude to me, Mason Holt," she says, but she's smiling. We've always had a sibling type of friendship, and we grew even closer over the years. She misses her sister, though she rarely talks about her, but I don't either. The memories are too painful.

"Fine, if you don't want to talk about him, then tell me how Sophie's doing."

I groan, not sure if I want to discuss that with her either.

"Oh, come on. You can tell me." She nudges me with her elbow. "She okay?"

"I'm worried about her. Some of her behavior is similar to the way I acted after Emma's death, and it scares me," I tell her truthfully. "The pulling away, not doing things that once made her happy, blaming herself. She's put all this burden on her shoulders, and she's gonna sink if she doesn't learn how to let some of it go."

"She's pushing you away?" she asks as if she already knows the answer.

"Yeah." I frown, then take another drink. "Wants us to take things slow. Like sloth speed."

"She broke up with you?"

"Not exactly, but my heart feels ripped out of my chest, nevertheless. We're in limbo, basically. Not *not* together but keeping distance."

Serena gives me a sad look, which I hate. "She'll come back to you," she says with so much certainty it gives me hope.

"Fuck," I mutter. "I need her more than I want to admit and losing her would kill me. I'm afraid too much space will bring us right back into a friendship-only zone."

"Didn't she wait like…three years for you?" she taunts, and I roll my eyes in response. "Yeah, Liam told me all about it."

I grunt. "Of course he did."

"You needed that time, didn't you? You were still punishing yourself over Emma and knew you weren't in the right headspace to be with anyone. Once you got your head out of your ass, you found someone who wanted you for *you*. So give her time. I doubt it'll take three years but show her she's worth the wait."

"Trust me, I'm trying. I have to actively remind myself not to touch her when it's all I want to do to prove I'm here for her. I make breakfast, and we eat across from each other, not talking, but being together. We're on, then we're off, and it's making my head spin."

"And it might have to be like that for a while. If she loves you like she says, she's struggling with it too."

Serena's right but talking about this makes my chest ache.

"Okay, well enough about me. Tell me about the last guy you hooked up with?"

"Mason!" She swats at me. "You don't ask a woman that."

"What? I thought that's what we were doing here. Having a girly gossip session," I taunt.

She groans. "It's a wonder we're friends at all."

Liam strolls in moments later with two large pizzas and a six-pack of beer. "Didn't know you'd be here, or I would've brought more."

Serena smacks him over the head before stealing one of his

beers. "Funny. Those pizzas both for you?" she asks as he sets them down in front of us.

"It's my cheat day," he says proudly, hitting his stomach.

"And what were the past four years?"

"Don't worry, Mom. I *exercise* plenty." He grabs a slice, then shoves it into his big mouth.

"Oh yeah? What're their names? Can you even remember?" Serena asks, taking a piece and lounging back on the couch.

"Does it matter if I'm never gonna see them again? Britney, Sarah, Kelly. Pick one. I've probably hooked up with them." Liam shrugs, takes his beer, then plops down in the recliner.

"You're such a pig."

"Oink, oink," Liam mocks around a mouthful of food.

"You two children need to be separated?" I intervene.

Liam grabs the remote and starts flipping through the channels before settling on some crime TV show.

"Do we have to watch this?" I complain. "I see enough of this shit every day."

"That's why you should love it," he says. "Better than watching bounty hunter shows. It's all fake."

"And you think this shit isn't?" I argue. "They glamorize it."

"So you're saying you don't walk into a crime scene in slow motion with a badass song playing in the background?" Serena mocks, her eyes widening as she pokes fun at me.

We get through one episode and two pizzas before the front door swings open and Sophie walks in. She hadn't texted me all day, and I didn't want to bother her, so I managed to restrain myself from checking on her.

"Hey." I smile, standing to greet her.

"Hey." Her eyes catch on Serena and glances between us before pulling away. "What're you guys doing?" She shifts her gaze to Liam.

"It's pizza and beer night. You missed out," he says.

"I can see that. My sisters and I grabbed dinner anyway."

"Hey," Serena chimes in.

"Hi," Sophie says. "I'm gonna grab a bottle of water, then head to bed. I'm worn out."

"So how'd things go?" Following her into the kitchen, I reach for her elbow, then drop my hand. She digs into the fridge before turning to face me.

"Pretty good. She specializes in emotional trauma and grief, which is perfect. Only time will tell, though." She shrugs, then takes a drink of her water.

"That's great to hear. How was it with your sisters?"

"It was fine, Mason," she says sharply, then walks around me.

Scrubbing my hands over my face, I remember what Serena said and try not to take her edginess personal. When I walk back into the living room, Sophie is gone, which means she already went to her room for the night.

"I'm gonna get going." Serena stands, grabbing her bag. "Text me if you need to talk, okay?"

"Bye, Liam," she singsongs. "Stay out of trouble."

"Never," he retorts.

Once Serena's gone, Liam comes and sits next to me. "What's up, dude?"

"God, not you too." I roll my eyes, not having the strength to talk about it again.

"I can sense some tension," he continues.

"Wow, you must be a psychic."

He pierces me with his eyes, not taking my shit. "What happened?"

"Weston. Dalton. My father. Emma. Need more?" I deadpan.

"You two break up?" he asks seriously.

"No, but she wants space, so that's what I'm giving her," I explain, keeping it short.

"Yeah, you did that too after Emma." He nods. "Sophie is strong. One of the strongest women I know, and for some reason, she's crazy about you, so I have no doubt when the time is right, she'll be ready to move forward with you again."

I glare, not appreciating his half-ass dig.

"She'll be okay," he reassures me.

"Doesn't keep me from being terrified of losing her."

"You're strong, too. I have no doubt you two will figure this out."

"Thanks, man."

"And that's my TED talk for the night." He waggles his brows. "I'm off to bed."

"You're annoying." I roll my eyes.

After sitting in the living room for a half hour by myself, I leave to take a shower. I'm so goddamn tense, and my head is a fucking mess.

Standing under the hot stream, I jerk my dick until it's hard. My strokes are punishing and fast. Images of Sophie flood my mind as my head falls back on a moan. As I hold myself up with one hand against the shower wall, I picture her cheeks hollowing when I slide my cock between her perfect lips and how sexy she'd look on her knees in front of me. It wouldn't be the first time I've fantasized about her, but the timing is all wrong. Yet I'm desperate for her touch.

I squeeze my eyes closed as I imagine her hands on me. My fingers tighten as I pick up my pace, harder and faster, and soon, I'm unraveling, releasing into my palm and moaning Sophie's name.

With my body soaked, I stand and try to catch my breath. Fuck me.

I love her so damn much, yet I still feel like it's not enough. I can't lose her after everything, and I'll do whatever it takes to keep her. If that means keeping my distance and giving her space, I'll do it. But I'm not letting her walk away from me—from *us*.

CHAPTER THIRTY-FIVE

SOPHIE

It's been a week since my first therapy appointment, and I've been trying to implement breathing techniques when I'm anxious or stressed. After my gut reaction to Serena sitting close to Mason was that she wanted him, I went to my room frustrated as hell. The rational part of me knows I'm overreacting, but the overly sensitive and emotional part of me wonders if she'd be better for him after all. The thoughts are dangerous and toxic, and I'm not usually the jealous type, but my insecurities definitely got the best of me.

Today's the day of my second appointment, and I wake up in cold sweats, my body trembling as I try to push away the thoughts of the nightmare that woke me. Before it used to only be Weston who'd visit me in my sleep, but now Dalton has started showing up too.

Sitting up, I put my feet on the edge of the bed and look at my violin case. I haven't had any desire to play since the incident. I squeeze my eyes tight and count to ten just as Mary taught me. Sadness washes over me when I think about playing. Music used to be my escape, but now I can't seem to find the strength to lose myself in it. There's still so much I need to work out in my head and process. However, I'm growing more concerned that feeling like this is my new normal.

Once I returned from Utah, I called my director, and thankfully, he's given me permission to take personal leave for as long as I need. He knows that creative people can't be forced to create. I'm grateful he understands because I'm not sure I could play right now even if I tried. Just going out in public is hard, but being around people is too much. I'm more comfortable staying inside the house, where I'm safe and no one asks me shit about the incident. I'm not forced to talk about anything unless I want to. Mason and Liam know that I bring it up when I want to and don't push me. My sisters don't force conversation on me either, which I'm more than grateful for. Since talking to a professional, it's confirmation that maybe I'm more normal than I thought. Everyone works through their demons in different ways.

I'm looking forward to talking with Mary again today, sharing how things have been since our last meeting. Not much has changed between Mason and me this past week. We talk, and I see him before and after work, but as far as progress goes, I'm still taking it one day at a time. At night, I cling to his shirt like it's my lifeline. I miss him, and he misses me too, and it's destroying me that I have to put this space between us right now.

After I get ready for the day, I drive across town as I chat with my mother on the phone. My parents have been worried about me ever since I visited Utah, and I've promised to keep them updated with what's going on with me. I've been added to every prayer list available, and while I appreciate it, I don't want the attention.

Pulling into the parking lot, I take a deep breath and walk inside the office. I sign in, and it doesn't take long before Mary grabs me from the waiting room.

"Hey, Sophie," she greets with a warm smile. We exchange light conversation about the weather as I follow her into her office.

Once we both take our seats, she crosses her legs and gives me all of her attention. "So how has this past week been? During your first session, you told me all about the trauma you've endured. What have been your biggest obstacles since the incident?"

As easy as it would be to gloss over my emotions and say I'm fine, that won't do me any favors. I'm *not* fine.

"Trust issues, the guilt I feel about Dacia's death, the harsh reality that I put the people I love in danger. Knowing I should've been more guarded after Weston, but I allowed a stranger in my life and didn't see the signs. I'm struggling with anxiety for the first time in my life and don't know how to deal with it," I admit.

She studies me. "That's very understandable. PTSD affects everyone differently, especially in harmful traumatic events such as yours. It triggers anxiety and stress and most definitely trust issues. When you think of those concerns, can you tell me what specific things come to mind that trigger anxiety?"

I inhale a sharp breath, swallowing down my fears and reminding myself to be open. "Specifically, the knife he taunted me with. How he threatened to slice my throat and the way it felt when he cut me." I glance down at the mark on my arm that's nearly healed now, but it's left a scar

"How do you cope when you feel anxious? What do you do?"

"Honestly, by usually crying or hiding in my room. Burying myself in bed or trying to drown out the external noise with TV or music."

"And does that help?"

"Temporarily, but not usually that long before those thoughts flood back in," I admit.

"What does it feel like when they return?"

"Like I have no control and may never get over this. I'm afraid this'll haunt me for the rest of my life."

She nods, leaning toward me. "One of the biggest obstacles that people endure from trauma is feeling out of control—of their feelings and the aftermath. You need to gain that back without the fear of what's already happened, of what you can't change."

She clears her throat and crosses her arms over her lap.

"Alright, next time you find yourself feeling that way, I want you to try something. Visualize the scene in your head. Put yourself back to that night as best as you can. Right now, this is your biggest fear—that someone is gonna hurt you again. In order to work through that aspect, I'd like you to try some imaginal exposure."

My breath hitches. This sounds insane. The last thing I want to do is force myself back into the nightmare that nearly killed me.

"I'm gonna guide you through this…" she informs. "Close your eyes and walk me through Dalton holding the knife in front of you."

Tears surface as I do what she asks. Starting slow, I describe what it was like to be taped to the chair and how helpless I felt. Being restrained, having no control, fearing for my life.

Mary asks questions and navigates me through, encouraging me to continue and combat the fears that now overlap with my everyday life. I've actively tried to push the thoughts of that night out of my head, but in this scenario, I'm standing on the edge of a mountain, and she's pushing me right over, falling fast into the darkness.

With tears down my cheeks and my arms wrapped around me, holding me securely, I manage to get through the exercise. Once I've opened my eyes and wiped my face, I inhale a deep breath. The anxiety I had before feels a little less heavy on my chest.

"You did really well, Sophie," she tells me. "I can tell how hard that was for you, but I can reassure you this type of behavior therapy has been very successful for many of my clients. I think it can help you too, if we continue to practice. Taking control of your emotions and fears inevitably gives you back the power."

I nod, proud that I got through it too. I'm so grateful for her and being able to take this time to work on myself.

"We still have some time left, Sophie, so why don't you tell me how things are going with Mason. You told me that you've asked him for some relationship space. Is that still the case?"

I grin when I think about him, though I've been mostly distant and in my own head this past week. "Yes, and he's been very understanding. He's here for me, and he doesn't push my boundaries, which I'm grateful for, but I feel bad for putting him through this. I still worry I'm too broken at this point to ever be what he deserves. After Weston's emotional abuse, I still have to fight the thoughts he implanted in my head. It's hard not to believe them although the rational part of me knows they were all lies."

"Weston used emotional manipulation to break you down so you'd believe what he told you. Abusers like him make you truly believe that you're unworthy of happiness or healthy relationships. He wanted you to think all the bad things he did were your fault. The only thing you're guilty of is being a good person and trying to see the best in everyone. You *are* a good person."

I let out a sigh. "I am."

"Do you find doing your breathing exercises helps when you feel anxious?"

"Yes, for the most part," I tell her. It's something the counselor taught me in Utah.

"That's great. Keep it up. I'd like to give you a project for the next time we meet. It can often be hard for a person to realize how far they've come or what part of their treatment has helped, so I'd like you to start an anxiety journal. Every time you feel fear, out of control, or anxious, write down the moment. Then record what you did to cope with it and whether it helped. Keeping track can allow you to see any patterns or triggers. Even if it's things you think are stupid, write it down so we can talk about it." Her voice is soft and sweet, and I focus on it as I agree with her suggestion.

When our session ends, we set an appointment for the same day next week. When I walk outside, I feel a sense of clarity. I need to take it one day at a time and focus on the right now.

I walk to my car, and as soon as I get inside, I lock the door and pull my phone from my purse, and see I have a text from Maddie.

MADDIE

I got the dates for the fall ballet recital and wanted to send them over to you! Last Friday of Sept. You're coming, right?

I quickly open my calendar app and don't see anything scheduled for work. Though I'm not playing now, every performance is penciled in for the year.

SOPHIE

Definitely! Wouldn't miss it for the world.

MADDIE

Awesome. Wanna invite everyone for me too?

She has a way of making me laugh.

SOPHIE

You mean invite Liam?

MADDIE

Thank you! He needs to see how flexible I am
and how many different positions I can put my
body in, if you know what I mean.

SOPHIE

You are so relentless. Which I find admirable.

MADDIE

He'll crack eventually. It's only a matter of time.
Guaranteed!

I snort. She's had a thing for him since the first time she met him and refuses to give it up. Maybe eventually she will break through Liam's thick shell, but I'm not so sure. He's not the kind of guy who settles down with anyone, and if he hurt Maddie, I'd chop off his balls, then Lennon would feed them to him. Hunter considers Maddie and me his sisters, so I wouldn't be surprised if he'd kick his ass on principle alone.

SOPHIE

I'll invite everyone. I'm sure they'll come.

MADDIE

Thank you! I love you! Gotta go back to class.

I crank the car and drive home thinking about Maddie and how I hope she stays safe. I don't want her to go through what I have, and I'll do everything in my power to protect her from all the crazy assholes out in the world. Rushing into a relationship with anyone isn't worth it, and although she has a thing for Liam, I'm not sure that's ever going to happen. She's beautiful, sassy, and sometimes a little naïve, which makes me worry about her that much more.

Soon, I'm pulling into the driveway, feeling relieved to be home. Before getting out, I look around, making sure nothing seems out of place or suspicious. Grabbing my purse, I hurry inside and quickly lock the door behind me. That's when I realize this is the kind of thing Mary wanted me to write down—when I'm anxious.

Once I'm in my room, I grab a notebook I've used for work stuff and go to an empty page and jot down what I felt and the thoughts that surfaced. Then I put how the anxiety had me rushing inside and double-checking locks. The paranoia reminds me that I need to take some slow, deep breaths and try to relax before I irrationalize the situation and have a full-on anxiety attack.

Once I'm done writing, I place my notebook and pen on my nightstand since I'm sure there will be more times I'll need it. Then I sit on my bed and go to my happy place, deep breaths in, slow breaths out. After a few moments, some of the anxiety melts away, and I'm content enough to stop for the time being.

I remember I promised to give Lennon an update about therapy, so I quickly send her a text letting her know things went well. Then a text from Mason comes through.

He's been a lifesaver in more ways than one, and I don't know how I'll ever be able to repay him for everything he's done for me.

SOPHIE

I don't care. What do you want?

MASON

I asked you first!

I wonder if this is what real couples do, go back and forth about what's for dinner. I realize I'm smiling, and it feels good, but Mason seems to do that to me. Always has.

SOPHIE

Pasta?

MASON

No, I'm not in the mood for that.

SOPHIE

Pizza then.

MASON

That's too greasy.

I groan and roll my eyes at his pickiness.

SOPHIE

So tell me what you don't want and then I'll decide!

MASON

Just choose something else.

There's one food he'll always agree to eat. With a lifted eyebrow and a smirk on my lips, I send him a text.

SOPHIE

Tacos?

MASON

Yeah, that sounds good!

I head to the living room and sit on the couch with a book but end up falling asleep. The sound of Mason walking through the door wakes me. He has bags of food in his hands and a smile on his face. I can't stop staring at him in his dark blue button-up shirt and black slacks. He doesn't always dress up for work, but when he does, it's hard to keep my eyes off him.

"I hope you're hungry. It was buy one, get one free tonight, so I loaded us up," he says as he sits down next to me, placing the bags of food on the coffee table. His hand brushes against my leg and goose bumps trail across my skin. My heart says yes, but my head says no. Every day is a battle because I don't want to rush and ruin our relationship before it has a chance to start.

"I'm starving."

He unloads street tacos along with chips and salsa. The faint smell of his cologne grabs my attention as he heads to the kitchen. He returns with two plates, and we make small talk about our days while we eat. If I don't think about what we've been through or our pasts, it's easy to fall right back into where we were before the Dalton shit happened.

"Mmm, tacos were a good choice." Mason smiles, leaning into me.

I can't help but notice the way his eyes shine when he looks at me. The electricity that streams between us is undeniable, even after everything.

"I thought so." I smirk, knowing he can't deny tacos. "How was work?"

"Good. I think people are realizing I'm not just there because of who my dad is, which should've happened a long fucking time ago, but you know how it goes. People know I'm a Holt and see the similarities between my father and me, and they jump to conclusions. I should find out about the promotion next week."

"Glad everything seems to be working out," I say around a mouthful, knowing how much this means to him and how hard he's worked over the years for his big break. "You deserve it," I tell him sincerely.

"If I don't get it, I swear I might lose my mind," he admits, and I love that he's able to be vulnerable with me, considering he doesn't talk about work very much.

"You know you're a shoo-in. You know that for a fact, so I wouldn't worry about it. What *should* happen *will* happen."

"You're so damn smart."

I shrug and laugh. "Nah, I have a therapist who gives me catch phrases like that."

"How'd it go today?" When my eyes meet his, I can tell he genuinely wants to know.

"It went well. We talked a lot about my anxiety since the first incident, and she had me visualize that night and how facing that fear will release the out of control feeling. It sounds odd, but in a way, it felt like it was a good start to my treatment. She also told me to write in a journal when I'm anxious, so basically, I'll be writing in it all day long," I chuckle nervously. "I started today when I got home. It's gonna take months to process what's happened, but it will get a little easier each day as long as I work on it. I don't think I'll ever forget the incidents, but hopefully, I'll be able to live with it without the memories barging into my thoughts."

Mason wraps his arm around my shoulders, and while I want to lean into him and stay there forever, I don't. I linger, then go back to my tacos.

After we finish eating, I help Mason clean up our mess. After we put the leftover tacos in the fridge, we both sit back down on the couch and get lost in Netflix.

"Want to watch *Lucifer* or piss off Liam and watch his show?" He flashes me a shit-eating grin, which causes me to laugh.

Liam's been working a shit ton, so I haven't seen him as much lately, and the last episode left us on a cliffhanger, so I'm contemplating it.

Mason glances at me, and I smirk. "We promised Liam we wouldn't watch it without him."

I bite down on my lower lip and shrug. "I won't tell if you don't."

"Deal. Let's Netflix cheat on his ass."

For the next few hours, I get lost in the town's bad boy and small Southern town drama, and it's everything I love getting lost in. Eventually, I yawn a few times, and Mason notices.

"Tired?" he asks, yawning too. "Damn, I caught it." He chuckles, yawning again.

I nod. "Yeah, but I don't know why, considering I didn't do much today except go to therapy. Apparently, being in my head is exhausting," I joke.

He gives me a look. "Let's go to bed," he tells me, grabbing the remote and turning off the TV.

I glare at him.

Mason snickers. "Hey, if I don't turn it off, you know we'll watch the next one and then the next one, and then we'll be on the next season. Netflix makes it too easy."

I giggle because we've done it so many times. It's hard to break away from him when we're hanging out. I never want our time to end. Mason stands and stretches and holds his hand out. I grab it, and he helps me up.

Neither of us moves to walk away, and I notice the way he searches my face. "You sure you're okay, Soph?"

"I will be."

Mason brings his thumb to the corner of my lips. "Got a little sour cream here."

"Oh." I chuckle, embarrassed. It's probably been on my face this whole time. "Thanks."

His deep brown eyes I've gazed into dozens of times look at me with so much love, it's hard to break away. Then he tucks loose strands of hair behind my ear, and my eyes flutter closed when he cups my cheek. Softly, his lips press against mine, and for a moment, I lose myself in his taste, in his touch, in him. I feel as if I'm falling as his tongue twists with mine, and he releases a groan, sinking deeper against me. His other hand slides down my body until it grips my hip, pulling me against him. Moaning, I wrap my arms around his waist, clinging to the feeling that surfaces at this moment. Kissing Mason is a dream, a fantasy come to life, but then reality smacks me in the face. Although I want to get lost in him and forget about everything, that sneaky bitch anxiety comes barreling in, and I remember it's too soon.

"I can't do this," I whisper-pant, pushing against his chest. We both lost control. The moment I see his sad expression, guilt pours over me, and I frown. "I'm so sorry, Mason. I just—"

"I know." He cuts me off. "You're not ready. I'm sorry. I shouldn't have…" He swallows and brushes a hand through his hair.

I nod, taking a step back. "Good night, Mason."

He sucks in his lower lip. "Good night, sweet Sophie." He winks before turning around and heading upstairs.

I walk to my room and lean against the door. My heart gallops in my chest, and I close my eyes, trying to hold back the tears. Mason deserves to have more than a sliver of me, and right now, my heart is still too shattered to give him anything.

CHAPTER THIRTY-SIX

MASON

THE PAST THREE weeks have been both interesting and strange. After that night when Sophie and I kissed, I've been careful to keep my distance and watch for her cues so I don't overstep her boundaries.

After she said she wasn't ready, I felt like the biggest asshole in the world. I shouldn't have lost control, but it seemed right regardless of how wrong it was. It's been difficult to keep my feelings closed up, but that's what she needs right now.

I think back to when I lost Emma and how I wanted to do nothing but sleep and drink the pain away. At least Sophie is functioning after what she went through. I'm trying to give her all the time she needs, even if that means I have to wait for years, because I will.

The timing has always been wrong for our relationship because when one of us is ready for more, the other isn't. However, I refuse to give up on her, give up on *us*. The guilt of crossing the line with her has consumed me. Though I've apologized more than once, and she acts as if it's no big deal, I know better.

I pushed her too far, too quickly, and felt like a selfish bastard. But it's hard not to be selfish when it comes to her.

A couple of weeks ago, I was offered the promotion, which has helped keep me busy. Most nights, I'm exhausted when I walk in the door. Although I wish I was spending more time with her, it's probably best that work distracts me for the time being.

Another early morning comes, and after I get ready for work, I head to the kitchen like always. Once the coffee finishes brewing, I pour myself a cup and make one for Sophie the way she likes it, knowing she'll be joining me soon. After my mug is half empty, I grab ingredients from the fridge and whip up some scrambled eggs and toast.

Like clockwork, Sophie shuffles into the kitchen. I look over my shoulder as she sits at the table, taking a sip of her drink. Her hair is a mess, and she offers me a sweet smile. My heart lurches forward anytime I look at her and have to remind myself to bury my feelings. Something I should be used to by now, considering I've been doing it for years.

Doesn't mean it's been easy. Finally getting to a place we've both wanted and then having the rug pulled out from under us has brought an internal battle I wasn't ready for.

"Morning," she says.

Her sleepy voice is so damn sexy.

"Morning. Sleep well?"

She shrugs. "No worse than usual."

I place the eggs and toast on two plates, set them on the table, then sit across from her. We don't talk much in the mornings, but we don't have to. I'm happy to be around her and that she's here with me. After we're done eating, I clean up and rinse our dishes before putting them in the dishwasher.

"How's work going?"

"Great. Got a few cases to oversee, which is a nice change. Instead of doing the bitch work, I'm assigning it. Finally." I laugh.

The sweet smile she gives me is everything. She may tell me she can't, but her unspoken words tell me she still feels the same. It's enough for me.

"Any big plans today?" I ask, trying to keep the conversation flowing.

"Going to see my therapist for my weekly appointment. Might go grocery shopping so we aren't always living on pizza and tacos." She lets out a breath as if she's nervous about going out in a public space. "Other than that, nothing much. Maybe read a book if I don't fall asleep."

"Do you think you'll go back to work soon?" I ask. It's the elephant in the room, and something she's been avoiding for a while. I don't want to force her into anything, but I know what playing the violin means to her. Plus, Lennon has been asking Hunter to ask me if Sophie's been playing, and still, she hasn't. The last time I helped her carry her clothes to her room, I noticed the case hadn't moved from the corner for over a month.

She shrugs, then leans on the counter by me. "I was thinking next week. I need to practice again for our upcoming shows and want to be ready. Plus, I can only take so much leave before it looks like I'm taking advantage. God forbid something else happens that I need to take off for." She sighs with a quiet groan, almost as if she's anticipating more stuff going wrong in her life.

I tilt my head, then rest my hand on her shoulder, giving it a small squeeze. "Nothing else is gonna happen. Well, unless Hunter passes out when Lennon gives birth because he nearly did the last time." I chuckle. "But take all the time you need, Soph. You don't have to rush back into something you're not ready to do."

"That's what Mary says too," she admits. "I think I'll be fine to go back on Monday. Maybe it'll help get me out of my head for a while. Music has a way of healing the people in my family."

"Good, I hope so." I wink.

"Need anything from the store?" She walks past me and pours more coffee in her cup. Her arm brushes against mine as my back leans against the counter, and that familiar electric current streams through me. By the way she looks at me with hooded eyes, she feels it too.

"Nah, I'm good."

Though, I'd be better if her lips were pressed against mine.

"If you change your mind, you've got my number."

"I do. Even got it memorized."

"Oh yeah?" she asks playfully.

"I only have three numbers memorized, and one is my own so you should feel special that I know yours too," I tell her, which makes her laugh.

"Trust me, I do." She blinks, lowering her face as if she's trying to hide her blush.

She goes to the fridge and adds more creamer, then lets out a sigh after she takes another sip.

I check the time and realize I need to get going. I'm trying to set an example by being punctual although I'd rather shoot the shit with Sophie instead.

"Have a good day, Soph," I tell her after I refill my to-go mug with coffee.

"You too," she says, looking me up and down with a cocked eyebrow. It takes all the willpower I have to walk away, and I'm not sure how I do it.

"Wait…" she calls out. "Who's the third person's number?"

Smirking, I shove one hand in my pocket. "Our dumbass roommate."

"For all the times he's had to bail you out of jail?" she taunts with a side-grin, and it feels good to banter with her again.

I point my finger at her, smiling. "I'm changing your contact name to Sassy Sophie now." Then I wink, turn around, and get my ass out of there before I do something stupid like take her up against the door.

On the way to work, she's all I have on my mind. Watching her become more like her old self each day gives me more hope than she knows.

Jerad walks over and gives me a head nod when he checks his watch and sees I'm more than twenty minutes early. "Working on another promotion so soon?"

"You got jokes before eight? Shocking."

Jerad laughs. "Still a smartass no matter what time of day it is. Morning to you too, Holt."

I smile, happy to be here, working my dream job. A stack of

files sits on my desk that I need to look over and see if we missed anything that might help solve the case. There's been a few that don't have any leads on suspects, and it's critical we put all the pieces together to understand what happened. It's going to take me the rest of the week to look over the evidence and photographs that were collected, but I don't have any issues with it. This is what I've worked so damn hard for.

I flip through the photographs of the first case. Murder. DNA evidence was collected, but it didn't match anyone in the system. Logging into the computer, I go to the database that has the digital images stored and zoom into something in the corner of the room that catches my eye. Making sure I'm not imagining things, I hurry and flip through all of the pictures from the case. I grab the file and go to Jerad's office. Busy typing away on his computer, he gives me a pointed look for interrupting him, then goes back to what he was doing. I swear he lives to agitate me.

"Did anyone realize there's something on the wall here?" I ask.

Jerad scans over the photos and logs into the digital files on the computer and zooms in. "It looks like a fingerprint, doesn't it?"

"It does. I didn't see any information about fingerprints collected in the system. Just hair. But I think there was talk that it might be her roommate's."

He rubs his hand across the scruff on his chin. "You might be able to go back out there and see if the apartment is still taped off. It only happened a few days ago, and I remember the complex manager said they were gonna work on renovations early next week."

I suck in a deep breath, knowing this could help solve this case and give this girl's family some closure and justice. "I'll go," I tell him.

"Take Greg with you."

I give Jerad a look. "The intern?"

He releases a chuckle. "You were the intern for years. Don't discredit him because of it. The kid knows his shit."

"He's egotistical and thinks he knows everything." I groan and roll my eyes.

"So do you," he throws back at me.

"Touché. I'll grab him, and we'll go and see if we can get access."

Jerad hands me the files, and before I leave, he praises me for a job well done. It makes me feel like a badass although the work has only begun. Greg sits at his desk, shuffling papers, and looks up when I walk by. He's so fucking young, but I refuse to be a hypocrite and treat him the same way everyone treated me when I was fresh blood in the office.

"You're coming with me today. Grab your shit, I'm leaving now." I don't stop or give him a choice, and he catches on quickly because I hear him behind me seconds later.

"Where're we going?" Greg was smart enough to grab a sample kit and a camera, which is already saving me time. Maybe having an intern with me won't be so bad after all.

"I think something was missed in this investigation, so we're gonna check it out to make sure."

Greg's eyes widen. "What did they miss?"

"I think a fingerprint."

He furrows his brows and makes a face. "How the hell was *that* overlooked?"

I unlock my truck, and he climbs into the passenger side as I climb into the driver's seat. "You'll see when we get there. It's in the corner of a room, and a piece of furniture is somewhat blocking it. I saw it in a photo that was taken at a weird angle. It might be nothing, but my gut tells me otherwise, and it's usually not wrong."

He nods and grins. "Nice."

We drive across town and park at the main office for the apartment complex. Once I go inside and show my badge to the apartment manager, I let her know we're back to take another look so I need her to unlock the door for me. Greg carries the gear and listens to the woman explain they'll be cleaning out the apartment tomorrow, so it sounds like we made it just in time. Yellow tape is still crossed over the door, but she unlocks it for us and gives us a bored look.

"Make sure it's locked before you leave," she says.

"Will do. Thank you so much," I tell her before she walks away.

Bending down under the tape, I walk in and cross the room toward the corner and see the faint smudge of blood on the wall. Greg's brows pinch together. "How the hell did you see *that* in a picture?"

"It stuck out like a sore thumb, but there used to be a chair and a lamp here. It wasn't in any of the other photographs, only that one. The accident happened at night, and the lighting wasn't the best in here when they were called in to process the scene."

I can tell by the way his mouth falls open that he's impressed. Moving closer to the wall, he's mere inches from the small smear. "It's definitely a partial fingerprint. There's no doubt about it."

I stand over him. "I wonder if it's enough for the system to scan in." We don't always need a full print to get a match with our technology, but only when it's the right part of the print. There have been many times it hasn't been enough, and the whole case fell apart.

Smiling, he opens the kit and pulls out his brush and powder. Jerad was right. Greg knows what the hell he's doing and takes his time, not rushing. Now, I'm the one who's impressed.

"Good work," I tell him after he gets it onto his tape sample.

"So what happened here?" he asks after putting his supplies back in his kit.

"Lover's quarrel, they suspect. Her boyfriend has an alibi and was conveniently with friends out of town, but he has a record of abuse, so he could easily be lying. There's no proof it was him, but the girl's roommate said he had a temper." Talking about it makes me think of Sophie and everything she went through with Weston. This could've been her fate if he hadn't been stopped. My jaw clenches thinking about it.

"So they let him go after questioning because there wasn't enough evidence to keep him?" Greg asks, but I have a feeling he already knows the answer to that.

"Absolutely. And from what I've learned, men like that do it again and again until they're caught." Or brought down, but I'm not going to open that can of worms with him today.

We lock the door as the manager instructed, and we continue our conversation as we walk toward the truck. "How much longer do you have until you're finished with school?"

"A year left of grad school." He groans.

I've been there. I lived that life.

"It'll fly by," I tell him as we drive to the office.

Once we're back, Greg and I give the fingerprint tape to one of the forensic scientists in the lab, Monica, who agrees to process it as soon as she can. She's swamped with a million other things, but we give each other shit regularly and always do favors for each other. I let Jerad know we've returned and move on to my next case, though I can't seem to stop thinking about this poor young woman. I go back to her files, read the witness statements, and look at all the evidence collected. Perhaps I'm jaded, but I think it's more than obvious the boyfriend is lying.

"Innocent until proven guilty, my ass," I whisper under my breath, hoping this fingerprint comes through, and we can find out who's responsible for this girl's death.

Sophie comes to mind again, so I text her.

MASON

Thinking about you! Hope you're having a good day.

SOPHIE

Weird, I was just thinking about you too, but only because your underwear were mixed in with my clothes.

She sends over a pic of my boxer briefs lying next to her sexy little panties. Mmm. Hot as hell. Is she trying to kill me?

MASON

Stealing my underwear now? My T-shirts weren't enough?

I'm messing with her, which she knows. She takes my shirts, and I pretend it doesn't feel like a knife to my heart that I can't be the one wrapped up in her.

SOPHIE

You know it! Better keep an eye on your jeans. They're next.

MASON

I'll keep that in mind.

SOPHIE

So I thought I'd plan a get-together at our favorite bar tonight for your promotion. We haven't celebrated, and you deserve it.

A smile touches my lips.

MASON

I'd love that. What time?

SOPHIE

When are you leaving work? What about after?

MASON

Six works for me.

SOPHIE

Alright! Consider it done. See you then

I love it when she's easygoing and playful like this. Those are the times I used to take for granted but not anymore. It warms my heart to hear she wants to plan this because honestly, I wasn't making a big deal out of it. This proves how caring she is because lately, we've been staying home. It's her safe space, so it's a big step for her to want to go out with our friends.

I meticulously sort through the cases Jerad gave me for the rest of my shift. The guy who had this position before me retired, which means I've had to pick up right where he left off. While everyone knew he'd be leaving, there wasn't a handoff period, so

I've been playing catch-up since the moment I accepted the position, but I can't complain.

Before I head over to the Coliseum, I get a text from Serena asking to hang out since she's in the area. I explain where I'm going and invite her to come out with us to celebrate my promotion. It'll be like old times.

It doesn't take me long to get there, and when I walk inside and see everyone sitting together, I smile. I didn't realize how much I've missed this until now.

When I get closer, I hear Sophie and Lennon laughing about something. Sophie instantly stops talking when her eyes meet mine, and she gets up and gives me an unexpected hug. She wraps her arms around me, and I do the same, inhaling the scent of her sweet shampoo before she pulls away.

"Congratulations, *officially*!" she squeals, and they all chime in after her.

"About damn time! They should've given you that position forever ago." Liam lifts his beer, then chugs it. "Tab is on you tonight since you're rich now."

Maddie snorts, and I roll my eyes as I sit across from Sophie. Before I can say anything, Serena's voice echoes behind me. She tells everyone hello and sits in the chair next to me.

Serena leans over and gives me a hug. "Look at you, dressed all nice, looking professional." She tugs on the collar of my shirt, making a show of it, and I shake my head at her mocking tone.

"You need to come around more often if you think this is out of the ordinary." I laugh, smoothing my hands down my shirt.

Hunter goes to the bar and orders a round of drinks for all of us except for Lennon, who is stuck with water and lemon. "Sometimes being pregnant sucks." She groans with a frown after we all get our glasses.

Maddie sips on her soda. "Sometimes being twenty sucks! But I mean, if any of you wanna buy me a drink, I won't tell. It can be our little secret."

Sophie gives her a pointed look, and we all crack up.

"You're gonna be a handful when you turn twenty-one," I tell her.

"*Gonna be* a handful? As in she's not already?" Lennon gives Maddie a wink.

We order food, and while we wait for our food, Serena leans in close to prevent the entire table from overhearing and asks, "You been doing okay? You haven't been answering my calls. I need to talk to you about something. Something *important*."

"Yeah, everything's as fine as it can be," I say honestly. "Just been working a lot."

"So that merits ignoring me?" she teases.

"Sorry, Mom. You gonna spank me for being bad?" I mock her mothering behavior.

I hear Sophie inhale a sharp breath and realize she's heard that last bit and probably not the first part of our conversation, and I'm not sure how she's interpreted it. When I look at her, she quickly shifts toward Maddie who's talking Liam's ear off. Not sure what to think of her reaction, I finish my drink, then use it as my opportunity to speak to her.

"Soph, you want another one?" I ask, trying to grab her attention.

She glances and shakes her head. "No, thanks."

I purse my lips and don't respond. Once I'm at the bar, Hunter joins me, standing next to me with a cocked brow.

"What did you do to Sophie?" he asks.

My mouth falls open, and I roll my eyes at his accusation. "Nothing. I didn't do anything at all, but I'm glad to know I'm not imagining shit. Things seemed fine, and then all of a sudden, something changed. Hell if I know."

He shrugs. "Women. Probably hormones."

I chuckle, ordering us both a shot of whiskey and a beer for me. "If only that were it."

"I'm sure it is," he tells me as we clank our shot glasses together, and we shoot them down.

When I'm back at the table, Serena flashes a mischievous smile. "Thanks for bringing me back a beer. What a gentleman…"

I smirk, then let her have it before returning to the bar for another. While I'm waiting, I watch the table and notice how Sophie acts when Serena tries to talk to her, and that's when it dawns on me what her issue is…she's jealous. Leaning against the bar, I continue to study her and how stiff and rude she's being, and while Serena may not notice, I certainly do.

Wanting to see if my theory is correct, I go back to my chair and see the side glares Sophie throws at her. Serena tries to start a conversation about the symphony, but Sophie isn't having it. All the answers she gives are short and to the point. Maybe I'm reading the situation wrong and she doesn't want to talk about work since she hasn't been there for the past month, but my gut tells me otherwise. She sees Serena as a threat, which is crazy to me. After our dinner arrives, and we finish eating, Hunter and Lennon have to go pick up Allie from the sitter, so they say their goodbyes.

Then we end up by the pool tables like old times.

"Wanna play with me?" Maddie asks Liam in such a seductive tone, it causes me to nearly choke on my drink. Liam tilts his head at Maddie, looks her up and down, and there's no denying the attraction. I laugh when Liam adjusts himself and actively looks away from her. I don't know how long their little cat-and-mouse game is going to last, but it's hilarious to watch.

As the two of them allow their competitive nature to take over, Sophie sits at a high top table and drinks her martini, but she's quiet. Taking advantage of getting her alone, I walk over to her and smile.

"Everything okay?" I ask, then take a sip of my beer. "Liam's playing your favorite game."

She nods without looking at me, putting a brick wall between us, one so tall, there's no way I'm getting over it.

"Are you sure?" I ask again, just as Serena walks up and loops her arm through mine.

"Wanna play after them? See if I can beat you for once?" She shoots me a wink.

Sophie continues to sit with her jaw locked and her gaze on

everything but me , and I don't know why she's being like this. Serena is a close friend, always has been. Plus, Sophie knows our history.

"One minute," I tell Serena, loosening my arm from her grip, and she glances at Sophie, finally noticing how pissed she is.

"Okay. I'll be right over there," she sheepishly says and leaves us be.

"Go ahead." Sophie tilts her head toward Liam, Maddie, and Serena.

I suck in a deep breath, wishing she wasn't acting like this, wishing she knew she had nothing in the damn world to worry about. "Soph."

"I'm about to go home," she says matter-of-factly, pushing her still full martini away. She looks at me, grabs her clutch, and goes to Maddie to say she's leaving. Maddie volunteers Liam to take her home since they're not done with their game. Seconds later, Sophie's walking out of the door with keys in her hands and no goodbye.

Liam looks at me. "What the hell did you do?"

"I think I'm gonna head out too," Serena interrupts before I can respond. "Call me so we can talk later, okay?"

I give her a nod and thank her for coming.

"I didn't do shit," I tell Liam. "I tried talking to her, and she gave me the cold shoulder."

Maddie shakes her head.

"What?" I snap.

"Sophie's pissed."

"Thanks, Captain Obvious. Gonna tell me why now?" I wait for her to answer, and all she does is laugh.

After crossing my arms and glowering at her, she continues, "If you haven't figured it out yet, you're stupider than I thought." She turns with the cue stick in her hand, then leans over and hits a solid into a side pocket. I don't wait around for her to talk shit like usual before I head out too.

By the time I make it home, I've had too much time to think about tonight. The attitude, the annoyance, the dirty looks Sophie threw Serena's way—there's no reason for any of it, and by Hunter's and Liam's remarks, I wasn't imagining things.

When I walk inside, Sophie's sitting on the couch, already changed into different clothes. She doesn't look and focuses all of her attention on the TV.

"What's your problem?" I ask. Crossing my arms over my chest, I stand at the end of the couch.

She shrugs. "Not sure what you're talking about."

"Not sure? You're not sure?"

She narrows her eyes, her face expressionless as she speaks firmly. "Please tell me you're not *that* dense, Mason."

"Enlighten me then." I lift my arms and let them smack against my sides.

"Serena. Why did you invite her to something I arranged for you tonight?"

The question confuses me.

"Because she's my friend. She's done a lot for me over the years, and when she asked about my plans tonight, I thought she'd want to celebrate my promotion too. She's like an annoying big sister." Which is the truth. She's always looked out for me and has never given me any indication of wanting more.

Nevertheless, I notice she's growing more frustrated with me. "Never mind," she snaps, turning off the TV and walking to her room, then slamming the door shut. Refusing to make it that easy for her to drop this, I follow and walk inside her room.

"We're having this conversation right now." By the look on her face, she knows she can't escape me.

"Fine," she says, sighing. "I see the way she looks at you, Mason. And the way she touches you, flirts with you, how her eyes shine when you give her the tiniest bit of attention."

"That's not true," I argue.

"Really?" Sophie tilts her head at me. "She leans into you when you talk to her. I watched her touch your arm. We're in limbo, so it's not like it matters anyway. I'm not sure why I'm even upset. If you want to be with her, you should be. You two would probably make a better couple, anyway, considering you have so much in common. Not to mention she'd at least put out for you."

"Jesus, Soph." I take a step toward her, feeling like she slapped me across the face. "It's not like that. Serena's a flirty person and has always been that way. You're looking for something that's not there, but I don't know why."

Her mouth falls open as if I've slapped her. "Leave. You're treating me as if I'm making this shit up, and I'm not. You need to leave right now before I say something I might regret later."

"That's how you feel? That I should be with Serena? Take her out on dates and make her my girlfriend and fuck her?" I'm so pissed and wish she'd realize she's the only woman I want. The only one I've wanted for years.

Sophie tenses as if my words affected her. "I can't give you what you need, so you might as well. Considering she's so willing…"

I shake my head and drop my arms. "Don't you realize how absurd this is? I'm standing here fighting for you, telling you I don't want Serena and asking you to see what's right in front of you. Why are you looking for a fight? Haven't we been through enough to get to this point?"

She stands and points to the door, her chest heaving as my words sink in. "Just leave. I don't want to talk about this right now and want to be alone."

"Soph," I whisper, pleading with my eyes for her to stop pushing me away. She's all I want. Why can't she see that? She stands her ground as my heart deflates. "Alright, fine." I walk out of her bedroom, then climb the stairs. I notice Liam's door is open down the hall and poke my head inside.

"Everything okay?" he asks, flicking on his TV.

I sit on the edge of the bed and scrub my hands over my face. "I want to be there for her, give her everything she needs, but anytime I make some sort of progress, she slips through my fingers, and I have to start over. The moment we get closer, she pushes away again."

He unpacks a duffle bag of clothes, and I can only imagine how long they've been in there. By the smell, a while.

"Well, she's not wrong about Serena." I narrow my eyes at him, and he shrugs. "She's not. I don't know if Serena wants you or wants to screw around, but she's flirty around you. Whether or not it's harmless, it obviously bothers Sophie. She's in a fragile state of mind right now, so everything probably feels escalated, but perhaps validating her concerns instead of brushing them off would tell Sophie that you respect her feelings."

"Of course I respect her feelings. Our friendship has always been like that. Serena checks up on me like an older sibling, and I tease her for having no other friends. It's how we are. It doesn't mean she wants something more."

"Have you ever thought of asking her?"

"No." I wince. "Up until recently, I hadn't realized I needed to. I've made it very clear that I'm in love with Sophie. Plus, Serena and me—no." I shake my head. "She's Emma's sister. I don't see her that way *at all*."

"Well, might want to think about asking her, that way the air is cleared and you'll know for sure. Otherwise, what other explanation is there for why she's been coming around so much?"

"She's worried about me, though she doesn't have to be. She thought I'd spiral down again after Weston and Dalton. But she also saved my ass."

"Or…" A booming laugh fills the room. "It's because you're available. You and Sophie haven't progressed, so maybe, in her mind, she thinks she has a chance."

My brows pinch together at the thought. "I don't want her. I *never* wanted her. There's nothing there, and that line has never been crossed—*never* will be crossed," I declare.

"Yeah, but it doesn't mean she doesn't want it to happen. Put yourself in Sophie's shoes. She's trying to get her head right and wants to be the woman for you but in her own time. It's already difficult enough for her as it is, but then Serena comes around flaunting her tits and batting her eyes at you every second she can. I know you don't want her, but does Sophie know that?"

"Well, I tried telling her tonight, but she wasn't having it. Said maybe I'd be better with her anyway."

Liam chuckles, shaking his head.

"What, Dr. Know-it-all?"

"You honestly know nothing about women, huh? I'm shocked you ever got laid."

I roll my eyes. "Jesus fuck. Get on with it…"

"That's her way of pushing you away because of her own insecurities on top of what she's already feeling guilty about— your weird relationship status that is. So with all of that and then seeing you with Serena tonight, I can see why she acted the way she did. She planned this for you tonight, and you essentially brought a date."

"Oh my God," I groan, my head falling back as my temples throb. "A friend. I brought a friend! You came tonight. Does that mean you came as my date too?"

"Well, you did buy drinks," he mocks. "Serena's different, and you know it. She's at the house a lot, and you two have a friendship Sophie can't understand because it's still new to her. You're gonna need to do more than just *tell* her. You need to show Sophie that she's the one you want."

"Well, it's hard to describe Serena's and my friendship because we have a bond most people don't, and after all this time, I've never noticed her changing how she acts around me. But I guess I can see how it looks from the outside, even if it's nothing," I say. "But I guess I'll have to show her, then."

"Thatta boy, now you're learning." Liam slaps my shoulder with a shit-eating grin.

Standing, I slap him right back. "Thanks, Dr. Liam. Who knew you had so many special skills? Wait, don't answer that. You're your own biggest fan."

"Ha!" He beams. "And my pleasure. But next time, I'm charging you."

Shaking my head, I walk out of his room and go to the bathroom. Right now, after this revelation, I need a cold shower.

CHAPTER THIRTY-SEVEN

Sitting on my bed, I stare at the wall. My emotions are going crazy like I might break down at any moment. Watching Serena touch Mason and laugh at everything he said made something inside me snap. Noticing the way she responded to him, it was more than obvious she has feelings for him, and the thought blinded me. I could hardly concentrate at dinner. While I feel bad for how I acted, I know I'm not going crazy in thinking Serena is after him.

Or maybe I am.

Needing to know if it was only me or not, I text Lennon because she'll be honest. It's not too late, and I'm sure she's just settling down for the night.

SOPHIE

So. I have a question.

LENNON

Go for it. I'm sure I have an answer.

I pause before I type the message and wonder if I'm being a jealous girlfriend. Then I laugh because our relationship is on hold, which means I have no right to be. Mason should be able to do whatever he wants, and it's my fault because I took the lead and put us on pause. I want to give him all of me, not shards of who I used to be, and that's going to take time. If only I knew how long.

> **LENNON**
>
> Did you fall asleep or something? I'm waiting on edge for this question.

A nervous laugh escapes me, but Lennon won't judge. She never does.

> **SOPHIE**
>
> Do you think Serena has a thing for Mason?

After a few moments, the text bubble pops up. It stops and disappears, and then her message comes through.

> **LENNON**
>
> She may, but it doesn't matter what other people want, it's more than obvious he doesn't want her. He loves YOU.

> **SOPHIE**
>
> Are you sure? What if he does because I'm broken over here?

> **LENNON**
>
> I don't think you have anything to worry about. Right now, focus on healing, and everything else will work itself out. I promise. It always does.

I let out a breath and take her words to heart. It's hard not to worry when it's been the only constant in my life for the past few weeks. Am I letting my insecurities get the best of me? Am I starting fights for no reason because of my rocky emotional state? Maybe I am. If Serena wanted him, why didn't she pursue him all the years he was single? Could I be seeing something that isn't there? Dozens of questions flood my mind, driving me crazy.

Trying to push the thoughts out of my head, I thank Lennon

for chatting with me and turn off the lights with hopes to fall asleep.

It's been five days since Mason and I had our small argument, and today's the day I go back to work. He hasn't brought it up since that night, but neither have I. It's been rustling around in the back of my head ever since, even when I try to push it out. Though he was in denial about Serena, I know what I saw, and I'm not stupid. Mason's a catch, and any woman would be lucky to have him—including me. Although Lennon's words gave me some hope, I hadn't been able to approach the subject since then.

I get out of bed and go to the bathroom. For the first time in a long while, I feel okay about going to work. The thought makes me smile because playing violin professionally isn't like a normal job. I show up and get to do what I love, which is more than most people can say. There's a lot in my life that I shouldn't take for granted, and being able to play is one of them.

After I brush my teeth, I practically glide through the living room in my sleepy haze to the smell of coffee brewing in the kitchen. Mason continues giving me the space I need, but now I feel like I'm losing him. I don't expect him to wait for me forever, and it's something I've been thinking about lately.

After everything that's happened, it feels like the universe is telling us to slow down. Not that I can't trust Mason—hell, he's saved my life more than once—but I want to make sure I'm ready when it's time to take the next step. I don't want to rush into a relationship and ruin something that could be great for us both, and I know he understands that more than I could've ever imagined, but still. It hurts to know I'm the reason we can't be together the way we deserve to be.

When I sit at the table, he brings me a cup of coffee made the way I like it. The cream makes it the perfect temperature. Mason places some scrambled eggs and sausage in front of me, and I give him a thankful smile in return.

My eyes wander down his bare chest to the jogging pants that sit haphazardly on his hips. The sound of him clearing his throat brings my eyes back to his.

"I said, good morning," he repeats with a smirk as he sits in front of me and starts eating. I'm a woman of little words in the morning, a habit I've been trying to break since moving in but have failed miserably. Instead, Mason conforms to my ways and lets me drink my coffee and eat in silence, something I used to crave with my last roommates.

There are a few elephants in the room. One has Serena's name on it, but we've both been avoiding that conversation. Then again, I don't have anything more to say about that.

"Ready to go back to the rehearsal hall today?" he asks, squirting ketchup on his plate.

Sucking in a deep breath, I nod. "Yeah. I think so. It's gonna be weird, though."

"Because you haven't played?"

I knew he'd ask me about it, considering he hasn't this whole time, and I nod, focusing on my food.

I've been counting down to this day, but I feel ready, which is great since I didn't know if I'd be okay when I gave a return date to my director. Though my therapist said she'd write up the paperwork to allow for a longer medical leave, I refused. I desperately want to get back to my routine, and this is the first step.

It grows awkward between us, and I'm not sure what to say, but thankfully, Liam walks in and interrupts us. He's standing in his underwear with messy hair and no fucks to give.

"Dude," Mason says when Liam takes a piece of sausage from his plate.

Liam tries to lean over and give Mason a kiss on the cheek, but

Mason pushes his face away. "Sometimes you're the most annoying human on the planet."

He shrugs, pours himself a cup of coffee, and plops at the table as if the room isn't thick with tension. "What were you two lovebirds discussing?"

I roll my eyes at his loaded question. "Your mom."

He lets out a big fake laugh. "Oh man, Sophie. Maybe you should become a comedian. You're so quick with the jokes!" Liam raises his mug with a smirk.

"Good, because it's my plan B when I get kicked off the symphony." I glare without really meaning it.

"Oh, is that today?" he asks apologetically, and I hate that I've made him feel bad about it.

"Yep, which means I better get moving so I'm not late on my first day back." I stand and put my plate in the sink. "Thanks for breakfast, Mason."

Our eyes meet, and for a moment, all I want to do is get lost in him, but I notice Liam staring, so I force my legs to move. I go to my room and get dressed for work, but it proves to be more difficult than I expected. Nothing feels or looks right, and I change my outfit four different times before settling on something more comfortable—black slacks and a cream blouse.

It's been a while since I've been around my colleagues, and I'm more concerned about the looks and questions I'm going to get. However, I'm rusty from not practicing too. Today, there will be no playing from memory, and I'll be forced to sight read every piece of music I have.

I check the time, then grab my violin case and rush out the door. Before I set it on my passenger seat, I open the case and make sure it's still there. Slowly, I run my fingers across the smooth grain of the wood before shutting it. Taking in a deep breath, I start the car and drive across town. Though I'll be early, it'll give me enough time to find a dash of courage to go inside. On the way over, I listen to music, hoping to keep my mind busy, and it works until I pull into the parking lot.

My nerves are on edge, so I focus on the positives. Other

musicians begin showing up, and I finally decide to join them. People greet me, but no one brings up the obvious of me being gone for weeks, which helps me relax. Mr. Tanner enters and greets me with a kind smile, but that's as far as the conversation goes. As everyone arrives, I sit and begin warming up, and I realize how off I am. I'm already struggling.

We start at the beginning of our set, and within the first few measures, I miss a note, then another, then another. By the time we've played through two songs, I'm so damn frustrated with myself that I can barely concentrate. The mistakes I'm making are novice ones. Anxiety slaps me in the face, and I worry that coming back was a bad idea. The confidence I once had when I play has disappeared.

By the time we take our midday break for lunch, I'm nearly in tears as I walk to my car. It's as if Mason knows because I get a text from him.

MASON

How's it going?

SOPHIE

TERRIBLE!

MASON

Oh no. I'm sorry. Is there anything I can do to help?

Of course, his thoughtful words fill me with warmth. He's always trying to save me, but he can't save me from this.

SOPHIE

No. I think I'm gonna go home.

MASON

Do it if you need to. You don't have to rush into anything until you're ready, Soph.

SOPHIE

Thanks. I appreciate that.

MASON

Anytime. Oh hey, I'm probably gonna be staying
late at work today, but we should watch a movie
or something later.

SOPHIE

Deal.

Instead of returning, I take Mason's suggestion to heart and
decide to text my director and let him know I'm going home and
will be back in a day or two. I feel like a fucking failure and so
deflated. He doesn't have any issues with it and tells me he'll see
me then. I've kept him in the loop of what's been going on, and
he's been more than supportive.

Once I'm home, I want to crawl in bed and bury myself under
blankets for a week, but instead, I set up my music stand and
chair. I'm more than determined to get this right, and there's no
excuse for how I performed today.

Basic missed notes are unacceptable and performing like that,
even during a rehearsal, means I could be replaced. I've worked
too damn hard for this, and before I go back to work, I need to be
more prepared. I'm pissed at myself for thinking I could walk in
there and nail every song. I'm good, but I'm no maestro, especially
after not playing for weeks. So for the rest of the day, I practice.

I practice until I'm fatigued.

I practice until I close my eyes and picture the music notes on
the page.

I practice until my arms and fingers hurt.

I deserve this. I deserve to feel the pain.

Page after page, note after note, I repeat bars and measures until I
nail each one. But I'm growing more frustrated with myself because
I begin to make new mistakes. I stand, stretch, use the bathroom,
then go back to my chair, and start at the beginning again.

At some point, I obsessively repeat one melody and play it
over and over and over until a knock rings on my door. I ignore it,
but my door cracks open.

"Soph," Liam says cautiously, looking at me with soft eyes.

"What?" I snap. "Don't you see I'm trying to practice?" I don't mean to project my agitation toward him, but I can't help it.

"You've been playing the same song for over three hours." His voice is calm, and I can hear the concern behind his tone.

I'm nearly shaking when I let out a breath. "So what? I have to do this, Liam. I'm fucking up too much. I felt so damn stupid in there today making mistakes I haven't made since I was fourteen years old. It was ridiculous and embarrassing."

He walks inside and crosses his arms over his chest. His demeanor grows more serious as he takes the violin from my hand and sets it on the bed. I'm ready to punch him in the face for pulling me away, but maybe he's right.

"Doing the same thing over and over and expecting a different result is the definition of insanity…I think." He chuckles. "If you keep on, you're gonna send yourself into a nervous breakdown. Hell, you might send me into one too. If I hear those notes played one more time, I'm admitting myself into the psych ward."

I swallow down the lump in my throat and groan. I became too focused. "I'm sorry. I just—"

"I get it," he interrupts. " I do, but maybe you should take a break. You don't want to push yourself too hard, too soon. It's not productive."

I stand and stretch again, realizing how stiff I am, and he smirks because he knows he's right.

"Look, it's after five. Let's go out and have a drink or something."

Shaking my head, I look at him like he's lost his mind.

"Come on. Please? I'll pay!" He gives me big puppy dog eyes as he continues to beg.

"I don't feel like it. Being around people is the last thing I want to do right now," I admit.

"*Sophie*. Pretty, pretty, pretty please. Just one drink. That's all, I promise." Liam is ridiculous, and it's hard for me to say no when he acts like this.

"Ugh," I say with a groan.

"So does that mean yes?" A smirk plays on his lips.

"I guess! You're so dramatic," I tell him. He holds out his hand like he wants a high five, but I totally leave him hanging.

"We're leaving in ten minutes. I don't want to give you any time to change your mind," he singsongs and walks out of my room.

I put my violin in the case, but I'll practice again tomorrow with a clear head and be more than ready in a couple of days. The last thing I want to do is to let down my director, my colleagues, and more importantly, myself. After I change out of my work clothes, I walk out of my room, and he's already waiting by the door.

"Why are you dressed so nice?" I look at him from head to toe.

"To impress the ladies," he says matter-of-factly, causing me to snort.

"I'm telling Maddie," I tease as we walk out to his truck.

"Don't. She's the biggest cock block out there."

And we all know that's the truth. Maddie's become braver over the past few months, marking her territory and scaring off any girl who comes within a five-mile radius of Liam when she's around. It's quite funny to watch.

Instead of going to one of our regular hangouts, Liam drives us to a wine bar. We walk inside and sit, and I'm excited to try all the different wines they have. The list is a mile long.

"I hope you're not expecting me to put out after this." I glance at him after seeing how expensive everything is.

"Nah, but maybe you could do my dirty laundry," he taunts, but I don't think he's kidding.

I order a white zinfandel, and Liam gets a Pinot Noir. Jazz music plays in the background, and light from the candles along the bar flicker against the wall. The mood is dark and quiet, not loud like most of the places we typically go to, and I'm grateful he brought me here. It's relaxing.

"You know, sometimes when I visit places like this, I like to make up stories about other people in the room. Pretend they're millionaires who like to slum with the common folk or drug lords. Like that guy over there…" Liam tilts his head.

I peek around and look. "The guy with the mustache?"

"Yeah, he has four wives, and they all live together. Right now, he's waiting for his girlfriend to arrive so he can propose to her and make her his fifth wife." Liam narrows his eyes then chuckles.

"Oh my God. You're ridiculous," I say, but it is funny. "So what about that woman over there?"

"She killed her husband so she could cash in ten million dollars' worth of insurance money. Her dream has always been to buy a private island, and once she gets the money, all her dreams are gonna come true," he says so confidently I almost believe the silly story.

"And the bartender?" I ask.

"Trust fund baby but runs an underground drug ring and uses his inheritance to fund it all. Next."

"You're way too good at this. Who would've thought you had such a wild imagination." I'm laughing, smiling, having a good time, and it feels so nice.

"I know. It's how I occupy myself in airports, considering I've been traveling so much lately. There are so many people in there it's easy to think about how crazy their lives could be. Who knows, it could be true although there's like a one in a million chance."

He finishes his wine and orders another, and I get one too, but this time, I switch to a merlot. For the first time all week—hell, all month—I have a sense of calmness, and I'm grateful for Liam's friendship, more than he knows. It's almost as if I feel like myself right now at this moment, and I don't want it to end.

"Talk to Mason today?" he asks, abruptly moving the conversation to me.

Our new glasses are placed in front of us. Sipping my wine, I give him a nod. "Yeah, he told me he'd be home somewhat late, but that's about it." Before he can continue with Mason as the subject, I quickly change the subject. "So you're coming to Maddie's recital, right?"

"You already know I'm gonna be there. You're trying to deflect. But I'm not gonna allow it." He smirks when I groan.

"Then I'm gonna need another glass of wine," I bemuse, and Liam makes it happen.

"I know you two are going through a rough patch and things have been rocky, but he loves you, Soph. A lot. The other night, I heard you arguing about Serena…"

"And? I'm not crazy, right?" My heart races as I think about it.

"You're crazy, but not about that," he teases. "I just want you to know that you have nothing to worry about. If you told Mason to jump, he'd ask you how high. If you wanted him to wait for you for a decade, he'd wait a decade plus a year. Hell, he's been waiting for a woman like you for a long ass time, and he's not gonna give that up. Trust me. I'm his best friend. I know him better than he knows himself. When Mason Holt falls in love, he falls hard, and he's not ever gonna let that go. In case you haven't noticed, in the past three years of knowing him, he's never had another girl around. Never."

Heat rushes to my cheeks, and a small smile plays on my lips. Liam's right, which makes me feel bad for fighting with him and assuming he wasn't going to be patient with me. The alcohol seems to hit me all at once. I haven't eaten anything since breakfast, which was probably a bad idea, but I finish my third glass of wine anyway. "I think I've had too much to drink."

I hiccup. "I'm a lightweight, aren't I?"

"Oh man, drunk Sophie has come out to play, hasn't she? Maybe we shouldn't have ordered the eight ounce glasses?"

Laughter overtakes me. "Can we get a pizza on the way home?"

"I said I'd pay for your drinks. I never said anything about dinner."

I poke my bottom lip out. "Please? Sophie needs food."

"You're lucky you're one of the few chicks I can stand." He rolls his eyes with a smirk.

"Thanks, I think?"

After he closes our tab, Liam orders a pizza just the way I like it. My head is spinning, and I'm on cloud nine as we drive home. Liam wouldn't lie about Mason. He has no reason to, and if there's anyone who knows him best, it's Liam. I stare out the window, lost in my head when I laugh.

"What's so funny?" Liam asks as we pull into the driveway.

"I was thinking about all those stupid stories you made up about those people at the bar," I tell him, noticing Mason is home.

Before he climbs out and gets the pizza, I grab his arm. "Thank you."

He laughs. "For what?"

"For being a good friend. Albeit a stubborn one, but a good one."

Liam shrugs as if it's no big deal. "Being stubborn is the easy part."

I snort, knowing Maddie would wholeheartedly agree.

CHAPTER THIRTY-EIGHT

MASON

It's nearly dark outside, and I've been staring at the computer screen for nearly twenty minutes. Instead of wasting more time, I leave. Sophie agreed to watch a movie with me, and I'm not going to pass up the opportunity to spend time with her. I've been trying to shift us back to where we were in our friendship before the Serena argument and without all the awkwardness. It's still a struggle, being up and down, but I won't complain. After what she went through, I'm still so proud she's come this far and continues her therapy to help her.

I try to give her space and let her do things in her own time, but I also refuse to let her go through it alone. Sophie is sometimes too proud to ask for help, to ask for anything. She's always so concerned with everyone else, she often forgets about herself, but that hasn't changed since the first day I met her. Nothing can change her kind soul, not Weston and not his brother either.

On the way home, I pick up a pizza, just the way Sophie likes it. There's little to no traffic tonight, and it takes me no time to arrive, but then I notice that Liam isn't home. While I love his company, I'm happy to spend some alone time with Sophie since he rudely interrupted our breakfast this morning.

When I walk in, all the lights are off. I call for Sophie but don't get a response.

Setting the pizza down on the coffee table, I go to her room and knock on the door. When I don't get an answer, I crack it open, but she's not inside. Her violin case is on her bed, and her music stand has sheets on it. Knowing she played today makes me smile because of how much joy it brings her when she's not pressuring herself.

Though I talked to her earlier and know she didn't have the best day, she still came home and practiced. That's the type of determination that can't be taught. Some people have it, and some people don't. Sophie's a fighter.

"Soph?" I call out again into the house but don't get a response. I check the upstairs and downstairs bathrooms, but they're both empty too.

I grow more worried but make another walk around the house to double check. I release a frustrated groan and pull out my phone. Before I can text her, the door swings open.

Sophie and Liam barge in loud as fuck, laughing about God knows what, and Liam's carrying a pizza in his hand.

"Where the hell have you been?" I ask Sophie, and my tone comes out harsher than I intend. Sucking in a deep breath, I calm my panic because my mind went to a dark place when I couldn't find her.

Liam shakes his head and sets the pizza on the table next to the one I picked up.

"Pizza?" Sophie asks, giggling. "Great minds."

I narrow my eyes as she plops down on the couch.

"Are you drunk?"

"Oh, Mason," she singsongs.

That's a yes.

Opening the box, she grabs a slice, then takes a large bite . "Oh my God, this pizza is giving me so much life."

I glance at Liam. "What the fuck, dude?"

He shrugs and stuffs his face with a piece, then sits in his recliner. "You should've told us you were grabbing dinner. I wouldn't have stopped."

Sophie laughs and grabs my arm, pulling me down next to her. "Chill out. There's no such thing as too much pizza."

I can't help but notice the way her head falls back on her shoulders and how free she seems right now. It makes me miss her so goddamn much. I can't put it into words how seeing her like this makes me feel, but it's nothing more than a façade, a mask she's currently wearing behind the alcohol.

"So you get my girlfriend drunk, then bring her home?" I ask Liam.

He gives me a smirk at my slipup.

Sophie shakes her head, but she grins. With a mouthful, she says, "I'm not drunk, scout's honor." Then she attempts to do the salute and fails when she can't figure out if it's two or three fingers.

"Listen, I offered to buy her a drink, not my fault she drank an entire bottle of wine in an hour," Liam says, then grabs another piece.

"Seriously? In an hour?" My eyes grow wide with annoyance. She's gonna be sick as hell tomorrow. She hasn't drunk like that in forever.

"Are you trying to parent me, Mason?" Sophie lifts her eyebrows as if she's daring me to keep talking. "Should I call you daddy now?" She snickers, and I give Liam the biggest you-motherfucker glare.

He bursts out laughing as I hold back a groan. "Jesus fuck, Soph. Don't say shit like that." I brush a hand through my hair, then decide if I can't beat 'em, I might as well eat too.

Liam and Sophie practically destroy an entire pizza by themselves, and I have a few slices too, but I'm not in the giddiest state of mind like they are. Eventually, Liam decides to go upstairs. When the house is quiet, I study Sophie who looks like she's dreaming of rainbows and unicorns.

Her hair falls into her eyes, and I can't stop staring at how damn beautiful she is. Looking at her right now, I know without a doubt how I feel about this woman. I'd give her the whole world if she'd allow me to, and while she won't right now, I'll always be waiting.

As if she reads my mind, she stands, then falls into my lap. I hold her close to my chest, smelling the freshness of her hair and feeling the warmth of her soft body pressed against mine. I want to be this close to her for the rest of my life, and it nearly pains me when she pulls away to sit next to me. Instantly, I miss her touch although we're still close.

"I was worried about you," I admit, staring at her.

She peers up at me, and I notice the way her tongue slides out of her mouth and swipes across her bottom lip, and I've never been so damn jealous of that tongue. I want to taste her again so fucking badly.

"I'm okay, Mason. I am. I promise." The small smile plays across her lips. "Liam wanted me to break away from playing because I wouldn't stop. I needed tonight."

"I understand. I just…I thought something happened." Perhaps I have PTSD from almost losing her. I worry every damn time she leaves the house, but I can't ask her to check in with me every second of the day, not if she doesn't want to.

"The only tragedy that happened tonight was I didn't get a glass of champagne. Liam cut me off," she says with an adorable pout as she shifts closer.

She's being overly flirty, and I have to remind myself it's the alcohol loosening all of her inhibitions. I tuck her hair behind her ear, and she leans into my touch.

"I've missed you," she admits, and it causes my heart to lurch forward. "So damn much."

"I've missed you too. But you know I'm always here for you, sweetheart. Right?"

Her hand rests on my leg, and I take any part of her that she's willing to give me. Just being this close to her is driving me absolutely crazy.

Sophie clears her throat as if she has something serious to say. "Listen, I'm sorry about last week when we fought about Serena. I should've been more understanding of your friendship. I can't say I'm not jealous because I am, but I should trust you enough not to let my insecurities get the best of me."

I release a deep breath and rest my hand on top of hers, relieved to hear those words. The last thing I want to do is fight with her, especially when the undeniable electricity streams between us. "I am too. I should've also understood where you were coming from."

"Mason, you didn't do anything wrong. I feel guilty for ruining your celebration dinner. I acted like a jealous ex-girlfriend when I had no right to." Her breath hitches when she realizes the words she said, and I notice the way her chest rises and falls with every ragged breath.

"You didn't ruin anything," I reassure her. "And you technically can't be a jealous ex-girlfriend. If you ever take the girlfriend label, trust me when I say there will never be an *ex* in front of it, only a Mrs." I wink, though I'm being one hundred percent honest. Our relationship being on pause or limbo—or whatever the hell it is—wouldn't stop me from marrying her tomorrow.

Sophie playfully rolls her eyes, not taking me seriously. "For real though, I'm sorry for getting upset about Serena." She chews on the corner of her lip, and I have to remind myself not to lean in and kiss her, but resisting the temptation has been one of the hardest things I've ever had to do.

"You have nothing to worry about, ever. Serena and I are just friends, and that's it. I promise."

"That's good to know. I hope *she* knows." She blushes, then yawns. "I think I'm gonna go to bed, so I can be somewhat functional tomorrow. I've had a long day." She stands, then takes a few steps away, and when I think our time is up, she looks over her shoulder at me. "Coming?"

I raise my brows when she holds out her hand. It's hard for me to tell her no, and she's testing every bit of willpower I have left. If I'm not careful, it's going to fucking snap.

Slowly and wobbly, she leads me through the living room and

to her bedroom. She closes the door and looks up at me with a sexy little smirk playing on her lips.

"I *need* you, Mason," she whispers, then sucks in her lower lip like a temptress.

Fuck. Me.

"Soph," I say cautiously, cupping her cheek and rubbing my thumb over it like I've done dozens of times before.

"Please?" she asks, nearly begging.

"I can't," I begrudgingly say.

Not taking no for an answer, she begins to take off her clothes. Carefully, she pulls off her shirt and drops it to the floor. Not waiting another second, she unbuttons and unzips her shorts, then kicks them away while keeping her eyes locked with mine. She stands in only her bra and panties, and my hands ball into fists to keep myself from reaching out and touching her. I bite down on my bottom lip and swallow hard as I study every soft curve of her body and grow harder with each passing second.

"Soph," I growl. "We can't."

She walks around me, and I watch as she pulls back the sheets, then lies down on the bed, batting her lashes at me. When I move closer toward her, she crawls under the blankets and curls her finger at me to join her. I swallow down the lump in my throat, knowing this is not *her* right now. As if she sees my hesitation, she goes a step further and takes off her bra, then dangles it outside the covers with a sultry grin, teasing the shit out of me. I close my eyes tight and tell myself to get the fuck out of there. I'd never take advantage of her after she's been drinking, but she's seriously testing me right now.

"Coming in?" she asks.

"No."

She pouts out her lower lip, giving me her best sad eyes. "Why? Are you out of condoms?" She asks the question so innocently, I bark out a laugh that's mostly strained with a *fuck my life* groan as I pinch the back of my neck. "I can't, Soph. You've been drinking."

The words nearly cause me physical pain because if she weren't drunk, she wouldn't have to ask twice.

"Will you at least hold me then?"

Sucking in a breath, I nod, and she scoots over for me to climb in behind her. She presses her ass against my erection that obviously has no shame or willpower. Her breath hitches when I nuzzle my nose and lips against the softness of her neck. She reaches for my hand and interlocks her fingers with mine, then rests it against her stomach, which is way too close to both her pussy and bare tits. Forcing myself to close my eyes, I take in this moment, the way she smells and how she feels, until we both fall asleep.

The next morning, I wake up in a stupor, not knowing where I am until I realize Sophie is still in my arms. I'm relieved it wasn't a dream, and she really asked me in here because too many times I've woken up disappointed. In my sleepy haze, I somehow find the strength to slip out of her bed without startling her.

The first thing I do is go upstairs and take a cold shower because goddamn, just thinking about her body against mine is making me hard all over again. As I stand in the shower, my dick nearly breaks off when I grab it and squeeze it tight. Placing my hand against the wall, I roughly stroke myself to thoughts of her. I think about all the dirty fucking things I want to do to her, kissing her from head to toe, then making love to her until her body convulses. Remembering the night in the bar bathroom and the softness of her moans as she comes makes me see white. Grunts escape me as the orgasm takes over. My heart races, and I breathe erratically as I try to calm down, but that's not going to happen until I can have her again. *And again and again.*

After my shower, I go to my bedroom and slip on some jogging pants. Considering eating together in the mornings is our tradition, I make breakfast for us, but this morning, she's getting French toast because after drinking a bottle of wine, she's going to need something heavier in her stomach.

I start the coffee, then pull out the ingredients. Just as I place the bread inside the egg wash, footsteps shuffle behind me.

When I glance over my shoulder, I hold back a smirk at how rough she looks. At least she put her clothes on.

"Oh my God, I think I'm dead." She takes a seat at the table and puts her head down but faces me. "Just kill me now and put me out of my misery please."

I set a cup of coffee and the bottle of creamer in front of her. "Liam will get you in trouble every *single time*. Remember that for next time." I grin, then move back to the stove and continue cooking. As the bread sizzles, I grab my coffee and sip it as she puts her hands over her face. She's a hungover mess, and I can't stop chuckling.

"Also, please tell me I didn't come on to you," she says, then narrows her eyes when I smirk. "Please tell me that's not why I woke up almost completely naked."

I burst into laughter. "Oh yeah, about that."

Dread covers her face, and her cheeks turn pink, which I find adorable. Even after everything we've been through, she still blushes around me.

"Wow. I suck." She smacks herself on the forehead. "You're a saint. That's all I have to say."

"I've told you once, and I'll tell you again…" I remind her, repeating my words from the night we met, "I'm no saint."

She bites down on her lip again, and it drives me crazy as hell. By the look on her face, she's also reliving the moment. I place the French toast on a plate and grab the syrup, then set it in front of her.

Leaning down, I rest one hand on the table and one behind her on the chair as I lower my voice and whisper in her ear, "The next time you beg me to fuck you, I won't say no. So you better mean it and be sober because my restraint is hanging by a thread."

Her breath hitches, and before she can respond, we're being startled by Maddie waltzing into the kitchen like she owns the damn place.

"Oh my God." She freezes in her tracks. "Did you two finally have sex again?" Maddie looks back and forth between us.

"No," we say in unison, and she snickers at our deer in the headlights expressions. I pull myself away and back to my chair since Maddie's ruined our moment.

"Are you sure?" She narrows her eyes.

"Shut up!" Sophie snaps, looking embarrassed. "Why are you here, anyway?"

Maddie shrugs, ignoring the question, and pours herself a cup of orange juice. Sitting next to her sister, she steals some of Sophie's food off her plate. "So, how was last night? I got your stupid drunk texts this morning, and I'm pissed you didn't come pick me up when you knew you'd be going out with Liam. Seriously, you're a cock block."

I snort.

"Funny, he calls you the same thing," Sophie retorts, which causes Maddie to scoff dramatically.

"Ironic, considering he's the one who runs away every time I'm around," she says around a mouthful.

When she flips her hair, I look at her butterfly tattoo on her wrist. It's sweet and dainty, a contradiction to her strong and fierce personality. Knowing their parents' strict religious values, I'm surprised she has one, but then again, she's known to rebel against rules. It's a wonder why Liam hasn't taken up her million offers, but I have a feeling it has more to do with his own fears about relationships than the fact she's in our inner circle.

"Maybe after a bottle or two of wine, he would've been more than ready to take my virginity, if I don't sell it to a guy for a hundred thousand. Do you have any idea what I could buy with that money? I mean, it's only one time, and he'd probably finish in less than five minutes. I—"

"Maddie," Sophie groans, drawing out her name. "Shut your French toast trap. My head is killing me, and you're talking *way* too much."

"What're you doing here?" I interrupt and ask her.

"Well, after I got your messages, I was worried, so I scheduled an Uber." She shifts her eyes between us again. "You both look guilty."

Sophie focuses on her food, and Maddie turns toward me. "You might not have had sex, but you almost did." She wrinkles her nose and leans into me. "I can sense it."

"Oh my God. You're a weirdo," Sophie quips.

"What're you, a psychic or something?" I retort, finishing the last of my food, then placing my plate in the sink.

Maddie giggles because she knows she's right. "No, but the sexual tension is—"

Liam walks in the kitchen and stops when he sees her. "What're you doing here?"

"So what were you saying about sexual tension?" Sophie taunts, glancing at Liam who's walking around in his boxer briefs, *again.*

Maddie's eyes widen as she looks him up and down, focusing heavily on his ass, and you'd think he's naked by how she's gawking. "I think I just died and went to virgin heaven," she whispers to Sophie, but we all hear it.

"What's she doing here?" Liam asks, grabbing himself a cup of coffee. He's loud enough for Maddie to overhear.

Sophie and I shrug.

"Why do I feel very unwelcome here?" Maddie asks after she's asked for the third time why she's here so damn early.

I walk out of the kitchen, and Sophie follows me, leaving Maddie in the kitchen with Liam. She talks a million miles per hour again about how he should've picked her up regardless of the fact she's underage because she's great company. Liam groans, and I only feel a little bad for leaving him with her. When Sophie lies on the sofa, I quickly run upstairs and grab some Tylenol from the medicine cabinet and then grab a bottle of water from the fridge.

Maddie's in tight booty shorts and a crop top, and although Liam's trying to ignore her, he's failing miserably. I walk out of the kitchen and hand Sophie the meds and water.

"You're always saving me," she murmurs before swallowing them down.

"And I always will." I wink.

At that moment, every sound disappears, and it's just her and me like old times. The only thing that brings me back to reality is Liam.

"I'm not babysitting today!" he shouts from the kitchen. Maddie's still talking, not taking the blatant hint from Liam, and all we can do is laugh. At least she's determined.

CHAPTER THIRTY-NINE

SOPHIE

Since Maddie's recital is tonight, and I was at rehearsal all day, I jump in the shower as soon as I get home.

It's been two weeks since the drunken episode when I embarrassed myself and begged Mason to sleep with me. Though I drank way too much, and I'm a lightweight, I can't forget the way he looked at me and then held me all night long. A part of me blames Liam for forcing me to go out for a drink, but I fully understood why he did it. I was drowning in my own personal failure, and Liam brought me to shore. Though I didn't want to chat about anything serious, he brought up Mason and wasn't going to allow me to avoid talking about it. Liam, being the big brother I never had, wanted me to understand how Mason feels. But of course that one drink turned into three within an hour, and the only person I can blame for that is myself.

After Liam and I got home, and I realized how worried Mason was, I felt bad for not giving him a heads-up sooner. Considering everything, I should've let him know before we left. He looked like he was memorizing every single inch of my body, and that old, familiar flame deep inside me started to burn again. I'm thankful he said no because I know he'd never take advantage, but I'd be lying if I didn't admit to being a tad disappointed too.

When it comes to Mason, I don't want to regret anything we do, and because the alcohol was numbing all my inhibitions, I might've. Once that door opens between us, it will be hard to close it again, and I don't want to deny him any more than I already am.

I told my therapist all about it, and she asked me a slew of questions, including how I felt then and the day after. The relief I felt to be able to fully talk about my feelings and have someone listen without judgment helped me work through my embarrassment and shame. I've continued my weekly appointments, and while I'm still working through everything, I'm getting stronger every day.

As I finish rinsing my hair, I decide my thoughts have wandered on long enough and turn off the shower. I wrap a towel around my body and get ready. I'm nearly exhausted by the time I finish blow-drying and curling it and then hurry down to my room to slip on a nice dress and some heels. After I apply makeup, I'm ready to go, so I walk into the living room where Mason waits on the couch. As soon as he sees me, he instantly stands and smiles.

Scanning his eyes down my outfit, he walks toward me. "You're breathtaking," he whispers, and his words cause heat to rush through my body. It's hard to keep him at a distance when he looks at me with so much love and admiration.

"Thank you," I say, knowing I'm blushing but don't try to hide it this time. "You don't look so bad yourself." And he doesn't. He looks good enough to eat.

Before he can respond, Liam nearly stumbles down the stairs. We look at him, and I arch a brow at his getup. There's no denying he went the extra mile to look nice for the recital, and Mason beats me to a smartass comment.

"If I didn't know better, I'd say you were trying to impress Maddie," he quips, causing me to giggle.

Liam rolls his eyes. "Don't you know basic etiquette when you go to a performance of any sorts?"

"Okay, he has you there."

"Mama didn't raise no slob. I know how these things work. Could be all the classical music I listen to or the theatrical performances I saw in college," Liam says matter-of-factly.

Mason snorts. "Spare me. There's no need to pull the elite card out of your ass."

"Good, because it's made of diamonds and hurts to flash." Liam winks.

"You're disgusting."

He lowers his gaze down my body, smirking. "Who're you trying to impress? Oh wait…" He waggles his brows. "It's for me, isn't it?"

"Shut up," I say, nudging him in his ribs. He pretends to fall over, but the truth is he's built solid. My elbow didn't do shit to him.

Mason glances at his phone and rounds us up. "We should probably get going if we want good parking."

"Lennon and Hunter might beat us there. We have front row tickets because I want to see the sweat beads roll off the dancer's foreheads." I snicker, knowing Maddie won't sweat a drop. She's in such good shape, a two-hour performance is nothing for her. Nothing at all. The girl could dance in her sleep and wake up refreshed.

Mason leads the way to his truck, and I look at Liam as he walks to the back. "You even wore a tie. You know she's gonna want you to tie her up with it," I tease with a chuckle. He groans and flips me the bird. "Don't say I didn't warn ya."

Giving him shit is going to be the highlight of my night, and it's only begun. When Maddie sees him wearing a black button-up shirt with a red tie and slacks that squeeze his ass, she might straddle him right then and there.

Mason drives us to the university theater where it's being held. When we walk inside the auditorium, Mason places his hand on the small of my back, and it causes every hair on my body to stand.

Of course Lennon and Hunter are already here. Liam sits on the other side of Hunter, and I sit between Lennon and Mason.

As soon as Lennon sees Liam, she says something about his outfit.

"Maybe we shouldn't sit in front. If Maddie sees you dressed like that, she's gonna drop dead." Lennon giggles, and Liam responds with an annoyed groan. "Even a tie…" She pretends to tug on it, and Hunter's already smirking and shaking his head.

"That's what I said," I agree with Lennon.

"Great, I have to listen to both of you riding my ass?" he snaps.

"Oh Hulk, it's all in good fun. Just don't laugh, you might pop a button and rip your shirt right open."

He crosses his arms, and I can't stop chuckling.

"Don't make him cry, Soph," Mason taunts.

Liam flips him off, then proceeds to flip every single one of us the bird.

"What was that you said earlier about etiquette?" I remind him with a wink.

"I hate you all."

"Mmhmm." Lennon continues to poke the beast.

Before we can add anything else, the lights flicker, giving the five-minute warning. I look around the room and see it's packed full. I'm so happy I'm able to be here, supporting Maddie and watching her in something she's so passionate about. I think about my past and how all of this would've been ripped away and stolen from me if things had ended differently.

"You okay?" Mason whispers in my ear as I try to keep my emotions in check.

"Just grateful." I smile.

The lights lower, the curtains open, and the music begins. The melody starts off slowly and builds to a giant crescendo when the ballet dancers rush forward. Maddie glides across the stage so effortlessly. Though I've been watching her perform since baby ballet, there's something so incredibly mesmerizing about her when she's doing pointe. The stage is hers, she's the queen, a true performer, and all eyes in the room are on her, especially Liam's.

The songs flow together, creating a full show, and though no words are spoken, it's obvious it's a performance about two lost lovers, determined to find the other, and Maddie's the star, the leading lady, fighting all the outside sources to find *the one*.

It's easy to pretend she doesn't have a smart mouth or isn't full of sass when she moves across the stage like it's glass, looking like a porcelain doll with perfect skin. She so effortlessly supports her entire body on one leg as the other extends directly behind her, using the music to draw a reaction from the crowd. Then in a blink, she's soaring through the air, spinning like an ice skater, willing her legs and arms to complete impossible movements. She extends and bends and so eloquently moves and leans her body in unimaginable ways, and I'm in total awe watching her. Talented doesn't even begin to describe Maddie. She's more than that. She's absolutely incredible.

When she finally gets to be with her lover, a dancer dressed in black rips him away. The music spirals into dark, ominous tones, and the finale begins with a dramatic emotional dance where it's obvious the man she loves has died. After all the fighting to be together, death ultimately tore him from her. Tears fill my eyes, and Mason interlocks his fingers with mine, rubbing his thumb across the softness of my skin. It's a simple gesture, and one I appreciate more than he knows. The stage lights turn bright white, and Maddie purposely and dramatically dances to the ground where death takes her too. Finally, the two are able to be together eternally, forever. The emotion behind it all is almost too much for me to handle, but based on the sniffles in the room, I'm not the only one.

I lean toward Mason, wanting to be as close to him as I possibly can. Tears stream down my face as the lover's dance ends. The stage fades to black, and the curtains close. Before the house lights brighten, I wipe my cheeks. I'm actually speechless. It was the most beautiful dance I've ever seen in my life. One of my favorites she's ever done, and while it was tragic, it was so damn deep and beautiful.

I let out a breath when the curtains open, and the dancers take their bows. Maddie is the last to come out. The crowd goes wild over her, and we all know why. She stole the show, no doubt about that, and should be proud as hell for the emotions she was able to draw from hundreds of people.

"That's my sister!" I shout, hoping she hears me over the applause as the room gives her a standing ovation.

When her eyes, full of tears and happiness, meet mine, she blows me a kiss and winks at Liam. Laughter escapes me, and I'm so damn honored to call her my sister that I can barely contain myself. She's a shining star, burning so brightly, and deserves the world. When the curtains close again, we leave the auditorium, and I hope Maddie hurries and changes so she can meet us in the foyer.

When I look at Mason, he's as taken aback as I am. "Wow." It's all he can say.

I glance at Lennon who's as teary-eyed as I am. "Our sister is a badass," she says proudly.

Liam's mouth is hanging wide open, and I lean over and place my finger under his chin to shut it.

"Speechless?" I tease. "Maddie's really gonna like that."

We wait for about ten minutes, and as if she was summoned, she comes from behind us wearing a huge smile on her face. "You liked it?"

I go to her and pull her into my arms. "I loved it, and I love you. You were amazing." She's worked so hard for this and deserves all the praise she's receiving.

She rolls her eyes. "You're just saying that because you have to."

"I don't have to," Mason says, giving her a friendly side hug. "You were incredible, Mads. Like, for real."

Lennon barrels her way through with her baby bump and pulls Maddie into a big hug. I'm still wiping away tears, but I'm smiling the whole time. While Hunter is giving her all the compliments, she studies Liam.

"Well, Hulk?" She smirks, giving his tie a hard tug. "What'd you think?"

I wondered how long that'd take. Apparently only a couple of minutes.

Liam places his hand on her shoulder, and Maddie melts into a puddle. "You were phenomenal." He shakes his head. "I really have no words."

A blush hits her cheeks, and Mason wraps his arm around my body. I lean into him, welcoming his touch as Liam compliments Maddie. She's eating it up, and it makes me happy that everyone now has seen what Lennon and I have seen for years.

"Thank you," I tell Mason, squeezing him.

"For what?"

"For always being there for me." It was like watching that performance made something click deep inside my soul, and I'm still trying to process it all. To find a love so great and then for death to rip it away in the blink of an eye feels a little too close to home, a little like reality.

Fans eventually bombard Maddie, so we give her space. We wait for her to make her way back to us.

"So I get a drink to celebrate tonight?" She perks up although she already knows the answer.

"No, but I did plan on kicking your ass at darts tonight. Gotta knock you down a few pegs," Liam teases, but I notice the way his eyes soften as he speaks. Maybe Maddie finally kicked through his wall with her ballet shoes. I laugh to myself, and Mason notices.

"I don't even want to know what you're thinking."

"You don't," I agree as we walk out to Mason's truck.

Maddie and Liam sit in the back seat, and Maddie continues to talk shit about how she's going to kick everyone's ass at darts and how she deserves a drink because she's worked so hard.

"Oh whatever," I interrupt. "You made it look so freaking easy. Like you were making soup."

"It's because I'm so flexible." She chuckles.

I glance over my shoulder and roll my eyes at her obvious

We pull up to the Coliseum, and Hunter and Lennon are waiting for us at the front. Maddie is on cloud nine, fluttering around because Liam is finally giving her more than five seconds of attention. Mason and I walk behind them, giving them distance.

"Do you see what I see?" He nods toward Liam and Maddie.

A grin fills my face. "He's in trouble now. Give her an inch, and she'll take ten miles."

Mason chuckles. "Yep, although I have a feeling he'll always think she's too young for him."

"Well, if we're talking maturity years here, then they're basically on the same level." I snort.

"Eh, more like he'd be too young for her then. He wouldn't even have his driver's license," Mason mocks, opening the door for me.

We sit at the table, then order drinks and food. After the guys have their beers, we all bombard Maddie. With a performance like that, it's almost impossible not to. Of course, she's so modest about her craft, and she blows it off like it's no big deal. Maddie won't always take the compliments about her dancing, but she's polite and appeases us.

As she continues on about the underlying theme of the dance, Liam listens intently to her every word with bated breath. After we get our food and eat, we decide to go over to the game room area and play darts. We gave Maddie the choice since it's her night.

Mason lazily hangs his arm on my shoulder as we stand off to the side and watch her and Liam battle, but it's not without smack talk from either of them. Lennon walks over to me, and Hunter decides he wants to start in with the trash talking too. The three of them have me nearly bending over with tears from their comebacks, but it doesn't surprise me that Maddie can hold her own. She had lots of practice growing up with Lennon and me as sisters.

Lennon gives me a smile, then yawns as she sits on a barstool.

"How are you doing, Mama?" I lean over and rub her belly.

"Tired, but good. This pregnancy is so much different than the last one," she admits as I impatiently wait to feel a kick or something. She's not due until March, but we find out next month what she's having, which is so damn exciting.

"Is Hunter still dead set on it being a boy?" I ask, glancing over as he smacks Liam on the back.

"Yeah, and he might be right. For his sake, I hope he is, or he's gonna have a house full of women, and he can barely handle two." She snorts.

"And we all know how Dad turned out after us," I admit. "But if you do have a girl, you can always try again for a little boy." I waggle my brows, making my hint more than obvious.

Instantly, she starts shaking her head. "No, I think after this one, I'm done. If I survive being a mom of two toddlers, that is." Hunter walks over and places a quick smack on Lennon's lips and then gives Mason a high five.

"You're all way too competitive for my taste." I point at each of them.

Mason scoffs. "Says the girl who nearly had Liam naked the first time you came to the house."

Lennon giggles, and we all remember the night of strip pool. It seems like a lifetime ago now. The guys walk to the bar for a refill, and Maddie comes over to us with rosy cheeks and a mile-wide smile.

Lennon shakes her head.

"You're way too transparent," I tell her.

"I'm determined to break him down, and I think it's working this time." She falls back into an overly dramatic ballet pose, her body nearly bent in half. I don't know how she's so damn flexible. There are times when I can barely tie my shoe.

"He saw my moves, and now he can't stay away," she says with a bow.

Lennon nearly spits out her water, and it causes me to laugh at both of them.

Soon the guys return, and they go back to playing darts.

"I might make a million dollars soon," Maddie says to all of us.

"How?" I ask, and she gives me an evil grin.

"Selling my virginity. I read an article about a girl who sold hers on eBay. She *literally* auctioned off her V-card," she tells us, and Liam's jaw nearly snaps.

Maddie notices too, which only encourages her further. "Apparently, she used the money to invest in some tech company, and it basically saved her life. She almost went homeless."

"Don't be stupid," Liam tells her, his expression hard as stone.

"Stupid or smart? I could make *a lot* of money," she retorts. "I'm not rolling in the dough here. Or dick. So…" She shrugs.

"It's probably a fake article. You can't believe everything you read on the internet," I remind her.

"What if you get some weirdo or some old guy with shriveled up balls?" Liam's trying to reason with her, and all she's doing is teasing the hell out of him.

"If you're so worried about it, I'll give you the link when I make the listing, and you can place your own bid," she quips, going back to her darts.

Liam grunts.

"What? Worried you'll lose? Not a gambling man?"

When I look at Liam, he's tense as fuck, and I think Maddie might've actually hit a nerve.

As Liam and Maddie go back and forth, Hunter notices how tired Lennon is, and they decide to call it a night. We all exchange hugs, and after Maddie completely destroys Liam and Mason in two more rounds of darts, we leave too. The entire ride to her dorm, she has me laughing to the point where my face hurts, and it feels good. There's no worry or stress, and right now, I feel more like myself than I have in a month.

We pull into the dorm parking lot, and when Maddie gets out of the truck, Liam volunteers to walk her to her door. Mason and I watch as he chats all the way up the sidewalk with wide eyes.

"I'm shocked," he says. "I think she's really getting to him."

I snicker. "She said it was her dance moves."

"It might've been."

The air in the truck is thick as he gazes at me with bright eyes. "Next week, my aunt wants us to have dinner with her."

"What? I thought she would've forgotten by now," I exclaim, and he shakes his head with a smirk.

"Nope, and it's gotten to the point where she texts me twice a day to remind me. She said Tuesday. Will that work for you?"

I catch a glimpse of Liam smiling at Maddie, and I wish I could hear what they're talking about. "Hmm," I say, stalling.

"If you say no, I'm giving her your number so she can text *you* all day," he threatens.

I lick my lips, wishing he'd kiss me, but he won't cross the line. "Yeah. I'll go."

He grabs my hand and kisses my knuckles. "Thank you. She cooks a mean spaghetti and meatballs and doesn't serve small portions, so wear your stretchy pants."

A giggle escapes me. "She better because I can put away a lot of food."

Unspoken words linger between us, but my thoughts are interrupted by Liam climbing into the truck.

"Did you kiss her good night?" Mason quips.

"Shut the hell up and take me home," Liam snaps, and it makes me wonder if Maddie's now playing hard to get. I think she might actually have him where she wants him.

CHAPTER FORTY

MASON

THE WEEKEND COMES and goes and so does Monday. When I drive home from work, my nerves get the best of me because tonight I'm willingly taking Sophie over to my aunt Sylvia's house. She's my dad's sister, has zero filter, and can be obnoxious at times, but I love her, and she typically means well. Regardless, she's going to spill all my business on her expensive floor, and Sophie will know everything about me by the time we leave, but I want that. I want her to know everything about me, and Aunt Sylvia doesn't forget and won't leave any stone unturned. She has the memory of an elephant, hence her bothering me about this damn dinner for the past few months. The unpredictability of it all is what makes me the most nervous.

When I walk inside the house, Sophie's sitting on the couch wearing black jeans, boots, and a nice sweater. Though it's only early October and the temperature hasn't dropped significantly since summer, she's been dressing in more fall outfits, which I love on her. As soon as she sees me, she stands with a grin. "I'm ready."

"You look great," I admire. I empty my pockets, placing my keys and phone on the coffee table. "I'm gonna change into some jeans, and then we can go."

She gives me a nod and sits back down. I climb the stairs two at a time and quickly change.

When I come back downstairs, I shoot Sophie a smile and notice her mood's dramatically changed. "Everything okay?"

She shrugs and hands me my phone. I look down and see a text message from Serena. I open it and read what she sent. Considering I have preview set up, I know Sophie saw it.

SERENA

How are you and your girlfriend?

Without responding, I lock my phone and shove it into my pocket. That's one text message I won't be replying to, not now and not ever. While Serena means well, my relationship with Sophie needs to stay private. It's something she and I share while we try to figure everything out. I can tell the text bothers Sophie, which concerns me since I've already explained our friendship several times.

"You have nothing to worry about," I remind her as she stands and releases a sharp breath.

"I know." She forces a smile, and all I want to do is change the subject, but luckily, Liam does it for me. He bursts through the door sweaty as hell from working out.

"Where're you two going?" he asks, then takes off his shirt and wipes his forehead with it.

"Dinner with Aunt Sylvia."

He snorts and lifts his eyebrows at Sophie. "Have fun. She's nuts."

"Shut the hell up," I say.

"Hey, the fruit doesn't fall too far from the family tree." He chuckles as he jumps up the stairs.

"Don't get me started!" I warn, then glance at Sophie. "Come on."

She lets a real smile escape, which gives me hope that everything is going to be fine.

We drive across town, and Sophie tells me about her rehearsal today, and I'm so damn thrilled things are finally going better for her. It's been a few weeks since she returned, and at first, it was rough, but she's seemed to have worked through a lot of her emotional issues.

Though my aunt lives nearly thirty minutes away, it feels like I only spent five minutes with Sophie since we chatted the whole time. That's one thing I love about her—time seems to fly by when she's near. So many times I wanted to interlock my fingers with hers, but ever since she took my hand at the recital, I've been trying not to push my luck. We seem to finally be heading in the right direction, and I don't want to jinx it. Each time we've made progress in the past, something happens, and she pushes me away. I want to avoid that this time.

We pull into the gated community where my aunt lives and park in her driveway. Sophie's eyes go wide. "This house is gigantic."

"Yeah, it is. She's my father's sister, remember? They're all about appearances." Sophie sucks in a deep breath, and I shoot her a wink. "She's harmless, though."

We get out of the truck, and I lead her up the sidewalk with my hand on her back. I look at the perfectly trimmed bushes, and before we make it to the door, it's swinging open. Aunt Sylvia greets us with a charming smile, not a hair out of place as she waves her hand for us to come inside.

"I've been expecting you two lovebirds," she singsongs, pulling me and then Sophie into a hug. Sophie looks around in awe at the high vaulted ceilings, chandeliers, and ridiculously expensive sculptures in the foyer. The marble floors are so shiny, I can see my reflection in them. Numerous political parties have been held here over the years, and I'm sure many more will be too. We enter the kitchen, and Sylvia has cooked enough food for a dozen people.

"Expecting a small army?" I ask, walking over to the counter where the gigantic meatballs, noodles, sauce, and homemade garlic bread are laid out.

"Nope, just us," she says. She divorced her husband years ago, and my cousin has long since moved out. Sophie and I help her carry the dishes into the formal dining room where the table is set up all fancy. When I notice Sophie's fidgeting with the hem of her sweater, I hope her nerves aren't getting the best of her. As we walk back to the kitchen, I place my hand on the small of her back, hoping she relaxes a tad.

Aunt Sylvia grabs an expensive bottle of wine, and I grab the glasses. After we take our seats, she fills our plates with a mountain of food. I glance at Sophie and grin at her expression. I warned her and wasn't kidding about the portions and stretchy pants.

As soon as she tastes one of the meatballs, she hums. "Oh my God. I think that's the best meatball I've ever tasted in my life. Ever."

Sylvia grins at me. "She's a keeper, Mason."

"Seriously," Sophie continues, then eats another meatball. I can't blame her, though. They are good. She could open a restaurant and make a killing, but being a county judge is her passion, and she'd never give it up. Just like my father, she's caught up in the attention. But unlike my father, she still has her moral compass.

"How's Crystal?" I ask about my cousin. Ignoring the pressure of following in her mom's footsteps, she became a nurse and was one of the main reasons I found the courage to choose my own path too. I knew my dad would get over it. Eventually.

"Doing great. She works a lot. I invited her to join us tonight, but she's on swing shift so wasn't able to. You'll have to come over again and meet my daughter," she tells Sophie, who agrees with a mouthful.

"Saw your dad last week," Aunt Sylvia adds, and I instantly tense. I was hoping she wouldn't bring him up, but that was wishful thinking. "Is he still married to that *child*? The secretary?" she asks suspiciously.

I stuff my face and give her a nod, but she continues chatting.

"Hmm," she says, but now my curiosity is piqued.

"Why?" I ask.

She shrugs. "No reason."

"This wine is great," Sophie says, taking a big sip, thankfully moving the topic away from my dad. I chuckle because the last time she drank wine was with Liam and got trashed, which by morning I found adorable because of how embarrassed she was.

"Oh, have more." Aunt Sylvia nearly refills Sophie's glass to the brim.

"She's a lightweight," I tell Sylvia, who waves me off.

"We all are sometimes. Plus, she's not driving." She shoots Sophie a wink, who then giggles.

After we've eaten our weight in spaghetti and meatballs, we help her clean up. I'm so full that I'm miserable, and I think Sophie is too, so we both refuse dessert. Aunt Sylvia tells us to grab our wine and follow her. By the smirk on her face, she's more than determined to embarrass the piss out of me tonight. She leads Sophie and me into her study, where she has a shelf full of photo albums. She begins pulling them down one by one and places them on her desk.

"Look at how adorable Mason was." Aunt Sylvia flips through photos of Crystal and me in diapers.

"Those eyelashes," Sophie says, glancing over with a smile. "Oh my gosh, you were the cutest baby."

I scoff. "I'm still cute."

Blush hits her cheeks as Aunt Sylvia goes on and on about the stories Crystal and I used to make up. "They would write plays and perform them in the living room. And the ballet moves Mason had," she continues.

"Ballet?" Sophie tilts her head. "I'll have to tell Maddie."

I shake my head. "Oh hell no."

Aunt Sylvia giggles. "He wanted to be an ice skater too."

"This is so embarrassing," I admit. I forgot about all of that. We shuffle through the pictures and come across some of me with my parents. I stare at it for a little while, and Sophie notices.

"Your mom is beautiful," she says.

"Have you met her yet?" Aunt Sylvia asks.

Sophie shakes her head. "Not yet."

"Soon," I say.

"Well, now I feel special. Have you met his father, Michael?"

"Once or twice," Sophie admits but doesn't expand on it or sound thrilled.

"He means well, but he's often stubborn like Mason." Aunt Sylvia pats my leg.

Sophie chuckles, glancing at me with hooded eyes. The signals she's throwing my way are not going unnoticed. So many stolen glances and unspoken words are exchanged as we continue to flip through the pages. After we've gone through every album and Aunt Sylvia has embarrassed me beyond means, we decide to call it a night.

Before we leave, she puts the leftover food in to-go containers and makes us promise to come back. Thankfully, Sophie agrees. As Aunt Sylvia walks us to my truck, she thanks us for spending the evening with her.

"So when's the wedding?" she asks with a wink. "You know, I can marry you two right here and now. We could deal with the paperwork another day." She waves it off as if she's talking about the weather.

Sophie tenses.

"Wait, are you two not together?" Aunt Sylvia's eyes ping-pong between us. "I know you said you're roommates, but…I'm not blind." She snickers, and it grows awkward.

"It's a technicality right now," I explain and silence her with a hug and thanks for dinner. Sophie repeats my words as Aunt Sylvia hugs her next. The two of us climb in and wave as I back the truck out.

"What?" I ask with a laugh after watching Sophie grin the past fifteen minutes.

"Nothing," she singsongs.

"Oh, you've got to tell me now."

She pretends to zip her lips, but a smirk takes over and is

replaced with out of control laughter. "You wanted to be a ballerina."

"I was five!" I exclaim.

"Maddie is gonna lose her shit."

"You better not tell her. Soph," I playfully warn.

She shrugs. "We'll see."

We pull into the driveway, and I'm thrilled to see Sophie in high spirits. The past few times we've gone out have given me hope that things will eventually go back to how they used to be.

"Thanks for taking me with you," she says, carrying our food as we walk toward the house.

"I wouldn't have gone without you," I admit, and time freezes for a moment. The only thing that pulls us away is the sound of laughter on the other side of the door.

"Is that…"

"Maddie."

Both confused, we walk inside and find her and Liam playing cards on the couch. By the sounds of it, she's kicking his ass.

"What the hell?" I ask. "What're you doing here?"

Maddie glares at me, then smiles at Sophie. "You brought me dinner?"

Sophie narrows her eyes. "What *are* you doing here?"

Standing, Maddie comes over and grabs the containers from Sophie's hands, then goes to the kitchen and returns with a fork, already eating from the Tupperware. Manners? I'm not sure she has any. "This is delicious!" she says loudly.

"You should share that," Liam whines. "Aunt Sylvia may be a weirdo, but she's a damn good cook." He holds out his hand, waiting for Maddie to share. Instead, she pulls it away from him.

"I was bored sitting in my dorm, so I came over to visit, but then realized you two lovebirds weren't home, so Liam let me in, and we've been hanging out while I waited for Soph."

I arch a brow at Liam as Sophie takes the other container into the kitchen.

He shrugs helplessly. "I couldn't tell her to go away. Her ride had already driven off."

"Mmhmm." I doubt he's been hating it either.

"It's the truth," he snaps when Sophie walks back in, and she's smirking at the way Liam's all flustered over Maddie. I grab a beer from the fridge, and Liam follows.

Liam crosses his arms with a glare. "I don't know why everyone has something to say about me being nice to her. Better than being a dick and treating her the way you used to treat Sophie."

I glare at him. "Yeah, well. I actually *liked* Sophie. What's your excuse?" Popping a brow, I dare him to admit he likes her, but he shakes his head and heads back into the living room. When I walk behind him, I notice Maddie purposely puts her legs up on his lap after he sits down next to her.

"This is everything," she says with her mouth full. Yep, she's officially disgusting.

Sophie sits in the recliner. "So. How's the millionaire quest going?"

Maddie shrugs. "Still working on the listing. I ordered a new bikini for some new photos. Then I'll work on my sales pitch, which they probably won't read once they click through my photos."

I snicker at her humility. "Want me to take the pictures for you? I do take them for my job and all." Granted, they're for crime scenes, but still.

"Don't encourage her," Sophie scolds, but she knows Maddie's stunt is all an act.

I look at Liam, who tenses as Maddie talks about selling her virginity nonchalantly like it's an antique piece of furniture she can sell for top dollar.

"Well, you have to go on dates if you want to find someone."

Maddie snorts and straightens, putting her feet underneath her. "I have! I've gone on a handful of them, and they've all ended badly the moment I don't let them hit a home run. It's all fun and games until I tell them no. Plus, most of them wouldn't know how to treat a woman right even if it was spelled out for them. I'm not trying to get taken advantage of by some idiot who can't spell

Mississippi. This way, I can be in charge of my own body, and it will strictly be a cash transaction. No feelings, no dates, no disappointments."

Liam tenses and I wonder if it's because Maddie's never discussed dating anyone.

Maddie continues, "I nearly castrated one guy who didn't understand that no meant no. I'm not kidding. I've never pulled a knife off a counter so quickly. I wasn't afraid to use it either." She holds her hand up like she's about to shank someone.

Sophie looks horrified.

"Oh, the stories I could tell," Maddie goes on between taking bites . "One douchebag thought he could get me drunk, but I didn't take a sip of anything he offered because I had a feeling he was trying to drug me, which he *was*."

"You're not dating the right kind of guys," Liam interjects. I can tell he's pissed, but hell, so am I.

Maddie turns toward him with an eyebrow popped and a fork in her mouth. "So what kind of guys should I be dating? Strong bounty hunter bad-boy types?" She puckers her lips, daring him to argue.

Maddie's a firecracker and gives zero fucks about being blunt. She'll cross boundaries anytime she feels like it, which is why shit's always interesting when she's around.

He shakes his head, then stands. "I'm done with this conversation. I'm going to bed. Night."

With a pout, Maddie tells him good night. Once he's out of sight, she looks at Sophie. "Think I pushed him too far?"

I chuckle. "I think you did."

"Do you want a ride home?" Sophie asks, yawning.

"No, I was thinking I'd stay. You're a bed hog, so I'll sleep out here. You have an extra pillow and blanket?" She teases, but she's not joking when she stretches her long legs out until her feet touch me. I look down at them and am terrified. They're what nightmares are made from.

"What? You've never seen a ballerina's feet before?" Maddie giggles, wiggling her toes and trying to touch me with them.

"Man, these springs might kill my back. Think I could share Liam's bed with him?"

Sophie stands, shaking her head. "Oh my God. Bad idea," she tells her before going to her room to grab an extra pillow and blankets.

"You're pushy as hell," I scold Maddie.

She shrugs. "Gotta be, especially when he treats me like I'm his little sister."

"You kinda are."

"I am *not*. You all treat me like I'm a child when I'm a grown ass woman. Just because you're a few years older than I am doesn't mean anything. Age is just a number, and neither of you guys knows what I've been through."

I can tell she's getting upset, and I give her a soft smile. "We're just in a different place in our lives than you, Mads. He's five years older and has a tough and demanding career. He's been through a lot too, and relationships aren't easy for him. You're still in college. Your age doesn't discredit anything, but you have to realize where Liam is in his life right now. I mean, what do you expect, to get married before your twenty-first birthday?"

Sophie returns and notices Maddie's expression, then hands her everything.

"I don't expect wedding bells. Just a chance and not to be treated like a kid. To be looked at like the woman I am."

"You'll always be my little sister. You've still got a lot to learn about relationships," Sophie says, sitting on the couch next to her.

"I know," she says, then looks at me. "Sorry. I'm just sexually frustrated."

I burst out into laughter. "Aren't we all?"

Sophie tenses, and I take it as my opportunity to leave them to chat. As I'm climbing the stairs, she talks to Maddie and I freeze.

"You don't need to rush into anything. Seriously, one of the biggest mistakes I made in my life was rushing into a relationship. Let everything happen organically, and if it's meant to be, it will happen. I promise you," Sophie says so sweetly and patiently.

"You'll find a nice guy, someone who treats you right, and when you meet him, you'll know he's the one without a doubt."

It goes quiet for a second, then Maddie speaks up. "I knew the moment I met Liam."

And not even I can argue with that because when you know, you know.

Just as I know Sophie's the one for me.

CHAPTER FORTY-ONE

THE TEMPERATURES HAVE FINALLY STARTED to drop now that the middle of October is upon us. I've been waiting for this for months, though I've been wearing sweaters and boots for weeks. Fall is my favorite season, and I count down to it every year.

This morning, I'm meeting Lennon at the doctor's office so we can find out if I'm getting another niece or a nephew. As I make a cup of coffee to go, Mason enters the kitchen.

"You're up early," he says, running his fingers through his messy hair.

I take a sip of coffee and look him up and down, taking in all his muscles and the way his pants hang on his hips. Would it be inappropriate to show my therapist a picture of him so she can see what I have to look at every day? Sometimes, I think I'm ready to take our relationship to the next step, but then I second-guess everything and don't.

Mason's been so damn patient, letting me take the lead and never pushing me. Hell, even I'm getting blue balls at this point. But I'm making amazing progress in therapy, and the nightmares and anxiety have slowly drifted away. I still get anxious at times, but I'm way better at managing it than before.

"Lennon's appointment is at eight, and it's across town, so I have to get through early morning traffic," I remind him.

He pours himself a cup and leans against the counter. "Oh yeah. I forgot. Any bets as to what you think she's having?"

"Hmm." I pucker my lips and tap my finger on the outside. "I think it's a boy and so does Hunter. Lennon doesn't have a preference. Maddie thinks it's a girl. Well, she's convinced it's a girl."

Mason grins, and I love the way his cheeks have a little dip in them. Sometimes, he catches me staring at them but doesn't call me out on it. "Maybe it's twins."

"Nah, she'd know that by now, but hell, stranger things have happened." I check the time and realize I need to finish getting ready and get going. "Love the view, but I gotta go," I say, admiring him one last time.

"You can look anytime you want." He shoots me a wink.

"Would it kill you to wear a shirt once in a while?" I tease, knowing damn well I don't mind.

"Would it kill you *not* to wear a shirt once in a while? Then we can be twinsies." He waggles his brows, and I snort and roll my eyes at his pathetic joke.

"Ha-ha. Bye." I walk away before I do something stupid like reach out and touch him.

While driving to meet Lennon, a smile touches my lips. It's finally Friday, and I've had a good week so far. Actually, the past few haven't been bad. I write in my anxiety journal a little less each week, and playing my violin feels normal again. I've also thought about calling my old students to take up tutoring again. Right now, I'm in a good place mentally. The only thing I need to work through is Mason's and my relationship, but I'm taking my own advice and allowing it to happen organically. Mason's not some fling to me. He's more than that. He always has been, and I knew the moment I met him that he wasn't just *some guy*.

When I pull into the parking lot, I park next to Lennon's car. I take a huge gulp of coffee, then grab my clutch and head out. As soon as I enter the waiting room, I find Hunter, Lennon, and Maddie all cracking up as Allie babbles.

"Allie Cat," I say, holding my hands out, and Lennon happily hands her over.

"I need coffee." She groans. During her last pregnancy, she refused to drink a drop, and she's worse than me when it comes to coffee time, so she's still struggling.

Allie's in a good mood. "You're getting so big. Did you miss your auntie Sophie?" She's almost ten months old and could start walking any time now, and then she'll be into everything.

I sit on the other side of Maddie and bounce Allie on my lap. She giggles, and it's the cutest thing. I can't believe how much she looks like Lennon, but I see features of Brandon too.

"So any final guesses before we go in the back?" I ask Lennon.

"Nope!" She stays firm with her answer. "I'll be happy either way."

"It's a boy," Hunter says matter-of-factly. As if it'll be true if he keeps saying it.

"Girl, one hundred percent." Maddie sticks her tongue out at him. I think she chose the opposite sex so she could fuck with Hunter. She loves getting under his skin and teasing him, but I don't think he minds it. He always talks about how we're the sisters he never had.

A woman calls Lennon's name, and we all follow through the hallway into the ultrasound room. It feels so surreal being here again while holding Allie. The last time we were here was when we found out Allie was a girl, and we were all so excited. So much has changed in so little time for all of us. It almost makes my head spin thinking about it.

The ultrasound tech introduces herself as Cassie and explains everything beforehand although Lennon has an idea of what to expect. Once her shirt is lifted and her jeans are lowered, Cassie places the wand on Lennon's belly. Lennon's watching the screen while Hunter sits close, holding her hand, not letting her go. The love they share for each other can be felt by every person in the room.

"The doctor wants me to do a series of measurements, and then I can check the gender if you want to know…" Cassie grins, tapping buttons on her machine.

"We do!" Maddie answers for everyone, and I chuckle.

"He or she is definitely active today. You must've drunk something sweet," Cassie says.

"I had OJ this morning," Lennon admits. "And I haven't peed yet, so don't push that too hard on my bladder," she teases, but I remember with Allie she did the same.

Cassie continues taking measurements and taking pictures of the brain and heart before she asks, "Ready, Mom and Dad?"

"Yep!" Lennon smiles. "Mostly because I want to put this argument between them to rest." She glares at Hunter and Maddie.

"Ahh, plain as day…" Cassie zooms in and snaps a photo.

"It's a boy?" Hunter stands, waiting on edge for confirmation.

"Oh, you want to know right now?" She teases, then nods as she types something over the screen: *It's a Boy!*

I bounce Allie on my knee. "Sweet girl, you're gonna have a baby brother! How exciting for you!" She has no clue what I'm saying, but I like to pretend she does.

Hunter bends down and cups Lennon's face before kissing her. My emotions bubble over at how happy they are. After their adorable moment, Hunter turns and holds out his hand. "You owe me fifty bucks, Mads!"

"Wait, you bet for real?" I ask, laughing at Maddie's annoyed expression.

Once Cassie finishes getting everything she needs for the doctor, she prints off half a dozen ultrasound photos. After Lennon cleans off her belly and readjusts her clothes, Hunter helps her up and whispers sweet nothings that make her blush. Then Maddie takes Lennon's phone and forces all three of them to pose with the printout. Cassie tells us to get together so she can snap a photo for us although we're all crammed into the little room.

Before we make it outside, Lennon's on FaceTime with our

parents, letting them know the exciting news. She's crying and keeps saying she doesn't know why she's crying, but I do. Happiness like hers is hard to keep in. Not to mention, her hormones are going haywire.

As we're walking through the lobby, I hand Allie over to Hunter. As he carries her outside, he tells her she's going to be the best sister in the world, and it's so cute the way he talks to her. As we walk to our cars, Lennon stops in the middle of the parking lot. "I forgot to tell you the other good news! Pregnancy brain!"

"More good news?" Maddie asks.

"You're getting a puppy?" I ask.

"Nope." Lennon grins.

"You bought a house?" Maddie bounces on her feet. "With a spare room so I can move in?"

"Oh hell no," Hunter blurts.

"Language!" Lennon gives him the evil eye. "We don't need our kid's first words being that."

"I give up," I finally say.

"Same," Maddie agrees.

"We chose our wedding date," Lennon exclaims.

I pull her into a hug. "Oh my gosh, that's so exciting. When is it?"

"May seventh. It gives me a little time after the baby's born to get back in shape, and then we can focus on finding a house after all the wedding planning is done."

"Aww…I think it's perfect." I give her a hug, and then her tears start again. "You're a hormonal mess."

We laugh. "I know. God. I cried over a diaper commercial yesterday. It was the stupidest thing. The baby was happy and walking, and I burst into tears."

I snort.

"Have I mentioned how I can't wait to start practicing making babies?" Maddie blurts, looking at her nails with a smirk.

Lennon and I both glare at her.

"Practicing making babies *actually* makes babies." Lennon points down at her tummy. "Don't forget that."

Hunter agrees as we make it to their car, and he puts Allie in her car seat and buckles her up. "So much truth to that."

"Well, don't forget that after this one is born," I tease. "Then again, I want more nieces or nephews so…"

"Can I have this baby first before you're pushing for a basketball team?" Lennon groans.

"I guess. But just know, they'll be waiting a while before they get cousins, so they need siblings to play with for now." I flash her a shit-eating smirk because she knows I'm right.

"Well, I don't know…" Hunter begins. "According to Maddie, she's ready to have Liam's offspring yesterday."

Lennon rolls her eyes and nudges him. "We aren't encouraging that."

Snickering, I pull Lennon into another hug and tell her how much I love her. Maddie wraps her arms around the both of us and we stand together in an emotional mess.

"I love you two so much," I murmur. "I don't take a day of being here with you guys for granted."

Lennon's bottom lip trembles. "Stop, or I'll be crying all damn day."

Hunter shakes his head with a smile.

I wipe my face. "Okay. Okay, I'm going now. Maddie, you need a ride?"

"Nah. I'm gonna bother Lennon and Hunter for a few more hours."

Lennon looks at me. "She volunteered to babysit, so Hunter and I can have brunch without food being thrown on the floor."

"Ahh, alright then. Love you. I'll see you both sooner rather than later, okay?"

We say our goodbyes, then I go to my car and climb inside. I suck in a deep breath, feeling elated for Lennon and Hunter, considering they wanted this so badly. After not knowing if Hunter could have children, to finding out he could, and then not immediately getting pregnant, it's been an emotional ride for them. In the end, it worked out the way it was supposed to.

I wipe away my happy tears, then drive to work. I show up to rehearsal a little late and play my ass off since our fall concert is set for the end of the month.

At first, I thought I was too broken and had lost my passion for playing again, but once I got over my mental block, I was able to find myself in the music again. Instead of dreading being around my colleagues, I've started looking forward to it. No one has asked me any questions about what happened, and I'm grateful most musicians are introverts and mind their own business. There's zero drama, which is what I need. I've had enough to last me a lifetime.

We play through our setlist several times, then we're released an hour early. Most of us could play the songs in our sleep anyway. Instead of going back to the house right away, I go to the grocery store and pick up some steaks and potatoes for dinner tonight. Being the nice roommate I am, I grab some for Liam too.

I'm excited to tell Mason and Liam the news about the wedding and the gender of the baby. Though, I'm sure by now Hunter's already texted and told them, and if not him, then Maddie definitely spilled the beans to Liam. She'll use any conversation starter to talk to him.

As I pull into the driveway, I see Serena's car parked in my spot. A lump forms in my throat, and I try to swallow it down as I grab the grocery bags and my violin. I remind myself that they're just friends, Mason doesn't want her, and I have nothing to worry about. But when I walk into the living room, she's laughing and leaning her head on Mason's shoulder.

Why is she so close to him?

Why does he let her touch him like that?

Am I being unreasonable for not wanting another woman all over him?

"Hey, Sophie," she says when she notices me.

With flared nostrils, I narrow my eyes at the two of them, then walk to the kitchen. Liam instigates the situation by telling Mason he's in trouble now. After I put the food in the fridge, I grab my violin and walk past the three of them.

"Well, hello to you too," she mutters under her breath.

I stop and turn on my heels. "What're you doing here? Why are you *always* hanging on Mason?"

"What's your problem?" she asks.

Mason shifts away, creating the much-needed space between them, but before he can intervene, I continue my rant.

"What's my problem?" I repeat her words with disdain. "Call me crazy, but I don't particularly like other women hanging all over my boyfriend. He's mine, which I think you know at this point. So back the fuck off." I glare, daring her to push me.

Her mouth opens and closes, staying silent.

"Soph…" Mason says my name soft and calmly, but I'm not calm. He stands, but I point my finger at him.

"Don't." I turn on my heels and walk to my room.

I hear Liam in the living room hollering and clapping. "Oooh, girl fight. Fifty bucks on Sophie. Sorry, Serena." He snickers, which only enrages my emotions.

If he doesn't shut the hell up, I might kick his ass after I kick hers. My heart's racing, ready to burst out of my chest. I take in a few deep breaths through my nose and release them through my mouth. I repeat this a few more times, and once I've calmed down, I walk out of my room where I find Liam and Serena. Mason's nowhere to be found.

"What're you still doing here?" I look at Serena. I'm not afraid of her or her attitude. She crossed a line, and I'm more than pissed at this point. I've taken it over and over and am tired of it. From the text message she sent Mason weeks ago, she knows damn well Mason and I are in a relationship.

"Seriously?" She snarls like I've lost my mind, and maybe I have. Seeing her that close and touching him was my last straw, and I've cracked.

"I'm dead serious."

"GIRL FIGHT!" Liam stands, starting shit again. "Rip off each other's clothes!"

"Shut up," we say in unison.

Mason enters with a bottle of water, and Serena stands. He stops in his tracks as if he's glued to the floor.

Serena turns to Mason. "I guess I'm no longer welcome here." Then she faces me, her eyes narrowed. "Just know, Sophie. I was here *first*." She grabs her Louis Vuitton off the coffee table.

"Bye." I wave my fingers and stand my ground as she storms past me and slams the door behind her.

I glare at Liam, pointing my finger at him. "You're a dick."

"And you, my friend, were a total baddie. Proud of you." He smirks and holds out his hand for a high five, but I leave him hanging. He between Mason and me, noticing the awkward tension, then says he's going to get a drink. We both watch as he grabs his keys and leaves. I should feel guilty for how I reacted, but I don't.

Mason clears his throat. The air's so thick, I can't breathe.

"You hungry?" he asks, effectively changing the subject, and my head almost spins.

I swallow hard when I look into his eyes. He should be mad for the way I screamed at his friend, and I'm pissed he allowed her that close to him. But arguing with him won't change anything, and I'm so tired of this are-we or aren't-we situation. So I don't push it.

"Starving. It's why I bought the steaks."

"I saw the potatoes. Let me cook for you." Mason heads back to the kitchen.

After I follow, I watch as he pulls two wine glasses from the cabinet, then fills them. I take it willingly, but I nearly break my jaw as I clench my teeth, thinking about Mason and Serena together.

As I take a seat at the table, I accidentally release a frustrated groan, and Mason looks at me with a small smile before he throws our steaks in a skillet and our potatoes in the oven. Luckily, he doesn't push the matter either. I'm mesmerized as he works around the kitchen, preparing the food. It seems like he magically cooked everything because soon he's placing our steaks on a plate and putting butter and cheese in our baked potatoes. We've exchanged no words, just stolen glances.

Silence fills the room, and I don't know what to say, but the wine has helped calm me down for now. My steak is cooked exactly the way I like it, and it nearly melts in my mouth. When I look up at Mason, he's studying me with a cheeky grin.

I swallow down my food. "What?"

He shrugs and continues to cut into his steak. "Nothing."

"Thank you for cooking. This is really good," I say, then sipping my wine.

"No problem." He winks, and I can't help but wonder why he's so giddy.

After our plates are cleared, he picks them up and rinses them in the sink. I finish my wine, making sure to get each drop and so does Mason. We walk into the living room, and he still has that goofy smile plastered on his face.

I grow more agitated, placing my hands on my hips and glaring when he faces me. "Do I have pepper in my teeth or something?"

Mason takes four steps forward, removing all the space between us. My breath hitches as our eyes meet, and I immediately feel as if I'm falling. His hands land on my hips, and he pulls me to his chest. "You called me your *boyfriend*."

"*That's* what you're focused on?" I half-chuckle. "I was two seconds away from taking her out."

"I wasn't worried." Mason arches a brow as if he's waiting for me to confirm those words came from my mouth.

"Well, are you expecting me to deny it or something?" I ask with an eyebrow popped.

He smirks. "Well, we've been in limbo so—"

Before he can finish his thought, I wrap my arms around his neck and pull his mouth to mine, tasting the wine on his lips, wanting to devour him whole. I'm breathless as his hands trail up my back, and I can't get close enough to him as our tongues dance together. When I push away, I'm lightheaded and nearly stumble as if he stole my breath. I'm literally weak in the knees, and he holds me close to his strong body.

"Soph," he whispers, then swallows hard. Before he can say anything else, I place my fingers over his mouth. I don't want the moment ruined. I don't want broken promises or expectations. I just want him.

It's so fucking hard to pull away from him, but somehow I do and immediately feel the loss.

Mason places his palm on my cheek, and I lean into it, my eyes fluttering closed.

"I'm gonna walk away and go to bed before I do something I'll regret." He inhales a sharp breath as if holding back is physically hard. "Thanks for eating dinner with me." Then he kisses my cheek and drops his hands. "Good night, my sweet Sophie."

"Good night, Mason," I whisper, my chest pounding so hard I'm sure he felt it.

He climbs the stairs, then disappears. I worry I've let Mason walk away forever by not stopping him.

But the truth is my heart longs for him so damn much, and he deserves to know.

CHAPTER FORTY-TWO

MASON

I HADN'T EXPECTED tonight to turn out the way it did.

I especially didn't expect Sophie to go off on Serena, and I was almost too stunned to do anything about it. Knowing how Sophie felt about her, I should've realized that we were too close, but I honestly didn't think about it because we're always this way. Before Sophie, Serena was the only woman in my life, and though I think of Serena as a sister, I should've been more considerate of Sophie's feelings and moved away from her the moment the lines were crossed.

As I think about it in bed, I'm not sure how I'm going to fix this feud between the woman I'm in love with and the woman who's been there for me through all my shit. I'd rather they get along, but if Liam is right and Serena is hoping for a romantic relationship with me, then there's definitely no way our friendship can continue. I'd be upset about it, though, because she's been a great friend.

Tossing and turning, unable to get comfortable and thinking about Sophie's soft lips against mine, I groan. She kissed me. *She* made the first move, something I've been patiently waiting for, but I didn't want to push for anything more. It's a step forward and hearing her call me her boyfriend is enough for me. It means she's as protective of me as I am of her.

Just when I'm able to calm my pounding heart, feet pad in the hallway, and then a second later, my door swings open.

Sophie.

The light from the hallway filters behind her as a smirk marks her face. She's only wearing a long shirt that leaves nothing to my imagination. *My* T-shirt. Pulling the covers back, I swing my legs off the bed and stand, studying her gorgeous silhouette. She shuts the door, then stalks toward me.

"What're you doing? Are you okay?"

"I'm perfect," she says in that sweet, seductive tone of hers that always gets me hard. "Are you okay?" The streetlights shine through my blinds, but it only brightens the room enough for me to focus on her eyes and lips.

"Uh yeah," I say, chuckling and wrapping a strand of her hair around her ear. "Especially when my stunning *girlfriend* sneaks into my room without pants."

Or hell, without a bra too.

Silently, Sophie pushes against my bare chest, and I stumble backward onto the bed. I catch myself on my elbows, and before I can say another word, she's on top of me, straddling my lap.

Grinding herself against me, I wrap my hands around her waist, then slide them down to her luscious ass.

"Baby, what're you—"

"I want you." She leans forward, whispering against my lips. "You left me a little hot and bothered down there, and I'm ready."

"Sophie," I growl, arching my hips to meet hers. "Fuck, are you sure?"

"You're the only thing I'm sure about these days, and I don't want to wait any longer. I love you, Mason."

If that doesn't sound like fucking heaven coming from her, nothing does.

"I love you so much, Soph. You have no idea." I palm her cheeks, bringing our foreheads together as she rocks against me. "Jesus, you're driving me insane already."

"Do you have any condoms?" She searches my face, her voice softer as if she's embarrassed to ask. I haven't had a need for condoms, considering she's the last person I had sex with years ago. However, the moment Sophie and I became more than friends, I made sure to buy some for when the time came.

"Yeah, I bought a twenty-four pack," I tell her honestly, smirking.

"Oh my God." She laughs. "A little presumptuous, don't you think?"

I shrug with a cocky grin. "Well, buying in bulk gives you a better cost per unit. I was being price savvy."

"Riiiiight." She chuckles, wrapping her hands around my neck. "*Savvy.*"

I squeeze her ass cheeks as our bodies move together, and my cock is wide-fucking-awake. Her little whimpers and moans are enough to get me off in seconds. However, I'm not about to let that happen. Not after all this time.

Swinging her body to the bed until she's under me, I tower over her and slant my mouth over hers. I slide my tongue between her soft lips as I settle between her thighs. Sophie wraps her legs around my waist, and the pressure between us is enough to make me combust.

"Soph…" I murmur, desperate to take my time with her and not waste a second of this. "I want to taste you, baby."

I worship Sophie's body, pulling up her shirt and feathering kisses down her stomach. Her fingers in my hair, her soft moans echoing in the air, the way she arches her back—I'm a fucking goner. My jaw moves across the band of her panties before my fingers pull them all the way down, and I toss them. The moment I smell her sweet arousal, I nearly lose all control.

"Jesus Christ, woman," I growl, flicking my tongue against her clit. I tease her swollen bud, then slide my finger down her slit until I'm inside her. Twisting my wrist, I go deeper and suck hard.

"Holy shit," she mutters, jerking her hips.

Using my free hand, I push her thigh higher, needing more

access. Then I slide a second finger inside and feast while bringing her closer to the edge.

"Mason…oh my God, please," she begs, and when I look up, she's fisting the sheets with her eyes rolled back. She's so goddamn close.

"You wanna come on my face, sweetheart?" I muse, then blow cool air against her skin. "You taste fucking delicious."

"Yes, yes…" She nods, opening her eyes to watch me.

Leaning up slightly, I spread her legs wider and lick up and down her slit, feeling her shake against me. Then I wrap my lips around her clit and slide two fingers back inside her. I devour her like I've fantasized, and when her body quivers, I know she's about to explode.

Pulling my hand back just enough to add a third finger, Sophie screams loud enough to rattle the walls, and I smirk against her pussy, knowing that if Liam was home, he would've heard her. I wouldn't feel bad, considering the years I've had to listen to his panty parade next door.

"Goddamn," I whisper, and seconds later, she's unraveling, squeezing my fingers with her cunt. I lick her clean before moving back up her body. "You have any idea how fucking hot that was?"

"I can feel how much." She grins, and I push my cock against her.

"Wanna see how amazing you taste?"

When she nods, my smirk deepens before I slide my tongue between her lips and kiss her deeply. Our bodies burn for each other, hot and ready.

"Do I get a turn now?" she asks when we break apart, and I settle my body between her legs.

"I don't want to come in your mouth, baby, and if your mouth is anywhere near my dick, I won't be able to stop myself." Her thighs tighten around my waist, pushing us closer together. My cock aches to be inside her, but the moment I feel her soft, smooth pussy, I'm going to lose all control.

Sophie chuckles and blushes, and I love how comfortable we are with each other. Being with someone has never felt this way for me, has never *meant* this much to me, and now that Sophie's mine, I'm never letting her go.

Leaning up on my elbows, I reach over to my nightstand and pull out the large box of condoms. She giggles at the size of the box. "Should we see how fast we can go through it?"

"If you just bought it, why was the box already opened?" she inquires, raising an eyebrow.

"Because I imagined myself scrambling to open it in the dark and didn't want to embarrass myself," I tell her honestly, chuckling.

Once I have a foil packet, I lean back on my knees. "Let me," Sophie says, pushing herself up. I give it over to her and watch as she pulls my boxer briefs down, then strokes my cock. I moan at her touch, my eyes rolling to the back of my head. My willpower is about to snap, so I stop her and tell her she better hurry. She slides it down along my length, and I nearly hiss at how amazing her hands feel on me.

I reach for her T-shirt and pull it off her body, and then she lies back, bare and waiting. Kicking off my shorts the rest of the way, I tower over her as she rests her legs on either side of me.

"I love you," I whisper, brushing strands of hair from her cheek. "So damn much."

Sophie reaches for me, pressing her lips to mine. "I love you, too. So much it scares me sometimes."

"Don't be scared, sweet Sophie," I tell her, pressing a kiss to her forehead. "I'm yours."

"And I'm yours," she repeats the words that melt my jaded heart.

Then I position myself against her entrance and slowly slide into paradise. Her breath hitches as her head falls back, and I sink deeper. Fuck, she's so goddamn tight. Sophie widens her hips for me as I grab her wrists and pull them above her head, linking our fingers together.

"You feel so good," she mutters. "Faster, Mason."

I gradually increase my pace, sliding my hand down her arm, then cupping her breast and teasing the nipple. Her tits are so soft, and her skin is so smooth. I want to devour every inch of her. Kissing along her jaw and neck, Sophie brings a hand down my back, encouraging more. I know she's not fragile, but knowing what she's been through, I can't fathom causing her any amount of pain.

"Harder…" she says, panting. "I won't break, baby."

Pulling back until I can look into her eyes, I frown. "Sweetheart, I know you won't, but I don't want to hurt you. Even if it's meant to bring you pleasure, the thought of hurting you tears me apart."

"You could never, Mason. As long as I'm with you, I feel safe and secure. But you don't have to hold back. Stop handling me with care." She pleads with her gorgeous brown eyes.

"I only want to make you feel good, Soph," I tell her.

"You do. Fuck, you do." She arches her hips with a moan. "But I want you to give me all of you. Take me like you really want to. Hard, deep, fast, rough—I want it *all*."

Jesus Christ.

Her words barely leave her mouth before I'm pulling out and ramming back inside her. She groans at first, tightening her hands on my arms, and then releases a long-drawn-out moan. I palm her breast, my fingers digging into her soft skin as she explodes, squeezing me like a vise grip.

"Oh God, yes…" The corner of her lips tilts up in a flirtatious smile. "More, Mason. I want *more*."

I lean back and push her knees to her chest, then drive back inside her.

"Hold your legs, baby," I order, thrusting deep and hard as she squeezes her legs together. "Fuck, you feel so tight."

Sophie's breathing is erratic as I grip her hip in one hand and rub circles against her clit with the other.

"You came so hard on my cock, baby. Do it again," I demand.

She nods, pulling her bottom lip between her teeth. I focus on her swollen bud as I drive faster, and soon, she's screaming my name again as her body shakes and her legs fall on either side of me.

Before Sophie can catch her breath, I pull out and cover her pussy with my mouth, licking up her arousal. Once her body settles, I tell her to flip over.

"Stick that ass out for me, Soph. Arms above your head," I demand, lining myself up with her entrance. Sliding in, I smack a cheek and smirk when she lets out a yelp. "You like that, sweetheart?" I whisper in her ear, wrapping a hand around her waist and rubbing her clit. "You like me smacking your ass when I fuck your tight cunt?"

Sophie responds with a shattering explosion. This time, I can't hold back, and I come long and hard, grunting her name. She feels so good, and I don't want to let go, so I thrust a few more times until she's unable to keep her body up.

She falls flat to the bed, letting out a loud breath that causes me to laugh. Once I dispose of the condom in the trash, I lie down next to her and pull her into my arms.

"I love you, Soph. That was—"

"Fucking amazing," she finishes for me.

"Yeah, that about sums it up." I chuckle.

"Had I known what I was missing all these weeks, I would've snuck into your room sooner."

"Oh really? Had you forgotten from three years ago?" I tease, brushing my fingers down her slick arm. "Because I could never forget. In fact, I was actively *trying* to forget."

Sophie leans up on my chest, locking her eyes with mine with sincerity. "Of course I never forgot. I had to get a vibrator after you gave me the 'Let's just be friends' speech."

That confession makes me laugh. "You're lying."

"I swear! A girl has needs!"

"Is that so?" I lean on my side and wrap my arms around her. "This vibrator. You still have it?"

Her chuckling and blushing are all I need to confirm that she *definitely* still has it.

We fall asleep wrapped up in each other, and I'm woken up with Sophie's hot mouth on my dick. Blinking, I clear the fog from my eyes and fist my hand in her hair.

"Baby. Shit, that feels good."

She slides her tongue up my hard shaft before wrapping her wet lips around my tip.

"Fuck," I hiss, arching my hips.

My grip tightens as I bob her head up and down my length. Her little gagging noises have my eyes rolling to the back of my head. Sophie pulls back slightly, stroking me hard and fast. Then she takes me by surprise when she settles deeper between my thighs and starts sucking on my balls as she jerks me off.

"Sophie, baby," I moan, ready to die. Her sweet torture is enough to push me over the edge, but I don't want to yet. I love her hands and mouth on me.

She hums, moving back to my tip and teasing me with her tongue as she circles it around.

"You want to fuck my throat, don't you?" Her little taunting voice has my dick jerking.

"Woman." I groan. "You better get up here and ride me before I do."

She crawls up my body, slowly kissing my stomach. With my fingers in her soft hair, I yank it just enough to get her attention. "Get your tits up here, sweetheart."

Her smirk deepens as she straddles me, leaning down enough for me to wrap my mouth around her nipple. If I stroked out right now, I'd die a happy man.

"God, your body drives me wild, Sophie. I can't stop touching you."

"I don't want you to," she tells me, rocking her body against my waist.

I grab another foil packet and put my hands behind my head as she slides it down my cock. Then she rises above me and slowly lowers herself onto my hard shaft.

"God, Mason…" She settles before she leans over and starts rocking against me. I grab her hips and arch up to meet her thrusts. "Why does it feel so good?" she whispers, her head hovering above me. "Better than I could've imagined."

I brush the hair from her face. "It's meant to be good when you're in love, can't live without the other person, and would literally die for them. But it's not just good, baby. It's fucking magical, and every moment I get with you is *perfect*. So goddamn perfect when it's with the right person."

Sophie squeezes her eyes as a tear falls. I catch it with my thumb, then cup her face and cover her mouth with mine. I kiss her soft and slow, then hard and fast, for all the years we lost and the missed opportunities. I kiss her as though it's my last dying breath.

We make love until the sun rises, and when we're both panting and nearly passed out, I pull her into my arms and whisper, "*I love you.*" She looks up with sleepy eyes and repeats the very words that I never thought I deserved to hear again. And for the first time in years, I allow myself to be truly happy without remorse.

CHAPTER FORTY-THREE

I WAKE up in a tangle of limbs, the sun blaring in through the windows, and wearing a goofy smile on my face. Mason's warm chest presses against my back, and his arm is around my waist, holding me close. I've never felt safer in my life than I do right now. He's my protector, and I'm certain he'd never let anything bad happen to me.

Considering what I know about him, I see how far he's come. How much he's done for me and all the sacrifices he's made to get here. The way he loves me is beyond anything I could've ever imagined. Most days, it seems like what we have is too good to be true. The thought of giving my whole heart to him terrifies me, and it makes me vulnerable and emotionally dependent. He has the ability to ruin me, but I trust him wholeheartedly. I don't want to walk on eggshells anymore or allow the *what-ifs* to keep me guarded. I'm all in.

"Good morning, sweetheart," he murmurs gruffly against my ear. He stirs, pushing his erection into my back. "You in the mood for a morning quickie?" I feel him grin against my neck.

"I'd say we're past that, seeing as it's almost noon," I taunt, knowing we stayed up late and slept in. "Afternoon quickie?"

"Afternoon, evening, night—let's make it an all-day marathon."

"I've unleashed the beast now, haven't I?" I chuckle and wiggle my ass. "You're addicted."

"Fuckin' right, I am. Addicted to you. To your body, your soul, your amazing tits." He slides his hand up and squeezes my bare breast.

"I think you might need to seek counseling…addiction can be dangerous," I tell him.

"Oh, baby. This is one addiction I never want to be cured from." Then Mason rolls me toward him and climbs over me. "In fact, I need another fix right now."

Before he lowers his mouth to kiss me, I block him with my palm. "Wait!" I squeal, and he pops a brow. "I have morning breath." My cheeks flush. "Let me brush my teeth and take a shower. And maybe eat something. You know, to gain more energy."

Mason's head falls back with a loud laugh. "Am I depriving you of fuel?"

"Well, you did work me quite a bit. Perhaps the hot water will help my muscles. I feel like I did a full-body workout."

"Oh yes, I like the idea of taking a shower." He winks, and I push him off me with a chuckle.

"I meant *alone*."

He pouts, sticking out his lower lip, which causes me to burst out laughing. "You're pathetic."

"I'd prefer love-sick." He grabs my hand and helps me stand.

I go in search of my clothes, and I blush at the sight of the condom box we dug into four times last night.

"You shower. I'll start lunch." He cups my face and presses a quick peck to my lips. "And for what it's worth, I'd kiss your stinky breath any fucking day." He winks and walks out of the room in only his boxer briefs.

Once I've successfully showered, brushed my teeth, dressed, and thrown my hair up in the world's messiest bun, I meet Mason in the kitchen. Leaning in the doorway, I grin as he places two sandwiches on one plate and two more on another. Then he grabs a handful of chips and places half on mine and half on his. He opens the fridge, grabbing two sodas, and when his gaze meets mine, he smirks.

"You gonna watch me all day?"

"I've spent many days watching you. You were just too busy avoiding me," I tell him, walking toward him and inhaling the scent of the coffee.

"You ever gonna let me live that down?" He snickers.

"Oh no." I shake my head. "That's going in our wedding vows."

Mason sets the cans down, then wraps his arms around my waist. "Wedding vows?" He pops a brow. "I think the guy is supposed to do the proposing, but…"

"That was *not* a proposal," I say pointedly, but I can't wipe the smile off my face.

"Why not? We're already living together. Have *amazing* chemistry." Mason leans down and presses a kiss to my nose. "Pretty sure you're obsessed with my cock. *You love me.*"

I smirk. "And you're clearly humble."

Mason cups my cheeks, claiming my lips and stealing my breath away. "Amongst many other qualities, right?" He winks before sneaking another kiss.

I snort at the way he waggles his brows. "Just feed me."

"You've got it, woman."

After devouring our food, we sit on the couch with mugs of coffee and catch up on *Lucifer*. Mason rubs my feet as we settle into a comfortable silence, laughing at the TV and sneaking side glances. I rub the heel of my foot against his dick, knowing it won't take much to get him hard. Though I'm a little sore from our marathon sex last night, I can't get enough of him. Things feel so natural, so *right* with him, and I love spending these quiet Saturdays together with only the two of us.

As soon as the thought enters my mind, the front door bursts open, and Liam barrels into the living room wearing the same clothes he left in last night.

"Afternoon walk of shame?" I tease.

Liam wrinkles his nose, sniffing. "It smells like sex in here. Did you guys finally do it?" He narrows his eyes. "Wait. Did you do it in *here*?"

"Have you two ever had boundaries?" I ask Mason.

"Nope. Not for lack of trying, though."

"Yeah, you two totally did it," he says, walking into the kitchen. "About damn time. But that means I'm gonna need noise-canceling headphones. I bet Soph's a screamer." He laughs to himself, then walks back into the living room with three beers in his hands. "Am I right?"

"Might be time to have that boundaries chat again." I pat Mason's leg with a mischievous grin and grab one of the beers. "I'll be in my room." I round the couch, then wink before leaving the two of them alone.

It takes Mason less than five minutes to charge into my bedroom and lock the door behind him. I'm sitting propped up against my headboard with a book, my eyes scanning the sentences when I feel him between my thighs. I hold back a smirk, keeping my gaze glued on the pages in front of me. He slides his hands up my legs, under my shorts, and finds my sweet spot.

"What're you doing?" I ask without looking at him.

"Oh, nothing. Keep reading your little book."

"I'd hardly call it little," I muse. "It's a Teddy Leigh novel."

"Oh, right. Your loverboy. Well…don't mind me then." He pulls my panties to the side and pushes a finger in. My breath hitches, but I don't move. I'm not reading a damn word on the page, but I'll gladly play his teasing game.

"Don't worry, I won't. This book is too damn good anyway."

"Is that so?" He adds a second finger, thrusting harder and faster. "How about now?"

"I'm sorry, are you doing something?" I playfully yawn, flipping the page.

Mason rubs circles around my clit with his thumb, and my hips arch to greet him.

"I think you like that." I hear the smile in his voice, but I'm not giving in yet.

"Not sure what you're talking about." I bite down on my lower lip to stop from moaning. Then the bastard increases his pace, calling my bluff.

"Your wet pussy knows what I'm talking about. Fuck, it's squeezing my fingers so goddamn tight." Mason's words have my eyes rolling to the back of my head as he takes my body closer to the edge.

"Fine, you win," I say, tossing the book to the floor. "Don't stop doing that." My back nearly flies off the bed as he sinks deeper.

Mason yanks his hand away, and when my eyes pop open, he's shoving both fingers between his lips, then sucks them. "Always so fucking sweet."

"You enjoy messing with me, don't you?"

"Oh, Sophie. Haven't you learned by now?" He crawls over my body until we're face to face. "You've been the one messing with *me* for years. You just didn't know it. Watching you shake your hips, your tits bounce, you sucking on that lower lip. It was torture."

"That's what you get…for friend-zoning me," I tease, fisting his shirt and pulling him closer. "We have a lot of making up to do."

"Fuck yes," he growls, stealing a kiss. "Let's start now."

It's a miracle I can walk by Monday morning. Pretty sure it looks like I've done a thousand squats and spent all day at the gym. I was exercising but not with workout equipment. Now that Mason and I have crossed the line from waiting to complete sex fiends, we can't seem to get enough of each other. If we don't end up in bed together, we're making out in the shower, and it ends with one of us on our knees. It's truly like nothing I've ever felt before, but now that I have it, I'm scared as hell it's going to be taken away from me again.

The rug has been pulled out from under me more times this year than in my entire life. Mason makes me feel things I've only read about in romance novels, and the fact that my reality is better than fiction is terrifying.

But I trust Mason more than anything and believe in the relationship we're building together. I can't stop the smile on my face, nor do I want to. He makes me the happiest I've ever been.

MASON

I miss you already. Skip work and come back
home. I'll make it worth it 😏

Chuckling at his message, I blush and bite my lip. I hadn't made it down the block, but I have no doubt Mason would make a day of playing hooky worth it.

SOPHIE

I just left! You haven't had time to miss me yet.

MASON

Then why is my dick hard already?

SOPHIE

That's a good question, considering you snuck in
the shower with me this morning!

MASON

You liked it 😌

I chuckle and roll my eyes then put my phone down when the light turns green. That man is insatiable.

Feeling more like myself and on cloud nine, rehearsal goes smoother than ever. The fall recital is soon, and I've memorized each piece by heart. The director even came up to me during one of our breaks and praised me for doing so well. He tells me how happy he is to see the passion back in my eyes. His words have me nearly skipping to my car afterward.

It's no secret my therapy has progressed very well these past few months, but I certainly didn't do it alone. Mason has been by my side the entire time even when he was giving me space. When it didn't feel like I was getting better, I'd read my previous journal entries, and it reminded me of how far I've come. For the first time, I'm right where I'm supposed to be, and the timing is *finally* right.

Since Mason always works later than I do, I text my sisters and see if they want to hang out. Lennon works until four, and Maddie has dance practice, but we can squeeze in a couple of hours of sister time.

SOPHIE

Can we meet up tonight? Lennon's house? 5:30?

LENNON

Sounds serious…everything okay?

MADDIE

I have a life, you know. Two hour's notice is not very much for me…

SOPHIE

That's fine. I'll just tell Lennon all the juicy news. See you at 5:30, Lennon!

I'm messing with her, knowing that'll get her sassy ass in gear.

MADDIE

No, you will not! You better wait for me and tell me every detail!

LENNON

Wait? Is this sex gossip? Not fair, I can't drink!

I chuckle at Lennon's crying emoji.

MADDIE

Me neither!

SOPHIE

More alcohol for MEEEE!

I send an emoji with a tongue sticking out, and they both send back angry faces.

LENNON

I gotta pick up Allie from Mrs. Locke's, and then
I'll be home!

SOPHIE

Great! I'll bring dinner!

MADDIE

Chinese food for me!

SOPHIE

You're not even coming, Miss Too-Popular.

MADDIE

Shut up. I've been waiting three years for this
story! Pick me up!

SOPHIE

☺

MADDIE

Maddie, the mature sister.

Once I'm home, I head upstairs to quickly freshen up. I look around the bathroom and notice Liam's dirty clothes in a pile. *Ugh.* He's lucky I love his slobby ass so much. He left yesterday morning for work, and I'm not sure when he'll be back this time. Grabbing his crap in my arms, I walk to his bedroom and throw them in his overflowing hamper. Deciding I'll be nice this one time, I grab the basket and take it downstairs to the laundry room. He works so much, and if I don't clean his clothes, it'll attract flies.

I reach into the pockets of his jeans and empty them out before shoving them into the washer, and in the third pair, I find a receipt and a gambling chip.

What the hell?

The receipt is for sixteen thousand dollars, and the chip is worth five hundred dollars. Even stranger, it's from the Bellagio. Liam never said anything about being in Sin City. He's always traveling for work and could've made a pit stop, but that's a lot of money to win in Vegas. Wouldn't he tell us or want to celebrate or something?

Deciding to ask him about it later, I put all of the crap from his jeans on the kitchen counter after starting the washing machine. Then I head out to pick up our food.

SOPHIE

I'm hanging at Lennon's house for dinner. Stop over if you aren't working too late. I'm bringing Chinese and could grab you something for later?

MASON

Hang out while the three of you talk about our sex life? Think I'll pass on that one 😜

I chuckle because he knows us Corrigan sisters too damn well.

SOPHIE

They don't want to hear about that, trust me.

MASON

You're a horrible liar, babe. Even through text.

I send him a smiley face emoji before replying with an *I love you!*

Once I grab our food order, I pick up Maddie, then head to Lennon's. She talks my ear off the entire ride there when I refuse to talk about Mason. She's too impatient to even wait twenty minutes.

"C'mon, just tell me one little detail! Anything. Wait. It wasn't little, was it?" Maddie pinches her fingers together and arches a brow when I finally park in front of Hunter and Lennon's apartment.

"How would you even know what's considered *little*?" I tease, grabbing the food, then getting out of the car.

"Um, excuse me. I've watched porn before. Plus, I've fooled around with a few guys," she states matter-of-factly, but I'm not buying it. Maddie is always way too eager to share information.

"Okay, *one* guy. Like two years ago. But still. Big, yay or nay?"

"Don't you dare tell her anything without me!" Lennon shouts from the staircase.

"You two are relentless!" I laugh, greeting Lennon with a hug. "I doubt Hunter wants to hear that about his friend anyway."

Maddie follows and gives Lennon a side hug then pushes her way into the apartment and immediately grabs Allie from her highchair.

"Don't worry," Hunter calls from the kitchen. "You and Maddie are the reason I bought sound-proof headphones." He smirks when he pops his head into the doorway.

"Har, har. I think you mean *Maddie* only." I set the bag of food on the table where Lennon already has plates and silverware set out.

"I'm sure you two were here years before me, so I can't be the one to blame." Maddie puts Allie back in her chair.

Hunter comes in with a plate for Allie and sets it in front of her with a little baby fork and spoon. We all take our seats and eat.

"So what's Liam think about you two finally hooking up? He's probably not used to that." Hunter laughs.

"He's hardly home but is convinced we're doing it all over the house and keeps asking if we've done it in the living room or kitchen. I'm afraid it's because he *has* done it all over the place."

"Good thing you've cleaned that house from top to bottom," Lennon says, snorting. "Especially since you two are in that honeymoon phase."

Maddie groans, and we all turn to her rolling her eyes. "The nonstop doing it phase, am I right?"

We all snicker.

"I'm totally selling my virginity."

"Maddie!" Lennon points at Allie, who is oblivious to any adult conversation happening as she stuffs little pieces of chicken into her mouth. She's getting so big, and I can't believe she'll be one in only a couple of months.

"She doesn't know what that word means!" Maddie argues.

"But I'd still like that not to be in her vocabulary!" Lennon scolds.

They do this fight and dance at least once a month, which cracks me up.

"Fine! I'm selling my…flowerpot. Happy?" Maddie flashes a snarky smile. "To the biggest…water hose."

Hunter nearly chokes on his food as he coughs, then tries swallowing it down with his drink. Lennon laughs as she slaps his back. "Water hose trip you up?"

"You've been saying you're gonna 'sell it off' for months," I say, rolling my eyes at her. "Either do it or quit whining about it."

Maddie responds with a glare. "I'll be twenty-one soon, and then I'm gonna get…"

Lennon clears her throat and motions to Allie with her eyes as a reminder to watch her words.

"Gonna drink some happy juice." Maddie grins, wide and taunting. "And get very, very happy. Then I'm gonna pick my water hose and be a full-blown bloomed flower."

I snort, shaking my head at her. "Just wait until you find the right person. It makes it extra special," I say with a dreamy sigh. "Trust me."

"Except you didn't wait, so why should I trust you?" she fires.

"Because I wish I would have!" I point my fork at her, daring her to keep challenging my older sister knowledge.

"Isn't it so much better when it's with someone amazing?" Lennon says, looking at Hunter like he hung the moon.

"It really is," I agree.

"All you two are missing are the floating hearts above your heads and cartoon stars in your eyes." Maddie groans, wrinkling her nose in disgust.

"Take it from me, Mads," Hunter intervenes, grabbing a container of food and dumping it on his plate. "I had a lot of meaningless one-night stands, and they made me feel empty and gross. Then Lennon happened, and it was nothing like I'd ever experienced before. It was beyond special, and it meant everything. I knew I loved her for years before, but getting to experience that shared love is indescribable."

"Aww, baby…" Lennon coos.

Maddie mimics a gagging noise, and I snicker.

"You two are relationship goals," I tell Hunter and Lennon. The moment they finally got together, I knew I wanted what they had. Lennon had a second chance at love after Brandon died, and I'm so happy she took the risk. Hunter's perfect for her and Allie.

Once we finish eating and clean up, Hunter offers to give Allie her bath and get her ready for bed so Lennon can socialize with us. Lennon gives him a deep, passionate kiss.

"Didn't know we were getting dinner *and* a show," Maddie blurts.

"Hey, you be quiet!" Lennon scowls before releasing Hunter, then he walks down the hallway so we can finally talk.

"Baby kicking?" I ask as she takes a seat on the couch next to me. I rub her bump and beg for movement. "Ooh, was that it?"

"Let me feel!" Maddie pushes me aside.

"Relax," Lennon says, laughing. "Pretty sure that was gas. I have a food baby in there too."

Lennon kicks her feet up on the coffee table, and I chat about Mason and me. I want to be respectful of the intimate details of our relationship and knew I wanted to take things slow after the incident with Dalton.

"It was…amazing," I tell them with a dreamy sigh. "Friday was completely unplanned. Serena was there being overly touchy with Mason, and I flipped out. Once she and Liam left, he cooked dinner, but we weren't really talking about what happened. He was acting a little too giddy for the way I told off his friend, and then he called me out for saying he was my *boyfriend*. Something changed for me that night. I didn't want to wait any longer because being with him felt right. I love him so much, and I wanted us to share something special. We ended the night, he kissed me, and we went to our separate rooms."

"And then what? He snuck into your bedroom and jumped you, right?" Maddie waggles her brows.

"Actually, it was the other way around." I blush. "I snuck into his room and told him I was ready."

"Then you spent the entire weekend naked and didn't come up for air until this morning. Amiright?" Lennon smirks.

"Basically!" I laugh. "I couldn't get enough, and neither could he. We ate and refueled in between."

"And now I want to barf," Maddie says dramatically. Lennon narrows her eyes at her, which causes me to smile. "I'm happy for the two of you, but I hate being the only sister who can't contribute to these stories."

I pat her leg. "You will one day. Then it'll be 'Maddie's Sex Stories' nonstop."

"Ooh, I like the sound of that. Should totally be a book." Maddie beams with excitement.

We laugh and chat for another hour before Lennon suggests we FaceTime our parents since the three of us are together.

"That feels wrong after the conversations we just had…" I bite my bottom lip, then shrug. "As long as Maddie doesn't blurt anything inappropriate, we should be okay."

"Considering I'm the one who knows both of your secrets, you should know I'm a pro at acting completely normal with Mom and Dad. It's you two sex addicts who will blow our covers."

"They know by now not to say anything to me," Lennon gloats.

We end up talking to our parents for twenty minutes before Lennon uses Allie as an excuse to hang up. They could chat for hours if we didn't find a way to end the call. We all love them so much, but they will pry into every detail of our lives if given the chance.

"Thanks for bringing dinner." Lennon gives us hugs before we head out.

"You're welcome!" I smile. "Oh, don't forget my fall concert is next week. You're all coming, right?"

"Of course! We wouldn't miss it. Mads, I'll pick you up," Lennon directs at our little sister. "Don't be late."

"You're the one with the baby, and I'm gonna be late?" She scoffs, and it's funny the way we both give her shit, but it's our job as the older sisters. She's growing into a young woman, and it's hard to believe she'll be legal to drink in a few months.

Once I drop Maddie off, I come home to Mason on the couch. Lying down with one arm behind his head and the other over his chest, he's fast asleep. He's been working so hard since he was promoted, and I know he wants to prove himself, but I still worry about him burning out.

"Baby…" I whisper, brushing my hand over his cheek. "Go to bed. You won't be comfortable out here."

"Mmm…" He stirs. "I was waiting for you. What time is it?"

"Just after nine," I tell him. "You fell asleep early."

"Pretty sure I fell asleep the moment I walked into the house," he murmurs, his eyes still closed.

"Did you eat something?"

"I downed a couple of sandwiches, but I skipped dessert. Get your ass on my face."

I burst out laughing. "Smooth."

He finally opens his eyes. "Did you girls have fun tonight?"

"Yeah, we ate dinner, chatted and then FaceTimed our parents."

"Oh yeah? Did you tell your folks about me yet?" Mason smirks, knowing how strict and religious they are.

"Totally. Confessed that I'm living with you in sin, and we're now fucking regularly. They told me to give you an attaboy!" I playfully punch his shoulder, and he grins.

"We've already discussed wedding vows, so it's best they're

caught up to speed here." He sits up and pulls me onto his lap. Mason brushes his fingers along my cheek and tucks loose strands of hair behind my ear. "Then I can tell them all about how much I love their daughter and would do anything for her. How I'll provide for her, care for her, and love her until my dying day. I gotta compete with Hunter now, so…"

I laugh, but my eyes fill with unshed tears at his admission. "You're too sweet to me," I tell him softly, leaning my forehead against his.

Mason cups my cheeks and kisses my lips, soft and quick. "I mean it, sweetheart. Until my dying day."

Nodding, I choke back my emotions. "I know you do. It's why I love you so damn much."

CHAPTER FORTY-FOUR

MASON

Sometimes I hate my fucking job.

I knew what I was getting into, but days like today are hard. Crime scenes with children are my hard limit, but I don't always have the choice. Suicide is another for me, but I use my experience to get through it, knowing the family will want answers. The *why* and the *how* usually, and although it's not something we can always give them, I strive to. They want closure.

But today was an act that doesn't hit close to home, rather it hits right in the gut. As I sit in an office and peruse the case files, I'm disgusted by how much politics and our government control the healthcare system. It's one of the many reasons my father and I butt heads so much. Our views differ greatly, and nothing he says will ever convince me that money and power are worth more than a human life.

An elderly man in his seventies shot his wife of forty-eight years and then called 911 to let them know he was going to shoot himself. He said she was sick, and they couldn't afford her prescriptions or hospital bills. The gentleman also had his fair share of health concerns, and the financial burden was too heavy for him to carry. He was his wife's caretaker, and somehow, he got it into his head that killing her and then himself was the best solution.

Sadly, his story is only one of many.

Without their medications, they would've eventually died, but probably while alone and sedated in a hospital bed. At least this way, he could make their own fate without suffering. I don't get how our own system could fail so many people, and on some level, I understand this man's thought process as painful as it is to admit.

"The letters are the saddest shit I've ever read," my colleague Jada says as we file. "And I've seen some sad shit."

Jada is one of my mentors, and I admire her greatly. She's in her forties and tells it like it is, something I also appreciate. There's never any guessing with her.

"You can tell his hand was shaking when he wrote some of them," I say, looking over the photographs we took. "As if he was questioning his decision for a bit but then found the strength somehow not to change his mind."

"In the last few notes, his writing gets sloppier as if he had his mind set and just wanted it to be over." Jada frowns, looking over the pictures. "It's a tragedy."

Nodding, I agree. Filing is grunt work, but I also get more responsibility now. Some days, I'm grateful for it, and other days, I'd rather not have to think about the hardships of life that bring someone to go this route.

Ever since revealing my past to Sophie and being in the field at work, Emma's been on my mind more than usual. For years, I've blocked it out, not wanting the memories to surface. However, now I like thinking about her—when she was happy—when *we* were happy. Sometimes, it seems like a lifetime ago, and other times, I remember it like it was yesterday.

Sophie can tell when I'm having one of those days. She doesn't push or force me to talk about it. Rather, she'll lay with me and let me hold her. Nothing will ever convince me that Emma's death wasn't my fault. I failed to react to the signs. Even if she'd cried wolf so many times before, I should've known better than to leave her alone. She'd been going to therapy and group sessions, but she was damn good at putting on an act when she wanted to. That much I know, and she proved it time and again.

"What're you thinking?" Jada's voice has me blinking away my thoughts.

Clearing my throat, I set the files down on the table. "I was wondering if there had been warning signs. If they'd called anyone to tell them they loved them or sold off any of their items. The typical things you see in planned suicides like this."

"According to Briggs…" She grabs one of the files from the pile and flips through a few pages. "He spoke with the daughter, and she seemed distraught but also not shocked. She'd been surprised he had a gun, but not that the father did it."

I furrow my brows. "I wonder why that is. Why her father being the killer wouldn't surprise her?"

"That's not our job, Holt," Jada warns as she always does. I want to dig into the nitty-gritty details, but our jobs are to process the scenes, establish the murder weapon, and help figure out the *who*. All the other stuff is unnecessary to solve the case. Even if it could help a family member find closure to know those details or just so I can sleep at night, it's not our responsibility.

"Yeah, yeah," I grumble.

"So how's that girlfriend of yours doing?" she asks, handing me the files so I can put them in the proper box.

"Amazing." I smile thinking about Sophie. "Went to her fall concert last week and watching her play is always incredible. She's so damn talented and special. Sometimes, it's hard to believe she picked me."

Jada gives me a pointed look and opens her mouth, probably to yell at me for putting myself down, but she must think better of it and doesn't say a word.

A minute later, she asks, "Has Daddy Dearest met her yet?"

"Only a couple of brief times," I tell her. "The most recent time, he showed up uninvited. They exchanged greetings, but that was about it."

"And what about Serena?" She smirks, resting her hand on her hip. "Has she met Sophie?"

"A few times." I snort but don't get into that whole story of the two of them. "Why are you so curious, anyway? You want an invite or something?"

"Well, you talk about her so damn much, I practically know her. Plus, we spend a lot of time together at work, so maybe she wants to know who you're spending your days with?"

"I purposely don't talk about work much. Being home is my safe zone," I explain. "Sophie listens when I need to vent, but otherwise, if I don't bring it up, she doesn't either."

"From what you've told me, both of you have gone through some tough shit. Remember not to hold your feelings in, even if it's hard to talk about. Trust me, I'm on my third marriage."

I chuckle, shaking my head when she smirks at her own dig. "Third time's the charm, huh?"

"Lord, I hope so. I've applied for marriage licenses and changed my last name so many times, the workers in the clerk's office know me personally." Her smirk widens.

"They probably run away screaming when they see you, knowing all the paperwork you're about to make them file," I tease, loading up the evidence box and putting the lid on top.

"Ha-ha." Jada rolls her eyes. "Joking aside, I locked up my emotions, which is something we're taught to do in this job. However, at home, you need to release them and let your partner in. If you're having a crap day because of what you saw, then express it. Otherwise, they think it's about them, and that's when shit goes downhill."

"You're probably right." I grab a Sharpie and label the box. "Sophie's a great listener too. She'd be open to talking about work, but I hate bringing negative energy home when being with her makes me so damn happy."

"Yeah, you have that sick in love glow about you." She circles a finger around her face to mock me.

"And I'm not sorry about it." I grin, taking the evidence and walking toward the exit. "I'm leaving after I put this away. Unless you need me to help you with anything else?" I press my back against the door, waiting.

"Nah, you're fine. I'm gonna sign these docs, and then I'll be done too."

"Have a good night then, Jada." I wink before heading out.

The moment I get home, I smell food cooking in the kitchen. When I find Sophie at the stove, stirring something, I quietly walk closer and softly brush her hair off her shoulder. She shivers but doesn't say a word. Instead, she tilts her head slightly, giving me the access I crave.

Lowering my face, I press a kiss below her ear and then down her neck. Sophie continues stirring the pasta sauce, and if I wasn't so damn hungry, I'd tear her ass away and haul her into the bedroom.

"Mmm…Liam. You're home early." She moans, releasing a deep sigh.

My eyes pop open, my hand stalling on her waist.

"I hope you're hungry," she continues, her voice sweet like honey. "Because I was thinking we'd start with dessert first." A deep growl escapes my throat. Then she wiggles her ass against my dick. "Mmm…what do you think?"

I cup her ass cheek after slapping it and earn a squeal in return.

"Ooh, dessert first it is." Sophie arches her back, sticking that ass out further. Then she glances over her shoulder and bursts out laughing. "Oh, come on! Nothing?" She chuckles as if she's the only one in on this joke.

Because she *is*.

Sophie turns off the burner, then spins around to face me. "You're no fun when you don't play along." She gives me a pouty face.

"You called me *Liam*…" I step back, crossing my arms.

"Hence, the joke!" She cackles. "Not funny?" Sophie bites her bottom lip as if she's trying to hold back a smirk.

"Not even close." I grab her waist, then haul her over my shoulder. She shrieks, and I smack her butt again. "And after the day I've had, I'm about to show you just how *not* funny that was."

"Mason!" she shouts, hitting my back. "Put me down."

"I'm about to make sure you never forget my name again…" I walk into her room and lock the door behind me. "Starting with stripping you naked."

"I didn't forget your name…" she argues with a playful tone.

I toss her on the mattress, then tower over her. "In fact, I should tie your naughty little ass to the bed."

"Mason…no." Her panicked voice sets off alarm bells, and I immediately regret the words. That asshole Dalton taped her to a chair, leaving her helpless and scared for her life.

"You know I'd never hurt you, Soph." I lean down and kiss her, rubbing the pad of my thumb against her cheek. "If I tie you up, it'd only be to *please* you. Never anything else."

Sophie nods, then wraps her legs around my waist and pulls me on top of her. "I do know that, but maybe instead of tying me up, you can use handcuffs." She waggles her brows. "I have some."

I pull back. "You do?"

"They were a gag gift," she explains, shrugging. "But they work."

"Okay." Leaning back, I reach behind my neck and tear off my shirt. "I have a few ideas."

She points to her nightstand. After digging to the bottom, I find them, and once I've stripped her down to her bra and panties, I cuff her hands in front of her.

"Keep your arms up, baby…" I tell her, raising them above her until they reach the headboard. "Don't move."

I slide my tongue between her lips and cup her cheeks. The kiss turns hot and passionate, and I have to push her hands back twice.

"Hands *up*," I remind roughly.

"Mason…" she whines, moaning. "You're torturing me."

"I'm just getting started, baby." I lower myself down her body, feathering kisses between her breasts and down her stomach.

Once I'm between her legs, I move her panties to the side and slide my tongue over her.

Sophie moans and wiggles underneath me, but when I slip two fingers inside and suck on her clit, she shakes and arches her hips. I love how her body responds and how hot she gets when I touch her.

It's been two weeks since our very first time, and when we make love, it never feels like enough. We always want more—more of each other, more togetherness. After breezing through a dozen condoms in only a few days, Sophie suggested we get tested together, and since she has an IUD, we didn't have to worry about an unexpected pregnancy. The moment our results came back that we were both clean, we ditched them and have gotten a bit carried away. In the shower, in the kitchen, on the table, her bed, my bed, the dining room.

Knowing Sophie's history, I always make sure to ask her before doing anything she might not like. Although she told me not to treat her like she's fragile, I also know how triggers work, and the last thing I want to do is remind her of something those assholes did to her.

I bring Sophie to the edge, teasing and licking her until she's screaming my name. She tries reaching for me, but I give her a look that tells her she better get her arms up or else. When her breaths have steadied, I slide off the bed and smirk. "Ready?"

She pinches her brows together. "For what?"

Once I've removed my slacks and boxer briefs, I grab her hips and flip her onto her stomach. She squeals, glancing over her shoulder and deadpans, "Thanks for the warning."

"Oh, sweet Sophie…" I muse, sliding my finger up her arm. "The only warning you need is knowing you won't be able to walk when I'm done with you."

"Mmm…I like the sound of that," she purrs, licking her bottom lip.

I kneel on the bed next to her and slide off her panties. Teasing her, I circle my finger over her swollen bud, and she moans before I push inside her. I admire every inch of her body—her round ass, the curves of her waist, the sides of her breasts. I don't know how I ever kept my hands off her. There were a lot of cold showers, that's for sure.

Towering over her, I bring my lips to her shoulder and kiss her smooth skin. Her dark hair cascades to one side, and I fist a handful, pulling slightly. "I'm gonna take you from behind, baby, but keep your legs together."

"What?"

"It's gonna feel really fucking good," I reassure her. She's already so goddamn tight. She's going to squeeze my cock even more. "Trust me?"

"Yes." She blinks, looking at me. "Of course I do."

Leaning down, I kiss the tip of her nose. "If you don't like it, tell me."

"I will."

She's probably sick of me telling her that, but open communication is so important to me. I never want her to feel obligated to go along with what I'm doing if she's not enjoying herself. Sophie's sex drive matches mine, but sometimes, I have to hold myself back because I don't want to hurt her. It's so easy to get lost in the moment.

I straddle below her ass and slide my dick up and down her crack. Once I reach her pussy, I coat the tip with her arousal and tease her until she moans my name. "Mason, please," she pleads, arching her back.

"Keep your ass up like that for a second…" I tell her, stroking my length before pushing inside her. I enter slowly, gradually stretching her, but once I'm fully seated, I slide out, then ram back in.

"Oh my God!" she squeals, trying to open her legs, but I don't allow it.

With her legs together like this, the sensation is tight as hell and so goddamn deep. "Fuck, baby. You feel so good…" I lean down slightly and press a kiss on her back. Then I reach up with one hand and grab her wrists, making sure the cuffs aren't too tight in this position.

I lean back on my knees until I'm straddling her legs and increase my pace as I spread her cheeks apart. Sophie pushes her body to meet my thrusts, and soon, we build a rhythm that has her coming undone, shaking beneath me.

"That's my girl." I give her ass a little slap before pushing deeper. "Fuck, I'm not gonna last much longer."

Sophie's heavy breathing and moaning are all it takes for me to come deep inside her, grunting her name. I love being able to feel her bare, making our connection even more intimate, which didn't seem possible. I'm one hundred percent addicted to her.

Towering over her with our breaths mingling together, I tilt her chin until our lips meet. "I love you, baby."

Sophie rewards me with the sweetest, most tender smile. "I love you, too."

After Sophie and I clean up and get dressed, we head to the kitchen hand-in-hand and finish preparing dinner. The sauce thickened in the pan, but it only takes a few minutes to warm it back up. I boil a pot of water for the noodles, and we work side by side as we exchange glances and smirks.

"Can I ask you something?" Sophie's voice is quieter than usual as if she's nervous or embarrassed.

"Of course you can. Anything," I tell her, adding in a pinch of salt to the water.

"Are you sure you've never *liked* Serena? I understand she's Emma's sister, so it might be weird to ask that, but I don't want there to be any secrets between us. So if there ever was an attraction there or still is, I just want to know." She bites down on her bottom lip.

I raise my brows, surprised by her question after the way things went down the last time Serena was here.

"Never," I tell her honestly. "Not then, not when she moved in, and not now."

Sophie nods as if she understands, her cheeks reddening.

I tilt her chin so our eyes lock. "When I said before that I had no interest in dating after Emma, I meant it. Didn't look at women, had no desire to move on, didn't feel like I deserved to. That was, until I met you."

She blinks at me with sad eyes. "Really?"

"You lit something inside me that I can't explain. I met girls at bars, but I didn't take any of them home, or to bar bathrooms…" I tease. "But you were different, and although I couldn't get you off my mind, I wasn't ready to date. I didn't want to *be* with another woman until I met you. Soph, you ruined me." I wink, wrapping my arms around her waist.

"I think Serena likes you in more than just a friend kind of way," she tells me, her cheeks flushing. "So I wanted to ask if there was something more there than your shared history."

"The only history Serena and I have revolves around trying to get her sister help. We've only ever been friends, and that's all we'll ever be. I can promise you that."

"Do you think she's on the same page now?"

"Well, she's aware that I'm head over heels in love with you. That's all she needs to know." I shrug, confident Serena wouldn't interfere with a relationship that makes me this damn happy. "She's so career driven, she'll probably end up with someone in the same field."

"I'm kinda surprised Liam didn't try to score with her once she moved in," Sophie says, laughing.

I snort, nodding. "You and me both. But Liam's smart enough to know you don't shit where you eat. Sleeping with someone who lives with you would be his definition of stupid."

"Why doesn't he want to date?" she asks, emptying the noodles into the boiling pot of water. "I know he travels for work a lot, but has he ever dated for real?"

"Nope, not since I've known him. From what I gather, he doesn't want a relationship because he doesn't trust himself not to hurt the other person. He's jaded when it comes to that stuff." I stand behind her and wrap my arms around her. "He has issues. Eventually, the right girl will come along and change him. And he'll marry her in a heartbeat."

"I sure hope so. I'd like to see him happy with someone." Sophie smiles. "When he's ready to settle down, that is," she adds.

"You might be waiting a while." I chuckle.

"Oh, that reminds me of something. Does Liam gamble?"

"Like poker? He did in college but mostly for beer. Why?" I furrow my brows, then reach into the cabinet and grab two plates. After setting them down on the counter, I grab us both a drink.

"Well, I was doing his laundry, and when I checked his pockets, I found a receipt and a poker chip from a casino in Vegas. I found it weird because he never mentioned going there to either of us." Sophie turns down the burner before stirring the pasta.

"He must've been there for work or something." I shrug. "Was it for a lot?"

"Yeah, sixteen grand," she says, and I spit out my beer. I took a drink at the wrong time.

"What? Really? Holy shit. That's definitely something he'd be way too happy and brag about." I grab a napkin to wipe the beer off my shirt.

"So it's weird, right? Do you think I should ask him?"

"I don't know. Maybe say something when you give him the chip back, but without it coming off like you're being nosy." I smirk, knowing Sophie will want to pry anyway.

She thinks about it for a moment, pursing her lips back and forth, then smirks. "Yeah, I think I can do that." She fists my shirt, pulling my mouth to hers. "And then you're gonna tell me about your day while we eat."

I can't hold back the grin that forms because my girl knows how to read me so damn well.

CHAPTER FORTY-FIVE

SOPHIE

"So now that your fall concert is finished and you're not stressing about rehearsal, you think I can take you on that official first date?" Mason asks me over breakfast. "I mean, it's only about three months overdue. Plus, you did introduce me as your boyfriend to your director, which is pretty serious if you ask me." He's being playful and is in high spirits this morning, which I adore.

I smirk, taking a sip of my coffee. After the performance last weekend, Mason surprised me with a gorgeous bouquet of roses and looked so damn handsome in his suit and tie. I kissed him, and of course, we weren't alone, so I introduced him to the other violinists and our director. Now Mason looks as though he's won the lottery, but I'm clearly the lucky one.

"It took me calling you my boyfriend in public for you to consider us serious?" I tease. It's Saturday morning, which means we don't have to rush out the door and go our separate ways. Mason's been so busy with work, and sometimes he doesn't get home until after eight.

"Oh no, baby. We were serious long before either of us were willing to admit it." Mason winks, and even after all this time, it still gives me butterflies. We finish eating, then move to the couch but not without filling our mugs full.

"Okay, so this first date. What'd you have in mind?" I ask, setting the cup down on the coffee table.

"I'm thinking it has to be epic." He smirks, inching closer to me. "Probably a long weekend."

Arching a brow, my eyes widen. "Aren't you usually on call?"

Although he got his big promotion, he has to be available if they need help. I hadn't realized until Mason explained it that forensic investigators aren't always fully staffed, which means if there are a lot of cases, they'll need extra people to collect and process a crime scene. He's been called in at three in the morning and then had to work an entire shift afterward.

"Not over Thanksgiving weekend. It's my off holiday, which means I'll be one hundred percent *yours*." He leans into me until our lips touch. "So what do you say? Will you go on a date with me, Sophie?"

"Hmm…a holiday weekend. That sounds *super* serious."

"We could have three full days of just the two of us. No interruptions." He waggles his brows, his implication clear as day. "I mean, unless you're busy and have plans with another boyfriend during that time."

"Well, if we're rotating holidays, then I better check my schedule to be safe." I hold up my finger, then grab my phone. "Let me take a look." I click on the calendar app and scroll through the months. "I think you're in luck. I'm free that weekend."

Before I can set my phone down, Mason lunges for me and towers over my body. "You're quite sassy, you know that? I might have to punish you."

"Oh yeah?" I wiggle beneath him, wrapping my arms around his neck. "What kind of punishment?"

"Mmm…my sweet Sophie." Mason hums in my ear, brushing his nose along my skin. "Always taunting me, aren't you?"

My legs wrap around his waist, arching my hips to feel his erection. Our bodies move together, the friction building between us. "We better move this into the bedroom before Liam catches us," I say, half-laughing, half-moaning when he sucks above my collarbone.

Before we can move, the doorbell rings.

"Motherfucker," Mason hisses, causing me to chuckle. This isn't the first time we've been interrupted by someone at the door. "Ignore it."

Hard pounding on the door comes next. Then another ding.

"For fuck's sake." Mason growls, getting to his feet, then helps me up as I adjust my clothes.

"Might want to…" I point at his sweatpants that don't hide a thing. That earns me a small smirk before he sighs, then leaves to answer the door.

"Father…"

My eyes widen at Mason's booming tone, and I can only imagine the daggers he's throwing right now.

"What do you want?"

"We need to talk. Can I come in?"

Before Mason responds, I hear shoes against the hardwood floor coming my way.

"Oh," he says and freezes the minute he sees me. "Sophie, right?"

"Yes," I say, forcing a smile. "Nice to see you again, Mr. Holt."

"If you hadn't barged inside, I could've told you my girlfriend lives here and that now wasn't a good time."

"Well, perhaps she wouldn't mind giving us some privacy." Mr. Holt shoots his gaze at me, and I'm appalled by his directness. I already had one man push me around and nearly kill me, and I'll be damned if I allow him to control me.

Before Mason can respond, I straighten my spine and give him a straightforward smile. "With all due respect, this is my home too. If you wanted privacy, you should've called Mason ahead of time and let him know you needed to speak with him instead of coming here unannounced. It's rude and inconsiderate." I keep my hands folded in front of me, locking my gaze on him.

"However, if you'd like to speak with him in my presence, feel free. Would you like a cup of coffee?"

I steal a glance at Mason who's standing tall and proud with a wide grin on his handsome face.

Mr. Holt's jaw clenches with frustration as if he's expecting Mason to defend him. When he doesn't, Mr. Holt returns his gaze toward me.

"Sure, cream and sugar."

"Of course. I'll be right back." I walk into the kitchen, my body shaking with the reality that I spoke that way to the district attorney. I don't know where it came from, but enough is enough. He's pushed Mason over and over again and then to come here and act like a total asshole was my limit.

"Have a seat, Dad," Mason says.

I'm purposely taking my time to give them some privacy but I can still hear them. Hopefully, Mr. Holt will quickly say why he's here, then leave. "What do you want?"

"I need a favor," his dad responds with a heavy sigh as if he's not used to asking anyone for help.

"Really? What kind of favor?"

"I'm in a bit of trouble," his dad says, which by his defeated tone, he's nervous to admit.

"Spit it out," Mason demands, and I can tell he's anxious. "What do you need from *me*?"

"I need you to claim to be the father of a woman who's pregnant with my baby."

Everything goes silent as I nearly drop the bottle of creamer I grabbed from the fridge. My heart is pounding so hard, I feel it throbbing in my head. *What did his father just say?*

Mason starts laughing as if he's sure he's heard him wrong too.

"You can't be serious. Do you ever learn your goddamn lesson?"

"This isn't funny," his father snaps. "This involves you more than you realize. If news comes out about the affair, it'll come back to you."

"What the fuck? How? Please enlighten me how your

wandering dick involves me? Or rather, how about you learn to keep it in your pants for once?" Mason's tone is sharp and cruel, and I want to go in there and support him. However, I'm not sure I should be in the same room as Mr. Holt at this point because I might junk punch him myself.

"Don't you talk to me like that, Mason. Remember who pays for this house. Who's paid your tuition. Who's gotten you out of murder charges and from going to prison. Without me, your life would've been fucked up ages ago, son."

"Yeah, and you use every chance to throw it in my face, don't you?" Mason's voice goes up an octave, and I'm scared shit's about to go down if I don't intervene.

"Okay, sorry it took so long…" I say sweetly, carrying a mug, then handing it to Mr. Holt. "Careful, it's hot."

Mason sits on one end of the couch, and Mr. Holt is in the old recliner on the other side. Knowing they were about to rip each other's throats out, I plop down between them.

"He won't have time to drink it because he was just leaving," Mason says between gritted teeth.

"Mason…" his dad pleads, setting down his coffee. "If a scandal breaks out and my character is questioned, they could dig into anything they wanted to prove I'm not suitable to be the DA. All of my cases, *your* cases. Our family. You, your girlfriend, your friends. Is that what you want? After everything you've been through?"

Mason scoffs, crossing his arms over his chest. "You don't know what I've gone through nor have you given two shits about it. You haven't a clue what it's been like, so stop acting like you know."

I don't want to help Mr. Holt any more than Mason does, but if what he's saying is true, and it could affect his previous case or our personal lives, I want to know more.

"What would he have to do?" I blurt, directing my gaze to Mr. Holt. "To prevent the scandal," I clarify. "What would Mason have to do or say?"

"Soph—" Mason starts, but Mr. Holt interrupts.

"Claim that he's the father of the baby and that any rumors of an affair with me are false. State that he was seeing her before you two got serious, and that he's taking on the financial responsibility to raise the child. That way it'll leave me out of it, and no one will go digging, and the baby can still keep the Holt name," he answers as if he rehearsed it.

"You're crazy," Mason huffs. "I'm not putting Sophie through that, and I'm not lying for you. This is too far."

Mr. Holt sits up straighter and swallows. "It's your lawyer," he says, his tone quieter than before.

"What?" I say. At the same time, Mason says, "Excuse me?"

"Serena. She's pregnant."

I gasp, my jaw nearly falling to the floor. I hadn't expected that news in a million years. Mason looks like he's chewing glass, and he has every right to be upset. His friendship with Serena is special, but this is unreal. He looks betrayed.

"Get out," Mason says in a tone that sends shivers down my spine, and not the good kind. "Get the fuck out of my house before I call the cops and have you removed."

Mr. Holt stands, not the least bit shaken by his threat. In fact, he chuckles darkly. "Think about it." Then he buttons his suit jacket and shifts his gaze to me. "Thank you for the coffee, Sophie."

I nod but don't move. I want to slap his shit-eating grin off his face. The woman he knocked up wasn't just a random nameless homewrecker. The person I worried wanted Mason and had the potential to interfere in our relationship is now the woman who could ruin *everything* for him—for us.

Our perfect Saturday together ended the minute Mason's father came knocking. Liam comes stumbling down the stairs in only his boxer briefs, hair sticking straight up, looking all kinds of fucked up. He came home from his work trip late Thursday, slept most of yesterday, and partied last night. Then he stumbled in at six this morning.

"What's with all the yelling?" He raises his arms above his head, stretching as he lazily makes his way to the couch. "You two?"

Liam looks worried, and I quickly shake my head but don't say anything.

"Mason? What is it?"

I look at my boyfriend who hasn't blinked in the past few minutes. His jaw is set tight, and I don't know what to do or say to him. I feel helpless. His father put him in an impossible situation.

"Soph?" Liam turns toward me again. "Who was here?"

Inhaling a deep breath, I release a sigh. "Mr. Holt."

"What was that fucker doing here? Was it about you?" he asks me. "About the Westbrooks?"

I shake my head. "Not directly." I guess it could be if this scandal breaks and people look into the cases he worked on or assisted, inevitably anything to do with me or Mason.

"Serena's pregnant," Mason blurts, grabbing Liam's attention. "With *his* fucking child."

My heart breaks for the man I love so damn much. I see his pain and can feel and hear it in his voice.

"As if my father could infuriate me anymore, he has an affair with the only person I trusted after Emma's death. One of my friends. Someone I lived with and confided in for years." Mason's head falls as he rests his elbows on his knees. "I can't believe she'd do that to me. She knows how much I hate him."

"Holy fuck," Liam says, blinking. "Serena and your dad? There's *no* way."

"According to him, there is…already has," Mason says. "The worst part? You ready for this?" Mason's voice switches to a crazy high-pitched tone. "He wants me to claim it, tell the press it's mine to cover up his goddamn affair."

"Jesus Christ." Liam brushes a hand through his hair, shocked. "And why would he think you'd do that?"

"Oh, he thinks if news gets out, they'll question his character and dig into his history. They'll look for anything suspicious, and once they find it—which if he's so concerned means there is something for them to find—they won't stop. He's suggested it could come back to me, considering he's been a key player in all of my legal cases. I'm being coerced to cover his ass or have my skeletons dragged out of the closet too."

"Can they do that? Can they reopen cases and charge you?" I ask.

"You know he's full of bullshit," Liam says before I get an answer. "They'd have to find something first to give them probable cause to re-investigate everything. He's just trying to rattle you, so you'll do it."

"Well, it's fucking working. This is the last thing we need right now. Not to mention, it's not fair to Sophie. Lying for my father… it makes me fucking sick to even think about."

"Mason…" I move closer and wrap my arm around him. He's so worked up, he's shaking. "I'm not leaving. You have me by your side no matter what, okay?" I lean my head on his shoulder, but a second later, he pulls me into his chest and hugs me.

Liam stands in front of us and cracks his knuckles. "Want me to rough him up a bit? Tell him he made his bed and now he can lie in it?" He flashes a knowing grin, but I roll my eyes at his awful timing of a joke.

"What I really want is to hear it from Serena. She owes me an explanation," Mason says. "Because until then, I won't believe it."

CHAPTER FORTY-SIX

MASON

I HIT send and hold my breath when the jumping dots appear on the screen. Then they disappear.

I toss my phone, shaking my head, not wanting to believe it. Being betrayed by my father is nothing new, but Serena? She was the closest thing I had to a sister. Now I don't know what to think. My dad's a sleazeball, and he'll never change. How the hell did Serena end up with him?

Deciding I need to blow off steam, I pack my workout bag and head to the gym. Tyler isn't there to box with me, so I work solo with a punching bag until my hands are sore and sweat drips into my eyes. The pain feels good, and it helps clear my head as usual, but the frustration returns once I'm home, and the memory of my father telling me the news returns.

After I shower and hide in my room for a half hour, I hear a knock on my bedroom door, and Liam slowly opens it, giving me a pitiful look. Sophie knew I needed some time and left me to wallow alone. She wants to be here for me but didn't push when I insisted I needed a minute to think this through.

"You've got a visitor," he finally says.

I furrow my brows, not in the mood to talk to anyone. "Who is it?"

Liam glances at the floor, then at me. "Serena. She looks like shit. Like she's been crying."

I groan, letting my head fall back. "Fuck." Brushing a hand through my hair, I push myself up and follow him down the hall. When I get to the bottom of the stairs, I frown when I notice how distraught she is.

"Can we talk? Please?" she asks when I stand in front of her. I look over my shoulder at Sophie who's sitting on the couch with a book. She meets my gaze and gives me a small smile and nods.

"Yeah, let's go in the back room." I lead her through the living room and kitchen until we're there. The pool table sits in the middle, and it's been untouched for weeks. "Want a drink?" I ask as she takes a seat on one of the chairs against the wall. "Of water," I add.

"No, I'm okay. Thanks, though." She wipes away the tears on her cheeks. "I'm sorry to show up like this, but I didn't want to talk over text. You deserve an explanation face to face."

I sit across from her, leaning back with my arms crossed. "I agree."

Serena inhales a sharp breath. "I tried telling you so many times but kept chickening out. It's why I was coming around more. The guilt of what I did was eating at me, but every time I told myself I needed to rip off the Band-Aid, I got scared of losing you."

"You should've told me," I snap. "A lot fucking sooner than this."

"I know." Her face falls into her hands before she looks up again. "I caused so much shit between you and Sophie when I should've been up front, but like I said, I was scared to lose you as a friend and also worried after everything you two had been through."

"I could've handled hearing it from you, Serena. But having to hear it from the man I hate was a real low blow."

Serena nods, wiping her cheeks. "We weren't like hooking up regularly or anything, in case you wondered. It only happened twice. Not that it matters at this point, but I don't want you thinking I was sneaking around and lying to you."

"So how'd it happen? You being with my dad alone?" I ask, not wanting the gross details, but I need something to help ease this frustration that weighs heavy on my chest.

"He asked to meet with me a few weeks after your plea hearing, and so I did, thinking it was about your case. I mean, it started that way. We discussed the Westbrooks, and he didn't think you were out of the woods yet, then asked me to keep an eye on you. Then he started asking me questions about us, like if we were dating. When I explained our friendship, something shifted. We started drinking, mostly because I was nervous around him. He's the DA, and the last thing I wanted was to make a bad impression because I'm your lawyer. After shit went down with Emma, I wasn't sure how he'd treat me. Then as the conversation moved to things more personal, I let my inhibitions go and allowed the alcohol to direct my actions. It's not an excuse, and you have every right to be pissed or hell, hate me, because I hate myself a little right now too."

"So you got drunk and slept together? That's what happened?"

"The first time, yes. It was reckless, and I should've known better. The second time was the night Sophie and I had that fight, and I left here upset. I ended up at the bar and stupidly drunk texted him. I don't know what I was thinking, and that's a shit excuse, but he picked me up, and we hooked up again. I regretted it the moment it happened. Last week, I realized I was late, and that's when I took a pregnancy test. He didn't take the news very well, as you can imagine." Her bloodshot eyes lower. She's been crying a lot.

"What'd he do when you told him?" I ask harshly. My father isn't a sensitive man, so I doubt he was kind.

"Told me he wanted to pay for an abortion. When I told him I didn't want that, he threatened my career. When I still didn't fold to his demands, he said he was gonna make a deal so no one found out."

"Did he explain what the *deal* was?" I ask.

"Only a few hours ago. He called and said that you offered to take responsibility and that from now on, I was to have no contact with him until a paternity test could be done. He said if it was confirmed, he'd pay financially but that was it."

"Such a fucking asshole," I growl. "He marched in here, throwing around threats for me to clean up his mess. I told him to fuck right off."

"Mason, I'm so sorry," Serena says between sobs. "I don't know why he thinks he has to involve you. I'm not gonna tell the media he's the father anyway."

"This is his way of covering his tracks in case you decide to blast him anytime in the future. His whole job is doing damage control for all his shady practices. Perhaps you should sell your story. Someone needs to burst his image bubble." I huff.

"That puts you at risk, Mason. I'd never do that to you."

I shrug. "He can't be sure of the outcome, so he's throwing out theories. Even if one of my cases gets reopened, I have the best lawyer in the state to help me fight it." I wink, and she smiles for the first time since she got here.

"Mason, are you sure? You tell your dad no, and he's gonna lose his shit."

"He's tried to control me my whole life. I'm not about to let him start now. He can walk around looking over his shoulder for once, waiting to see if you blow his cover."

"I'm not gonna say anything, but it'd be nice to have the upper hand by letting him think I could." She smirks, which makes me grin.

"Thatta girl. Don't let him be a douchebag to you. Make him pay child support and anything else you need, and don't allow him to get away with this. If he didn't want to jeopardize his name, then he should've thought about that years ago."

"Thank you," she says softly. "I've been sick over this and how to tell you. You're one of my best friends, and I royally fucked up."

I stand with a smirk, and I pull her into a hug. "Come here."

Serena wraps her arms around my waist, and I hold her tight against me.

"You know the baby is gonna technically be my sister or brother."

She giggles. "I know. Weird, right?"

I pull back, laughing. "Very."

We stroll into the living room, and Sophie quickly sets her book down. "Hey. Everything okay?"

"Yeah, it will be," I tell her, glancing at Serena. "My father's a fuckwad, but that's nothing new."

"Serena, I want to say how sorry I am for the way I acted the last time you were here. I never should've—"

"No, you have nothing to apologize for," Serena cuts her off. "You're protective of your relationship with Mason, which confirms how much you love him. No need to be sorry for that." Serena smiles. "I *really* am happy you two are together."

"Thank you," Sophie says. "Congrats on the baby, even if the circumstances aren't what you expected."

Serena wipes away her tears. "Thanks. I'm excited to be a mom and have a baby. Even if I have to do it alone."

"You won't be alone," I immediately tell her. "You know I'm not going anywhere."

"My sister Lennon is pregnant with her second, and I'm sure she can give you mom tips. You two would get along."

"You're both more than I deserve." Serena gives Sophie a hug, then me. "I'll keep you updated. I have my first appointment next week."

"You have everything packed?" I ask Sophie the morning after Thanksgiving.

It's been three weeks since I learned about Serena and my dad. After telling him to kiss my ass and that neither me nor Serena were going to lie on his behalf, he basically told me to "prepare" for the worst. Then I told him to fuck off and blocked his number.

He should be kissing *my* ass, considering I could tell his wife, and she could do whatever she wants with the information. But knowing Hallie, she won't do anything. She loves her luxurious lifestyle too much to rock the boat. On top of that, it'd be my little sister Michaela paying the price, and I don't want her involved in any of his scandals either. She's only five, and even if our father's a piece of shit, he spends time with her and gives her anything she wants. I'd rather she have some kind of father figure than be left with nothing.

"Just about ready!" she calls out.

When I walk into her room and lean against the doorframe, I smirk at the mess on her bed. "What're you doing?" I ask with a chuckle. It doesn't look like she's started.

"Wondering if I have room for one more book…" She digs through three large books and hums.

"You plan to read on this date?" I tease, walking in and spinning her around. "Because I'm thinking you're gonna be a little too busy."

Sophie wraps her arms around my neck and pulls me in for a kiss. "Haven't you learned by now that I'm quite good at multitasking?"

"You think that's funny, but…"

She cuts me off with another kiss.

"It's funny because it's true. Plus, I don't know where we're going, so maybe I can read in the car. I don't know what type of clothes to pack." She turns toward the empty suitcase. "Sweater weather?"

I tighten my grip on her stomach as my chest presses against her back. "You're gonna be naked, so you don't need clothes."

She smirks over her shoulder. "Well, I'm not gonna go out to eat naked, so tell me what to bring."

It's in the sixties this time of year, so I tell her to take some sweaters and mostly comfortable clothes. That seems to be helpful enough for her to grab things out of her closet.

An hour later, we're zipping our suitcases, and once I finish loading up my truck, I walk inside to grab my wallet and phone. "I better not come back to a trashed house," I warn Liam who's sitting on the couch eating a huge bowl of cereal. He's practically naked and already acting like we aren't home.

He snickers. "I'll have my dates clean it up. Don't worry."

"Don't burn the house down," Sophie adds. "Towels don't belong on the stovetop."

"That was one time!" Liam defends, but neither of us laughs at his stupidity from a couple of weeks ago.

"We're coming home to ashes, aren't we?" Sophie deadpans.

"You two act like I've never been home alone before…" Liam finally glances at us over the couch. "If I promise not to cook, will you two finally leave?"

Sophie laughs, then leans down to give him a hug. "Be good, Hulk. Stay out of my room."

"Mine too," I add for fun.

"Yeah, yeah. Go have a *banging* weekend. Ha! Get it?" Liam laughs at his own joke while Sophie rolls her eyes.

"So what're you gonna do for the next few days?" Sophie asks.

At first, she felt bad leaving him behind on a holiday weekend, but I doubt it's going to be a hardship for him, considering how much he travels alone. He's used to it and probably prefers it.

"Eat chocolate and watch porn," Liam answers without a beat.

"And that's our cue to go."

"What? There are some good videos on there!" Liam calls over his shoulder as we make a beeline for the door.

"Sadly, he's not joking," I mock with a laugh.

"Bye, Liam!" Sophie calls out before we shut the door and walk to the truck.

I open her door and kiss her before she gets inside. I can't wait to surprise her. This date has been months in the making, and there have been some holdups, but it's finally happening. If all goes right, it's going to be the most magical weekend of her life.

Over two hours later, we arrive at Tahoe City, and the look on Sophie's face is worth every moment of planning it took. "Oh my God. It's beautiful here!"

I booked three nights at a lodge resort where we'll be able to do some hiking, eat at a romantic restaurant overlooking the water and mountains, and enjoy the cozy fireplace inside our suite. I have a couple's massage schedule for tomorrow, and then we'll go on an afternoon boat ride.

"Have you been here before?" I ask, taking our locked hands and kissing her knuckles.

"No," she answers with a smile.

"Good. I wanted to take you somewhere super special for our first date." I wink, then cup her face and slant my mouth over hers.

"I have a feeling it's gonna be the best first date I've ever had."

"Well, I hope it's your last first date." I smirk and waggle my brows at her.

Sophie blushes, then grins. "Maybe, if you play your cards right."

Chuckling, I bring her lips back to mine. "That sweet mouth is sassy."

Once I grab our luggage and we check in, we're led to a large suite. As soon as we enter, Sophie gasps. "It's beautiful! Oh my God, it's perfect!" I look around and see the large bouquet of roses I requested, then drop our suitcases. "You did good, Mason Holt."

She launches herself into my arms. I catch her and hold her to my chest, inhaling the sweet scent of her strawberry shampoo. "I want everything to be perfect for you," I tell her. "You deserve it, baby."

"It's been one hell of a year, hasn't it?" she asks earnestly.

"Simultaneously the worst and best," I tell her honestly. "The worst was thinking I'd lost you. But the best was how it brought us together, and even after the challenges that tried to push us apart, we only grew stronger together."

Sophie looks up with tears in her eyes. "I couldn't agree more."

I cup her beautiful face and press a soft kiss to her mouth before sliding my tongue between her lips and taking more of her. She melts into my chest, and soon, we're a tangled mess of limbs falling on the bed.

"Just so you know, I don't usually have sex on the first date," I tell her when I lay between her legs, kissing down her jaw.

"I think you lost your right to say that when you pulled me into a bar bathroom," she retorts, and I chuckle against her neck.

"Aren't you the one who said it'd take more than one drink to seduce you?" I taunt. "Pretty sure you were flirting with me."

"You bought my drink without asking!" she fires back. "Just assumed I'd want you to buy me a drink."

I lift up and look into her gorgeous brown eyes. "I didn't hear any complaining." I smirk, arching a brow because I know I have her there. "In fact, I remember a lot of moaning…"

"Okay, smart-ass," she says, laughing. "We'll call that our prequel date."

The corner of my lips tilts up. "Prequel to what?"

"To a wild, exciting, sometimes scary ride. I don't regret a thing, though. Not when it brought us here, to this very moment."

"I like to think we would've eventually found our way to one another. Maybe."

Sophie's brows shoot up, clearly not agreeing with me. "Oh really? If I recall, you were hell-bent on pretending I didn't exist. Took three years to get that fire burning under your ass."

My head falls as I laugh in defeat. "Hey, I had my reasons."

"I know, babe. We weren't ready back then, but nothing could tear us apart now. I think we've proven that time and time again this year."

Brushing a strand of her hair behind her ear, I smile at the woman I love more than my own life. She's talented, sweet, and so damn caring. She doesn't have a mean bone in her body, and my world starts and ends with her.

"I love you, Sophie." Cupping her face, I kiss her. "I never thought I'd be ready to say that again after Emma, but with you, saying it to you for the first time was effortless. So many crazy circumstances may have brought us together, but my life is a million times better with you in it."

"Thank you." Sophie brings our mouths together for a searing hot kiss, wrapping her legs around my waist and arching her hips to create friction against my erection.

"For what?" I ask softly.

"For loving me the way you do." *A kiss to my cheek.* "For not being afraid to love again." *A kiss to my other cheek.* "For telling me how much I mean to you." *A kiss to my nose.* "For not giving up on us when I needed time." *A kiss to my forehead.* "And lastly, for loving me for who I am. I know I come with a lot of baggage at times, and I've gotten us into bad situations, but you were always there to save me. I don't know many men who would've stuck around after all that." *A kiss to my lips.*

I hold her mouth captive, not letting her go. It grows desperate, heated, and eager. Sophie is my everything, and not one bone in my body doubts that we belong together.

"Soph..." I moan against her swollen lips. She's rubbing her hot body against mine, my dick hard and threatening to burst out of my jeans. But this can't wait. Not anymore.

She smiles. "Hmm?"

"Will you marry me?"

CHAPTER FORTY-SEVEN

MY HEART LAUNCHES into my throat, choking me as I try to suck in air.

Oxygen. I need oxygen.

As I try to breathe, my eyes flutter, wondering if I heard Mason right. We were making out, about to tear each other's clothes off, and then he dropped a bomb.

Will you marry me?

I finally clear my throat and look up at him. He's staring at me, waiting for a response as if he didn't drop a bombshell of a question.

"What did you say?" I whisper, the beating in my chest echoing loudly in my ears.

Mason shifts off me and kneels on the bed, then grabs my hand and helps me upright. Face to face, he looks at me with a beaming smile and sparkling eyes. He takes both my hands in his and gently holds them. "I had planned on waiting until our final day here, but it feels like the perfect time to ask you right now. So without letting this moment go by…" Mason slides off the bed, reaches into one of his bags, then returns with a black velvet box.

I gasp, my throat too dry to form words. He smirks, grabs my hand, and helps me stand, then he drops to one knee in front of me. "Oh my God," I whisper, my free hand trembling as it covers my mouth.

"My sweet Sophie…" He squeezes my left hand, then presses a soft kiss to my knuckles. "I wouldn't be the man I am today without you, and I want to be the very best man for you, always. I love you more than words can express, and if you'd allow me to, I promise to spend the rest of my life showing you how much you mean to me. Would you do me the honor of becoming my wife and marrying me?"

Tears fall down my cheeks before I have time to catch them. I can't believe this is happening. The man I love more than anything is asking me to marry him, and I'm speechless.

Finally, I find my voice as I frantically nod. "Yes! Yes, of course!"

"Yes?" he repeats with a wide grin.

"Yes!" I fall into him, wrapping my arms around his neck and holding tight. My entire body shakes as tears take over my vision, and Mason stands with me in his grip.

Once we're both on our feet, he pulls back slightly and brushes his thumbs under my eyes. "You really said yes?"

Chuckling through my emotions, I nod again. "I did!" When I finally get them in check, I clear my throat and wipe my face. "I'm just so shocked."

"I can tell," he says, smirking. "Do you want to see the ring?"

"Oh my God, I forgot to look!" I laugh. "Yes, show me!"

Mason grabs the box that fell to the floor, then opens and reveals the most stunning diamond I've ever seen.

"Wow, it's gorgeous." My jaw drops as he slides it onto my finger. A perfect fit. "I can't believe you picked this out."

He shrugs. "Well, Maddie helped."

"Maddie knows?"

"Actually, no. I didn't tell anyone except Liam. However, Maddie has not-so-subtly been sending me pictures of engagement rings for the past three months," he explains, and I laugh. That little shit.

"Subtle isn't in her vocabulary." I snort.

"I wouldn't say so, but it was actually helpful. She would send them randomly and tell me that she thought you'd like this one. Then she'd find another and would say if my budget allowed it, to get it instead."

"I hope you weren't thinking I was putting her up to that because I had no idea!"

"Oh, no. Maddie has a mind of her own."

"That she does. In fact, we should probably be prepared for her to send baby and parenting magazines to the house now."

"And then I'll slip them into Liam's room."

I burst out laughing. "That'd give him nightmares."

"I know." Mason smirks, knowing damn well about Liam's lack of commitment.

Staring at my finger, I twirl the ring around, and it feels so foreign being there. "You know what this means now, don't you?"

I look up at him, biting my lip. He furrows his brows.

"You're gonna have to meet my parents. My father isn't gonna like that you didn't ask his permission first."

"I was afraid of that…" He chuckles. "But hopefully, he'll understand since we live in different states and haven't met."

"Well, he forgave Hunter for lying about being married to Lennon, so I'm sure you'll be fine," I taunt. "Though, he did swoop in and care for the baby too…"

"Shit. He had brownie points to start. Wouldn't saving their daughter's life give me something?" His brows crease as if he's thinking hard about this, which makes me smile.

"Oh, it definitely does." I wink, pulling him closer. "It gives you *all* the brownie points."

Mason wraps his arms around me, and we fall to the bed. We strip off each other's clothes, and soon he's inside me, stealing my breath, panting as our bodies collide together.

"Fuck, baby. You feel so good. *We* feel so good," he mutters into my neck.

I arch my back, meeting him thrust for thrust. My heart is so full right now, and all I want to do is feel every inch of him and give him every inch of me. "Oh my God…" I moan as my head falls to the side. My heels dig into his ass, pushing him closer into me, and when he hits the right spot, I cry out his name.

Mason flips us around until I'm on top and straddling his waist. He palms my breasts and jerks his hips up into me. "Ride my cock, sweet girl. I want to see all of you."

Biting down on my lower lip, I flatten my hands on his chest and rock against him. I love watching his facial expressions when I'm on top, knowing I'm giving him as much pleasure as he gives me.

"Fuck yes, baby. Just like that." He grips my hips, moving my body faster. His thumb finds my clit, and when he rubs hard and faster, I come undone, arching back until I surface again. "Jesus," he hisses. "That was so goddamn hot."

Blushing at his words, I lean on top of him and devour his lips. With my forehead pressed against his, I increase my pace, knowing he's close. "Yes, right there, babe. Don't stop," I encourage him when he slams into me, our bodies slapping together loudly. Moments later, he stalls, digging his fingertips into my skin and groaning out his release. I love watching him, the way the veins in his neck pop, and how tense his body goes.

"Christ, sweetheart." Mason breathes out, his arms going limp next to him. Then he brings a hand up to my face and rubs his thumb along my cheek. "I fucking love you so much."

I shift and slide off him, falling into his arms as we lie side by side. "I love you, Mason. I can't believe we're getting married!" I squeal because I'm still in shock.

"I can't wait, baby. You're gonna be the future Mrs. Holt. Damn, that sounds hot."

"Sophie Holt." I test it out. "Mr. and Mrs. Mason Holt." I grin. "Mrs. Mason Holt."

Mason chuckles as I practice out loud. "Better stop that. You're getting my dick hard again."

I snicker, snuggling into his side and wrapping my arm over his chest. "So…do you propose on all your first dates?"

He shakes his head, laughing. "Only on my very last first date."

Three days fly by way too quickly. Every moment we spent at the resort was perfect. From the fancy dining and boat rides to the hiking and the midnight room service, it felt like a honeymoon before the wedding. In fact, I suggested that we get married there.

Knowing Hunter and Lennon are getting hitched after the baby is born means we'll hold off on making any plans for a while. Plus, it gives me more time to break the news to my parents. We want to enjoy being together and not rush this. Everything is perfect as is but knowing we're building a future together makes me the happiest woman in the world right now.

"So you think the house is still standing?" I tease as Mason takes the final exit off the highway before we get to our street.

"Well, he didn't leave any frantic voicemails, so I'm thinking it's safe."

"Think my sisters will be surprised to hear the news? I can't wait to tell them!" I gush, smiling thinking about it. They're going to lose their minds.

"I think they'll be surprised but not shocked. They know we're meant to be." Mason smirks, still capable of sending butterflies to my stomach by just looking at me. I'm so damn happy, my heart is going to burst out of my chest.

Mason parks in the driveway, and we both grab our luggage from the trunk. "Let me grab them for you, *fiancée*."

"Ooh, that sounds weird." I giggle. "Fiancé." I try it out. "I suppose I could get used to it, though."

When I hand him my bag, he leans down and gives me a quick kiss. "Broke all kinds of first date rules for you."

"Don't tell me you get married on the second date…" I tease, shutting the door.

His smirk deepens. "Don't tempt me, sweetheart. We'll get a marriage license and call Aunt Sylvia right now."

My eyes widen, and he chuckles. Before I can respond, Maddie flies out the front door with her arms open as she races toward me.

What the hell?

"Ahhh! Lemme see! Lemme see!" She's screaming, and I have no idea why.

"What?"

Maddie nearly tackles me to the ground, but Mason catches me before I can fall. "The ring! Let me see!" she says between catching her breath. When I furrow my brows at her, she continues, "Oh my God. You said yes, right? Shit, did Mason chicken out?"

"How did you know about the ring?" I ask, then glance over my shoulder at Mason. "I thought you said you only told Liam?"

"Yeah, and Liam told me," Maddie explains.

Mason growls, shaking his head.

"Okay, well, to be fair, I made him tell me," she adds, which makes me laugh. I don't doubt for a second that Maddie could squeeze information out of Liam or anyone, for that matter.

"And why are you here?" Mason asks as we all walk into the house. That's the question of the hour every time she's over, which causes me to laugh.

"Well…there was a fire on campus and—"

"What?" I squeal, interrupting her. "Did your apartment burn down?"

"No, thankfully. The one next to us, however…anyway, they evacuated us because of smoke damage. I packed all my shit and called Liam."

I smack her shoulder. "Why didn't you call me? I'm your sister!"

We all walk into the living room where Liam is lounging in the recliner with a beer. Mason sets our luggage down and scowls at him. Liam responds with a grin.

"Liam texted me before you guys left and told me I wasn't to bother you! He said it was your *special* weekend, and if I needed anything, he was on call. Of course, that sounded fishy as hell coming from Hulk, so when I did ask him to come get me, I bugged him enough until he finally told me and said I wasn't allowed to reach out to you."

"Way to play it cool, man," Mason teases.

"Well, I didn't expect her to actually need something! Go figure the one weekend you guys leave, she gets evicted."

"I was not evicted!" Maddie defends. "Anyway, I'm not sure when they're gonna allow us back inside. It's pretty bad, though."

"Don't worry, you can stay here as long as you need," I tell her, knowing Mason would agree with me. Whether or not Liam does is up for debate.

"Well, I'm glad because I have nowhere else to go, and I've been sleeping in your room. Also, I'm broke as fuck so…" She shrugs as if it's nothing new. "Now." She grabs my hand. "Let me see this rock."

"Isn't it stunning?" I beam proudly at my fiancé.

"Yeah, it's perfect." Maddie gives Mason a knowing grin. "Wonder how he knew what you liked?"

"No clue," Mason intervenes. "Guess I'm just that good."

"Oh, don't even play!" Maddie pushes a finger into his chest. "You're welcome."

"Pfft. I would've figured it out, ya know?"

"Mmhmm, sure." Maddie snickers. "Aren't you so excited to have me as a sister now?"

"Yeah, I didn't quite think this through…" Mason makes a face and scratches the back of his head. "Might need to reconsider that proposal, Soph…" he taunts with a smirk. "Two Corrigan sisters."

"Just tell them both that you're their favorite and they'll leave you alone."

"I'm gonna unpack and do laundry since I have to be back at work tomorrow," Mason tells me, then presses a kiss to my forehead. "Guess you're sleeping with me tonight." He waggles his brows as he walks backward toward the stairs.

"Oh hell, I'm gonna need earplugs, aren't I?" Maddie groans, crossing her arms.

"I have an extra pair," Liam chimes in. "Bought them in case."

"Oh my God, you guys act like we're shooting an adult film or something." I shake my head at them. "And you should talk, Liam!" I take a throw pillow off the couch and chuck it at him. "If I'm greeted by your morning wood one more time, I'm buying you a robe!"

"I'm not sure if coming here was a good thing or not…" Maddie grimaces. "You guys fight like siblings."

"This is how they show love," Mason teases before making his way upstairs.

"So did you tell Lennon about the proposal?" Maddie asks as she follows me into my room. I need to unpack and do laundry too, which means I have to beat Mason to the washer. I chuckle to myself, knowing he'd let me have it first anyway if I asked.

"Not yet."

"How do you think Mom and Dad will react?" Maddie sits on the bed, making herself at home. "You two are making it hard for me. By the time I have a baby or get married, they're gonna be expecting the worst."

Laughing, I shrug. "Perks of being the little sister."

"They're not perks! But maybe that means they won't give me any shit for anything I do. You two will have worn them down by then."

"See? There ya go. You're welcome." Once my suitcase is emptied, I take my hamper to the laundry room and put in a load. "I think after Lennon put them in their place, they've toned down a bit. Mason and I living together won't be such a shock," I tell her once I'm back in my room. "It's the being engaged before they met Mason that might hurt them. But it's not like it's on purpose. We don't live in Utah, so it makes it harder to introduce them to the guys we're dating."

"Well, and if you factor in the first time you guys hooked up, you've been dating for over three years."

"Ha-ha, funny. I'm not gonna tell them that, and neither are you." I point my finger at her. "They know our story, and once they do get to meet him, I have no doubt they'll love him."

"They totally will," she reassures me. "I'm so excited for you guys. You two deserve it so much."

Maddie stands and gives me a hug. "Thank you. I'm still in shock, I think. But it was awesome to spend the weekend together with just the two of us, so…thanks for not calling." I burst out laughing when she scowls at me. "Oh, I bet you loved being here alone with Liam anyway."

"It hasn't been so bad, I guess. I mean, it's only been two days, and he sleeps till noon."

I nod. "Yeah, he does that when he's between bounties because he doesn't sleep that well on the road. He stays up for long hours at a time, plus hotel beds suck."

"It was nice to hang out. I'm gonna wear him down eventually."

Smiling at her determination, I wrap my arm around her shoulder and squeeze. "I have no doubt that you will."

EPILOGUE

MASON

SIX MONTHS LATER

"Mmm…you're so warm," Sophie murmurs against my chest, which causes me to laugh, considering California has hot as fuck summers and it's the middle of June. "Ignore the alarm and stay in bed."

I silence my phone and wrap my arms around her. "Wish we could, baby." I drag my nose along the planes of her face until I find her lips. "Let's go take a shower together. Then we'll have twice as long."

Sophie wraps her leg over my hip and pushes my erection against her pussy. She hums with a smile, keeping her eyes closed. "Soph…" I warn, watching as she bites her lip.

Since Maddie moved in after Thanksgiving, Sophie's been in my bed every night, and it's exactly how I want it. My future wife should only ever be in my bed.

Although the students in Maddie's apartment got relocated to another building while they remodeled, Sophie liked spending more time with her, so she asked her to stay through the summer. At this point, I wouldn't be surprised if Maddie moves in, considering the room is available anyway. She has one more year of school before she graduates, but when Sophie and I get married, we'll find a place of our own.

Sophie reaches down between us and strokes my cock. My head falls back as she increases her pace and pushes my shorts down.

"Baby," I mutter, but it's useless. I'm a fucking goner for her.

She's not wearing bottoms, so when she presses the tip of my dick to her entrance, it doesn't take much for her to slide her panties to the side and then arches her body into mine. Surrendering, I grip her hip and push inside. Sophie moans, and I pull out before sliding back, harder.

"Fuck," I hiss with our foreheads touching and our breaths mingling. Grabbing her thigh, I raise it higher and go deeper. "You're gonna have to come fast, sweetheart."

We're supposed to be getting ready to go to Hunter and Lennon's housewarming party in an hour, and I could make love to Sophie all day.

"Mmm, yes…right there. Don't stop." She moans loudly, and I kiss down her jaw, then suck on her neck as I thrust harder. Sophie plays with her clit, and I know the sensitive part behind her ear sets her off every time.

"Come on my cock, Soph," I whisper-growl, then press my mouth to her sweet spot.

Her body shakes as she gets closer. We've become experts at morning quickies, considering my long work hours and her rehearsals don't always allow us a lot of time at night. I've been in my position for less than a year, which means I'm still working on-call shifts.

"So close," she whimpers, then wraps a hand around my neck. Seconds later, she screams my name as her pussy squeezes my cock.

"Christ, babe." I pant, my release following hers moments after.

We lie together in silence as we catch our breaths. "We're gonna be late," she finally says, chuckling. "Maddie's probably already waiting for us."

"Then I guess we better shower together after all." I lower my hand and smack her ass. Sophie squeals and laughs as I scoop her out of bed and walk us into the bathroom. "Not gonna be a good impression for your parents if we show up late as fuck."

Considering I've cut my father out of my life for good, her parents liking me and approving of our relationship is important to both of us.

After Serena came clean about everything, she kept her word about not going public with the affair, but to keep my father on his toes, she reminds him she can and will if he doesn't keep up with his financial responsibilities. She's seven months pregnant, and even if my father doesn't want to be involved in my little brother's life, I have been and plan to always be. Serena is one of the strongest women I know, and she'll get through this either way. Though I do hope someday she meets a nice guy who can love her and her son.

Once Sophie and I have showered and finished getting ready, we're only a few minutes late to the party. We're greeted by Hunter and their three-month old, Aaron, who was born in March.

After the baby was born, they finally got married in May in an intimate ceremony in Utah, where I met Mr. and Mrs. Corrigan for the first time. They didn't hate me, so that was a plus, but today will only be the second time I've been around them, and it makes me nervous. Although I don't need it, I want their approval for Sophie's sake. When Sophie announced we were engaged, they were speechless—literally.

Shortly after the wedding, Hunter and Lennon bought a house outside of Sacramento, and since their parents are visiting for a couple of weeks, they decided to throw a party for everyone. Sophie thinks the party is to keep their mom and dad occupied so Lennon and Hunter can have a break from entertaining them.

"Hey, guys. Come in." Hunter moves to the side and frowns when Maddie steals Aaron from him.

"It turned out to be a beautiful day for a barbecue," Sophie says, giving Hunter a side hug. We've been to their house several times before they bought it, but Lennon's gone crazy decorating it for the event. "Ooh, I love what she did with this foyer."

"Yeah? It cost a thousand bucks, so just a warning, these Corrigans are expensive," Hunter says, giving me a pointed look.

Sophie nudges him. "It's your home. It's supposed to be nice!"

"Let me guess, Hunter's complaining about how much money we spent?" Lennon walks toward us with a shit-eating grin. She scowls at Hunter, which is hilarious, considering they still act like they're in the never-ending honeymoon phase. In fact, I wouldn't be surprised if Lennon was pregnant again.

"I'd never, babe," Hunter says before either of us can respond. "I love what you did." He cups her face and silences her with a kiss.

She pulls back, laughing. "I might have mom brain, but I'm not that dense." Lennon rolls her eyes. Sophie and Maddie snicker while I give Hunter a shoulder smack of support. "So where's the Hulk? He bail on us?" Lennon asks, crossing her arms.

"No, his flight got delayed. He said he's coming right from the airport, though," I tell her. Once I checked my phone after our shower, I got his message about it.

"Well, come in and say hi to Mom and Dad. They're playing with Allie outside on her new swing set," Lennon says as she leads us into the kitchen.

"A new swing set?" Maddie squeals. "Is there a baby swing for Aaron?"

"Of course!" Lennon answers.

Sophie gives me a kiss before following Lennon and Maddie out the back door.

"Homeownership looks nice on you," I tease Hunter after he hands me a beer. "Husband, dad, homeowner. Who knew?"

"I knew," he states proudly. He was so in love with Lennon long before they were together.

"So, Liam's flight really got delayed?" he asks, searching my face. "Or did he get *held up* again?"

SOPHIE

Lennon, Maddie, and I talk with my parents and play with the kids outside while Mason and Hunter chat inside. The food is all ready to go, but they're waiting until more people show up. Liam could arrive at any time, so we've learned not to wait for him anymore. He doesn't usually mind either since he gets *held up* a lot.

When my parents follow Allie to the teeter-totter, I stand next to Maddie who's pushing Aaron in the infant swing. It's not a regular baby swing, so he's able to lie down and not have to worry about his head falling back.

"So any idea where Liam is?" I whisper loud enough so only she can hear me. "Have you talked to him since he left?"

Liam flew out on Thursday and was supposed to be back early this morning. He said it was a quick two-day job max, but he's been acting very strange lately. I found that casino receipt in his pants pocket six months ago, and when I asked him about it, he brushed me off and said he stopped for a quick trip on his way to a job. However, I could tell he was lying, and I've been suspicious ever since, especially when I overheard him telling Mason he would be late with his portion of the rent a couple of months ago. Either he's not making as much money as he lets on, or he's gambling it all away. Whatever it is, I'm worried as hell about him.

"He told me he had to pick up a fugitive in Nevada," she says. "We talked the morning he left, but that's the last time. Why?"

I snicker, knowing she has no idea that I saw them that morning.

"What?" she asks.

"So you're saying you haven't spoken to him since before he left?"

"That's right."

I purse my lips, wondering if she's going to tell me or not. When she doesn't continue the conversation, I figure she's not, and since he's coming home today, we need to have this conversation now.

"So…was your make-out session the first time you two locked lips, or have you two been sneaking around for a while?" I blurt quietly, and her eyes immediately widen in shock. "Yeah, I saw you two."

She tries holding back a smile, but I notice it. Maddie blushes too, which is ironic because she never gets embarrassed.

"I never kiss and tell," she taunts, which is a lie, considering how much she talks about selling off her virginity. "And no, I don't know what it means. He said we'd talk about it once he got back."

I squeeze her arm, wanting to squeal out to the gods that my little sister actually kissed Liam. A guy she's been not-so-subtly chasing for years. "How could you keep that from me?"

"I'm not foolish enough to think it changes anything," she says with a shrug as she continues pushing Aaron who fell asleep. "Liam's a player, and I finally broke through his hard shell, but that doesn't mean he wants to settle down with me."

"So Thursday morning was a goodbye kiss before he left?" I push, wanting more juicy details.

"I was grabbing food from the fridge to make breakfast, and he said he had to leave so he wouldn't miss his flight. I was giving him the cold shoulder. I don't want to get my heart broken, so I figured if I act like I don't care, then I can't get hurt."

My chest aches, seeing her this vulnerable, which isn't common for her. Maddie's a tough girl, always sarcastic and blunt, but deep inside, she's a marshmallow.

"I walked around him in the kitchen to grab a pan, and then he just grabbed my arm and spun me around. He pulled me into his chest and kissed me. Like *really* kissed me. Then he said we'll talk when he gets back, and that's the last I heard from him."

"*Oh my God, oh my God!*" I whisper-squeal, which makes Maddie laugh. "Well, from what I saw, it was *very* hot."

"You're a little creeper, aren't you?" She takes Aaron out of the swing and holds the sleeping baby to her chest. "I better get him into his rocker so he can nap."

"You guys ready to eat?" Hunter calls from the patio door. Everyone walks into the kitchen and starts piling food on their plates.

Mason and I sit with my parents to give us more time together, and although we didn't do things in the order they prefer, they've accepted us and like Mason a lot. It helps that Hunter and Mason are friends because they cherish Hunter so much, and he's told my parents what a good guy Mason is. They know Mason protected me from Weston and Dalton, and for that, they're very grateful.

As I sit next to my future husband and listen to him talk to my dad about sports, I can't help the cheesy smile on my face. I love watching the two most important men in my life get along and laugh together. I'm so madly in love with Mason and can't wait for us to get married and buy a house someday soon.

"So are you gonna get married in Utah, too?" my mother asks.

I look at Mason. "Uh, we're not quite sure yet." He grabs my hand and squeezes. "We're happy right now, and we'll make plans when the time is right," I tell them. Between our work schedules, it'll be hard to plan a wedding. I'd love a Christmas-themed wedding in the mountains, but I don't tell them that. The moment I give Mom any information, she'll continue to pry and push.

"Madelyn," my mom says, grabbing her attention. "Have you thought about what you're doing after graduation?"

Maddie plasters on a forced smile. It's no surprise our mother would ask although she has a year left. "Probably apply to some dance companies and hope for the best." That's her go-to answer.

"Well darling, you can't wait too long in that industry. You aren't getting any younger."

I hold back a snort and an eye roll. Maddie takes it much better than me, though.

"I heard twenty-one is the new forty," Maddie says in a serious voice, but her tone is filled with sarcasm.

Before they can continue their conversation, the front door flies open, and Liam finally walks in. But he's not alone.

Oh my God.

Maddie's jaw tightens as she stares at him, but Liam doesn't glance her way as he walks hand-in-hand with some chick. Maddie's eyes narrow as if she's about to murder him for bringing another woman here after he'd kissed her two days ago.

That motherfucker. I'm going to kill him myself.

"Liam, you made it!" Hunter walks up and slaps him on the back.

"Yeah, sorry. Damn delays."

"Hey, Liam," Lennon greets from the table. "Who's your friend?" Her tight, black dress leaves nothing to the imagination, and she's definitely overdressed for a barbecue.

"Oh, sorry." Liam smiles wide, which makes me want to knock his teeth out.

He wraps an arm around her waist and she does the same. She rests her hand against his chest. That's when I notice the big rock on her left hand.

"This is Victoria. My wife."

Find Liam and Maddie's story next in
Between Secrets and Obsession

A NOTE FROM THE AUTHOR

There are millions of women and men in abusive relationships that don't know how to leave or find proper resources. Like Sophie, they're scared and fear for their lives. Creating that fear is part of the abusive and controlling behavior from their partner. You're not alone. I hope if you're ever in a situation like her, you'll utilize the resources below.

Domestic Violence Support Hotline
Crisis Text line
Text 741741

National Domestic Violence Hotline
Call 1-800-799-7233

•According to the National Coalition Against Domestic Violence (NCADV.org) nearly 20 people per minute on average are physically abused by an intimate partner in the United States. During one year, this equates to more than 10 million women and men.

•1 in 4 women and 1 in 9 men experience severe intimate partner physical violence, intimate partner contact sexual violence and/or intimate partner stalking with impacts such as injury, fearfulness, post-traumatic stress disorder, use of victim services, contraction of sexually transmitted diseases, etc.

•On a typical day, there are more than 20,000 phone calls placed to domestic violence hotlines nationwide.

•The presence of gun in a domestic violence situation increases the risk of homicide by 500%.

•Intimate partner violence accounts for 15% of all violent crime.

•Women between the ages of 18-24 are most commonly abused by an intimate partner.

•19% of domestic violence involves a weapon.

•Domestic victimization is correlated with a higher rate of depression and suicidal behavior.

•Only 34% of people who are injured by intimate partners receive medical care for their injuries.

There are many more statistics at NCADV.org if you wish to learn more.

ABOUT THE AUTHOR

Brooke Fox is the alternate pen name for Brooke Montgomery. She lives in the Midwest with her husband, teenage daughter, and four dogs. She survives on iced coffee and afternoon naps.

Find her on her website at
www.brookewritesromance.com
and follow her on social media:

facebook.com/brookemontgomeryauthor
instagram.com/brookewritesromance
threads.net/@brookewritesromance
tiktok.com/@brookewritesromance